Paper

Married at his convenience!

**Three sizzling, modern romances from
three favourite Mills & Boon® authors!**

In October 2008 Mills & Boon bring
you two classic collections, each
featuring three favourite romances
by our bestselling authors...

PAPER MARRIAGES

Wife: Bought and Paid For
by Jacqueline Baird
His Convenient Marriage by Sara Craven
A Convenient Wife by Sara Wood

HIS CHILD

The Mistress's Child
by Sharon Kendrick
Nathan's Child by Anne McAllister
D'Alessandro's Child
by Catherine Spencer

Paper Marriages

WIFE: BOUGHT AND PAID FOR
by
Jacqueline Baird

HIS CONVENIENT MARRIAGE
by
Sara Craven

A CONVENIENT WIFE
by
Sara Wood

◎™ MILLS & BOON®
Pure reading pleasure™

*Harlequin Mills & Boon Limited,
Eton House, 18-24 Paradise Road, Richmond, Surrey TW9 1SR*

PAPER MARRIAGES
© by Harlequin Enterprises II B.V./S.à.r.l 2008

Wife: Bought and Paid For, His Convenient Marriage and
A Convenient Wife were first published in Great Britain by
Harlequin Mills & Boon Limited in separate, single volumes.

Wife: Bought and Paid For © Jacqueline Baird 2002
His Convenient Marriage © Sara Craven 2002
A Convenient Wife © Sara Wood 2003

ISBN: 978 0 263 86134 1

-05-1008

*Printed and bound in Spain
by Litografia Rosés S.A., Barcelona*

WIFE: BOUGHT AND PAID FOR

by

Jacqueline Baird

100 Reasons to Celebrate

We invite you to join us in celebrating
Mills & Boon's centenary. Gerald Mills and
Charles Boon founded Mills & Boon Limited
in 1908 and opened offices in London's Covent
Garden. Since then, Mills & Boon has become
a hallmark for romantic fiction, recognised
around the world.

We're proud of our 100 years of publishing
excellence, which wouldn't have been achieved
without the loyalty and enthusiasm of our
authors and readers.

Thank you!

Each month throughout the year there will
be something new and exciting to mark the
centenary, so watch for your favourite authors,
captivating new stories, special limited
edition collections…and more!

Jacqueline Baird began writing as a hobby when her family objected to the smell of her oil painting, and immediately became hooked on the romantic genre. She loves travelling and worked her way around the world from Europe to the Americas and Australia, returning to marry her teenage sweetheart. She lives in Ponteland, Northumbria, the county of her birth, and has two teenage sons. She enjoys playing badminton, and spends most weekends with husband Jim, sailing their Gp14 around Derwent Reservoir.

PROLOGUE

PENNY ran lightly across the field, leapt over the fence into the old stable yard, and headed straight for the back door of the house. She was late and Veronica would kill her. Penny had promised to return before five to babysit her half-brother, while her stepmother went to the hairdresser. But her boss in the antique shop had been late getting back, and then Penny had bumped into her best friend, Jane Turner, the local vicar's daughter, and Jane's brother Simon.

Simon had just returned from a trekking holiday in the Himalayas. A year older than the girls, he was full of his experiences, and waxed lyrical about his prowess as a mountain climber. Jane was delighted because her older sister Patricia, who was married and lived in New York, was coming home on holiday next month, and bringing her new baby with her. Penny was pleased for her friends but it had delayed her even more.

'Sorry, sorry,' Penny yelled as she dashed into the rear porch that led to the kitchen.

Veronica stood, baby James in her arms, blocking her way. 'About time! I'm going to be late and you know how important this dinner is tonight. We have invited Mr Maffeiano and his PA, and with a bit of luck not only will Maffeiano buy the land, and solve our immediate money worries, but also he might be persuaded into going into business with Julian. It could be the making of your father, and heaven knows we need the income to keep this place up.'

It was the familiar moan, and Penny shrivelled a little inside. Veronica wasn't a bad person; in fact, when she had first married Penny's father Julian eighteen months ago they had got on well. It was only when Veronica had given birth to a baby boy ten months later, and begun talking of when James would inherit the estate, and her husband had disabused her of the notion, informing her Haversham Park was always left to the oldest child, irrespective of sex, that she'd changed.

Penny's own mother had died of cancer when Penny was thirteen, and for a while her father had been depressed. But four years later he had met and married Veronica.

'Well, take him, for heaven's sake! I have to dash,' Veronica snapped.

'Sorry, Veronica,' Penny apologised again, reaching out and taking James into her arms. She adored her brother. But, casting a glance at her stepmother, she could not help thinking uncharitably that it was amazing how quickly Veronica had lost interest in Penny, and to some extent the baby, when she'd realised her husband wasn't as wealthy as she'd thought.

'Sorry isn't good enough—we really do need the money. Working in that dusty junk shop for a gap year before going to university will nowhere near cover the cost of keeping you at college for three more. Your father will have to pay. Heavens! We can't even afford a caterer! Feed James, and put him to bed, then keep an eye on Mrs Brown's cooking. The woman is far too old to work and she flatly refused to take James for me, saying she was too busy. The nerve of the woman.'

'Okay,' Penny agreed as Veronica swept out. Penny sighed with relief as she walked into the kitchen.

'She's gone and left you holding the baby again,' Mrs Brown, the live-in housekeeper, remarked grimly.

'I don't mind.' Penny grinned at the older woman and slipped a gurgling James into his high chair, then set about preparing his bottle and food.

''Brownie'', as Penny called her, had lived at Haversham Park since before Penny was born and Penny could not imagine the house without her. Much as Veronica complained about the woman, she had not tried to get rid of her.

However, this was probably because Brownie worked for a small salary and, more importantly, Veronica did not cook… In fact Veronica's one aim in life, as far as Penny could see, was to look good and be part of what she called the social scene. This apparently, entailed flitting back and forward to London for dinners and charity balls.

Penny grimaced; it was a ball that was responsible for tonight's dinner. Veronica had persuaded her father to take her to an exclusive charity event in London. As luck would have it, Veronica had bumped into an old friend of hers, a businessman, and had introduced him to Penny's father. One thing had led to another, and apparently the man was interested in purchasing land, perhaps for a golf course. Personally Penny could not see the point but, as her father had explained, there was no money in farming any more, and they needed money. Veronica was right; this was an ideal opportunity for Julian to make some money and her father almost always bowed to what Veronica wanted, Penny thought ruefully. Who could blame him? He was a man in his fifties with a beautiful young wife and he just wanted to keep her happy.

But Penny took heart in the fact they would still keep

the home she loved, a stone-built Tudor-styled house set in five acres of parkland, and she began feeding James with a smile on her face.

Once he was fed and happy, Penny left James with Brownie and set the large oak table in the dining room with the finest damask cloth and silver cutlery. Then, with a brief glance at her wrist-watch she dashed back to the kitchen.

A sleepy James stretched out his arms to her and she swept him up in hers, giving him a cuddle and a kiss. 'Bed for you, little man,' she murmured, and strolled out into the hall. Her foot was on the bottom step when the front door was flung open. Penny stopped and turned. Veronica was back quick.

'Ah, Penelope and my favourite boy.' Her smiling father walked towards her.

Oh, my God! She stifled a groan. The guests had arrived early, over two hours early by Penny's reckoning!

Solo Maffeiano entered the hall, and wondered what the hell he was doing here. Two nights ago he had spent a couple of hours of inventive sex with Lisa, his occasional mistress in New York. She was a lawyer, she knew the score and was very accommodating.

In a way it was her fault he was here now. On a previous date with Lisa months ago, he had been flicking through a year-old magazine while he'd waited to be picked up for the airport. The centre-fold picture of a wedding had attracted his attention: the marriage of Veronica Jones to a much older minor English aristocrat, Julian Haversham.

Solo had laughed out loud as he had known the lady seven years before, not in the biblical sense, but it had not been for the want of trying on her part. Veronica had been the girlfriend of an Arab business associate of his when they had spent a week cruising the Greek Islands. Bridal material she was not!

But the picture of the bridesmaid, the daughter of the groom, had caught his eye. The Honourable Penelope Haversham was a beauty, with pale blonde hair and milky white skin, and an innocent, almost fey quality about the small, slender figure that had intrigued him.

He had met Veronica and her new husband at a charity ball in London a couple of weeks back. Now following his PA Tina down the hall, he realised he should have taken her advice and had nothing to do with the proposition Veronica was pushing, the purchase of farming land and possibly a joint leisure development. If the house were included it might have been viable. But it would be sacrilege to alter it. It was a beautiful example of Tudor architecture, and Solo appreciated works of art. His hobby was collecting rare objects; his home in Italy was a treasure trove of *objets d'art*.

Probably because he had been brought up in the back streets of Naples with a whore for a grandmother and a mother who'd followed in the family tradition! He was the result of an American sailor's fling with his mother. He was named Saul after him but the name was quickly bastardised to Solo, and by the time he was ten he'd been on his own.

There was very little he had not seen and done. But blessed with a brilliant mind and a quick tongue, he had never fallen foul of the law. He had worked and acquired a formal education whenever he'd had the time and opportunity, ultimately graduating with honours in economics. But privately he acknowledged the economics of poverty and the street had proved to be a much

more valuable lesson, when dealing with the upper ech-
elons of international finance.

At thirty-four he was a success. Wealthy beyond most
people's wildest dreams, he was a whiz at playing the
markets and had also invested heavily in property
around the world. He could have any woman he wanted
without really trying. So why was he wasting his valuable time on the off chance of seeing the girl from the
picture? He wondered, his lips twisting in a self-
derogatory smile.

Then he saw her, and he stopped dead. The picture
did not begin to do her justice.

Penny held James a little more securely and, putting
a brave face on it, she said, 'You're early, Daddy. I'm
just going to put James to bed.' Her father was a tall,
slender man, with white hair and brown eyes, and she
loved him to bits.

'Not to worry, darling. Come and let me introduce
you to our guests.'

Penny's glance skimmed over two people. A red-
headed woman and a tall man, half hidden behind her
father.

'My daughter Penelope.' Her father stepped aside and
smiled at the couple, before glancing back at Penny.
'Solo Maffeiano, and his PA Tina Jenson, our guests
this evening. It was such a lovely afternoon we decided
to come down early and conduct our business here
rather than in a London office.'

The woman was tall and elegant. 'How do you do?'
Penny said politely. 'I hope you will excuse me not
shaking hands, but as you can see my arms are full.'

Penny looked up at the other guest with a polite smile
on her face, and her heart quite inexplicably began

thumping against her ribs. She simply stared, struck dumb by the sheer dynamic presence of the man.

Solo Maffeiano was the most devastatingly attractive man she had ever seen. He was wearing a tailored lightweight grey suit that fitted his elegant frame to perfection. He was well over six feet tall with wide shoulders that tapered down to lean hips and long legs. He was olive-skinned with thick black curling hair, his eyes were a piercing grey, his nose straight. His perfectly sculptured lips were curved in a smile over brilliant white teeth.

'Delighted to meet you, Penelope,' Solo husked. She was a vision of feminine perfection with a baby in her arms, and Solo felt an instant reaction in the groin area. It had not happened like that for him in years.

Her hair was fair, and it fell long and straight down her back like fine silk. Her petite features held a perfect symmetry, her lips full and sensually curved. Her eyes were a stunning green but darkening to deep jade as she watched him, the lashes thick and curling, and he noted the tinge of pink on her cheeks.

He knew the effect he had on women and for the most part ignored it, but he felt a stab of savage masculine pride that this dainty creature before him reacted so helplessly. In that instant he decided he wanted her, and he was a man who always got what he wanted.

Penny finally found her tongue. 'And you, Mr Maffeiano.' She swallowed hard.

'Please call me Solo.' He smiled again, and she was mesmerised.

'Solo,' she breathed his name, and at that moment young James decided he did not like his sister's attention diverted from himself, and grabbed a handful of her hair and tugged.

'Oh, you little devil,' she cried at the swift stab of pain, bringing her back to reality with a jolt, but she was grateful to James. It had stopped her staring at the man like a besotted fool. 'Come on, it's bed for you.' With the briefest glance at the others, she murmured, 'Excuse me.'

But before she could turn Solo Maffeiano reached out one elegant finger and slid it gently down James's chubby cheek.

'I hope you know how lucky you are, boy, with a beautiful girl to take you to bed.'

James gurgled happily and reached a chubby hand out to the man and the others all laughed. Penny shot a startled glance at the dark stranger, and blushed scarlet. She saw the knowing amusement lurking in his silver eyes; he knew exactly how he affected her. How he affected every woman he met, she thought, reality clicking in. He was a sophisticated, handsome beast—add wealth and power, and he had it all. He was way out of her league, she told herself, turning to her father and gripping James like a lifeline.

'See you later, Daddy. Veronica is not back yet, and I must get James to bed.' She was babbling, she knew, but she needed to get away from Solo Maffeiano and the peculiar feelings, the tension he aroused in her. 'I'll see you all at dinner,' she said and almost ran up the stairs.

Lying in the bath later when James was safely tucked up in bed, Penny told herself she had overreacted. Solo Maffeiano was just a man like any other. It had been shock at the early arrival of the guests that had made her react so oddly.

It was almost eight when Penny made her way back downstairs. She had herself firmly under control—she was nearly nineteen. no longer a giddy teenager prone to blush if a boy so much as looked at her.

Her grin vanished as she walked into the drawing room for a pre-dinner drink.

Conversation stopped dead and four pairs of eyes turned to look at her.

'Really, Penny, you must learn to be punctual. I said seven-thirty for eight.' Veronica's opening comment had her stuttering for a response.

Her father's 'Leave the child alone, you know how Penny adores playing with James and she loses all track of time,' and brief smile before he looked around the other three did nothing for her self-esteem.

Tina Jenson smiled politely at Penny, and turned back to Solo Maffeiano.

But he simply ignored everyone else and crossed the room to Penny. His cool grey eyes flicked over the mass of fair hair she had swept up and knotted on top of her head, roamed down over her small face, her elegant neck and slender shoulders, and lingered on the boat neckline of her dress that revealed the soft curve of her surprisingly luscious breasts. His intent gaze dropped lower to the indentation of her waist, flat stomach, and down to where her straight skirt skimmed her slim hips and ended some two inches above her knees, right down to where her small feet were encased in high-heeled black sandals.

'You look beautiful, well worth waiting for,' he said with casual charm, taking her arm, 'And your father must be blind if he thinks you're a child,' he drawled huskily so only she could hear.

The touch of his fingers on her bare flesh seemed to

burn through to the bone. Penny felt a wild heat surge through her body, and she did not know what had hit her.

Dinner was torture to Penny, although she persuaded Brownie to pretend her arthritis was bad so that Penny could do the serving.

Brownie gave her a quizzical look. 'Your stepmother won't like that.'

'Tough, I don't want to be stuck listening to boring business all night.'

A few minutes later Penny walked back into the dining room, carrying a tray, with the first course, melon and Parma ham.

'Where is Mrs Brown?' Veronica demanded curtly.

'Her arthritis is bothering her so I offered to help.'

'The trouble is good help is so hard to find when you live in a backwater like this,' Veronica began as Julian dealt with the wine.

Thirty miles or so outside Cambridge, the village was small, but it was also only about ninety minutes' drive into London, so hardly the back of beyond, Penny thought dryly as she put the plates on the table and took a seat next to Tina. Only then did Solo Maffeiano sit down directly facing her.

'I can imagine,' Tina Jenson drawled in agreement, while Penny kept her head down and tried to eat. 'But if Solo does decide to invest in the place I'm sure he will have no trouble finding staff. He never does,' Tina concluded with a smile at her boss.

Penny's head shot up at the words, and with a horrified glance at the man opposite, 'But the house is not for sale,' she blurted.

Solo leaned back in his chair, his silver gaze sweeping slowly over the delicate beauty of her features. He caught the tightening of her lush mouth, the tension she could not quite hide, before he captured her gaze with his own.

'Isn't that up to your father to decide?' he asked smoothly. 'After all, you're a very attractive young woman, some man is bound to snap you up before long.' One ebony brow arched enquiringly. 'Or are you already committed to some lucky man?'

Penelope heard her father's soft chuckle, and felt herself the object of all eyes around the table, and colour surged in her cheeks. 'No,' she responded quietly, 'to both your questions,' she concluded with a brief flare of resentment she could not quite disguise. Solo was deliberately needling her. She might be young, but she could recognise a chauvinistic statement when she heard one.

'Penelope is right,' Veronica piped up, supposedly in support of Penny, but then she went on to describe how Penelope stood to inherit the house. As Julian's wife Veronica only had the right to live in it, never own it, as did baby James.

Incredibly hurt by Veronica's implication that Penny was likely to throw her stepmother and brother out, she leapt to her feet, and whipped around the table collecting the plates. It was some consolation to hear her father say firmly, 'That is not quite true Veronica, I could sell if I wanted to, but I don't. Havershams have lived here for three hundred years, and always will as far as I'm concerned. And I have not the least doubt Penelope would share everything with her family. We Havershams always do.'

Penelope slanted her father a grateful smile for sticking up for her, and shot off to the kitchen without another word.

For the rest of the meal she kept quiet and listened.

But keeping her eyes from straying to the handsome man opposite was not such an easy feat. She couldn't help but look at him. Solo Maffeiano's voice was deep and melodious, his English had the slightest trace of an Italian accent, and his easy wit as the conversation flowed held her enthralled. But when Veronica started name-dropping shamelessly as she described the house party she and Julian were going to attend that weekend at Lord Somerton's, Penny had had enough.

She glimpsed the cynical smile on Solo Maffeiano's face, saw the contempt in his grey eyes, and she cringed. Looking down at the table, she placed her napkin by her plate before rising to her feet and declaring brightly to no one in particular, 'I'll go and get the coffee.' She couldn't get away fast enough.

'I'll help you,' Solo Maffeiano declared smoothly.

'No, no, please, you're a guest,' Penny flung over her shoulder as she scuttled out of the room and into the kitchen.

Breathing deeply, Penny crossed to the bench where the coffee percolator stood. Brownie had gone to bed, but she had left the tray, and the coffee on, bless her!

Not long now and Penny could make her own escape. She grasped the edge of the bench to steady her shaking nerves. What a meal! She had never felt so aware, so disturbed by a member of the opposite sex in her life. Solo Maffeiano had the power to make her heart shake with only a glance from his pale eyes, and she wasn't sure she liked it.

Sighing, she turned, only to freeze at the sight of the man in question strolling towards her. 'What are you doing here? I told you I don't need any help,' she snapped.

He didn't immediately answer. Instead he stopped

and captured both her hands in his and very slowly folded them behind her back, bringing her into intimate contact with his tall frame. A shiver rippled through her as her breasts pressed against his broad chest, her slender legs trapped against the strength of hard, masculine thighs. She tried to wriggle free, then gasped as she felt the stirring of his mighty body and its blatant masculine sign of passion.

A mixture of innocent embarrassment and not so innocent helpless heated arousal caused a tide of pink to sweep up over her face. Penny stared up at him and was paralysed by the blinding flame of desire in his eyes, her heart hammering against her chest so hard she could hardly breathe. Nothing like this had ever happened to her before.

'What I have ached to do since the minute I set eyes on you,' Solo declared, and smiled a slow, soft curve of his firm mouth. His dark head bent and too late she realised the danger she was in.

'No,' Penny gasped at the same time as his mouth covered hers. She had been kissed before, not very often, and never like this, was her last conscious thought.

The sexy male scent of him filled her nostrils, a hot, liquid sensation flowed through her body making her breasts tingle, and heat pool at the junction of her thighs, and his mouth! His mouth moved on hers with a soft, sensual pleasure, his tongue darting between parted lips, gently then fiercely plundering the hot, sweet interior in an erotic, wonderful kiss that quickly flared out of control.

Solo groaned and, freeing her hands, he slipped his own firmly around her waist, holding her in intimate contact with his hard body.

Penny felt his other hand sweep up under her breasts

and cup the aching fullness in his palm. Her slender body arched into him as his thumb stroked across the tip of her breast, bringing the tender nipple into a rigid peak against the fabric of her dress. 'Don't.' Her voice was a shocked murmur, verging on a moan.

Solo lifted his head, taking a swift breath. *Dio!* The girl was dynamite—he had come perilously close to forgetting where he was, and that had never happened to him before. He needed to tread warily and, wrapping his arms around her, he hugged her. 'I knew it would be like this between us.' He stepped back and released her.

Penny gazed bemusedly up at him. She lifted a hand to her full lips. 'You…we…' she stammered. She couldn't say *kissed*, she didn't have the breath. Solo Maffeiano; this incredibly attractive, virile man had kissed her, touched her. It felt more as if she had been hit by lightning. Powerful and sophisticated Solo, and yet she could have sworn she'd heard him groan as well.

'Us, you mean,' Solo amended throatily. 'And there is going to be an us. But not here and not now. The others are waiting for their coffee.' He slipped an arm around her waist to steady her. His eyes, dark as slate, stared down into hers and he saw her shock and confusion and knew she was exactly what he wanted. Innocent, well bred and maternal, she was perfect wife material. To a man who had everything, and had never considered marriage before, the thought of a wife and possibly a child suddenly held strong appeal. 'How old are you, Penelope?' he asked softly.

'Nineteen in September,' she answered without thinking.

'I'm thirty-four, a lot older than you.' And a hell of a lot more experienced, but Solo did not say it. He did

not want to frighten her off. She was like a perfect rosebud slowly unfurling. She came alive in his arms, all
heat and light and totally unconscious of her potent sensuality.

'Not too old,' she murmured, her fingers curling into
his shirt.

He chuckled. 'Good, Penelope, hold that thought, but
for the moment coffee.' He ran a soothing hand up and
down her spine. Then, cupping her face in his strong
hands, he smiled into her eyes and gently kissed the tip
of her nose.

'You get the coffee, I'll carry the tray, my hands are
steadier than yours are.' And smoothing a few stray
tendrils of hair back from her face, he added, 'There—
no one will ever guess I have been seducing you in the
kitchen.'

'It was only a kiss.' Penny finally managed to speak
almost steadily, embarrassed by her headlong capitulation to his overpowering male sexuality.

His slate-grey eyes hardened on her slight, tense
frame with a narrow intensity that made her shiver.
'Don't pretend with me, Penelope. The sexual chemistry
between us is intense, you know it…accept it, and I
promise you won't be disappointed.'

Their eyes met and meshed and something indefinable passed between them.

'Yes,' Penny murmured.

Solo's deep chest heaved and he stepped back a couple of paces. He had her, he thought exultantly. 'I won't
rush you, Penelope, except for the coffee!' he added
teasingly to lighten the atmosphere.

Walking behind Solo into the dining room, she had
to battle to keep down the blush that threatened, con-

vinced the others must know what they had been doing, but no one noticed.

Later she was stunned as they all stood at the front door saying their goodbyes and Solo managed to arrange to come back in two days' time—Saturday—the only time he had free to look over the land, and Penny was to be his guide, because of course her parents and James were going to a house party.

Later, lying in bed going over the events of the evening, she touched her lips and felt again the pressure of Solo's mouth. It had really happened, and she was seeing him on Saturday. She went to sleep with wild dreams of an erotic weekend ahead.

Solo guided the car through the country lanes deep in thought. Once he hit the motorway heading back towards London he turned to Tina. 'Tomorrow send flowers, and an expensive piece of jewellery to Lisa Brunton in New York with a suitable note ending the arrangement. I won't be seeing her again. You know the address.' His decision was made: he was going to marry Penelope Haversham, but first he had to cut all ties with his past liaisons.

'Good idea. I can imagine the dollar signs in her eyes,' Tina agreed.

Saturday morning Penny opened the door to Solo Maffeiano and stared. He was wearing a blue checked shirt, and blue jeans hung low on his hips and moulded his long legs like a second skin. He carried an overnight bag in one hand, and, when she dared to look up into his face, a spasm of sensation clenched her stomach sending her pulse rate flying.

Solo dropped his bag and swept her into his arms. A

long kiss later with her head swimming and her legs shaking, he finally set her free.

It was a weekend out of time. Penny introduced him to Mrs Brown, and Brownie insisted on accompanying them when Penny showed him to the room that had been prepared for him.

'I see we really do have a chaperone,' Solo said with a rueful grin when they finally walked out of the house ten minutes later, and got in the car. 'Not that I'm objecting—it is good to know you have been properly looked after.'

She shot him a surprised glance; it seemed an odd thing for him to say. Old-fashioned, but rather honourable, and her happiness ratio went up another notch.

They parked the car at the pub in the village, and walked across the fields. Solo was a fascinating companion. He told her of his travels around the world, and his home in Italy that he managed to go to as often as he could, but not as often as he would like. He made her laugh, and she made him climb over stiles, and hike for miles. But in between they exchanged brief and not so brief kisses, and he continued to tease her sexily until she was unable to think straight.

By the time they sat down to dinner that night, under Brownie's beady eye, Penny knew she was in love for the first time in her life.

Penny leaned over the crib and marvelled at the baby boy. 'He's beautiful—he's going to grow up to be a stunningly handsome man,' she told the doting mother, Patricia, her friend Jane's sister who had arrived from New York the day before. 'Though maybe not as handsome as Solo,' she sighed dreamily. Solo was never out of her thoughts—it had been the most perfect five weeks of her life.

'You are besotted with that man.' Jane laughed. 'You mention his name just about every other sentence.'

'I'm not that bad. Am I?' Penny queried with a grin.

'Do I smell romance in the air, Penny?' Patricia interjected, touching the baby's head. 'He is asleep,' she murmured before sitting down next to Penny on the sofa.

'Maybe.' Penny blushed; she could not help it.

'And you should see him, Patricia,' Jane cut in. 'Tall, dark and handsome does not cover it, add rich and he is every girl's dream.'

Patricia gave Penny a searching look. 'He sounds too good to be true. I hope you're being careful,' she went on bluntly. 'You don't want to end up another statistic in the unmarried mothers list.'

Chance would be a fine thing, Penny thought wistfully. Solo had taken her out every weekend, and she had just about offered herself on a plate. But he had a lot more self-control than she did. He always called a halt before they went too far. She admired him for his strong principle, but it did not stop her aching in bed every night.

'He is not like that,' Penny defended. 'He respects me.'

'My, my,' Patricia drawled teasingly. 'The boy must be a paragon of virtue, if he does not want to get into your knickers.'

'Please.' Penny blushed scarlet again. 'It is not like that.'

'Unless of course he is a virgin like yourself,' Patricia offered with a grin.

Jane spluttered, 'He is no boy, and I'd bet my life

savings he is no virgin,' and went off into paroxysms of laughter.

Penny had never thought of Solo with another woman, but Jane's words forced her to. Solo was a healthy, virile male, a lot older than she was; he was bound to have dated, even loved other women, and it hurt.

'Do you mind?' Penny snapped. 'It is not a joke. Solo is the man I am going to marry.'

'What?' Jane exclaimed, her laughter vanishing. 'The hunk has actually asked you?'

'Well, almost,' Penny amended, and did what she had been dying to do all week—she confided her secret hope to Jane and Patricia. 'When Solo came down last Saturday, he had a talk with my father, but then his PA called him and he had to leave suddenly. But when I saw Solo out to his car, he said he had something very important to ask me when he got back. Plus all week my father has been grinning at me, as if he knows something I don't.' The relief at being able to share her excitement with her friends was heady. 'Solo telephoned me yesterday. He is coming back tomorrow, and he has planned a special dinner in London for the two of us. What else could it all mean?' she asked, turning sparkling eyes on her friends.

'If you are right, this is serious,' Patricia said bluntly. 'You're only eighteen.'

'I'm nineteen next week,' Penny said swiftly.

'Even so, I thought you were going to Cambridge University with Jane.'

Shamefaced, Penny turned to Jane. 'I know we are booked into the halls of residence together for the first year, but I really do love him.' Then as another thought occurred to her a smile lightened her eyes, and she

added, 'Though maybe I can still go to university. Solo
has his work, and he has to go abroad a lot. We haven't
discussed it, but we could probably live between here
and Cambridge.'

'Wait a minute.' Patricia adopted her older-sister
mode, hands on hips. 'What's his name? Where did you
meet him? And what exactly does he do?'

'His name is Solo Maffeiano, he is an Italian businessman and he is gorgeous,' Penny began enthusiastically. 'And I met him when Daddy invited him down
on business. Daddy has sold him some of the farmland
to develop, I think.' But business was not Penny's interest, Solo was, and she lifted her head, smiling, but
was stunned by the look of horror on Patricia's face.

'Solo Maffeiano. *The* Solo Maffeiano?'

'That's his name,' Penny said cautiously, a sense of
unease curling her stomach. 'Why, do you know him?'

'I've met him once in New York. He's tall, dark and
very handsome but I know a lot about him. He dated
Lisa, a partner in my husband's law firm, for months.
Lisa was madly in love with him and she thought he
would marry her, so she was heartbroken when he finished with her four weeks ago.'

'It can't be the same man,' Penny said stoutly. She
had known him five weeks!

'There could not be two Solo Maffeianos in the
world. His financial acumen and his prowess with
woman are legend.'

'Yes, there could.' Penny clung onto the hope.

'Penny, the man is in the same line of business.'

'Well, even if it is the same man, maybe he realised
he didn't truly love your friend. That is not his fault,'
she said, trying to defend Solo.

'If that was all, maybe not,' Patricia said soberly.

'But when Lisa received a goodbye gift of roses and a diamond pin, she called him and discovered he had not even sent them but his PA. Tina Jenson. How low is that?'

Penny felt her heart shrivel in her chest at the mention of Tina Jenson. Patricia was right—it had to be the same Solo. 'Maybe he didn't have time,' she said faintly, but she was clutching at straws and she knew it.

'Oh, you poor kid, Penny. What have you got into? According to Lisa, Solo Maffeiano is a ruthless, powerful man. Nobody knows much about his early years, just that he had made his first million by the time he was twenty-two, and nobody asks too closely how! In fact, rumour has it Tina, his American PA, is his permanent lover. The only reason they are not married is she has a husband tucked away somewhere who won't divorce her.'

Penny felt the blood drain from her face. 'No. I don't believe it.'

'Penny, you're young,' Patricia said gently 'Maybe you're right and Solo Maffeiano is totally genuine in his feelings for you, but the man is too old for you. Give yourself time. Don't be rushed into marriage. You said Solo has bought some of your father's land. How do you know he is not after the house and park as well?'

'No…I don't know, but he is not too old for me.' she ended defiantly, wishing she had never come to visit Jane today and never heard Patricia's denouncement of Solo.

'Do me a favour, Penny. If Maffeiano does ask you to marry him, take your time before making a decision. You are an intelligent girl, with your whole future before you, a pedigree a mile long, and you stand to inherit a very desirable property.'

'Rubbish, nobody cares about things like that any more,' Penny exploded.

'Your stepmother Veronica does, and I think a man like Solo Maffeiano does as well. Promise me, before you do anything drastic you will at least start at university.'

'I'll think about it,' Penny murmured in a very subdued voice.

'If the man loves you, Penny, he won't mind.'

'Who loves our little Penny?' Simon burst into the room. 'Besides me,' he teased. Tall, tanned with blond hair, he grinned at the three women.

'Oh, shut up, Simon and get out,' Jane snapped.

Penny got to her feet. 'No.' She glanced at Simon. 'Stay. I have to go.'

'I'll see you out.' Jane jumped up, and, once in the hall of the vicarage, Jane put an arm around Penny's shoulder. 'Don't worry about university or me. Talk to Solo—I'm sure it will be fine. You know Patricia, she always was a terrible gossip. You don't have to believe everything she tells you.'

The sun was shining, it was a beautiful warm September afternoon, but to Penny the world had turned grey as she set off walking through the village, a deep frown marring her lovely features. She needed to think, and, turning, she trekked across the fields towards home.

Solo with another woman. She examined the thought and she didn't like it. He had finished with the woman within a week of meeting Penny, which she could just about get over. But what Patricia had said about Tina Jenson she could not dismiss quite so easily. Penny had only met the woman once, and she had taken Tina's position as Solo's PA at face value.

Solo had hinted to Penny he wanted to marry her, and she would stake her life on him being sincere. She loved him with all her heart. Was she really going to let Patricia's vague rumours and gossip spoil the love and trust she had in Solo?

No, she finally decided with the optimism of youth. Tomorrow Solo would be here and everything would be fine, and, holding that thought, she hurried on home.

Penny saw the black car as soon as she walked around the corner of the house. It was Solo's—he had come back early, and her confidence in his love rose sky high. She heard voices as she passed the open window of the drawing room, and paused. But it was the 'Solo, darling really!' that stopped her in her tracks.

She leant against the warm stone wall beneath the window, unable to move, and for once grateful for her lack of height. She had only heard the voice once before but it was unmistakably Tina Jenson.

'I have seen the amount of money you have paid for the land, and it's not worth it on its own. What are you up to?'

'It s a good long-term investment, and I'm thinking of going into a partnership,' Solo responded smoothly.

'I don't believe you. You always work alone.' Tina paused, then added, 'But then it's not like you to buy a lump of land. With the house and park, yes, I could understand. The building is historic, and with work could be turned into a luxury hotel. But even so the place is shabby, and it would cost a fortune to renovate. No, I have known you too long...You are up to something, Solo.' She ended with a chuckle.

Penny's spine stiffened, her pride in her home coming to the fore, and she waited for Solo to deny Tina's words.

'You obviously don't know me that well,' Solo opined, 'or you would know I have every intention of refurbishing this place and going into a partnership, but not necessarily with Julian Haversham. You seem to have overlooked the delightful Penelope, and it is about time I settled down.'

'What? Seduce the daughter? That child.' Tina laughed out loud. 'So she will go along with your plan for the house!'

Numb with shock and totally humiliated, Penny sank to her knees on the hard ground. She wanted to put her hands over her ears but a masochistic desire to know the worst made her hold back her cry of despair, and she made herself listen.

'Come off it, Solo, you can be ruthless in business, but you're not the type to seduce a young girl. Penny Haversham is lovely, but she is the kind a man has to marry, and I can't see you doing that. Solo by name, Solo by nature. You like your women to know the score. Sex without commitment. I should know. I have sent the flowers and picked out the jewellery often enough.'

'True, but only because you are much more sensitive to a woman's needs in that area,' Solo drawled with mocking amusement. 'But maybe I've reached an age when I want something different. A loving wife and a son or two holds strong appeal.'

'Oh, sure, a malleable little wife while you do what you like. I can see the appeal, but I hate to tell you, Solo, young girls have a nasty habit of growing up, and Penelope Haversham is no fool; unworldly, yes, but to get a place at Cambridge University she has to have a brain,' she said cynically. 'And have you thought of how you would explain our relationship to a wife? She would need to be enormously broad-minded,' she ended with a laugh.

'Nothing would change between you and I,' Solo said with a responsive chuckle. 'You don't need to worry on that score. I'll always love you...'

Patricia had been right, and, sick to her soul, Penny did not stop to hear more, but scuttled back around the corner of the house. Her eyes swimming in tears, blindly she ran and ran back over the fields and finally collapsed in her secret place, beneath a huge willow by the river.

Fighting to breathe, her body racked with gigantic shudders. She cried until there were no tears left. Her throat was sore and aching, but was nothing like the ache in her heart. Still the words of Solo and Tina, their shared laughter, echoed in her head like some horrific nightmare that would not go away. Her dreams of love and marriage completely shattered—it had just been an illusion created by the deceit of one man.

Solo had considered marrying her; in that she had been right. But he did not want her, did not love her, never had. It had all been a sophisticated game, a plan to acquire her acceptance for the changes in store at Haversham Park, and as the knowledge sank into her tortured mind she heard her heart break.

Penny slipped from her hiding place and stared at the softly flowing water, and wanted to die; she could not bear the pain. Lifting her head, she looked up at the clear blue sky, the only sound an occasional bird song and the gentle flow of the water over the stones. But as she stood there with the water swirling around her the familiar beauty of the place touched her soul, and she realised life was too precious to let a womanising devil of a man like Solo Maffeiano destroy her.

Slowly Penny walked back across the fields towards the vicarage. She couldn't go home yet… She could not face Solo.

She needed to build up her courage to dump the swine, and face her father. She could not bear the thought of him actually going into business with Maffeiano, and selling the house even though he had every right to do so, and if her rejection of Solo spoilt her dad's plans, tough… But she could see Veronica's hand behind this.

Penny consoled herself with the thought that at least her father had got the money for the land. He and Veronica would have to be happy with that. She was almost at the front door of the vicarage when it flew open and Simon appeared.

'What the hell happened to you?' he demanded. 'You look as though you have been dragged through a hedge backwards.'

Penny looked up into his friendly face and she could not help it, she threw herself into his arms. 'Oh, Simon, Patricia was right about the man I thought loved me—he doesn't at all. I am in a hell of a mess, and I dare not face Solo Maffeiano.'

'Hey, don't be upset. Your honorary brother is here to help.' His strong arms closed firmly around her, and he tilted her chin up to his. 'Jane told me you were involved with a man.'

'Not any more—I never want to see him again,' Penny said bitterly.

'This Solo wouldn't be a tall, dark, good-looking dude…?'

'Yes, why?'

'He's walking up the drive, probably looking for you. Follow my lead and your troubles will be over. He looks the jealous type. Kiss me and make it look good. Then tell him you were waiting for me, your boyfriend.' Simon pressed his lips to hers and Penny wrapped her arms around his neck and clung to him…

CHAPTER ONE

'I REALLY don't feel like socialising, Jane.' Penny made one last effort to get out of accompanying Jane to her firm's dinner-dance as they got out of the taxi outside an exclusive London hotel.

'Yes, you do.' Jane grabbed Penny's arm and almost frogmarched her into the impressive entrance foyer. 'After the shock you have had today you need company. Relax, forget your worries and act your age for once, instead of like an old spinster.'

'But I feel half naked in this dress.' Jane had insisted on lending her the dress, when Penny had tried to use the excuse of having nothing with her to wear. 'I never wear red,' Penny wailed as they handed their wraps in to the cloakroom attendant.

'You look great. Stop moaning and enjoy yourself.'

Solo Maffeiano walked out of the lounge bar and stilled, tension in every long line of his superb body. He looked and looked again at the lady in red. His grey eyes flared in shock: it was Penelope Haversham in person. But not a side of Miss Haversham he had ever seen before...which was hardly surprising as she had played the young innocent for him. It still rankled that she had managed to fool him.

But there was no mistaking the delicate profile. Her pale hair was swept up into an intricate twist on the top of her head. Her translucent skin. Though tonight there was a lot of bare skin, he thought with a cynical twist of his hard mouth. The slight coltishness of youth had gone and she had grown into a strikingly sensual woman. The shimmering red dress clung to her every curve; it was cut low at the front and even lower at the back. With her high, full breasts, a tiny waist and firmly rounded bottom, she had the perfect hourglass figure. Add shapely legs and the fact that she moved like a dream oozing sex appeal, and she became every red-blooded male's fantasy female. Nothing like the demure bridesmaid in the photograph Solo had first noted.

But what was she doing in his hotel? Had she come looking for him? Perhaps she thought she could seduce him into doing what she wanted more easily in the intimate surroundings of his suite, rather than waiting until their official appointment tomorrow. The thought was seductive, and she was certainly dressed for the part.

Then he spotted her friend Jane and the direction they were heading. He realised it was pure coincidence after all as the two women were swept up in a crowd entering the ballroom, and he felt the sudden jolt of desire again.

Damn it to hell! She still had the same effect on him. Even though he knew her for the two-timing, scheming little bitch she was. Red was a very appropriate colour for her type. His grey eyes narrowed menacingly, the anger was buried deep, but it was still there…

For a moment he was tempted to follow Penny and make his presence felt, but cynically decided not to. It would be interesting to see which Penny would appear in his office tomorrow—the-butter-wouldn't-melt-in-her-mouth Penny, or the sexy lady-in-red Penny.

Four years later he still smarted from the blow to his pride Penelope Haversham had inflicted. Since the age of twelve, no woman had ever turned Solo Maffeiano down, and no woman had deceived him so thoroughly

then dumped him. No other woman had even tried, only
Penelope, and she had succeeded.

His memory of their brief, disastrous affair four years
earlier still had the power to make his blood boil. It had
not even been an affair, because being an idiot he had
never taken her to bed. For the first time in his life he
had decided to commit to one woman for life and got
stamped on for his pains. This time would be different,
he vowed with a chilling smile that never reached steel-
grey eyes. He spun on his heel and re-entered the bar.
He had not expected to see her here tonight, and he
needed a drink.

Enjoy herself? If only she could, Penny thought, a
prickling sensation bringing her out in goose-bumps.
Convinced someone was watching her, she glanced
swiftly around and felt a fool. Her nerves must be getting the better of her—it was only a dinner-dance. Get
a grip, she told herself as they walked into the ballroom.

As for fun, there had been very little in Penny's life
recently. Her father and Veronica had been involved in
a rail crash nine months ago. Veronica had died instantly, and her father two days later without ever regaining consciousness, and it had changed Penny's life.

She had graduated from university last year with
Jane. Jane had got a job in the legal department of a
finance company, and rented a tiny two-bedroom ter-
raced house in London. Penny had planned on joining
her, having secured a job in the British Library, but the
accident that had killed Julian and Veronica had also
killed her plan to live in London.

Instead Penny had stayed at home to look after her
brother James, and grieved, while still having to deal

with all the details of two deaths and the ongoing accident investigation.

Today Penny had come up to London on business and to stay with Jane for two days. Jane's family was looking after James.

In a buoyant mood, Penny had actually thought she was beginning to get over the worst of her grief and feel hope for the future. It had been a perfect May morning when she had set off for her meeting with her publishing house, and to her delight she had signed a contract for four more children's books. The first was already at the printers'.

It had been James who had given her the idea. By the age of three he had already learnt to read simple books, and when Penny was at home he loved her telling him bedtime tales, that were often based on historical fact. She had looked for some early learning books on history and been unable to find any.

So she had written and illustrated one. James had loved it, and after her final exams were over last June, she had sent it to a publishing house. With the death of her father and Veronica, she had forgotten all about it, until she had received a letter saying they liked it and were going to publish it and suggested she wrote a whole series.

In the afternoon she had had an appointment with Mr Simpson, her father's lawyer. Thinking the will had passed probate, she had walked into his office, happier than she had been in months, and hoping for more good news.

Mr Simpson had gone over the will again. He had informed her Mrs Brown's pension was secure and there was a reasonable amount of cash divided between Penny and James equally, and in the event of Veronica's death Penny would be James's legal guardian. Penny had been aware of all this, and she'd already known Haversham Park was hers, because he had read the will out after the funeral.

'Now we come to the hard part, so to speak,' Mr Simpson said gruffly. 'Your father was a lovely man, but paperwork was not his forte. Another document has come to light, perfectly legal and above board, but the actuality is you only inherit a half-share in Haversham Park. It seems your father sold the other half to a third party.'

The news came as a complete body-blow to Penny. She could not believe it. 'What?' she exclaimed, her eyes widening in horror. 'A third party, I don't believe it! Daddy would have told me.' Someone else owned half her home! The thought was mind-boggling. What was she supposed to do—share her home, or split the house down the middle? She had the hysterical desire to laugh—the whole idea was ludicrous. But one look at Mr Simpson's serious face and she knew he was not joking.

Penny paled as a premonition that worse was to come filled her mind. She had to ask the question, but her mouth was suddenly dry.

'I don't know why he didn't,' Mr Simpson continued. 'But I have to tell you the inheritance tax on the value of your father's estate is quite considerable.' He mentioned a figure that had her mouth falling open in shock. 'If you don't sell your share of Haversham Park you can't pay the inheritance tax and you will eventually be declared bankrupt, and the house will be sold anyway by the Inland Revenue.' Things could not get worse, but they did...

'But it is not all bad. I have spoken to the other party.'

'Who is the other party?' Penny asked hoarsely, finally managing to speak.

'Well, that is the good news. He is an Italian gentleman, a Mr Solo Maffeiano.'

At the mention of Solo, the little colour left in Penny's face drained away, her stomach heaved. Solo Maffeiano owned half her home. No, no, no, she screamed silently. Life could not be so cruel. But as Mr Simpson's voice droned on she was forced to accept it could.

'He tells me you know each other, and he is quite agreeable to talk over the options available. You sell to him or you put the place on the open market and share the proceeds. Either way, Penelope, you will be all right.' Mr Simpson actually smiled.

Penny shivered, nausea clawing at her stomach, and she could not respond.

'You can buy a smaller place, much more sensible for you and James. The inheritance tax can be paid, and you will still have enough to live on plus the money to set up a trust fund for your brother's education.' Mr Simpson beamed and looked at Penny and he realised his client was far from happy. She looked terrified, as though the weight of the world had just fallen on her shoulders.

He stood up from behind his desk and walked around to Penny, putting a fatherly hand on her drooping shoulder. 'I realise it has come as a shock to you, my dear. But, believe me, selling is the sensible solution, the only solution.'

Penny shook her head, and dragged herself up on shaking legs. 'There must be something I can do,' she

pleaded, 'Rather than involve Mr Maff...eiano.' She
choked on his name. To have to sell her home was
horrific, but not half as bad as the thought she might
have to see Solo again. He had hurt her so much in the
past she couldn't bear to face him. 'If I must sell the
house, please, you arrange it for me, Mr Simpson.'

'Don't worry, Penelope, it is all in hand. I have taken
the liberty of setting up a meeting for you tomorrow at
noon at Maffeiano's London office.'

'Please could you go for me? Whatever you arrange
I'll accept, but keep me out of it.'

'I'm afraid I can't do that. Mr Maffeiano has insisted
on dealing with you personally. But it will work out
fine, I'm sure.' Mr Simpson pressed a card with the
address on it into her hand. 'Now, why don't you run
along and do some shopping, cheer yourself up?'

Mr Simpson looked pleased, while Penny looked sick
when she had finally left the lawyer's office. She could
not believe what had happened; it was her worst nightmare realised. She was dreading having to meet Solo
again, but she had no choice.

She could vividly remember the horrendous scene
when Solo had caught her in the arms of Simon.
Incredulous anger had been followed by a tirade of what
had sounded like curses in Italian and then, as if a
switch had been thrown in his brain, he'd stepped back,
coldly remote and in complete control.

Acting for all she was worth, Penny had told Solo
she was sorry if she had given him the wrong impression, but Simon had always been her boyfriend, and she
had only dated Solo because Simon had been away.

Even now she still shivered when she remembered
the look of icy contempt Solo had slashed at her, before
in the next moment Simon had played his part.

'Penny and I have been a couple for ages, and I know her well. When her stepmother asked her to be nice to you she was too soft-hearted to say no—she doesn't like to hurt people. You do understand, sir,' and the *sir* had simply accentuated the age difference.

'Yes, I understand perfectly,' Solo had drawled. His handsome face devoid of all expression, and his grey eyes cold and hard as the Arctic waste, had frozen her to the spot. 'Congratulations, Penny, I do believe Veronica has finally met her match.' And swinging on his heel, he had stalked off.

After the fatal day when she had lied to Solo and he had left, life had never been quite the same at Haversham Park. Her father had told her Solo had called but had had to leave in a hurry. Her father had continued saying he was sure Solo would be in touch as he was very fond of her.

Penny had responded, lying through her teeth, 'Maybe, but he is far too old for me, and I'm going to university with Jane. We are really looking forward to meeting other young people, laying the groundwork for a good career.'

Her father had looked shocked, and then worried, before sighing and saying, 'You're very young; I should have expected it.'

Three weeks later when Penny had left for university and there had been no contact with Solo, Veronica had realised something was wrong, and accused Penny of destroying the best chance her father had ever had of making a fortune.

'It was obvious Solo fancied you. You should have given him more encouragement. What girl needs an education when they can hook a millionaire like Solo

Maffeiano? You're an idiot.' Which had summed up Veronica's slant on life, Penny had thought dryly.

'For heaven's sake, cheer up, woman,' Jane's voice cut into her troubled thoughts. 'Sell the mouldering old pile and get a life like me.'

For the next couple of hours Penny did try. But the thought of the meeting tomorrow prevented Penny relaxing and she was glad when the evening was finally over and they returned to Jane's house.

At five minutes to noon Penny walked into the building that housed the London offices of the Maffeiano Corporation. She glanced across the marble-floored foyer to where a smart brunette sat at a long, curved desk, bearing the word 'Reception' on a gold plaque.

Taking a deep breath, Penny pulled the jacket of her black suit down to her hips and walked to the desk. 'Excuse me, I have an appointment with Mr Maffeiano.'

The receptionist's gaze slid over Penny's slender figure dressed in the neat black suit, with the white blouse beneath, the blonde hair scraped back in a bun, and the pale face. '*You* have an appointment with Mr Maffeiano?'

Bristling, Penny affirmed with a nod, 'Yes.' So she didn't look like his usual model woman, so what! At college she'd had no trouble fighting off a succession of young men more interested in her looks than her brain. Then during nine months as a mother to James she had developed a firm belief in her own intellectual talents, and ability to cope with any eventuality. This was business, strictly business, and she could handle it.

'I'll call his secretary. Take a seat.' The girl gestured to a seating arrangement surrounding a table holding magazines.

Penny was glad to sit down because her legs were suddenly weak. If the girl did but know Penny did not want to be here, only the decision had been taken out of her hands. She had not slept a wink last night, the enormity of what had happened was almost destroying her.

Over and over again she asked herself why her father would have done such thing, but could not find an answer. The only certainty was that she had lost the family home. The only decision left was where the house would go—to Solo or to a stranger—and that was not up to her, but to Solo. She dreaded the prospect of meeting him again.

'Miss Haversham.' A grey-haired lady in her fifties approached Penny. 'Will you come this way, please?'

'Thank you.' Penny tried a smile and followed the lady down a long, carpeted corridor.

The secretary opened a door at the end, and gestured Penny to enter before her. 'You can wait here. Mr Maffeiano is delayed, but he won't be long. Help yourself to coffee,' she said, indicating a coffeemaker that stood on a small table in one corner of what was obviously an office. The woman took a seat behind a large computer desk. 'You look as though you need a fix, my dear,' and she smiled, suddenly looking very human.

'No… No, thank you.' Penny returned the smile, her head turning when a double door that she surmised led to the inner sanctum was opened and a woman walked out. Penny stifled a silent groan. Tina Jenson…

'Hello—well, if it isn't little Penny Haversham,' the tall redhead drawled, then added, 'I'm surprised you have the nerve to face Solo after the stroke you pulled.'

'And hello to you too.' Penny said dryly. Why should she be surprised to see Tina? The woman was Solo's

Personal Assistant and long-time lover. If any stroke had been pulled, it had been by Solo Maffeiano on her father, she thought angrily. Her father had been no businessman, Penny would be the first to admit. Solo had to have tricked him, anything else she could not contemplate. She had adored her dad; still did, she thought sadly.

'You have nerve, I'll give you that,' Tina said shortly, and, with a goodbye to the secretary, swept out of the office.

Penny watched her leave with mixed feelings. It was only the second time she had met the woman, but Tina did not improve on acquaintance, she thought bitterly. Obviously Tina and Solo were still together, and Penny refused to believe the slight pain in her heart was anything other than a touch of heartburn. She had not eaten anything since yesterday.

Penny glanced at the coffee but dismissed the idea, and sat down on one of the chairs provided. All she'd had for breakfast were three cups of black coffee, and she was nervous and angry enough without having another shot of caffeine. She clasped her hands around her purse in her lap in a deathlike grip and waited.

'He will see you now,' the secretary announced as a green light on the console flashed, and, indicating the door to Penny, she added, 'But please make it quick, he does not have much time. His meeting with Mrs Jenson took longer than expected.'

I'll just bet it did! Penny thought unkindly. A kiss and a cuddle, or maybe more had delayed him! Rising to her feet, Penny straightened her shoulders and with a brief, 'Thank you,' in the secretary's direction she walked into Solo's office.

Warily she glanced around the elegant room. Dark

panelling, a polished wood floor with what looked like a very expensive carpet, a black leather sofa and chair, and by the massive window that filled almost a whole wall was an enormous mahogany desk and a high-backed chair. But no Solo Maffeiano!

She walked slowly into the room, her heart racing. It was hot. May and the central heating was still on. Not a luxury Penny could afford at Haversham Park, she thought wryly. She unfastened the jacket of her suit, and pulled at the collar of her blouse.

Maybe it was deliberate. Solo Maffeiano was the sort who would like to make a client sweat, she thought bitterly, taking a deep breath and slowly exhaling before she forced her feet onwards to the desk. She stopped at the edge, at a loss as to what to do next. She tried a polite cough, her throat tightening in the process.

Slowly the chair swung around and she saw Solo and her breath stuck in her throat. Their eyes met and she almost passed out. It was the fiercest electric connection she had ever experienced in her life. She blinked, and when she looked again, like a replay of her eighteen-year-old self, she was totally intoxicated by the sheer animal magnetism of the man that the years in between had done nothing to dispel.

To disconcert her even more Solo was lounging back in the chair, his jacket and tie discarded, the tailored white shirt fitting his broad shoulders to perfection, the collar open at the neck to reveal the strong, tanned throat and a glimpse of black chest hair. Her pulse raced, and her mouth went dry; she could not have spoken to save her life.

'The honourable Penelope Haversham,' he drawled sarcastically. 'Allow me.' He rose to his feet and walked around the desk.

She watched him move, six feet three of stunningly attractive male. She had forgotten quite how tall Solo was, and how he projected a power, a raw sexuality that made her stomach muscles clench in helpless response. From the top of his dark head, to the broad shoulders, to the dark pleated trousers that settled on his lean hips and long legs, he was the epitome of predatory male and she could not help staring.

Her fascinated gaze watched as he took a chair from against the wall and placed it beside her. Realising she was staring, Penny jerked back her head and felt a painful tide of red wash over her face. She was ogling the man like an idiot.

'Sit down,' Solo commanded coldly.

She was glad to oblige, as her legs were shaking. 'Thank you, Mr Maffeiano,' she murmured politely, and was aware of him resuming his seat at the opposite side of the desk.

'Mr Maffeiano,' he drawled mockingly. Ice-grey eyes cut like a laser into hers, then slowly swept over her slender body with a frigid disdain that even now, after so many years had the power to make her cringe. It was the exact same look he had given her when he had caught her kissing Simon, as though she was beneath contempt.

'Surely you and I are on first-name terms at least, Penny?'

She blushed even redder. 'Yes, of course, Solo,' she muttered, her tongue sticking to the roof of her dry mouth.

She was behaving like a fool. She was no longer a naive young girl, with a head full of romantic ideals of love and marriage, an easy conquest for a ruthless, so-phisticated man of the world like Solo. She should be

thanking her lucky stars that she had seen through the
devil in time, instead of sitting here, trembling and
blushing like a schoolgirl.

'Well, let's get down to business—I haven't much
time to spare.' His deep voice was curt. 'I have a lun-
cheon engagement at one.'

Warily she watched him as he shoved his chair back
a little, and flung one arm casually over the back.
Nervously she straightened the hem of her skirt over
her knees.

His grey eyes followed the movement of her hands
and narrowed to linger on her legs, and the charged
sexuality of the knowing look he swept slowly over her
body made heat surge in her face, and, to her shame,
another more intimate place. The shockingly helpless
flare of response made her press her knees together, her
body became taut, and she wanted to curl up and hide.

His expressive mouth twisted in a cynical smile. 'Still
as demure as ever, I see.' Solo had a vivid image of the
lady in red last night and wanted to laugh out loud at
the image Penny presented today in the black suit, the
conservative court shoes, and the hair scraped back.
Who did she think she was fooling? Certainly not
him...

Appalled at her own weakness, Penny murmured,
'Yes,' as she stiffened her shoulders, not knowing what
else to say. Simply being in the same room with Solo
again had a disastrous effect on her mental powers. One
look at him and every sensible thought vanished from
her head, and she knew she needed all her wits about
her to discuss business with the man.

He had been thirty-four when she'd first met him, and
well aware of his impact on the female of the species.
Suave and devastatingly attractive, he could charm the

birds right out of the trees. His deep, melodious voice tinged with a hint of sensuality had promised untold delight, with perhaps just a touch of danger. Now as she looked up into his cold eyes all she saw was danger…

Almost four years had left their mark. His curly hair was ruthlessly swept back from his broad brow. There was harshness about the firmly chiselled features, a ruthlessness in the grey eyes that met her own that said he was a man in firm control of himself and all those around him. A man to be respected for his immense power and wealth, but also a man to be feared.

'If you say so.' His gaze moved with leisurely insolence over her face, and lower to the firm swell of her breasts against the soft cotton of her blouse. 'It has been a long time but you haven't changed at all, Penelope.'

Penny's body responded with another sudden rush of heat that horrified her. Slender fingers curled into fists, her nails digging into her palms until it hurt, trying to distract her traitorous body with pain. What a choice! she thought dryly, and the sheer stupidity of injuring herself enabled her to relax her grip.

'Neither have you, Solo,' she said stiffly, hoping she sounded sophisticated and, praying her voice would not wobble, she added, 'And I'll take that as a compliment.'

'Take it any way you like,' he drawled. 'But back to business. What exactly do you want?' One dark brow arched enquiringly.

'Well. I…you… Mr Simpson said…' she stammered to a halt.

Solo rose slowly to his feet and in a few lithe strides was around the desk and towering over her. 'You seem a little nervous. Shall we start again? After all, we were close friends once.' Holding out his hand, he added, 'Good to see you, Penny.'

Penny looked at his hand as if it were a snake that might bite. She glanced up into his eyes and saw the mocking amusement in their silvery depths. The swine was laughing at her.

'Yes, of course.' she said firmly and placed her hand in his. His hand squeezed hers, sending a prickling sensation scooting up her arm.

Instinctively Penny tensed, and lowered her eyes from his knowing gaze. Her head was telling her to get out of there as quickly as possible, while her traitorous heart skipped a beat as the hand that gripped hers tightened fractionally, before he set her free.

Solo looked at her lowered head. 'You have changed, after all,' he drawled mockingly. 'At one time you were not afraid to face me.'

Pride alone made her tip back her head and look up. 'I'm not now,' she denied curtly. 'I'm just surprised you wanted to see me, instead of Mr Simpson, my lawyer, after the way we parted,' she said with blunt honesty.

'Some you win, some you lose.' One shoulder elevated in a shrug.

Penny's eyes widened in surprise on his dark, inscrutable face. He was as good as admitting it had all been a game to him four years ago, and she, poor fool that she was, had felt guilty over the blunt way she had dismissed him. The anger that had been simmering inside her ever since Mr Simpson had told her the news yesterday came bubbling to the surface.

'But you never lose, do you, Solo?' she said hotly. 'What I want to know is how the hell you conned my father into selling you half of Haversham Park.'

His silver-grey eyes hardened perceptibly, his handsome face an expressionless mask. 'Be very careful of throwing unfounded accusations around. I allow no one to cast a slur on my integrity without taking legal action, and, given the mess you are in at the moment, bankruptcy would be the result.'

'I'm not far from it anyway,' she snapped back bitterly, recalling the inheritance tax, and it was enough to make her clamp down on her anger. Insulting the man was not going to help her situation. She needed Solo's agreement, either to buy her out or to sell the house to someone else.

She had overreacted. Shock at seeing him had churned up emotions she had thought she had successfully buried. Solo Maffeiano might still have the charisma, the blatant sexuality that had the power to awaken old familiar feelings inside her. But she was older and wiser now, and knew it wasn't love, just lust, and easily denied. She only had to remember the way he had tried to manipulate her feelings for the sake of the house.

A wry smile tugged her mouth, the irony of the situation hitting her. With her late father's help it looked as if Solo would get the house anyway. But at least she was not stuck with a man who had quite happily toyed with her foolish heart, while betraying her with the elegant Tina Jenson.

The fact that Tina Jenson was still with him simply confirmed Solo's guilt in Penny's eyes. He was a ruthless, devious bastard, and she had had a lucky escape.

'That is a very secretive smile,' Solo prompted. 'Care to share the joke?'

'It was nothing,' Penny said, and in that moment she realised Solo was nothing to her, and she smiled with genuine relief.

'I don't want to waste any more of your valuable time. My lawyer informs me you own half my home. How, he wasn't quite clear.' She could not resist the dig and cast a swift glance up at him beneath the thick fringe of her lashes. She still did not understand why her father would have done such a thing, but he had, and she had to deal with the consequences.

'Strictly legitimate, I can assure you,' Solo informed her coldly.

'Yes, so I understand, and that is why I am here.' She lowered her eyes. 'I want you to buy me out or agree to put the house on the open market,' Penny stated simply.

She knew Solo had not developed the land he had bought from her father, apparently losing interest in the project. When Veronica was alive she had never stopped telling Penny that it was all her fault.

Penny had had no answer to her stepmother's accusations—well, none she'd wanted to tell her—and instead Penny had suffered in silence. While Solo Maffeiano had vanished from their lives and, as far as she knew, the acreage he had bought was rented out to adjoining farmers.

'My, my, you actually want to sell your home?' His sarcastic tone cut into her musings, and she glanced back up into his dark, sardonic face. 'And I have first refusal.' A slow smile twisted his hard mouth and chilled her to the bone. 'What an interesting scenario, and surprising. I seem to remember you were very attached to the ancestral pile. What has changed?'

'Apparently you own half,' she said scathingly. 'And I wouldn't share so much as a minute with you, given a choice. Therefore I have no alternative. The inheritance tax has to be paid, and I don't have the money.'

He knew all this; he was just trying to make her squirm. 'But you know all this. Mr Simpson spoke to you.'

'I do, but I wanted to hear it from your own sweet lips,' Solo said with cold derision.

Penny studied his hard face with bitter eyes. What he really meant was he wanted to humiliate her. Because she had had the temerity to dump him, and he was not averse to a little revenge. 'Yes, well, you have now, so can I have your answer?' she snapped back.

'No. I'll need to think about it, and it will take me rather more than a *minute*,' he drawled sarcastically. 'In the meantime you can tell me what you have been doing the last few years.'

He was supposed to be in a hurry—it didn't sound like it, Penny thought, simmering with resentment. And she wished he would go and sit down. He was too close and towering over her like some dark avenging angel. It was giving her a crick in the neck simply to look at him, and, fixing her gaze to a spot on his left shoulder, she began a catalogue of her life to date.

'I went to university for three years, got my degree. Then I secured a job at the British Library to start last September. I was going to share a house with Jane. But I never got the chance because Daddy and Veronica were killed in a rail crash. They had spent the summer in France as usual, and ironically the crash was when they were nearly home, only a few miles outside of London. So now of course I look after my brother full-time.' She saw no reason to tell him about her new career as a writer of educational books for children. The less he knew about her, the better.

'So where is James now?' Solo queried lightly.

'Jane's parents, the Reverend Turner and his wife, with their older daughter Patricia who is visiting from

America with her son, kindly offered to take him with them on holiday. It is the first time we have been apart since our loss.'

She did not add that the vicar and his wife, who were like honorary grandparents to James, had had to talk her into it. Mrs Turner ran the playgroup James attended and he knew them very well. Penny had only agreed after Mrs Turner had pointed out James would enjoy the holiday, plus Patricia's son would be there for him to play with. Nor did she notice the gleam of satisfaction in Solo's cold eyes as he turned his back to her.

'I was sorry to hear of your parents' death. I was in South America at the time and could not attend the funeral.' Solo straightened something on his desk and turned and leant against it.

Watching him leaning negligently against the desk, with a bit of space between them, Penny could almost convince herself this was a normal conversation.

'Thank you for the wreath,' she said quietly, remembering how surprised she had been at the funeral to discover Solo Maffeiano had sent flowers. Because after she had split up with him, as far as she knew, her dad and Veronica had never seen him again.

'My pleasure, your father was a decent man.'

He was to you! she wanted to snipe. Because even after seeing it in black and white she still had difficulty believing her father would have sold him half the house without telling Penny. But antagonising Solo would get her nowhere. Be civil, and get out as quick as you can, she told herself, so instead she agreed.

'Yes, he was, and I still miss him. But James and I are pulling through, and of course Brownie is an enormous help.'

'And what happened to the blond-haired Adonis?' He

slanted a glance at her ringless fingers. 'Simon, wasn't it?' The question was asked so casually Penny answered without thinking.

'The last Jane heard he was in Africa teaching English.' She smiled fondly, thinking of Simon. 'But Simon is not much of a letter writer, he could just as easily be living on Mars!'

'And this does not worry you?' Solo said smoothly, his heavy lids and thick lashes almost hiding his eyes.

'No, not at all.' Then suddenly Penny realised what she was revealing.

'Ah, the fickleness of women. Why am I not surprised?' he opined cynically, straightening up and taking a step towards her. 'You haven't changed after all.'

As clear as day, the conversation Solo had had with Tina Jenson rang in her ears. She remembered the humiliation, the heartbreak she had felt at the time, still felt, if she was honest. He had some nerve… Talk about the pot calling the kettle… Anger sparked in her eyes as she flung back her head and looked up at him. 'Ah, but I have. I am no longer the little innocent I was at eighteen.'

'I can see that.' Hard grey eyes captured hers in a look of stark cynicism. 'So now young Simon appears to have had his fill of you, and can't help you, you come to me,' he drawled in ruthless mockery. 'Perhaps you and I should explore the possibilities.'

Penny cringed inside, but she could not blame Solo. She had deliberately given him the impression that Simon was her lover, so it was no good being shocked when he believed it, but it still did not prevent her speaking her mind.

'That is a disgusting thing to say.' she snapped.

'But true,' Solo voiced and, with a lightning speed,

his hands grasped her by her upper arms and hauled her hard against his long body. 'Once there was something between us.' His dark head swooped, and before she knew what was happening he had covered her mouth with his own in a brutally demeaning kiss.

Penny wriggled furiously, her hands trapped between their bodies, but as the kiss went on she felt herself weakening, old, familiar feelings flooding through her. His hard mouth gentled on hers. His hand slipped to cup the back of her head, while his other hand swept around and up her spine, holding her firmly against his long, lean length. The familiar, masculine scent of him teased her nostrils, and the warmth of his body enveloped her in a seductive cocoon of sensations she had never quite been able to forget.

'As I thought,' Solo drawled, lifting his head, and to her chagrin, while she was breathless and burning up, his slate-grey eyes surveyed her without a flicker of emotion. 'The buzz is still there between us.' His hands spanned her waist, holding her close. 'The question is, what are we going to do about it?'

Humiliatingly aware of her own abject surrender to his kiss while he looked like the original Ice Man, she sought solace in anger.

Scarlet-faced, she spat furiously, 'I don't want to do anything.' She placed her hands on his chest and tried to push him away. 'All I want from you is a straightforward answer about the sale of the house, and that is all there is between us. Either you buy my share, yes or no,' she demanded, with a swift glance up into his hard face, and as quickly away again. He was dark and dangerous, and she must be mad to challenge him.

Solo had to fight hard to keep the knowing grin off his face. The determinedly averted angry green eyes could not hide the flush of arousal on her smooth cheeks or the fact a pulse beat madly in her neck. He wondered what she would do if she knew where his thoughts were really leading, that it was taking all of his famed control not to pick her up and spread her on the desk, and strip her naked.

'Have you finished?' he said.

'That's no answer.'

Solo had been expecting this demand from her ever since he had heard of the death of her parents, but he saw no reason to make it easy for her. Not after the way she had deceived him with Simon. He slid his hands slowly from her waist up over the curve of her breasts and fastened them on her shoulders.

To Penny's horror her breasts hardened against the fabric of her blouse at his insolent caress. 'Let me go,' she said, trying to hold herself rigid, but helplessly aware of her body's response.

Solo felt her shudder, and was content, for now, and moved her gently but firmly out of his way. Then he glanced at the gold watch on his wrist, and back at her pink-tinged face. 'I have to go, my lunch date awaits me. But in answer to your question…' Penny held her breath—at last… But the smile he bestowed on her was totally lacking in humour.

'I have tomorrow free. I will call at Haversham Park and survey the merchandise before I make a decision. After all, four more years of use could have seriously damaged the…' he paused, his cold eyes raking over her from head to toe, before he added… 'structure, don't you agree? I do not want to buy a pig in the poke—I believe that's one of your English expressions.'

The only pig around here was Solo, Penny thought furiously. She was damn sure he had not been referring to the house, but having a dig at her. But she had no choice but to agree. 'Yes, all right. What time?' she demanded shortly.

'Fix it with my secretary. I have to go.' He flicked a dismissive glance her way, then opened a door in the wood panelling. He extracted the jacket that matched his trousers, and slipped it on, quickly followed by a conservative navy striped tie. Then to her astonishment he spun on his heel and left without another word.

CHAPTER TWO

PENNY paced the hall for the hundredth time in an agony of suspense. Twelve-thirty, the time she'd arranged with his secretary, had come and gone and there was still no sign of Solo.

She glanced around the familiar hall, and dejectedly sat down on a wooden seat next to the oak hall table. It was well after two. She had just returned from dropping Brownie off at her friend's house, driving like a bat out of hell in case she missed Solo. Brownie always spent Friday afternoon with her pal, shopping, and stopping for tea, and then the pair of them went to the bingo in the village hall in the evening. With James away it meant that if and when Solo Maffeiano arrived they would be alone in the house, which was not a prospect Penny particularly relished. She had hoped to show him around and out again within the hour, with Brownie for company.

The hurt and humiliation she had suffered the day four years ago when she had discovered the true nature of Solo Maffeiano had never really left her. She had hidden her pain well, and managed with the help of Simon to end the relationship on her terms. But yesterday had taught her a salutary lesson.

Much as she despised Solo for the ruthless, heartless type of man he was, when he had pulled her into his arms and kissed her she had felt the same old fierce physical longing that deprived her of what little sense she had.

She hated to admit it, but she didn't trust herself to

be alone with him. Which was a hell of an admission, she thought wryly just as the old iron doorbell rang.

Leaping to her feet, she tugged the edge of her bulky woollen sweater down over her jean-clad hips and went to open the door.

'It's blowing a gale and freezing.' A wet, windswept Solo brushed past her and into the hall, rubbing his hands. '*Dio!* Why anyone lives in England I will never know. The climate is the pits. It is more like March than May!'

Penny could only stare. His black hair was plastered to his head, and tiny rivulets of water trickled down his lean, strong face. He was casually dressed in a soft black leather coat that reached to mid-thigh.

'You've arrived,' she stated the obvious, eyes flaring with anger as she recalled how late he was. 'Almost two hours late. I'm surprised you could be bothered at all.'

With a shrug he divested himself of the coat and dropped it on the chair she had recently vacated. Straightening to his full height, he glanced around the hall, not a flicker of emotion visible on his sardonic features, his glance finally settling on Penny.

'Not the best way to greet a prospective buyer, Penny,' he drawled with a tinge of mockery, then arched one ebony brow in silent query. 'That is, if you have not changed your mind, and still want to unload this place?'

'Yes. I do.' Her innate good manners forced her to respond politely. 'Would you like a coffee? You look cold.' Meanwhile Penny was the exact opposite. Hot... Why did he have to be so gorgeous? She stared up at him, trying to still her racing pulse, but frighteningly conscious of the superb powerful male physique. A cream crew-necked cashmere sweater moulded his wide shoulders and every muscle of his chest in loving detail, snug-fitting black jeans followed the line of thigh and hip.

'Ever the lady. But I would prefer a stiff whisky,' Solo said swiftly, and, as though he already owned the whole house, he walked straight into the drawing room. 'Your father used to keep the best stuff in here.'

'Help yourself,' Penny murmured to his back, following him into the room. 'You usually do.'

'Not always.' Solo said with a wry twist of his lips. 'Pour me a drink, and try to act like the lady you purport to be,' he ordered, crossing to the fireplace and holding out his large hands to the flickering flames.

There was no answer to that, and Penny didn't try. She simply crossed to the drinks trolley and poured a good measure of whisky into a crystal tumbler and handed it to him.

For an instant his fingers brushed hers, and sent an electric pulse the length of her arm. She snatched her hand away, and moved to sit down on her father's old chair beside the fireplace. Thank goodness she'd had the forethought to light the open fire, and, leaning forward, she threw another log on the flames. She had thought it would make the old place look more welcoming, and perhaps distract from other more obvious faults. But at the moment she hoped he would think her face was red from the fire, and not from heated reaction to his slightest touch.

Fighting for composure, she took a deep breath and glanced up. She found Solo had slumped down in the armchair opposite, his long legs stretched out before him in negligent ease, his elegant fingers turning the crystal glass in his hand.

As she watched he lifted the glass to his mouth and took a long swallow. She saw the tanned throat move, and his tongue lick with relish around his firm lips, and she felt again the shameful pull of his physical attraction. How she was going to get through the next hour, she didn't know, but she had to try.

'Your father always did keep an excellent whisky.' His cool grey eyes sought her wary green gaze. 'Why don't you join me?' he queried, tipping the glass towards her. 'You look like you need a drink.'

'No, thank you, and when you have finished that I will give you the tour of the house,' she said quickly. 'You don't want to waste time. The weather is awful, and you have to drive back to London.' She was babbling, but she was so tense she could not help it.

'I am in no hurry,' drawled Solo, his silver eyes fixed on her in steady appraisal. 'It was a slow drive down, the rain was so heavy visibility was cut to about twenty yards, and, by the look of you, you need to relax.'

Immediately she felt guilty; of course he had driven through a fierce storm. Where were her manners? She got to her feet. 'I never thought—perhaps you would like something to eat? A sandwich, soup, anything?'

Solo finished the whisky and stood up, and, placing the glass on the mantelpiece, he came towards her, pausing only when he was within touching distance. 'No, I'm not hungry.' Derision glittered in his eyes. 'At least not for what you are offering. Let's go.'

Penny's face turned scarlet. She should not have said *anything*. She was only trying to be helpful, but he obviously thought she was flirting. He could not have made it plainer he didn't fancy her, she thought, drowning in embarrassment. But then why was she surprised? He never had, she reminded herself, and, straightening her shoulders, she swung one hand around the room.

'Well, this is the drawing room, as you can see, nothing much has changed since you were last here except...'

'Purple,' Solo said incredulously, finally noticing the surroundings instead of the woman. 'The walls are *purple.*' His eyes gleamed with wry humour as he stared down at Penny. 'When did this happen?'

'Veronica's taste.' Penny said grimly 'It matched her colouring, she thought.' Determined to be businesslike, she ignored Solo's soft chuckle. 'The dining room next,' she suggested.

'Lead on.' Solo placed a hand beneath her elbow. 'But tell me, am I in for many more shocks?'

She wrenched her arm away. 'It depends on your view of a scarlet dining room, a pink morning room, not to mention a rather virulent lime sitting room. Veronica was a colourful person.' She slanted him a cynical glance. 'As I'm sure you know—I seem to remember she was a friend of yours before she met my father.'

After Penny had split up with Solo she'd had a long time to think over the past and, from countless little digs Veronica had made, she couldn't help wondering just what relationship Solo had had with her stepmother.

His eyes narrowed and his expression became darkly forbidding. 'Veronica was never my friend, an acquaintance at best, but I think you better stop right there, and show me the rest of the place. That is why I am here.'

Penny gave a casual shrug, surprised to find she believed him, but refused to admit she was relieved he had denied knowing Veronica on a more intimate basis. Anyway, what was the use of raking over the past with the man? Best to get rid of him. With that in mind she led the way to the dining room.

Solo assumed the mantle of sophisticated buyer, and he asked pertinent questions as if they were two complete strangers as she showed him around all the rooms on the ground floor.

Penny told herself she was glad, an aloof, business-like Solo she could deal with; at least she thought so, until she had to lead him upstairs.

'I see what you mean about colour,' Solo drawled with a touch of mockery, walking into the master bed-room and stopping at the foot of the bed.' Knowing your father, I can't believe this bright fuchsia and leopard pattern was very conducive to a good sex life.'

The master suite was horrendous, Penny freely acknowledged, standing a couple of steps behind Solo and glancing around with sad eyes.

A bittersweet memory of another time, when her own mother was alive, and the décor was warm almond and elegant. The bed had been a place to curl up in as a child with her parents on freezing cold mornings. There had been no central heating then.

Veronica had been responsible for installing all the mod cons and the horrendous fuchsia wallpaper, not to mention the *faux* leopardskin bedcover. No one with the slightest taste would like this.

'I'm never going to sell this place,' she thought and didn't realise she had said the words out loud. Not without painting it, at least…

'Ah,' Solo said softly and turned to face her. He had wondered when she would finally admit she didn't want to sell the house, and what she was prepared to do to keep it. 'We get to the truth. I was wondering when you would show your true *colours*.' A steely note crept into his voice. 'I should have guessed you would choose the bedroom.'

Penny stared up at the grim lines of his face, lost in memories of the past; she hadn't the slightest idea what he was talking about.

'It is awful, but I could hunt out the old furnishings, and with a pot of paint it could be okay,' she said distractedly, thinking if she got rid of Veronica's worst excesses they might get a better price for the house. As it was it would make most people bilious.

'Or an interior designer, and a lot of money, my money,' Solo suggested with a cynical smile.

'Well, you could afford it,' Penny snapped as it hit her she really was going to lose her home anyway, whether to Solo or a stranger, it didn't matter. Determined not to let him see how the loss of her home hurt her, she pinned a bright smile on her face and glanced up at him.

'Come on...' She gestured towards him with one hand. I'll show you the rest was what she meant to say, but never got the chance.

A large hand curled around hers, and a lazy forefinger trailed a tingling path across her cheek to the edge of her mouth, where it delicately outlined the shape of her lips. 'Sweet, sexy Penny,' he murmured provocatively.

'Hey, what do you think you're doing?' Penny jerked her head back indignantly, her lips tingling where he had touched, and tried to wrench her hand free, suddenly aware of the intimacy of their position, alone in the bedroom.

'Agreeing with you, Penny.' And the hand holding hers effortlessly wrapped around her back and pulled her close to his large male body. With his other he dispensed with the band holding her hair in place so it fell in a tumbled mass around her face.

After the first shock and her own hair blinding her, Penny began to struggle, and launched a hefty, kick at his shin, but all she succeeded in doing was knocking Solo off balance so he tumbled backwards on the bed, with a dishevelled Penny sprawled on top of him.

'Get off,' she cried.

'I'm not on you,' he drawled sardonically. 'Yet.'

Then with one swift movement their positions were reversed, and Penny found herself flat on her back on the bed, with Solo's great body lying half over her. She struggled wildly in an attempt to free herself, and he let her, restraining her effortlessly with his superior size and strength until eventually she gave up and lay helpless and panting, looking up into his strikingly handsome face.

'Let me go,' Penny demanded, her eyes wide with fear and something more.

'Oh, no.' He smiled slightly, but only with his lips; the grey eyes remained watchful, and slightly cruel. 'This time I am going to sample the goods before I pay.'

'Pay! You mean—you—' She stopped, spluttering, then started again on a rising note of incredulity. 'You mean *me*? You think I am for sale with the house?' she screeched, renewing her efforts to scramble from under him.

Solo stopped her by grabbing her wrists and pinning them above her head in one strong hand, and throwing a long leg over her slim hips. 'I'm accepting your offer, Penny.' His grey gaze was intent on her furious face. 'So long as I get exclusive rights to your body for as long as I want.'

'My offer... My body!' she gasped.

'Yes.' His eyes didn't leave her face. 'Starting now,' he insisted with silken emphasis.

CHAPTER THREE

PANIC-STRICKEN, Penny arched up, trying to dislodge Solo's weight from her body, but it was a futile exercise as his mouth with unerring accuracy covered hers. Forcing her head back onto the bed, and prising apart her soft lips, he began a ravishing exploration with tongue and teeth in a kiss that shattered her romantic concept of a kiss for ever.

Before when he had kissed her it had been a gentle invasion, but now it was a blatantly sensual demand to possess, and to her shame she felt the rising heat of desire scorch through her, heating her blood to fever pitch.

As he sensed her capitulation Solo's mouth softened on hers, and with the tip of his tongue he soothed her swollen lips, before raising his head. Her glorious eyes were dilated with desire and her lips softly parted. She was his for the taking...

Penny drew in a deep, shuddering breath of air. She was so caught up in him she was hardly aware he had released her wrists. And before she could recover from the shock of his kiss his hands slid to her hips and in one swift movement had flipped her jumper up and over her head, and tossed it aside.

'I've waited a long time for this,' Solo opined huskily, his sweater removed in a flash. His eyes bored into hers with undisguised sexual intent.

'No. Please,' Penny breathed, shaken to the core by the devastating awareness of the powerful naked torso looming over her stirring a terrifying weakness in her. She was compelled to touch the hair-roughened chest so that her *no please* sounded weak even to her own ears. But he was not listening. His arm slid around her waist, and arched her slender body off the bed, removing the lacy scrap of bra with a deftness that smacked of long experience.

She spread her hands on his chest in a belated effort to push him away. 'No.'

'You invited me.' His face tightened, and his silver eyes glittered with a deep angry passion over her face and lower down to her firm, lush breasts.

Invited! Was he mad? 'No way,' she cried. 'I don't want this!'

Molten silver eyes held hers 'Your body tells me otherwise.' His gaze dipped sensually over her bare breasts as his long fingers tightened around then caressed her waist.

'You can't,' she whispered hoarsely, a peculiar weakness overwhelming her as she took in his bronzed semi-nudity. 'Let me go.' The blood pounded with increasing excitement through her veins. 'You can't force me,' and even as she said the words she did not really believe he would use his superior strength against her.

At eighteen she had ached for him, and he had controlled her girlish fervour with ease, but now he was unleashing the powerful expertise of his awesome masculinity on her and she had no defence. What little resistance she had left collapsing like a house of cards against his sensual onslaught.

Solo ate her body with his eyes. *Dio* but he wanted her, and he knew she wanted him. It was there in her pouting lips and in the jade depths of her gorgeous eyes. She was sex personified, and the fact she had once turned him down made the prospect of her ultimate surrender all the sweeter.

'I wouldn't dream of it,' he responded silkily, and cupped the smooth, creamy fullness of her breast, and trailed his thumb over the rosy tip, bringing it to rigid life, and watched her helpless, trembling response with cynical masculine satisfaction. He would seduce her slowly, and once he had her begging in his arms he would finally cure himself of the fatal attraction she held for him. She would be a body in his bed like countless others before her—until he tired of her.

Penny did not know what had hit her. One minute she was showing him the bedroom, now she was half naked on the bed drowning in a sea of sensations she did not really comprehend. The hands that had tried to push him away with a will of their own stroked over his satin-skinned shoulders, and when his head moved down to kiss her other breast her whole body shuddered in mindless delight.

'Don't lie, Penny,' he drawled against her hot skin, sprinkling tiny kisses back up her throat. 'You want me as I want you.' Once more he found her mouth, his tongue slipping between her teeth with a seductive sensuality until she forgot she was supposed to be fighting him and welcomed the intimate probing of his tongue with innocent, wild enthusiasm. Her fingers slid around his neck and into the silky black hair of his head, her breasts pressed into the hard heat of his naked chest as he held her closer, and she surrendered to the throbbing need his mouth and hands aroused in her.

So it was a brutal shock when suddenly Solo jerked away from her. Senses swimming, her green eyes wide and wondering, she looked up into his handsome face. Hard grey eyes stared back at her.

'This has been a long time in coming. Now tell me you don't want me.' His mouth curled mockingly, his gaze skimmed cynically over her full breasts, his hand flicking insolently over her rigid nipples. 'Deny the evidence of your own body.'

Penny stared back at him, too stunned to speak, and hating him for deliberately arousing her to a point of mindless surrender, simply to point out the weakness of her own flesh.

'Force does not come into it, Penny,' he drawled, his eyes boring into hers with stark demand. 'Make up your mind. You are no longer an innocent young virgin, so stop pretending and act like the mature woman I know you to be. Admit the need, the desire I can see in your eyes. Yes or no.'

Scarlet-faced, her body throbbing with unfulfilled need, she was vitally aware of Solo's half-naked form, the dark intimacy of the bedroom, and she shuddered, unable to subdue the fierce excitement flowing through her veins however hard she tried.

She had thought herself over him long ago, and she had never considered herself to be a particularly sexual person. She'd had no trouble rebuffing the young men she had dated at university, but now she was forced to face the fact that, where Solo was concerned, he only had to look at her, touch her, and for some inexplicable reason her untried body was perfectly attuned to his. It didn't make sense...

'Your silence is very telling, Penny,' Solo drawled throatily, his grey eyes burning into hers as he kissed each breast in turn, while his deft fingers unfastened her trousers and stripped them and her briefs from her body, and she let him... Hypnotised by his fiercely glittering gaze.

'You want to be persuaded. Very feminine,' he husked. Penny gasped out loud as slowly he slid his hand down over her stomach and swept along the length of her thigh, and then trailed his long fingers sensually down her leg with deliberate provocation. 'Very beautiful, and I'm happy to oblige.'

Penny trembled, mesmerised by the rapt expression on his strong, lean face, and the emotions surging inside her. Then lazily he stood up, and, taking her unresisting hand, he slowly lifted it to his thigh.

'See what you do to me, Penny.' He pressed her hand hard against him, and her palm seemed to burn as she felt the strength of his manhood through the fabric of his trousers. Fascinated and terrified at the same time, she would have pulled back, but he spoke in a throaty, seductive murmur. 'I need your answer, Penny.'

She gulped and then he was leaning over her; his other hand gently touched her shoulder and lower, her skin burnt. Why me? a tiny voice of sanity cried in her confusion. Why did this one man in the world have this devastating effect on her? Her fingers flexed. Horrified, she realised she was stroking Solo with tactile fingers of desire. Swallowing hard, she jerked her hand back and closed her eyes in mortification at her loss of control.

She did not know what she was, what she had become lying naked on the big bed, every nerve end in her body quivering with tension. She opened her eyes and tried to sit up. This had gone far enough, too far…

Solo was as naked as she was! Penny's stomach clenched at the sight of his magnificent bronzed body, the flagrant proof of his manhood casually revealed. She had never seen a totally naked man in her life, and she couldn't credit the rush of excitement that shivered over every pore of her skin simply from looking.

'Well, what is it to be, Penny?' Solo demanded, his voice deep and full of sensual invitation. His finger curled gently around her shoulder and eased her back down onto the bed. He draped his long body alongside hers and her pulse leapt at the contact of naked flesh on naked flesh. Rising over her, he slid his leg between hers as his mouth came down to claim her lips in a scorching kiss.

'Decision time.' Solo's mouth seductively glided along the curve of her cheek, leaving only a breathing space between them; his glittering eyes held hers, demanding an answer.

For a moment a nerve-jangling fear hit her, but with the heat of his body searing into her skin, and bewitched by the sensual promise in his silver eyes, she suddenly thought, Why not? Why deny herself the experience of making love with Solo? She had always wanted to, from the first time she had set eyes on him. No other man had ever been able to make her feel a tenth of what Solo could with a glance. Whatever happened in the future, at least she would have the satisfaction of knowing she had started with the best, she thought wildly, impulsively. 'Yes.'

One simple three-letter word, and Solo Maffeiano's heart leapt and so did another part of his anatomy. For the first time in his life he was speechless. He looked at the exquisitely beautiful naked girl beneath him and it took all his self-control not to rush. He stroked the elegant curve of her throat, the hollow of her collarbone, and his fingers trembled.

He shuddered, and Penny was aware of every inch of his huge male body and her own, the beating of his heart, the heat, the pressure of his hips against her inner thighs as he eased her legs apart.

Emboldened, she ran her fingers over his back and felt the contraction of muscle and sinew beneath her touch. She pressed her lips to the strong cord of his throat, tasting the salty tang of his skin. Then she gasped as his hand tangled in the long length of her hair and pulled her head back.

The bronzed skin was taut across his perfectly chiselled features as he fought a savage battle for control. But his eyes…his eyes burnt dark as night as he scattered gentle kisses on her cheeks, her eyes, her nose, and finally took her mouth.

His mouth searched hers with a sensuous, building passion and with a wild, uninhibited delight she responded, her tongue duelling with his, her hands stroking feverishly over his broad back, his firm buttocks. She felt the urgent thrust of his body as, with a hoarse groan, he broke the devouring hunger of their kiss.

His dark head bent to press hot, hard lips to her throat and lower to her breast, and she arched in wanton pleasure. Her fingers raked through his hair and slipped to his shoulders as he reared up. His hands cupped her breasts, kneading and pushing them together. His thumbs teased the rosy nipples, his blazing eyes watching in rapt fascination as the tips strained to hard, aching peaks beneath his sensuous manipulation.

'Exquisite.' He groaned and then swooped, his hungry mouth tasting first one and then the other in a compulsive, greedy passion.

Penny felt the pulsating waves of sensation flooding through her in ever-increasing force. She clung to him, and cried out when his head moved lower, to kiss her navel, and lower still. He kissed and caressed her slender body with a sensuality, a need that Penny had never imagined possible, and she exulted in the tremors that shook his great frame as she responded, her hands touching him, stroking him, wanting to give him the same incredible sensations.

When his caressing fingers slipped into the soft heart of her femininity, she shuddered violently. Every nerve end in her body was taut with a painful, aching need. She grasped his head and drew him to her, and she kissed him with a hungry, untutored, mindless passion.

Solo wanted to wait, to make it last, but he could not; he had waited years already and her aggressive kiss, the scent, the wet, silken readiness of her tossed him over the edge. A near-violent wave of desire surged through him and, with an animalistic growl low in his throat, he lifted her slender hips and drove forward into her moist, tight core.

Penny cried out, the breath left her body, the need was gone, and only the pain remained. The hand that had curved round his shoulder now hit out at him.

'*Dio*, no,' Solo groaned; his slate-grey eyes burnt into hers and his great body stilled. 'No, relax.' His deep voice caressed her cheek, her mouth as he murmured husky words in Italian, then added, 'Wait, Penny.'

He held her pinned to the bed. His magnificent body still linked to hers in the most intimate way possible. He pressed a soft kiss to her lips, and, easing very slightly from her, he licked the rosy tip of her breasts once more, and then, just as slowly, he moved again.

Gradually she became aware the pain had subsided, and an exquisite sensation of mind-bending pleasure bathed her in wave after wave of ever-building sensual tension. Slow then fast, pause…advance and retreat… He stretched and filled her body and soul, and miraculously her inner muscles clenched around him in ever-increasing need until she was once more mindless, lost in a passionate world she had no prior knowledge of.

Solo's darkened gaze flashed to her bemused molten jade one. She was with him every step of the way, he exulted, the cords and tendons of his face and neck etched in rigid lines of restraint. There was no sensual movement that he did not know, and with phenomenal control he utilised them all. With mouth, hands and body he used every refinement of eroticism to make it good for her, to drive her to the brink.

'Solo,' she helplessly moaned his name, pulsating with the exquisite torture of his possession.

It was his downfall. With one final thrust he drove them both over the edge into a tumultuous climax, his great body shuddering violently, the breath stolen from his lungs.

Penny lay there, the weight of Solo's body still pinning her to the bed, but she didn't mind; she was floating in a bubble of euphoria. This incredible man had shown her what it was to be a woman, and it was beyond her wildest dreams. So this was love; she sighed happily. 'Solo,' she murmured for the sheer joy of saying his name.

'I am too heavy for you,' Solo opined roughly, and rolled off her to lie on his back. He was still reeling from the fact Penny had been a virgin, and when he could think straight again he finally concluded the blond boyfriend she had rejected him for had to have been a fool. The thought cheered him no end.

Deprived of the warmth of the closeness of his body, and stung by his prosaic comment, suddenly Penny felt chilled, her euphoria vanishing as reality kicked in.

What had she expected? Avowals of undying love, or at least a little romance.

Instead she was lying naked flat on her back staring up at the ceiling in what used to be her parents' bedroom, having just been thoroughly seduced by Solo Maffeiano, a man she'd thought she hated half an hour ago. She wanted to weep. What had she done?

Panicking, she glanced wildly around and, spotting her sweater, she grabbed it and, swinging her legs over the side of the bed, tried to stand up, but a heavy arm curved around her waist and dragged her back against his broad chest.

'Where do you think you are going, Penny?' Solo levered himself up into a sitting position while keeping a firm hold on Penny. 'We need to talk, *cara*.'

Talk! She almost laughed out loud on the edge of hysteria. But, keeping her back determinedly to him, she managed to say steadily, 'I think it would be better if I got dressed first.'

Solo grinned smugly down at her bent head, his arm tightening around her midriff, his hand splayed under one luscious breast. He hadn't felt this good in years. Who was he kidding? He had never felt this good, ever!

'Are you all right?' he asked, his voice gruff with inexplicable emotion. Lifting his hand, he ran his fingers through the tumbled mass of her silken hair in a gentle gesture. Revealing the perfection of her delicate profile. She *was* shy, and now he knew why.

Solo considered himself broad-minded, a man of the world—he had to be with his parentage, he thought with a tinge of cynicism. He had never been the sort of man who was bothered about his female companions' past affairs. His only rule was monogamy for as long as a relationship lasted. He never asked about past lovers, and by the same token never told.

He let his fingers trail down the long length of Penny's blonde hair, loving the silken feel, the warmth of her small body against his chest, and he had to admit, on a purely primitive level, it gave him incredible satisfaction to know he was her first and only lover. She had rejected him once, but not any more...

'Yes. But do you mind?' Penny said, grasping long fingers that were edging ever closer to her breast, and trying to prise the arm from around her waist. 'You have had your fun, now let me go.'

Solo's arm tightened fractionally. She was doing it again...rejecting him. His silver eyes turned cold grey, and he withdrew his arm from her waist. 'Certainly.' And to Penny's surprise she was free.

Not daring to look at Solo, she scrambled off the bed and pulled her sweater over her head, not caring about underwear, and, finding her jeans on the floor, she quickly pulled them on.

'Why the rush to dress, Penny? I have seen a naked lady before, and I already know every intimate inch of you,' Solo prompted mockingly.

'Thank you for reminding me,' she said with icily polite sarcasm, incensed by his mockery. In her fragile state, she needed reminding she was one of a legion like a hole in the head...

Then she made the mistake of turning to look at him. He was lounging against the headboard of the bed, like some great, smug god of mythology, totally unfazed by his nudity. His magnificent olive toned body made her feel weak all over again. No man had the right to look so damn sexy.

'So polite.' Solo casually slid off the bed and pulled

on his boxer shorts and walked towards her. 'But, sex aside, we still need to talk about this place.'

Sex. That was all it was to him, Penny thought bitterly, the most momentous, mind-blowing experience of her life, and it was nothing to him. He stood there in black shorts, tall and powerful with the arrogance of a man who had complete conviction in his mastery over the female of the species, his slate-grey eyes staring blandly down at her. Suddenly, amid the chaos of all the emotional highs and lows storming through her brain, the one overriding emotion was anger.

'Why, you no-good, lecherous pig, you deliberately seduced me!' She waved a hand at the horrendous fake-leopardskin-covered bed. 'In that bed, and you dare stand there half naked and say we need to talk, as though it was a flaming board meeting.'

Solo reached out and dragged her hard against him, and plundered her mouth in a deep kiss. Penny tried to bite him, but it was a mistake, it gave him easy access to her mouth, and in moments her slender arms were wrapped around his neck, her slender body arching into his in helpless response. To her utter humiliation Solo grasped her hands from his neck and placed them firmly by her sides before stepping back.

'No more talk of seduction, Penny, we both know it's a lie.' His deep voice held a cynical edge 'Your *come-on* was just that. A come-on.'

Shamed by her instant surrender, she looked at him, the pull of sexual awareness impossible to deny, and something tugged at the edges of her memory. Oh, no! She silently groaned. Earlier she had smiled and said, 'Come on,' but he had never let her finish. Did he really think she had asked him to make love to her? In the next half-hour she had her answer.

'Wait while I dress and we will continue our business discussion over a drink.' Solo's cold, mocking eyes flicked over her tense body and to where her small hands curled into fists at her sides before he added. 'A whisky should hit the spot. It does not look as if anything else is on offer, except maybe a slap on the face,' and he had the gall to laugh at her gasp of outrage.

'I'm going to have a shower. I'll meet you downstairs.' Penny spun on her heel and marched out of the room, blinking rapidly to keep the tears of anger and humiliation at bay, and silently cursing the arrogant devil under her breath as she headed for her bedroom and locked the door behind her.

Her anger lasted until she had a shower, and stepped from the tiny *en suite* back into the room she had slept in all her life. She glanced at the cuddly toys arranged on top of a chest of drawers, oddly at variance with the opposite side of the room where a long desk took up all one wall, with her computer in the middle, and shelves of books above.

Suddenly the catastrophic events of the past two days hit her like a punch in the stomach. Her body aching in places she'd never known was possible, she sat down on the narrow bed and stared around. Her home was no longer hers to keep. James would never know the idyllic childhood she had enjoyed, the timeless sense of belonging. She wrapped her arms around her middle and, doubled over, she finally let the tears fall. How long she sat silently sobbing she had no idea until a knock on the door made her hiccup.

She heard the handle turn, and was glad she had locked the door. Quickly she rubbed her wet cheeks with a shaking hand. The last thing she needed was for Solo to find her red-eyed from weeping and naked but for a towel in a bedroom. She shuddered—whether in fear or remembered pleasure, she refused to acknowledge.

'If you are not downstairs in five minutes, I'll break the door down.'

'Yes, all right,' she snapped back, the cold determination of his tone telling her he meant it. Rising to her feet, she dashed into the bathroom and splashed her face and eyes with cold water. Returning to the bedroom, she withdrew clean bra and briefs from a drawer and a fine blue sweater, and slipped them on.

Solo Maffeiano was right about one thing, she admitted with brutal realism. Sex aside, she did have to talk to him. She stepped into her jeans and eased them up her legs.

Crossing to the mirrored dressing table, she snapped the fastener at her waist, and took a minute to brush her hair back behind her ears. She didn't appear any different, she thought in surprise. Without make-up and with her hair loose, she still looked like a teenager. It was the bane of her life, and why very few people took her seriously. Well, that was about to change as far as Solo Maffeiano was concerned...

Penny pushed her feet into a pair of mules, then opened the bedroom door, a light of steely determination in her green eyes. It lasted until she walked into the kitchen and found Solo leaning against the bench, two cups and saucers arranged before him, and waiting for the coffee to percolate.

'I thought you wanted a drink,' Penny said, refusing to admit she had been surprised to see the sophisticated, super-rich Solo doing something so mundane as preparing coffee, or that the sight of his long body dressed

again in black trousers and the cream sweater had the
power to make her heart miss a beat.

Shrugging one wide shoulder, Solo turned to face her.
'I decided against alcohol. I want you to have a clear
head for our discussion.' His grey eyes met and held
hers. 'So there can be no mistakes, or cries of foul later,'
he informed her with a tinge of sarcasm colouring his
tone.

'As if I would,' Penny denied hotly. How dared he
imply she was less than honest?

One dark brow arched sardonically. 'This from a girl
who once spent an unforgettable few weeks with me
years ago, and then declared it was a mistake.'

Unable to hold his gaze, and without a ready answer,
Penny pulled out a chair and sat down at the pine table
before raising her head and glancing back at him. 'I can
assure you our business dealings will be strictly legitimate.'

A cynical smile twisted his hard mouth. 'We will
see,' he said enigmatically, and, turning his back on her,
he filled two cups with coffee as she watched. 'Black
with one sugar?'

He had remembered, Penny thought, astonished.
'Yes,' she murmured, taking a deep breath to steady her
nerves, and when Solo placed a cup and saucer on the
table, and held out the other one to her, she managed
to take it with a firm hand. Then she took a deep swallow of the reviving brew, and waited.

Penny watched Solo pick up his cup and drain it in
one go before placing it back on the table, and could
hardly believe that not so long ago she had been naked
on a bed with the man. He was so firmly in control,
whereas she felt like a nervous wreck.

He swung a kitchen chair next to hers around, and

straddled it, his arms resting on the bowed-back. Involuntarily Penny's green gaze dropped to where his legs were spread over the chair, the fabric of his trousers pulled taut across his muscular thighs, and felt a swift curl of heat in her belly.

'Right, Penny. Haversham Park, and what is to be done with it,' Solo said crisply.

Penny lifted her head, embarrassed at where her wayward thoughts were leading, and, fighting down the blush that threatened, she said equally crisply, 'Firstly, to satisfy my curiosity. How did you acquire a share of my home? I still cannot get my head around the fact my father sold it to you without telling me.'

For years Solo had thought Penny must have been in on the deal he'd made with her father, a deceitful little gold-digger, but now he wasn't so sure. Her dismay at finding she had lost half her home was obviously genuine. But then she had always been a consummate liar. She had led him to believe their marriage had been a foregone conclusion, when all the time she had been waiting for her boyfriend to return. But it left him with the tricky question of what to tell her. The truth wasn't an option; he had no intention of appearing a bigger fool over Penny than he already had.

That last Saturday four years ago, he had formally asked her father's permission to marry her, and had told Julian obviously he had no intention of developing the land around what was his future wife's family home. Julian was disappointed, and hinted he needed money. So as a form of compensation, or, to put it more cynically, the price of his bride, Solo had parted with a large amount of cash and Julian had insisted Solo take a half-share in the house in return.

Solo had had to leave in a hurry, and so he'd been

delayed in asking Penny to marry him. When he had returned six days later, he'd been glad he had. Penny had not been around, but Solo had signed the deed with her father while waiting for her.

Then, with Veronica's information that Penny had been at the vicarage with her friend Jane, he had gone looking for her and found her with Simon. Fury did not begun to cover how he had felt at the time. Rejected and robbed in one week was not something he had ever contemplated happening to him. But it had reinforced the belief he had developed in his youth that women were not to be trusted, with his mother and grandmother as prime examples.

Remembering the fiasco now made his teeth clench. For once in his life he had let his guard down and as far as Solo was concerned the whole damn family had taken advantage of the fact to con money out of him. A half share in a house they had no intention of leaving or selling was of no use to Solo. He had been well and truly tricked.

'Well?' Penny said, the long silence praying on her already-taut nerves.

His eyes flickered, the pupils hard and black, dilating with what looked like anger. For a moment he stared at her, and then suddenly he smiled, his expression bland.

'As you know I bought some acreage from your father with a view to developing it. Your father was quite happy with the price I paid, but he had a very expensive wife in Veronica.'

'Tell me about it,' Penny muttered dryly.

One dark brow elevated sardonically. 'Yes, exactly. Anyway, I had a feasibility study taken on the profitability of the project, and it wasn't viable. Your father was disappointed, because he needed more money.

Veronica had very expensive taste, though not particularly good, judging by what she has done to the house.

'Knowing Veronica, I felt some sympathy for your father when he approached me and offered me a half-share of the house as collateral for a rather large sum of cash for an alternative investment he had in mind. I agreed because I felt a little guilty that we were not going ahead with the original project.'

'How very altruistic of you.' Penny said scathingly. 'But that does not explain why he never told me.'

'He was a proud man, maybe he was hoping to invest and make a profit.' Solo shrugged his broad shoulders indifferently. 'Perhaps he was hoping to remedy the situation before anyone knew. But I am sure he would have told you eventually. Even you must admit he couldn't possibly have expected to die so soon.'

That was true enough, Penny thought sadly. Veronica and her father had spent every summer in the south of France, while Penny had stayed home and looked after James. Veronica had always flashed the photographs around to all and sundry of the villa and yacht they'd leased.

'You're probably right.' There was a connection tugging at the edge of her brain, something that she was missing. But with a sigh she gave up. There was no sense in dwelling on what she could not change. 'So you buy me out or we sell,' she said flatly, getting back to the point of the talk.

'No,' Solo's steel-grey eyes met hers. 'There is another choice. In your case it's the only choice.'

'That sounds ominous,' she said, trying for a lightness she did not feel. 'In fact it could almost be construed as a threat.'

'Not a threat, a promise. I promise to restore

Haversham Park, and pay all your debts, plus your expenses, and you and James can stay here. In return...'

For a split second hope sprung in her heart. 'You turn most of it into a hotel and leave us with an apartment or something,' she finished for him, thinking with relief that it was an incredibly generous offer.

'Not quite.' Hard eyes stared down at her. 'It stays a private home, you will still run the place, but we share it.'

'*Share!*' she exclaimed, jumping to her feet. An unpaid housekeeper was what he meant, and Penny could imagine nothing worse than sharing a house with Solo, having to see him parade his girlfriends in front of her. 'No way.' She could not bear the idea and she did not question why.

Rising to his full height, Solo let his strong hands fall on her shoulders; she tried to shrug him off, but his hold tightened.

'So impulsive,' he opined hardly. 'But allow me to finish. We get married and you stay here but as my wife for as long as I want you.'

'Your *wife*?' She almost choked.

'Yes,' Solo said flatly. 'Then when we part the place is yours free and clear.'

Her stunned gaze lifted up to his. He had to be joking... His grey eyes stared back cold and implacable, and there was a ruthlessness about his hard, handsome features that told her he was not. The colour drained from her face; she could hardly breathe. Solo was a man who always got what he wanted—she should have remembered that.

A hollow laugh escaped her. Well, he'd already had her, to put it crudely; what had she got to lose? 'Why?'

Penny demanded stonily. 'What earthly benefit will it be to you?'

'What do you think? After what we did earlier, how can you ask that?' Solo looked at her, his smile filled with arrogant amusement. 'Or perhaps like most females you are fishing for compliments.' He shrugged slightly, his powerful shoulders lifting beneath the fine cashmere of his sweater, his handsome face expressionless.

'I don't mind humouring you. You were exquisite at eighteen, and the years in between have been very good to you. You have matured into a stunningly beautiful woman.' Blatantly he let his eyes drop to her high, full breasts clearly outlined by her blue sweater. 'My hobby is collecting perfect works of art, and to my utter astonishment I discovered you were one of that rare breed of woman, pure in body, if not mind.' he inserted cynically. 'I intended to be your lover four years ago, but you denied me, and I don't take denial easily. I figured you owed me, and today I collected,' he declared dangerously, and Penny erupted into angry speech.

'I owe *you*. You have some gall. I don't know how you did it but you have already stolen my home—what more can you want?'

'You,' he told her inexorably, his fingers biting into her shoulders. 'I was surprised to realise I was your first lover, so naturally I intend to hang onto you for as long as I want you.' His eyes glittered with ruthless disregard and Penny could not believe the colossal arrogance of the man.

She tilted her head back, a light of battle in her gaze. 'That is the most disgusting, chauvinistic statement I have ever heard. You can't own a woman like an object,' she flared back.

'I don't want to own you for ever. A temporary wife was what I had in mind,' Solo said mockingly, and she shrugged in an attempt to dislodge his restraining hands.

Penny shook her head. 'This is surreal. I don't believe I am having this conversation.'

Slowly his eyes drifted over her and her skin heated where his eyes touched. His mouth twisted in a menacing smile. 'Believe it, *cara*,' he commanded just before his mouth settled with deadly accuracy over hers.

CHAPTER FOUR

WHO said lightning could not strike twice? Penny thought inconsequentially as Solo pulled her hard against him, and, from ravishing her mouth, he moved to the soft curve of her ear. Already she could feel the swift flush of heat that signalled her instant arousal, but, now she knew what he could do to her, her body's anticipation was a hundred times more intense. She turned her head to try and escape, but his mouth hungrily followed the elegant curve of her throat, his hands sliding up under her jumper and the wisp of lace that covered her breasts. She moaned as his long fingers expertly teased the hard bud of her nipples, an unbearable spasm of excitement lancing from her breast to the apex of her thighs.

'Why fight it?' Solo demanded with sibilant softness. 'The choice is yours.' Slowly he moved his large hands down to span her narrow waist, his eyes locked onto her dazed green. 'Marry me, or I keep my share in the house. It will make a nice country base when I visit my London office.' Solo living in her home! Penny's mind boggled as he continued, 'And I would prevent you from selling until you go bankrupt and I snap up your share for peanuts. I don't mind either way, your choice.'

She gazed up into his hard face, saw the icy determination in his cold eyes. 'You actually mean it,' she said after what seemed like a lifetime had slipped by. In a way it had, she thought—her life, if she agreed to his outrageous suggestion. 'But what about love in a marriage?' She had to ask; was he really so unfeeling?

'Love is a lie, simply another word for lust believe me. But I never lie about sex.'

'Sex.' Penny looked at him with angry eyes. He couldn't have made it clearer he didn't believe in love. 'That is all this is about for you. Never mind this is my home, and my brother's—my *life*.' Fury mingled with an aching sense of loss.

'And possibly a baby, unless you happen to be on the pill,' Solo cut in bluntly.

'Oh, my God!' Penny exclaimed, the colour leeching out of her face. She had had unprotected sex. 'You—you—bastard,' she said, hitting out at his chest. 'Where was your common sense, your condoms?' she cried. A man like Solo should carry a permanent supply. 'How the hell do I know where you have been? You could have sentenced me to death.'

A violent change came over his features. He grasped her flailing hands in one of his and his other arm tightened around her waist. 'Stop right there.'

His eyes narrowed, a thin white line circled his tight lips, and a muscle in his jaw beat against his bronzed skin. She wasn't quite sure what had happened, she only knew he terrified her.

'I am not such a bastard as to put a woman's life at risk.' Solo was furious, because Penny was right, he should have used protection, he always had before. Only this woman staring up at him with her huge green eyes had the power to make him forget, and he bitterly resented the fact.

'So you say.' She swallowed hard. 'But...'

'But nothing.' His eyes glittered with cruelty. 'I have the medical proof. But you were never the shrinking violet; quite a tease, as I recall. You might have hung onto your virginity, but there are other forms of sex equally as dangerous.'

Penny stared at him in disbelief. 'You think… I…' She was lost for words.

'Not so nice when the shoe is on the foot.' Solo mangled the English saying.

'The other foot,' she corrected unthinkingly.

'Whatever.' His voice hardened. 'But we are straying from the point. You agree to marry me and you get the house. Obviously there will be a pre-nuptial. But any child I keep.'

She stared at him. His expression was unreadable, his jaw hard, his eyes steely grey. He meant every word. He let go of her hands, and they fell limply to her sides. Fear made her knees weak, and she was grateful for his supporting arm, but she knew better than to let him realise it. She lowered her eyes to fix blindly on his chest. If he sensed the slightest weakness, he would take advantage of it. She didn't know how, but he was that kind of man, a predator, and she was his prey, and he had caught her.

Penny thought of James, and any child she might have. It was a real possibility—it was the middle of her cycle, and, the way her luck had been running lately, almost inevitable. Glancing up through the thick fringe of her lashes, she could not deny Solo was a devilishly attractive, virile man.

Once she had loved him with all her heart, and she felt moisture glaze her eyes, and she blinked it away. Now she was numb with pain, hating him for what he was making her do.

'I'll be your lover,' she offered, her voice shaking,

and she kept her eyes lowered. She couldn't marry him, not without love.

'No, I can get a lover anywhere, but you may be pregnant. It is marriage or bankruptcy.' His free hand curved around the nape of her neck, and he tilted her head back, forcing her to meet his gaze. 'Yes or no?'

There was no choice. Even if she could persuade him to accept her offer of lovers, what would she tell James? Plus if there was a child, she would rather be married, and if they ever divorced there would be more financial support for any children.

'Yes, all right. I will marry you.'

'A very wise choice, Penny.' His silver eyes flared with what looked like triumph into hers. 'I knew you would see sense,' he concluded with arrogant self-assurance.

It was the arrogance that did it. From feeling like crying, Penny felt like screaming, anger bubbling up inside, and in that instant Penny changed her mind. His dark head bent, he was going to kiss her, but she placed a small hand on his chest. 'No, wait a minute, I've changed my mind.'

She cried out as his hand tightened on her neck. Contempt raw and violent blazed in his pale eyes. 'Already you are back to playing games.' Hauling her against him, he added, 'But no more, Penny.'

'No, you don't understand.' The colour surged in her cheeks. 'I want to marry you.' She looked defiantly into his eyes. 'But if there is a baby it has to be brought up and educated in England, here at Haversham Park with me.'

Something flickered in his eyes, and his heavy lids fell, masking his expression. 'I accept, Penelope,' he said, his deep voice not quite steady.

For a second Penny wondered if he was laughing at her, and if she had just made the biggest mistake of her life, then he kissed her, and it wasn't in the least amusing. He was taking her mouth with a hungry, raw possession, and she didn't care, because if he had been gentle with her she thought she would have cried, unable to stand the pretence. This way it was simply sex...

'Penny,' he groaned her name, his lips softening, gentling on hers.

Maybe not so simple as she was transported back in time to the first time they'd met, in this same kitchen, to their first kiss. She placed her hands on his broad chest, and responded with the same helpless longing.

She whimpered as he slipped his hands under her sweater and she felt his fingers hot on her naked flesh. She looped her arms around his neck. His mighty chest heaved, and then he took her hands from his nape.

'Not yet,' Solo said softly. 'I have too much to arrange.'

All Penny wanted to do was arrange his gorgeous body naked on the kitchen table and, with a guilty flush of colour at her erotic thoughts, she stepped back, avoiding his gaze.

'You said James was on holiday.' He reached out and cupped her face between his palms. 'When is he due back?' he demanded, staring down into her beautiful face.

'Eight days or so,' she murmured.

'That should be fine—and Brownie?'

'It's her bingo night. I drive down to the village and collect her about ten. Why the sudden interest?' she asked.

He looked into her eyes and smiled. 'Because you and I are going to Italy in the morning. With James away and Brownie here to look after the house, it is perfect timing. So pack a bag, and then let's have something to eat. I'm starving.'

'Italy! I can't go to Italy.'

Solo placed a kiss on her brow and set her free. 'You can and you will, but for now do as I say. I need the laptop from my car, and I'll use the study.' Slanting her an almost boyish grin, he left her standing in the middle of the kitchen totally confused...

Penny sliced carrots and wished she were slicing Solo's neck. What had she done? What did she actually know about the man she had agreed to marry other than she hated him? Solo was a very private man. The first time they were together all she had known about him was that he was a wealthy businessman, and he lived in Italy. She had asked about his family, and he'd told her he was an only child and his parents were long gone, and he had no relatives. Her young heart had filled with compassion and she had kissed him, thinking how awful to be so alone in the world. Now she wasn't so sure, if it weren't for James she wouldn't be in this mess...

Penny gasped, horrified where her thoughts had taken her; for a nanosecond she had actually thought if it weren't for James she would not happily, but willingly, have walked out of her family home, and out on Solo Maffeiano.

She loved her half-brother, and she glanced around the kitchen, the familiar room she had known all her life, the only home James had ever known. She could walk out, but she would still be stuck with a huge debt, and how could she explain to James they had no money, and no home?

Her lawyer's plan for her to sell up and start afresh

with James was finally consigned to the dustbin of useless ideas. Solo would not allow it. One didn't need to be a genius to see he could delay the sale for ever if he wanted to. He had the money and the power; he was in complete control.

She shivered, suddenly feeling cold. Gathering up the carrots, she dropped them in the pan with the chopped meat and onions. Solo was used to the finest food. Well, tough!

He was getting beef stew and potatoes.

Washing her hands under the kitchen sink, she dried them with the kitchen towel, and sat down at the table. Penny sighed and stared out of the window, at the overgrown garden, and wondered where her life went from here.

James's and Brownie's futures would be secure, which was a major consolation. They need never know the circumstances of the proposed marriage, never know the happy couple actually despised each other, if Penny was careful. Their lives would not change, except for the better, with Solo's money to make life easier.

Would it really be so bad? she asked herself. Apart from this visit to Italy Solo was insisting on, she might hardly ever see him once she was back. His interests were worldwide; he had told her he didn't get back to his home in Italy as much as he would like. So it was reasonable to suppose he would not spend much time in England.

She let out a breath. Her own innate honesty forced her to admit that being able to keep her own home, having great sex occasionally, and the possibility of a child of her own was not a bad deal. When had she become so cynical? Penny sighed, and, folding her arms on the table, she rested her head. Just for a moment.

The death of her father had turned her life upside down. Then, just when she'd thought she was over the worst of her grief, and was beginning to see the light at the end of the tunnel, Solo Maffeiano had walked back into her life, and turned it upside down again.

She was bone-weary and so tired. Once she had loved Solo so much, marriage to him had been her dream. Now it was her nightmare. Her long lashes fluttered over her cheeks, her breathing slowed, and she slept.

That was how Solo found her. She looked so young, so defenceless, and for a moment he questioned if he was pursuing the right course. He still had not got over the shock of discovering he was her first lover. The blond youth had to have been an idiot, or perhaps with the idealism of the young he had respected Penny too much.

He hardened his heart. Damn it to hell! She had not been that innocent. Penny had quite happily deceived her boyfriend and him... She owed him, and this time there was going to be no mistake. She'd marry him, and like it.

He reached out a hand. His first inclination was to shake her awake, but instead his fingers stroked gently down the back of her head. 'Penny, *cara,* wake up.'

Somewhere in the distance Penny heard the softly voiced command, and, eyes slowly opening, she raised her head. She felt the caress of a hand on her hair and jerked upright. 'Solo, what do you want?' She spoke sharply. He had surprised her but she could feel a much more dangerous emotion heating her blood, something that had to do with the sight of him smiling down at her.

'Something smells good.'

'Oh, hell! The stew!' Penny jumped to her feet and dashed to the stove. 'It's nearly burnt.'

Solo laughed and moved to stand close. 'What will you do about it?'

'Nothing—you can like it or lump it,' she said tightly. 'Sit down, it will be two minutes.'

He flicked a finger down her cheek 'Relax, I don't mind, anything will do.' He pulled out a chair and sat down, much to Penny's relief.

Filling the kettle, she moved around the kitchen setting two places at the table and, when the kettle boiled, pouring water onto some dried mash potato.

'Very cordon bleu,' Solo drawled mockingly, eyeing the plate of stew and mash she put before him warily.

'I never said I was a cook,' Penny shot back, taking the chair opposite, and, picking up a fork, she began to eat.

'Then it is as well I am not marrying you for your culinary ability,' Solo said, one ebony brow arching sardonically.

She looked up and suddenly, in a flash of clarity, she realised what had tugged at the edge of her mind earlier, when Solo had explained he had given her father the money against the house. But in the same breath had said it was not a viable proposition for development. Solo was a ruthless businessman—he would never waste money on a loser. But that was exactly what he had done, and was still doing.

She looked up, her eyes flashing. 'No—then why the hell are you marrying me?' she demanded, her smooth brow creased in a confused, angry frown. The deal he had offered her was marriage, and she got to keep the house. But that meant she had been wrong four years ago when she'd thought he was only after her for her home!

For a moment she wondered if she had made the most horrendous mistake of her life at eighteen. Then she remembered the other woman Patricia had told her about and the sound of Solo's laughter and his, 'I'll always love you,' to Tina Jenson, and she knew she had been right to walk out on him.

She searched his hard, handsome face seeking an answer. He was strikingly attractive, he could have any woman he wanted, so why her?

'Let's be blunt,' she said quickly before she lost her nerve. 'I am marrying you for money, but your reason escapes me. I'm sure you have never had to pay for a woman in your life.'

'A compliment, I'm flattered.' Solo said with a wry grin.

'It's not funny.' Penny replied. 'This is my life we are talking about. Is it because I dented your ego once when I said I preferred Simon to you? A touch of old-fashioned revenge?' Not giving him time to respond, she continued, 'I find that hard to believe—we both know you were not that bothered. It certainly isn't because you feel anything for me, and I cannot believe it is just for sex—you are notorious for your women.'

'Stop.' Solo's eyes locked onto hers. 'The past is not up for discussion.' He pushed the half-eaten plate of food away and rose to his feet. 'Suffice it to say I have my reasons, and all you need to know is that the wedding is arranged for three days' time in Italy.'

'Three days, just like that?' Penny shook her head in amazement at his arrogance. 'You say jump, and I say how high?' she said sarcastically.

His hands closed over her shoulders and he drew her

to her feet, his dark head bending towards her. 'You're getting the idea.'

'Am I?' She could feel the warmth of his breath against her cheek, and her throat constricting at his nearness. His lips brushed against her mouth and she trembled.

Solo felt her reaction and smiled. 'Oh, yes.' he drawled, lifting his head, grey eyes gazing intently on her slightly pink face. 'Now, if you haven't packed yet, I suggest you do it now, because in an hour poor Brownie will be standing in the rain waiting for you.'

'Oh, hell! The car.' She chewed her bottom lip in angry frustration. She'd left it out, and the old vehicle had a nasty habit of stalling in the rain. 'It is all your fault I forgot.' She jabbed a finger in his chest. 'If it doesn't start you can fix it. After all, you're supposedly the best at everything.' She knew she was being childish, but it was the only defence against him she had left.

'You've lost me.' Solo let his hands drop from her shoulders and stepped back. His own wide shoulders elevated in a shrug. 'I have not touched your car.' He had never met a woman who could switch so instantly from one subject to the next.

But he was grateful because if he'd had to explain why he was marrying her, he no longer knew the answer. He had told himself she and her family owed him big time, and no one got away with cheating Solo Maffeiano. But it wasn't strictly true. Julian Haversham had contacted him and offered to repay half of the money, and the rest when he could afford it. Solo had refused his offer, and told him he was quite willing to wait. The money wasn't really important, the amount was small change to a man of his wealth.

All he knew was every time he looked at Penny he

felt a fierce stirring of lust coupled with the old hatred and contempt he had felt when he had found her in the arms of a young man.

'I know that,' Penny said after a long pause. 'But the car does not like the rain and because you were late I had to rush down and drop Brownie off, in case you arrived while I was gone, and I left it outside. It's not the most reliable—'

'What?' Solo exclaimed, back to the present with a jolt as he remembered the car parked outside. 'You're not still driving your father's old car?' His brows rose in astonishment, when he realised what she was talking about. 'It was ready for the scrap heap years ago.'

'Not all of us are blessed with millions,' Penny replied bitterly. 'And the car is perfectly all right.'

'So long as it does not rain,' Solo said dryly.

She looked up, and saw the amusement in his eyes, and a smile quirked the corners of her full lips. 'Yes.'

'No problem, we will take my car.'

To say Brownie was surprised when a gleaming black car drew to a halt outside the bingo hall and Solo Maffeiano stepped out was an understatement. Penny sat huddled in the front passenger seat on Solo's orders as he said there was no need for both of them to get wet, and watched as he took Brownie's arm and led her to the car.

'This is wonderful news, Penny,' Brownie said, settling comfortably in the back as Solo started the car. 'I could hardly believe my eyes when I saw Mr Maffeiano, but I always thought he would come back.'

What news? Penny was about to ask when Solo cut in. 'How could I possibly stay away from you any longer, Brownie? I really missed your cooking.'

'Oh, Mr Maffeiano.' Penny looked on in astonish-

ment as Brownie moved forward and patted Solo on the
back. 'You are such a one.'

It got no better when they were safely back indoors.

'I better explain to Brownie…' Penny started to say,
but Solo ignored her.

'You will find a bottle of champagne in the fridge,
Brownie. Will you join us in a little celebration?'

Brownie smiled—well, more of a simper, Penny
thought nastily.

'Well, I don't usually drink, but for you, yes, I will.'

'For us, Brownie.' Solo moved to Penny's side.

'Wait a minute,' Penny demanded, turning stormy
eyes up to him. 'Where did the champagne come from?'

Dark and with a devilish grin, Solo curved an arm
around her shoulders. 'I brought it with me, darling, and
put it in the fridge while you showered after—'

'Yes, okay,' she cut him off, horrified he was going
to tell Brownie how they had spent the afternoon.

He squeezed her shoulder, his smile mocking the
blushing confusion she could not hide from him. 'Darling, Brownie must be the first to know we are getting
married.'

CHAPTER FIVE

'How do you feel?' Solo asked, his brow furrowed in concern. 'It never entered my head you might be afraid of flying.'

Strapped into a flight seat, one hand gripping the armrest as if her life depended on it, Penny managed to turn her head and glance up at Solo leaning over her.

Trust him to look incredibly attractive and disgustingly fit, while she felt like death. He was wearing a pale linen suit and a white shirt open at the neck. The suit had appeared from the back of his car yesterday along with the champagne and an overnight bag. Penny didn't believe for one moment that he always travelled with a change of clothes prepared for any eventuality as he had said. She suspected he had had a much more sinister reason. If she had not fallen into his arms so easily, she was prepared to bet he would have hung around until she did. He was a devious, manipulative swine at the best of times.

Not that she cared in her present state of health. But to give him his due, Solo had called the flight attendant and demanded some water for her, and impatiently he had vacated his safety seat and walked the length of the private jet to get the water himself, such was his concern.

'I didn't ask to come to Italy,' Penny said between clenched teeth. The water had eased her raw throat a little, but she was sure she was going to be sick again, and she had only been in the plane twenty minutes.

'Open your mouth and swallow this pill,' Solo demanded, his lean fingers reaching for her lips.

'What is it?'

'A travel sickness pill. Just swallow it, you will feel better, trust me,' Solo soothed, stroking the back of her hand that grasped the armrest. 'Try and relax, the nausea will pass.' Meekly opening her mouth, she felt his fingers against her lips as he placed the pill on her tongue. 'Now have another drink of water.'

With a hand that trembled she lifted the glass to her mouth and swallowed, then, feeling cold, she slid down in the seat in a state of near panic. Solo took the glass from her shaking hand and passed it to the male flight attendant, then sat down again.

'Feeling better?' His deep, husky voice was anxious.

'Not so you'd notice,' she tried to joke, but her nerves were shot to pieces. 'I don't like flying,' she said with feeling.

'Why didn't you tell me?' She saw him stiffen, his jawline taut. 'I could have done something about it.' Prising her hand from its deathlike grip on the armrest, he held it firmly in one of his.

'You never asked.' His skin was warm and his grip comforting and Penny laid her head back and closed her eyes, feeling marginally better.

'No, but it's not that unusual,' Solo said soothingly, slowly stroking the back of her hand. 'Lots of people are afraid of flying, but there are excellent medications available to overcome the problem.'

Penny's lips twisted in a wry grimace. Airsickness was the least of her problems. Her biggest problem was the man gently stroking her hand. It was hardly surprising she was ill after yesterday and a sleepless night.

She was an emotional wreck before she ever got on the damn plane!

Until three days ago, she had been a reasonably contented woman. Her childhood had been happy until the death of her mother, but she had battled though her loss, and accepted her father marrying again and loved her half-brother. The only blip on the smooth running of her life had been the summer when she had first met Solo and fallen headlong in love with him, or so she had thought...

But with grim determination she had got over what she saw as his betrayal, and gone to university, passing all her exams. The trauma of losing her father and Veronica was fading and she was on the first step of the ladder to being a successful author of children's books. She was quiet by nature, but with an inner core of strength that made her fight against adversity.

That was until yesterday afternoon. Before she had been an inexperienced girl who had not discovered the depths of her own sexuality. But Solo had changed all that in a couple of hours, when he had shown her what it was to be a sexually aware woman. She had been struggling with the emotional fallout ever since.

Last night she had watched him charm Brownie. Then he had stood at her side and listened while she'd rung Jane's mum on her mobile and told her she was going on holiday to Italy for a week, and while she'd spoken with James. Then Solo had called her a coward for not revealing their marriage plans.

Penny had been furious, but later, when he had walked her upstairs to her bedroom, to her shame she had been torn between hoping he would leave her alone, and then, when he'd kissed her goodnight at her door, wishing he wouldn't. No wonder she'd had a sleepless night.

'Penny.'

'Hmm,' she murmured, her eyelids fluttering open.

Solo looked down at her through thick black lashes, an intimate glance that made her heart miss a beat. 'Feeling better?'

As if he actually cared…Penny thought mutinously, but bit down on the childish response and hesitated for a moment, listening to her body. 'Yes, I think I am.' She sighed in relief. The nausea had gone.

Solo sank back in his seat, and breathed in deeply. Thank God she had got a bit of colour back in her face. Not willing to admit seeing her sick and as pale as a ghost had made him feel as guilty as sin. He had bull-dozed Penny into coming to Italy with him. But seeing her ill had terrified him. There were times when he wanted to wring her lovely neck for the way she had rejected him in the past, but other times, like now, when he wanted to cradle her in his arms and comfort her.

He must be getting soft in his old age—then he dismissed the thought; age was not something he wished to dwell on. He cast her a sidelong glance. She was resting her head back, the elegant arch of her throat exposed by the open neck of the blue blouse she was wearing, as was the shadowy cleavage of her luscious breasts. He felt a tightening in his groin. What the hell was he thinking of? The girl was ill!

'So, Penny, tell me,' he said, calmly determined to divert his wayward thoughts. 'How is it in the twenty-first century a woman of your age is still terrified of flying? Surely you must have tried to get over your fear before now. I know you and your family fly down to the South of France at least a couple of times a year.'

'There are such things as boats and trains,' Penny remarked, slanting him a wry glance. With her nausea gone, she had time to look around. The cream leather armchairs and the bar all portrayed the wealth of the man at her side. The fact she was still in the safety seat, and had no intention of moving until the plane landed, did not stop her appreciating the luxury the plane afforded.

'But as it happens I've never been to the South of France—it was Dad and Veronica's holiday. They stayed in England for Christmas, but when I came home for the Easter and summer vacations, they took off the next day. It was a chance for them to have a break on their own while I was there to look after James. I've never flown before. In fact, technically you could say I've never been outside of the UK.'

'You have never flown!' Solo declared incredulously. 'I don't believe it. You've never even been abroad?'

'Unless you call the Channel Islands abroad. No...James and I had a week in Guernsey two summers running. It is a nice journey by boat, and there is a lovely beach at St Peter's Port. The weather is generally better than in mainland Britain.'

'I need a drink.' Solo got to his feet. He also needed to think. 'Want anything?' he asked curtly.

'No, I'm fine.' Penny looked up. His eyes burned into hers. He was angry.

Solo shook his dark head in exasperation, and moved to the bar. For years he had naturally assumed Penny had benefited from her father's upturn in fortune at his expense. But now he was not so sure; either she was a great actress, or too soft for her own good. Unfortunately for him he was beginning to think it might be the latter.

JACQUELINE BAIRD

103

The red dress apart, Penny's clothes appeared to be classic but conservative. Today she was wearing a blouse and neat-fitting navy trousers, suitable for travelling. Her blonde hair was tied back and she looked the same as she had at eighteen. And she had never flown before!

To a man who spent half his working life travelling in his own jet the notion was unthinkable. Plus he had known Veronica, and he could easily believe she would dump her child on Penny and take off to the high life. He was a bit surprised that Julian Haversham had agreed, but then he'd been an old man with a young wife—what else could he have done? That thought brought Solo up cold.

Solo was silent for the rest of the trip, and Penny turned her head towards the window and stared out at the vast expanse of clear blue sky. He was probably angry and disgusted with her for being ill. Served him right if he was fed up with her already. The whole sorry mess was his fault, and on that thought she fell asleep. When the plane slowed and the noise increased, she started awake with a nervous jolt. But she did not have time to feel ill before the aircraft touched down.

Solo unfastened her seat belt. 'I think I better carry you,' he said, his mouth tight.

'No. No.' Penny struggled to stand up, knocking his hand away. 'I can manage, just lead me to a house on terra firma, and a bathroom,' she said with feeling.

Her mouth felt dry, her blouse was sticking to her, and it did nothing for her self-esteem to see Solo looking as cool and elegant as ever.

The customs officer waved them through without even looking at their passports.

'You must be well known,' Penny murmured as they

exited Naples airport. Unaccustomed to the heat and the brilliant sunlight, she shielded her eyes with one hand and glanced up at Solo.

But his attention was fixed on a white-haired, casually dressed man in shorts and a black shirt who flung his arms around Solo like a long-lost brother, and a rapid conversation in Italian ensued. Then the older man turned to smile at Penny with sympathy and Solo quickly introduced him as Nico.

When she was seated in the back of an elegant black car, Solo beside her, he explained. 'Nico and his wife look after my home, and they both speak a bit of English, so anything you need feel free to ask them.'

They drove for what seemed miles in silence. With each breath Penny took she was aware of the faint scent of Solo's aftershave. He was too close sitting beside her, his arm casually resting along the back of the seat, his jacket pulled open, and the white shirt did nothing to hide the breadth of his muscular chest.

When the car suddenly turned and she fell against him, she quickly straightened up and looked out of the window, and was glad of the distraction as the car was angling into a concealed driveway flanked by massive stone pillars and lined with trees.

She gasped when the house came into view. 'This is your home!' she exclaimed, turning stunned green eyes to his perfectly chiselled profile.

Amazingly, colour striped his high cheekbone. 'Yes, it is, and I like it,' he said, his voice hardening almost defensively, and stepped out of the car, opened Penny's door and held out his hand.

A pretty fantasy—there was no other way to describe it. The pale blue stuccoed house, with delicately carved white-painted shutters, had fantastic sculptured scrolls and smiling nymphs at each corner and marching along a stone balustrade at the base of the high slate roof were twelve sculptured figures. In the vast expanse of a paved forecourt were three fountains with elegant dolphins and mermaids. The design was quirky classical, but so *not* Solo…

He was an aloof, arrogant man, and if she had had to picture his type of house it would have been something impressive and solid in granite, with no frills, as hard as he was.

'Penny.'

She glanced up. 'Yes,' she said and, ignoring his hand, she got out of the car and looked around. Beyond the open courtyard there was a terrace with a riot of colourful flowers and shrubs leading to an oval swimming pool. A sloping lawn ended at a row of orange and lemon trees with a view of the sparkling blue sea beyond.

'Do you approve?' Solo asked, moving to stand beside her, and deliberately sliding an arm around her waist to hold her at his side.

'It's beautiful,' she answered honestly. 'But not what I expected.'

'Things rarely are. As I am beginning to realise,' Solo said enigmatically, and urged her towards the porch.

Nico preceded them in and a smiling dark-haired woman of about fifty waited for them. 'My wife, Anna.'

'Welcome back, *signor*, and this must be Miss Haversham. Good morning,' Anna said with a heavy Italian accent.

Was it still morning? Penny wasn't sure—the effect of Solo's hand on her waist, warm and possessive, added to her confusion and, glancing at her wrist-watch, she registered it was almost one. 'Good afternoon.' She tried to smile.

Solo grasped Penny's arm and led her across the marble-floored hall to the foot of the stairs. 'Penny has had a bad journey,' he explained quietly. 'Leave the luggage till later, Nico. I am going to take her up to her room. She needs to rest.'

'Wait a minute,' Penny said as her delighted gaze swept around the beautiful hall, the delicately painted antique Italian furniture. A roll-top desk against one wall, a gorgeous hall table. 'Can I—?'

'No, upstairs,' Solo said firmly and, striding forward, he almost dragged her up the curving staircase, and along a wide landing and into a room.

'Why the rush, I am feeling much better and I would like to have a look around,' Penny said as he released her and closed the door, her angry green gaze clashing with grey.

'Because you have had a very traumatic journey and you need to recover,' Solo said smoothly, walking towards her, his mouth curved in a brief smile, and to her astonishment he walked straight past her.

'Here is your bathroom.' She turned and he had opened a door, and beyond it was the gleam of cream and gold tiles and sparkling mirrored walls. 'Drink your tea, then take a shower and have a rest.'

He was ordering her around like a child. 'Now, wait a minute…' Penny muttered, burning with resentment and other feelings she preferred not to recognise, but, ignoring her, he continued.

'Your dressing room is over here, but don't waste too much time unpacking.' His grey eyes clashed with her rebellious green. 'On Monday you will be moving into the master suite as my wife.'

Wife hit her like a thunderbolt. She glanced wildly around, then back at Solo. He had moved to stand only inches away from her, and it finally registered in her tired mind—Italy, *this* man, *this* room, *this* was reality.

Her head jerked up and she stared at him. 'It's impossible, Solo. You can't get married just like that.' She was panicking. 'I mean, you need documents, a birth certificate, and papers.' She tossed back her head, and hoped he would not recognise her panic. 'What about my family, friends?'

'All arranged. I spent a constructive hour in your father's study. It wasn't possible for us to marry in England quickly. Luckily I have some pull in Italy and I have the documentation.' He was staring at her, his expression unreadable. 'I have an appointment with the relevant authority in an hour, and later today we are going shopping for some clothes for you.'

'There is nothing the matter with my clothes,' Penny cut in angrily.

His grey eyes made a slow, indolent appraisal of her slender form, and she was horribly conscious of her crumpled blouse and trousers. 'Not quite bridal finery,' he remarked, moving closer.

'I don't need you—'

He lifted one finger and pressed it over her parted lips. 'All you need to do is to look your usual beautiful self on Monday, and keep your mouth shut, except to say *sì*.' He looked at her mouth and then into her eyes. 'Everything clear?'

He must have gone through her father's papers in the study, and she had let him, she thought, angry with her own trusting stupidity. He tipped her head up, and her breath caught in her throat when she realised he was going to kiss her. She told herself it wasn't what she wanted, but when his lips replaced his finger on her mouth she welcomed his kiss with a soft sigh of surrender.

Solo lifted his head and looked down into her dazed green eyes, the softly pouting mouth, and offered, 'If you like we can have a wedding reception for your friends when we return to England.'

'That would be nice,' Penny said rather nervously as she glimpsed the deep, sensual warmth in his eyes.

'Good, because there is no going back,' he mocked. 'You're mine.'

Something Penny was made very much aware of at six o'clock that evening as, stripped to her briefs, she stood in the changing room of an exclusive boutique silently fuming.

She had slept for most of the afternoon. Anna had awoken her with a cup of tea and some very English cucumber sandwiches, and the information the master would be waiting for her downstairs in half an hour. Physically feeling much better, Penny had showered and dressed in a plain rose-coloured shift dress in fine cotton, a matching scarf held her long hair back and, with sandals on her feet, she had made it downstairs in time.

Solo had taken a brief look at her and said, 'Very nice, but I think we can do better than that for your wedding dress,' which did nothing for her self-confidence.

'In that case, you can't come with me. It is unlucky for the groom to see the wedding dress before the marriage service.'

With a sardonic tilt of one ebony brow, Solo said, 'Foolish superstition. A man makes his own luck in this world.'

Solo certainly did, Penny thought wryly, and did not bother arguing.

A short journey in a fire-red sports car saw them arrive at this exclusive boutique in Sorrento. The owner, a stunning-looking woman named Teresa, greeted Solo with a kiss and a hug, while Penny was subjected to a brief smile and a comprehensive examination of her slender figure, before Teresa turned back to Solo and a discussion in Italian followed.

Roughly Penny pulled the cream creation over her head and smoothed it down over her slender hips, her temper simmering. Half a dozen times already she had paraded out of the cubicle into the salon, and had to suffer the indignity of Solo lounging on a satin sofa and studying every inch of her body. Then discussing the relative merits of the garments in his native language with Teresa, before saying yes or no.

At least that was what Penny thought they were doing, but they could have been arranging a hot date for all she knew, and she felt like an idiot. She did not even bother looking in the mirror this time before she marched back out into the salon.

'So will this do?' she demanded, her green eyes flashing fire. Teresa was now on the sofa beside Solo. The woman might as well sit on his lap, Penny thought angrily. It was perfectly obvious they were very good friends and probably more. Not that she cared, she told herself...

Solo's grey eyes lifted, and an arrested expression crossed his hard features. Slowly his gaze raked over her face and down her throat, to her slender shoulders and lower. 'Beautiful,' he murmured.

She felt the heat of his glance down her body, like a flame, and looked down. Then blushed scarlet when she realised the strapless gown, embroidered in tiny seed pearls, revealed the upper curve of her breasts, and fitted like a second skin into her narrow waist and down over her hips to end above her knee. 'There is a jacket to go with it.' She spun around.

'No, wait,' Solo demanded and slowly she turned back to face him.

He had stood up, and moved to stop in the middle of the floor. She glanced up at him, a tall giant of a man with silver-grey eyes, and then quickly lowered her eyes as he slowly walked all the way around her.

She half turned. 'I'll get the jacket.' But long, tanned fingers closed over her shoulders and turned her back to face him.

'Not yet, let me look.' His grey eyes raked over her from head to toe. 'This is the one.' His deep, husky drawl feathered across her nerves as smooth as silk. 'You look incredible,' and, turning to Teresa, 'You agree?'

Penny made her feet move. 'Right, so that is that,' she said flatly, dashing back into the changing cubicle. But she did not escape quite so easily. By the time they left the boutique she was the owner of three formal gowns, a whole load of mix-and-match casual summer clothes, if one could call designer labels casual—the prices certainly weren't—and to her shame some very flimsy underwear Solo took delight in choosing for her.

'Did you have to ask Teresa what she thought of lace thongs?' Penny snapped when they finally got out of the shop. 'I have never been so embarrassed in my life.'

He slanted a mocking sideways glance at her as he led her to an outside table at the restaurant next door, and held out a chair. 'Sit, you're looking rather flushed, and your naivety is showing.' And he had the nerve to laugh.

'Well, I would never wear one,' Penny said sharply.

'Shame.' Solo smiled down at her, a wicked gleam in his eyes. 'I rather like the image of you in a tiny lace thong,' he murmured as he took the seat opposite her.

'You're disgusting.' Her flashing green eyes clashed with his. 'But then at your age I should not be surprised—you probably need all the titillation you can get!' she shot back, deliberately having a dig at his age in the hope of denting his massive ego.

His lips twisted into a cynical smile that held a hint of cruelty and his eyes held no humour at all. 'You're brave in public with a table between us,' he told her blandly. 'But beware of challenging me, Penny. You're a novice in the sexual stakes.'

He regarded her silently across the table for what seemed like an age, and it took considerable will-power to hold his gaze. 'But unlike you I am still young enough to learn.'

With a shout of laughter he threw his head back. 'Have you any idea what you have just invited, you foolish girl?'

'I am neither a girl or foolish,' Penny replied, infuriated by his laughter.

Reaching across the table, he grasped her hand in one of his. 'That could be construed as an offer for me to teach you everything I know.' He lifted his hand to his lips and kissed her palm, and she felt the sensual effect right down to her toes. 'Thank you, *cara*,' and at that moment the waiter arrived.

Penny wanted to rage at the arrogant devil, but, thinking over where her anger had led her, she could see his point.

'Champagne, Penny?'

'Yes, please.' Why not? Maybe getting drunk was not such a bad idea. Face it, she told herself, it is the only one you have left.

His slate-grey eyes raked over her expressive features, pinning her gaze. 'Not a good idea. Alcohol never solved anything. Trust me, I know.'

He was a mind-reader as well; why didn't that surprise her? Letting her lips curl in a brief smile, she taunted, 'You would, oh, mighty one, font of all knowledge, seducer of hundreds of women.'

'I will take that as a joke…this time,' Solo warned with a hint of steel, and she wondered at her own nerve in goading him.

'Have some champagne.' He poured the sparkling liquid into the glass provided. 'A toast to our marriage and us. It can be as happy as you choose to make it, Penny.'

'Why is it up to me?' she asked dryly. 'Unless I'm mistaken, it takes two to make a marriage.'

Solo leaned back in his chair, his handsome face expressionless. 'Because I know what I want from this marriage,' he declared with thoughtful deliberation. 'But I'm not sure you do.'

'I don't actually want to marry you at all. I simply want to prevent being declared a bankrupt and keep a roof over my brother's and my head,' she slashed back bluntly. 'And as you are hardly likely to spend much time at Haversham Park, and I am certainly not going anywhere else, it will be a temporary marriage of hopefully brief duration.' Her life was full enough with James and her fledgling writing career to look after. What the hell! As long as she wasn't pregnant, she could come out of the sorry mess smelling of roses, with

Solo the villain. After all, he already had a long-term mistress in Tina Jenson.

Lifting her glass, she pinned a dazzling smile on her face. 'To us,' and she drained the glass. 'But tell me,' she said, placing the glass on the table and glancing across into his flintlike eyes. He was so confident and incredibly attractive, he mesmerised and made her want to murder him in equal parts. 'How did your PA react to your news, or haven't you told her yet?'

One ebony brow arched sardonically. 'An interest in my business? You do surprise me.'

'Well, rumour has it Tina Jenson is something more than your PA,' Penny said with a brittle smile. 'I do hope you have informed her of your forthcoming nuptials, it is only good manners,' she ended facetiously.

His grey eyes became coldly remote on her mutinous face. 'Of course,' he drawled. 'Tina as my PA is aware of my movements at all times.'

Anger hot and instant scorched Penny's cheeks. 'I'll just bet she is.' To think Tina was his lover was bad enough, but to have it tacitly confirmed by the arrogant devil was too much.

He watched her with merciless eyes. 'As for the rest,' he said cuttingly. 'I never listen to rumour, and neither should you.'

'So you never slept with Tina?' The question just popped out and Penny could have kicked herself.

'I didn't say that,' he corrected silkily. 'But it is nice to know you are jealous, Penny, darling.'

CHAPTER SIX

PENNY watched him drink his second cup of coffee with bleary eyes. Solo had eaten a good breakfast, ham, eggs and three pastries, with apparent enjoyment, while she had struggled to swallow one of the delicious pastries. He seemed to be in an excellent mood, his silver-grey eyes smiling at her across the top of his cup.

'I've been in touch with decorators and Brownie, and with a bit of luck by the time we have to return to England at least the paintwork at Haversham Park will not be so bilious.'

'You've what?' she exclaimed. 'Who gave you the right to instigate the decoration of my home.'

'Our home, Penelope,' he drawled sardonically.

He was right again. They were seated at a table outside on the terrace, the sun was warm on her bare shoulders. Italy in May was a lot warmer than England and she had dressed accordingly in a cropped white cotton top and a short denim skirt. But suddenly she felt cold. She tilted her chin. 'You should have consulted me anyway,' she flared, her pride stung.

'I didn't think it was necessary. Brownie assured me she remembers all the original colours.' Solo shrugged. 'I thought that would do for now as I remember it being very attractively decorated.'

He had been talking to Brownie behind her back, and that hurt. Solo had taken over her home and now the loyalty of the one person Penny trusted above all others.

'Later we can discuss any alterations that need to be

made, perhaps a new nursery.' At her arrested gasp a glint of amusement flickered in his grey eyes. 'You must consider the possibility, Penny, as you so succinctly pointed out we took no precautions.'

'Well, if it ever happens again, you better make damn sure you do.' Penny hated him for stating cold, hard facts. It was all his fault she might be pregnant.

The amusement vanished from his eyes. 'Oh, it will happen again, and again, of that you can be sure,' he stated emphatically, shooting her a penetrating glance. 'As for protection, if the thought of having my child so horrifies you—' his mouth thinned in a tight, ominous line '—I suggest you wait until we see what nature intends this month, and then I will introduce you to my doctor, and you can take the pill.'

If Penny had not known better, she would have thought she had deeply offended him, but she quickly dismissed the idea. He had made it very plain their relationship was strictly sexual, and of a temporary nature. With Tina in the background it could never be anything else. Why the thought depressed her, she didn't dare question.

'We don't have to get married,' she said quietly.

'Yes, we do.' Solo eyed her with cool implacability. 'I was born a bastard and no child of mine will suffer the same fate.'

'I thought your parents were dead!' Penny exclaimed.

'My mother is, she died when I was ten; my father, I have no idea. He was an American sailor, and my mother a whore.'

'That's terrible,' Penny murmured, her tender heart aching as she pictured Solo as a small boy without family. 'I can't imagine not having a home and family.'

She lifted green eyes moist with sympathy to his. 'It must have been awful for you.'

'No, it was the making of me. The streets of Naples were my home. As for family, who needs one? Neither your father or your stepmother were particularly kind to you, or you would not be here now. Save your pity for someone who needs it,' he declared callously. 'Yourself perhaps, because you are still going to marry me. The arrangements have been made, and I will not be made to look a fool in my home town.'

Penny said nothing. But the insight into his upbringing or lack of it had a profound effect on her troubled mind. She could not get the picture of a young Solo having to fend for himself out of her mind. He had every material thing a man could want, wealth, power, stunning good looks, a home. A home filled with perfect objects, and who could blame him for collecting only the best, when he had started life with nothing? No wonder he had insisted on marriage, any child of Solo's would have everything the world could provide.

She cast him a surreptitious glance through the thick fringe of her lashes—but would the child have love? He was so cold, so controlled, but, beneath the hard exterior was he capable of love? As a teenager she had once thought so; he had been light-hearted and had made her laugh, for a few short weeks they had had fun... Later he had made her cry. Perhaps it was not impossible to recapture something of the past.

But for the duration of the meal the conversation was limited to generalities.

Later, acting as though he were a tourist guide, Solo showed her around his home. She stared in amazement at the paintings in the main salon. She recognised a genuine Matisse, and her eyes boggled at the exquisite oriental china, the bronze statues.

His collection of *objets d'art* was eclectic, but everything the genuine original. He had not been joking when he had told her he collected only perfect objects. His home was beautiful, and she told him so after leaving a purpose-built gallery that housed modern art, a Picasso and Jackson Pollock just two of about twenty.

'You are like a human magpie, Solo.' She slanted a smiling glance up at him. They were in his study, and even the desk was magnificent, made of polished walnut, and the silver and crystal ink set had no modern use but was perfect all the same.

His lips curled sardonically. 'If by that you think I am a thief…' he gripped her arm just below the elbow, his fingers biting into her flesh '…let me disabuse you of the notion. Everything I have I have bought legitimately, and that includes you.'

Then he pulled her into his arms, crushing her breasts against his hard, muscular chest, moulding her slender thighs and stomach into the rocklike contours of his body. He lowered his head and his hard mouth covered hers.

Penny could not move, so she did the only thing possible and clung to his wide shoulders as he kissed her with a deep, burning, angry passion.

At last he lifted his head and moved back and her legs trembled, her breathing ragged. 'I never meant…' She suddenly realised the insensitivity of her comment with a background like Solo's and wanted to apologise, but he didn't give her the chance.

'Shut up, Penny, and listen.' His chiselled features impassive, his expression was hard. Walking around the desk, he said, 'I have the pre-nuptial for your signature.

Read it, and I think you will find I have not robbed you, then sign,' he commanded cynically.

Penny looked warily at the papers he slid across the desk, rubbing her arm—she would probably have a bruise there tomorrow—then picked up the document.

'More than generous,' she said flatly into the long silence and signed it.

Penny's wedding day dawned bright and clear. Anna insisted on doing her hair—apparently she had been a hairdresser in her youth—and swirled the blonde tresses into a fantastic concoction on top of Penny's head. The final touch was a number of tiny rosebuds from the garden inserted in the soft curls.

Penny glanced at her reflection in the mirror, and hardly recognised herself. The strapless dress lovingly clung to her slender body, the tiny pearls glinting in the sunlight. She slipped on the short jacket with the pearl-studded stand-up collar, and she had never felt so elegant. The three-inch high-heeled matching shoes helped.

The ceremony at the civic hall was thankfully brief. Anna and Nico were the witnesses, and half a dozen other people appeared. Solo introduced her but she was too numb with nerves to take in their names. Penny stood still as a statue at Solo's side as he signed the necessary documents, and she took the pen from his elegant fingers and added her own name where he in-dicated, and it was all over. It seemed unbelievable to Penny that a few words in a language she barely un-derstood had changed her life.

She glanced up at the man who was now her husband looking as cool and remote as ever. Dressed in an ex-pertly tailored pale grey business suit and looking for all the world as if he had just concluded another business deal. Which she supposed in a way was what their marriage was.

Suddenly, as Solo cupped her elbow in his warm palm, and ushered her out into the bright sunlight, a dozen cameras all seemed to go off at once.

In the noise and confusion that followed Penny felt totally lost. Somebody shouted Solo's name and something else in Italian, and Solo chuckled, and the rest went off in peals of laughter. Penny did not get the joke. But then she didn't get much through the meal that followed in a very plush restaurant—the conversation was quick-fire Italian.

'You're very quiet,' Solo murmured during a lull in the conversation. 'Are you all right?' His mouth was close to her ear and she was aware of several things at once. Gleaming silver eyes alight with amusement, and the faintly cynical curve of his sensuous lips, and the gentle touch of his hand over hers on the table. She caught the glint of the gold wedding band Solo was wearing and wondered why he had insisted on them both wearing a ring. 'You look a little flushed.'

'It is rather warm,' she murmured. 'And I have had rather a lot of champagne.' She made the excuse because she could hardly confess she was worried about what would happen next.

Since signing the pre-nuptial Solo had treated her with cool indifference. In fact she had begun to think he had changed his mind. He had made no attempt to touch her or kiss her, and when she had suggested again last night after dinner that they did not have to get married he had looked at her with a sort of lazy possessiveness, and reiterated it was too late to change her mind.

'Not too much. I have been counting,' Solo remarked softly. 'But I think it is time we left.'

'Already?' Penny exclaimed, coming back to the present with a jolt. She glanced around the guests and saw they all seemed to be settled in for a long liquid lunch. 'But what about your friends?'

'Our guests, my dear wife,' he said pointedly, 'can take care of themselves. Whereas I have an overwhelming desire to take care of you,' Solo drawled silkily, standing to his feet. He caught hold of her arm and pulled her up.

Solo said their farewells and thanks in a mixture of Italian and English for Penny's benefit, and instructed Nico they would be away for three days, and began walking towards the door.

When they reached the street a sudden thought made her blurt out, 'Three days—where are we going?'

'A surprise.' Solo opened the door of the sports car and saw her seated before sliding into the driving seat. 'Obviously not far, as your penchant for being sick in an aircraft curtails the choice somewhat,' he mocked. 'I want you fit for our wedding night.'

She ignored his quip about the night ahead. 'But I have no clothes,' she declared.

'Anna has taken care of everything, just relax and enjoy the ride.' He flicked her a glance of mocking amusement. 'I know I shall.'

In the close confines of the sports car she was aware of several things at once. His long, muscular body, the faint scent of cologne mingled with the male scent of him, the gleaming silver eyes, and the faintly mocking curve of his sensuous lips. She shivered and closed her eyes, battling against the strange fascination this one man aroused in her.

She opened them twenty minutes later and glanced out of the window 'Oh, my God, no! You can't drive down there.' Penny grabbed Solo's arm. 'It's a cliff.'

'Trust me.' He slanted her a grin, his typical macho excitement at the drive ahead obvious. 'I know what I'm doing.'

'God save me from would-be racing drivers,' she murmured and squeezed her eyes shut, and did not open them again until she felt the car come to an abrupt halt. Warily she looked out of the window again, and saw only water.

'Where are we?' She turned to Solo but only his jacket and tie lay on the seat. He was already out of the car, and in a moment was holding the door open for her. Penny climbed out and the heat struck her. She slipped off her jacket and looked around, and looked again.

It was a complete suntrap. A tiny bay at the foot of a cliff with a small what looked like a log cabin perched on the very edge of a rocky outcrop, with a wooden deck and jetty reaching out a few yards into the sea. A small boat rested clear of the waterline on about twelve yards of beach. She turned and tilted her head back and looked up at what looked like a sheer cliff face, until she spotted the serpentine track cut into the rock.

'You drove down that?' Penny flung out a hand and cast Solo a horrified look. 'You must be mad!'

He briefly caught her hand and pulled her around before flinging out his arm in a wide, encompassing gesture. 'Look around you. Beautiful, no?' he demanded in a slightly accented voice, and, not waiting for an answer, added, 'The first time I landed on this bit of sand I was like you, scared stiff at the sight of the cliffs, but now I love it.' A satisfied grin softened his tone. 'The perfect hideaway, no television, no telephone.' He started walking towards the cabin.

The image of Solo afraid of anything was something Penny had trouble picturing. He seemed indomitable. She watched his confident stride, the movement of his buttocks as he walked, and a sudden rush of heat that had nothing to do with the bright sunshine flooded through her. Quickly she moved forward and stumbled in her high-heeled shoes.

'Sugar!' she exclaimed, and in a moment was swung up in Solo's strong arms. 'Put me down.' She tried to wriggle out of his hold, her jacket and shoes falling in the process.

'Stop it unless you want us both to take a dip in the sea,' Solo said dryly, pulling her closer and walking on, ignoring her struggles with an ease that was galling as he elbowed open the cabin door.

'Alone at last, Penelope,' Solo drawled mockingly, lowering her gently to her feet. He was so tense it took all his considerable self-control to speak normally. He wanted to tell her she was exquisite, he wanted to throw her on the bed, and feast on her beautiful body with eyes and hand and mouth. The brush of her body against his thighs as he set her on her feet was agony. He had never wanted a woman so much in his life. 'You like the place?' he asked quickly, but the question wasn't casual.

He had discovered the tiny bay as a child of eight. He had set out to sea in a rubber dinghy he had found on the beach at Naples, even at that age desperate to escape the gutter and a mother who he'd known would never miss him. The dinghy had deflated, he had swum until his arms had ached and had finally been washed up in this bay, and it had saved his life.

Then there had been only the ruins of an old fisherman's cottage and a rotten jetty, the place long since deserted, but it had become Solo's refuge. Whenever the city had got too much for him, he'd walked the miles from Naples and scrambled down the cliff path. Later, when he'd had money, he'd bought the land, built the cabin, and had the track cut out.

Solo could feel some of the tension seep from his muscles as he glanced around the familiar room; it was his sanctuary. He glanced down at Penny. It didn't matter if she didn't like it, he told himself, but for some indefinable reason he knew it did.

Penny's eyes skimmed around the room, and it was just one room. To one side of the entrance door was a kitchen and dining area that took up a quarter of the space. At the other side of the door a long sofa beneath a window, on the next wall an open fire, with bookshelves loaded with books either side. On the far wall, a large bed… She stood rooted to the spot, unable to move a step forward if her life depended on it.

'It's tiny,' she declared hollowly. Her stomach began a series of somersaults as she was struck by nervous dread at the thought of the three days alone in *one* room with Solo. No escape from his overwhelming masculine presence morning, noon and night… Penny glanced up at him. 'There is a bathroom?' she demanded, tension making her clip the words.

So she didn't like it. So what? 'Of course.' Solo frowned, indicating a door to the left of the kitchen area, his expression stern and remote. 'All the facilities are located through there.'

Penny raised an eyebrow. 'Thank God for small mercies.'

'I am not completely primitive,' he said coldly.

'That's a matter of opinion,' she muttered under her breath, and, without a word, he slid an arm around her waist and pulled her hard against his long body. His head bent and his mouth closed over hers with brutal savagery, forcing her lips apart in a kiss that shocked her into numb submission.

'That is primitive, my sweet wife.' Solo's eyes narrowed in a slow, raking appraisal of her slender form. 'You need to know the difference, because what happens next is your choice, but don't try my patience. I waited four years for you, and then another four days—symbolic maybe, but too long.'

She tilted back her head; her eyes, flashing with anger, clashed with his darkening gaze. 'Very symbolic—four is the number of the devil in Japanese culture,' she shot back defiantly.

'Then as you have labelled me a devil, you silly girl...' he grasped her chin between thumb and forefinger, and she could see the cold fury in his silver eyes... 'I am quite prepared to act like one. I would hate you to be disappointed,' he declared with mocking cynicism, his other hand sweeping around her back, and before she knew it his fingers had swiftly unzipped her gown.

'I am not silly or a girl.' She slapped his hand from her face and jerked free. 'You saw to that,' she hissed, burning with resentment and trying to grab at the front of her dress.

'And you loved every minute of it,' he declared sardonically, and, catching her hands, he held them wide, and to her utter humiliation the pearl-strewn gown sank to pool on the floor at her feet.

She heard his sharply indrawn breath and for a long moment he simply stared. 'I have been longing to do that since the first moment I saw you in that dress.'

Solo's voice lowered to a husky murmur as his eyes roved over her delicate features and lower to her firm breasts, the tiny waist, and the small white lace briefs that barely saved her modesty.

Struggling to free her hands and burning with embarrassment, she used the only weapon left to her and lashed out at him with her foot, connecting with a shinbone. But in seconds she was powerless to move as he linked her hands behind her back in one of his, hauling her hard against him and raking his other hand through her hair, sending rosebuds careering to the floor. 'Let me go,' she gasped, wriggling ineffectively in his grasp, the atmosphere suddenly raw with tension.

Solo laughed softly. 'Never.' His silver eyes held her furious green gaze, his teeth gleaming in a devilishly menacing smile. 'And you don't really want me to.' His gaze flicked down to her breasts heaving with her recent exertion, and back to linger on her slightly swollen lips, and then her hair.

'Your hair should always be loose.' Threading his fingers through it, he smoothed the silky mass down over her shoulders in an oddly tender gesture. 'That's how I always picture you.'

A warm tide of colour washed over her body—that Solo pictured her at all was a surprise to Penny, given the women he had enjoyed, and she was rather flattered at the thought. His face was close and there was something mesmerising about his silver eyes, his deep, husky voice.

She felt his hand at the nape of her neck, urging her head back as he lowered his own, and he brushed her mouth with his with an almost reverent gentleness, so different from what had gone before that she sighed her relief, the fight draining out of her. Her eyes fluttered closed as with practised expertise he kissed and caressed her silken skin until every cell in her body pulsed with aching need.

She felt herself being swept up in his arms and deposited on the wide bed, and the soft warmth of silken sheets at her back.

'That's better, my beautiful bride.' And Solo's warmth was withdrawn.

Better for whom? Her eyes flew open. Solo had shed his shirt, and was stepping out of his trousers. With fast-beating heart, she stared at him; his bronze body, all taut muscle and sinew, left her breathless. She gulped. 'What are you doing?' she cried inanely, casting him a nervous glance.

'Well, if you haven't guessed by now,' Solo drawled, his silver eyes gleaming wickedly, 'your education is sadly lacking,' he mocked, and he had the nerve to chuckle as he lowered his long body on the bed and curved an arm around her shoulders. 'But no matter, I will soon rectify your lack.'

'You have a vastly inflated ego,' Penny snapped back, his mockery infuriating her again, but the sight of his naked body had a debilitating effect on her anger. He was even more beautiful, more awesome than the picture that had haunted her sleep for the past few nights—incredibly handsome and with a body to die for. The trouble was she knew just how he could make her feel; her temperature was already shooting off the scale at the warmth of his naked thigh against her own.

'No, merely a vast experience with the female sex.' A smile quirked the corners of his mobile lips. 'Which I am putting completely at your disposal, Penelope mine.'

He was teasing her—the devil thought his vast num-

bers of lovers were amusing! Penny tore her gaze from
the latent sensuality in his grey eyes. 'I am not yours;
in fact, I think I hate you,' she grated, not for a second
admitting she was also madly jealous at the thought of
all his other women.

'You know the cliché: hate is akin to love, but at
least hate is an emotion.' Solo loomed over her, supporting his weight on one elbow, but his hand still
curved round her shoulder. With his other he held her
chin, his silver gaze burning into hers, his expression
solemn. 'Indifference is the real killer, Penny, I know.'

For a second a fleeting shadow seemed to dim his
glittering eyes, and Penny had the odd idea the powerful
domineering male she had just married looked vulnerable. Quickly she dismissed the idea. Solo was a typical
Alpha male, and she doubted if anyone, male or female,
could ever be indifferent to him. Whether it was love,
hate, admiration, envy, lust or jealousy, he aroused
strong emotions simply by being Solo Maffeiano.

'And whatever else you are,' his deep, husky voice
continued temptingly, 'you are not indifferent to me,
Penny, *cara.*' His thumb and finger brushed down her
throat, and lower until his palm cupped her breast and
the tantalising fingers tugged very gently at the nipple.
'My bride and soon my wife.'

Penny did try to resist, but his touch ignited a burning
hunger within her she was helpless to deny. Warmth
coursed through her veins, and with a low, inaudible
groan, her eyes wide and luminous, she stared up at
him. *Wife*, and he was her *husband*. Why deny her own
feelings? She wanted him, and which emotion fuelled
the craving she did not care any more. Instinct told her
despite her naivety that Solo would be a hard act for
any man to follow.

Reaching up, she traced the hard line of his jaw with her fingers, and up into the silken black hair at his temples. The marriage might be for all the wrong reasons, and, if she were not pregnant, would almost certainly be brief. She had no faith in her ability to keep and hold a man like Solo, even if she wanted to, but for now he was her husband.

'My husband.' She murmured the words out loud, and he grasped her hand and pressed a hot, hard kiss into her palm.

'Yes. Oh, yes,' Solo said huskily, and her eyes widened into huge pools of helpless longing as he lowered his head. His lips traced her own with incredible tenderness, exploring and teasing and urging her response. 'We can dispense with these.' He raised his head and she felt his hand peeling her briefs from her body. 'I want you naked against me,' he rasped. This time Penny reached for him.

She ran her fingers through his hair and urged his head down. She gave a shaky sigh and parted her lips, her tongue seeking the hot interior of his sensuous mouth. She felt his great body shudder against her, and suddenly he moved onto his back, leaving her stunned, and screaming with frustration.

'I want to take this slow,' Solo rasped, his breathing heavy. 'It's your wedding night.'

Why should he dictate the pace? He dictated everything else, Penny thought in a wild bid for independence. Pushing up, she leant over him, her mouth briefly seeking his before withdrawing teasingly and nipping at his lower lip. Fierce, primitive pleasure swept through her and she was caught up in a desire so intense nothing else mattered. She eased back and deliberately trailed her long hair over his wide shoulders, glorying in her feminine power over him.

'*Our* wedding night,' she amended, and bit lightly into his shoulder, her slender hand stroking through the soft, black body hair of his chest, her fingers scraping over a pebblelike male nipple with tactile delight.

Her green eyes wide and wondering, she traced the arrow of black hair that angled down to his groin, fascinated by his aroused flesh. Her body quivered in delight at the capitulation of his. She wanted to touch him, taste him, wallow in his masculine beauty, his virile power, and Solo let her for a while...until her pink tongue touched the vulnerable velvet skin.

Then suddenly, with a husky growl of need, he pushed her onto her back, held her hands down by her sides, and kissed her with a wild, passionate hunger that melted her bones. She trembled, the blood flowing hot and thick through her veins, as he trailed his lips down to the gentle swell of her breasts and with sensual delight he suckled each one in turn. She writhed as his mouth began an evocative journey to discover every pulse point, every erogenous zone, with an expertise that made every atom of her being spark with incredible heat.

With the air scented with sex, their breath mingled in a branding kiss as they lay, silken skin on skin.

Finally Solo knelt between her thighs. 'You're mine, Penny, my wife,' he said with an animalistic growl of triumph, and then in one deep thrust he possessed her. Penny arched up to him, her fingers digging into the flesh of his shoulder and his side, anything she could cling to as he drove her on and on into an explosive sunburst of heat and light.

*   *   *

'Good morning, Penelope.' Penny tried to stretch, and came up against a hard male thigh; she opened her eyes, and saw Solo grinning down at her. Her whole body blushed scarlet as the events of the night came rushing back.

'Did you sleep well?' Solo asked, his hand slipping beneath the silk sheet to curve around her breast.

Catching his hand with hers, she looked up into his handsome face. Black curls fell over his broad brow and a five o'clock shadow darkened his strong jaw, making him look tough but endearingly dishevelled. 'Not much, as you very well know.' There was no point in denial; they had made love countless times through the night.

His silver eyes gleamed down into hers with wicked amusement. 'Well, we could stay in bed a little longer, if you are still tired.' And they did.

Three days later Penny stood and watched as Solo locked the cabin door and walked towards her. It had been the most perfect three days of her life. They had gone swimming naked in the sea, and made love on the sand, taken out the boat and gone fishing with Penny demanding Solo put back any fish he caught. He had dropped one on her and then washed the fish smell off her in the shower, or so he had said, but it had just been an excuse to make love again.

She looked around the tiny bay, a tear forming in her eye. And she finally admitted what she had subconsciously known all along: she loved Solo, always had and probably always would, but she would never dare tell him. She was his only for as long as he wanted her body, and the tear fell.

'Ready, Penny?' Solo's long arm wrapped around her waist and turned her around to face him. 'Hey, what is this?' He flicked the solitary tear from her smooth cheek.

'The thought of the flight back to England.' She sighed. 'And I was wondering if I will ever get back here again, it is so beautiful.' She told him half the truth.

Solo looked at the woman in his arms, and his heart expanded in his chest. Penny did like his sanctuary. 'Of course you will.' He kissed the tip of her nose and led her to the car. 'If I have to I will drive you back and forward to England, whenever you want.' In fact he would drive to the ends of the earth for Penny.

The ludicrously emotional thought made him stop in his tracks and he let go of her. Solo knew himself that it was only with burning ambition and ruthless self-discipline that he had become the successful man he was today. Emotion played no part in his life.

'Solo…' Penny laid a hand on his arm. He looked ill—he had gone white beneath his naturally tanned complexion, the skin pulled taut across high, arrogant cheekbones. 'Solo…' Ice-grey eyes surveyed her, and every nerve in her body tensed.

'Get in the car, Penny.' he said harshly. What had he done? She hated him, she was only with him now because he had given her no choice and she needed his money to keep her young brother and that damned old house.

It irritated the hell out of him that from the moment he had seen her he had wanted her with a fierce, consuming hunger that had nothing to do with logic, but everything to do with lust. It angered him that he who had always prided himself on the ability to control his passion couldn't control it with Penny.

Her wide green eyes were staring warily up at him; her lush lips, still swollen from early-morning lovemaking, trembled slightly. He reached out a finger and traced the soft curve of her breasts revealed by the blue sundress she was wearing, and saw her catch her breath. He could take her now; without conceit he knew he was a good lover and he had taught her well. He had never met a more wildly responsive woman in his life. Penny was like a kid in a sweet shop, but he recognised it was because sex was new to her, and what was worse he also knew that her need was nothing like the wild hunger that ate at him.

Shrugging off the unpleasant truths, he dropped a light kiss on the top of her head and helped her into the car. What did he care why she was with him, as long as she shared his bed? he told himself, and frowned as he started the car, no longer sure he believed it...

CHAPTER SEVEN

'ACTUALLY, flying is not all that bad,' Penny said. Anything to break the tension that had sizzled between them since leaving the cabin. She glanced at Solo as he manoeuvred the sleek black car through the traffic. 'Those tablets really worked.'

'Good—in that case you can travel with me sometimes,' Solo remarked, flicking her a sidelong look.

'No,' she said immediately, panicked by the thought. 'I couldn't, there is James. And the house.' She had enjoyed the last few days in Italy, in fact more than enjoyed. She cast a surreptitious look at Solo's classic chiselled profile, and her heart ached.

Who was she kidding? She had loved their brief honeymoon; she loved Solo. He had the power to make her heart leap with a single look. But she knew she could never tell him, because she could never forget she was not the only woman in his life.

'We can hire a nanny, staff—it won't be a problem.' His grey eyes were enigmatic with a glimpse of something else less easy to define as they briefly focused on her. Anyone but Solo and she would have thought it was a silent plea. Which was ridiculous. She straightened in the passenger seat.

'No,' she said again. 'I stay at Haversham Park with James, that was our agreement, and you do as you like,' she reminded him with biting sarcasm. 'Anyway, you have Tina to accompany you on your travels; three is a crowd.'

'As you wish, my dear wife,' Solo drawled sardonically. 'But whatever you may imagine, Tina is not my lover, and be advised I will not tolerate anything except complete fidelity on your part, and I will accord you the same distinction as long as the marriage lasts. What you choose to think is your prerogative, but I will not be the subject of idle gossip, understand?' he warned implacably.

He had surprised her by his declaration of married fidelity; whether to believe him or not, she was not sure. As for his distaste for gossip, he was a vastly wealthy, powerful man. A very influential force in the world's money markets, governments listened to him, but as Penny was beginning to realise he had an exaggerated desire for privacy.

She recalled her surprise at first seeing the secluded villa that he called his home, and the amazing little wood cabin where they had spent the last few days. He obviously loved the place and yet he owned some of the most perfectly situated, luxurious hotels around the globe.

Recalling his confession about his mother, she could understand his fierce protection of his privacy, but in this day and age Penny did not believe it mattered. It certainly did not matter to her, and she opened her mouth to tell him so. But one glance at his grim expression was enough to make her close it again, and keep her mouth shut for the rest of the journey.

The difference was amazing. Brownie met them at the door, and insisted on showing them around all the ground-floor rooms. Everywhere had been painted and polished and scrubbed. 'I can't believe all this could

happen in less than a week.' Penny turned shining eyes
to Brownie. 'You must have worked like a slave.'

'Not a bit of it.' Brownie laughed. 'Mr Maffeiano
hired over twenty people. It was wonderful, all I did
was order them around.' Turning to Solo, Brownie
added, 'And the new bed arrived this morning. You and
Penny pop on up and have a look, while I get the lunch.'

Solo took Penny's hand. 'Come on,' he said curtly
and led her upstairs.

'What new bed?' she murmured, her pulse racing at
the warmth of his hand enfolding hers, and inexplicably
she felt nervous. It was stupid, she knew, given how
they had spent the last three days. But somehow knowing she loved him had made her more cautious, not less
so. Solo had seemed to change as soon as they'd left
Italy and he was once more the aloof, powerful businessman. Looking around her now, back in the house
where she was born, she felt their sojourn in Italy was
quickly becoming a distant fantasy.

In the master bedroom the garish colours had vanished, replaced by the colours she remembered from her
childhood. The only difference was a large four-poster
bed with elegant cream silk drapes tied back with
twisted golden tassels. A thick, quilted cover in the
same material and colour, with huge plump pillows,
adorned the bed.

'Incredible.' Penny sighed. 'How did...?' She looked
up. Solo was standing by one of the long windows, his
back to her, and there was something about the set of
his shoulders, a tension in his tall frame as he slowly
turned around, that froze the rest of the words in her
throat. As he walked towards her she was struck again
by his superb animal magnetism, an intrinsic male dom-

inance that fancifully reminded her of some lethal predator intent on devouring its prey.

'So was it worth it, Penny?' Solo asked, the words a barely concealed taunt.

'Was what?' She looked at him, mystified.

Solo saw the puzzlement and the slight darkening of her glorious eyes as she watched him approach, unable to hide her sensual response. But that was all it was, he reminded himself. His anger at her rejection years ago had faded, lost in the passionate abandonment of their love-making. But today her refusal to even consider travelling with him, and then walking into this house had brought back to him all too vividly the real reason she was his wife: money and the threat of pregnancy, and it angered the hell out of him.

A self-derogatory smile twisted his sensuous mouth. He had deluded himself into thinking a few nights with Penny in his bed and he would get her out of his system. But the violent, primeval passion he felt whenever he looked at her, or touched her, he knew was the reaction of the primitive male animal in him that lurked beneath the thin veneer of civilised sophistication he presented to the world. She was his mate, only his, and he wanted to keep it that way.

It was not a realisation he was comfortable with. She had bewitched and beguiled him with her mixture of innocence and sensuality, so that he only had to look at her to feel like a randy teenager again. He stared down at her, and gestured with one elegant hand around the room. 'All this,' he drawled, and, closing his hand around her slender wrist, he added, 'This house for my money.' A cynical smile curled his beautiful mouth. 'My body, my bed.'

Penny stared at him, genuinely shocked and then angry. 'I could ask you the same. But I would not be so crude,' she returned.

'Ah, of course, you are a lady…' Long, tanned fingers moved caressingly on the tender skin above her wrist. 'But to answer the question you are too polite to ask,' he said mockingly, 'so far you are repaying my investment admirably.' His ice-grey eyes flared, then narrowed on her angry face, and suddenly she sensed just below the calm surface was a violent rage waiting to escape. 'The highest-paid whore in the world could not have done better,' he opined in a deep, dark voice that slashed through her body like a knife.

A deep flush overlaid her pale skin. It had been insensitive of her to call a man with Solo's background crude, but his response shamed and horrified her. Now she knew what Solo really thought of her, and she collapsed on the side of the bed, only dimly registering that her legs were shaking.

'But I think it is time for another instalment,' Solo suggested, and, roughly hauling her up hard against him, he took her mouth in a fierce, brutal kiss.

'Don't.' She struggled against him. 'Solo…' He was frightening her.

'Yes, say my name,' he breathed, the violence in his eyes making her shake, and she pushed hard at his chest. 'Remember who you belong to.' He laughed, a harsh, cruel sound, and captured her mouth with his own as he tumbled her back on the bed.

The breath whooshed out of her body. 'No, please, Solo,' Penny cried and grabbed a handful of his hair to pull him away. 'I didn't…' was as far as she got.

He lifted his head and the scorch of his laser-like gaze burned into hers as he claimed her mouth again with a low, agonised groan that seemed to reach right into her body and pluck out her heart.

She tried to struggle, striking out at his chest. 'Wait.' Fear, stark and debilitating, made her shudder as his eyes, hard as flint, clashed with hers. One strong hand caught the hem of her dress and dragged it up around her waist.

'I don't need to. I might be crude but you are bought and paid for,' he snarled, and his lips came crashing down on hers again.

Penny battled to breathe, her fingers curved into his shoulder, her other hand pulled his hair, but slowly the heat, the hungry passion of his mouth got to her as only Solo could. His body, hard and taut with a need he could not hide, slid between her thighs, and the hand that pulled his hair turned to caress the silken locks.

'*Dio!*' Solo suddenly exclaimed, lifting his head. 'What the hell am I doing?'

She saw a flicker of vulnerability in his hooded eyes and her heart squeezed. Solo was the most arrogant, indomitable male she had ever met and yet... Something made her slip her arms around his back and hug him as he would have moved off her.

'I can make a guess,' she tried to tease, staring up into his sombre face, but he wasn't amused.

He jerked to his feet and glanced down to where Penny lay sprawled on the bed and gave her a long, brooding look, before spinning on his heel and walking away.

Penny watched him depart with sad, puzzled eyes. She saw him rake his hand through his hair as he went through the open door, but he didn't look back. The honeymoon was definitely over.

Slowly Penny dragged herself up to a sitting position,

and made an attempt to smooth her dress down over her legs. He could not have made it plainer the marriage was to be a short-term affair. Solo was a man who thrived on challenge; maybe she had been too willing and he was tired of her already. Then there was Tina…

A deep, shuddering sigh shook her. How long could Penny live with a man, love a man, when he treated her like a whore he'd paid for? What about every time Solo left on business—would she wonder if he was sleeping with his mistress? His avowal that he demanded strict fidelity in a relationship she had a suspicion should have ended in a caveat. *With the exception of Tina.* Penny could not live like that; it would destroy her.

Why had she let it happen? Because she loved him, her heart cried.

Dinner was a quiet affair. Penny, dressed carefully in one of the new gowns Solo had bought for her as a kind of armour against her raw emotions, tried her best. She made herself smile for Brownie's benefit and drink a toast in champagne.

Solo sat grim and brooding all evening and it was a relief when he said he had some work to do and she could escape upstairs to bed.

After showering and slipping on a scrap of blue lace that Solo had bought for her, Penny crawled into bed and fell into a restless sleep.

Her eyes fluttered open, a strong arm pulled her gently towards the warmth of a hard male body. 'Solo…' Penny murmured his name dreamily.

'I was a boar earlier, forgive me.' She felt his lips at her temple and then the warmth of his breath at her earlobe, before seeking the soft bow of her mouth, in a kiss of incredible sweetness.

'Yes,' she breathed. A large hand traced up her spine

and held her close to the muscular strength of his torso, and the kiss went on and on. She was boneless, floating in a sea of sensations, as long fingers stroked her breasts, the negligee sliding away.

Her lips parted and drank from his, and she felt his slight intake of breath before he moved down to the base of her throat and lower to suckle the small, tight nipples. She moaned softly and ran her fingers along the arrowing hair that spread down past his navel, her touch finding him.

Solo moved over her, his mouth finding hers again as his body took possession with a fierce passion that she met and matched, crying out as she climaxed in a tumultuous explosion of release.

She almost said she loved him but changed the words to, 'I love…the way you make me feel,' just in time.

'The feeling is mutual, *cara*,' Solo rasped, and sucked hard on her nipple, his hands lifting her hips as he thrust ever deeper to the very portals of her womb. Sweeping her through her climax, something she had never thought possible, and on and on until his great body shuddered in wave after wave of violent pleasure, and Penny convulsed around him again in a mutual relief.

They collapsed on the bed, Solo sprawled on top of her, their ragged breathing the only sound, and then Solo murmured something in Italian and rolled off her. He curved her possessively into the hard heat of his body, nuzzled her neck, and she wrapped an arm over his broad chest, her head on his heart, and in moments she was asleep. She woke up a long time later to a knocking on the door, and Brownie calling her name.

'Come on, sleepy head, your husband has been up for hours working, and James will be arriving back in about an hour,' Brownie said with a smile, and walked to the bedside carrying a coffee tray.

Wriggling under the covers into her nightgown, she sat up, and reached out and took the coffee-cup Brownie offered. 'Thank you, Brownie, but you really should not be running up and downstairs after me.'

'Your husband offered, but I told him I wanted you out of bed, not kept in it!' Penny blushed, and Brownie chuckled. 'What a man!' she said and, with an admonishment to hurry up, left the room.

'Penny, I'm home.' James ran into the hall, followed a few steps behind by a breathless Patricia.

Bending down, Penny swept James up in her arms and gave him a fierce hug, moisture stupidly blurring her vision. 'Hello, darling.' She pressed a kiss on his chubby cheek. 'I've missed you.'

Small arms wrapped around her neck, and he said, 'I missed you, but guess what? I can swim!' His beaming smile flashed out. 'Can we go to a swimming pool, Penny, can we? I want to show you.'

'Of course we can, darling, but not right now,' she said with a chuckle, depositing him on his feet. 'Say thank you to Patricia. Brownie is in the kitchen with your favourite…cake.' Before she had finished the sentence James had darted for the kitchen, screeching at the top of his voice, 'Thank you. Brownie, cake, cake, cake.' She watched him go with a shake of her head.

'I hope he wasn't too much trouble,' Penny remarked, glancing at Patricia.

'No, it was a breeze—he got on great with my little terror. But, hey, you are looking good. Mum told me you were going to Italy for a week, and it seems to have agreed with you. I told you, you needed a holiday, and

I was right.' Patricia stopped, an arrested expression on her face. 'When did this happen?' She pointed to the newly painted hall.

'Yes, well…' Penny blushed scarlet '…about that…'

'What is all the noise about?' a deep voice demanded, and Penny silently groaned.

Turning slowly, she watched as Solo, wearing black jeans and a short-sleeved black shirt, his great body exuding an aura of almost lethal male sexuality, moved towards her. 'James is back.' She smiled tentatively. After his moody behaviour yesterday and their passionate, almost loving reconciliation in bed last night she was not sure how he would react, but she need not have worried.

'Ah, that explains the noise.' Solo smiled into her eyes, touched his mouth briefly to hers and whispered, 'Good morning, *cara mia*.' His eyes gleamed with the smug, sensual satisfaction of a man who knew he had satisfied the woman in his life. Slipping an arm around her waist, he turned her to face their guest, easing her against his long length, her bottom fitting snug against his thighs, and it felt great. 'And this is?' He paused, politely smiling over Penny's head at Patricia.

'Solo Maffeiano. What the hell is he doing here?' Patricia exclaimed, her eyes out on stalks. 'I thought I told you to get rid of him years ago.'

'Please, Patricia, let me explain.' Penny felt the sudden stiffening in Solo's long body and abruptly he let her go, stepping to one side. The feel-good factor had not lasted one morning. Penny almost groaned aloud her frustration, and, glancing up, her green eyes were captured by narrowed grey ones.

'I don't think I know your friend, Penny, darling,' he drawled, his hard, dark face expressionless, but only a fool would fail to detect the steel beneath the silky smoothness of his voice. 'Introduce me.'

Now would be a good time for the floor to open and swallow her, Penny thought dryly, tearing her gaze from his, but one look at Patricia's bossy, big-sister-type expression, and then back to Solo's icy one, and she knew she was in trouble with both of them.

'Solo, this is Patricia Mason—Jane and Simon's older sister. Patricia and her child were on holiday with James and her parents,' Penny began to explain.

'Never mind the social niceties,' Patricia said. 'What is he doing here?'

'I live here,' Solo said with a sardonic arch of one dark eyebrow in Patricia's direction. 'And as far as I know I have never met you.'

'Well, you have once,' and she mentioned a première in New York. 'And I know all about you,' Patricia fired back. 'I told Penny—Lisa Brunton is a friend of mine.'

'And?' Solo prompted icily. Penny sensed the increased tension in his mighty frame, and slanted a brief glance at his chiselled profile. She saw his jaw tighten and a muscle jerk in his cheek; he was livid.

'Stop it, both of you,' she cut in firmly.

'Yes, let's have a coffee and be civilised.' Solo's hand snaked out, and his fingers dug into Penny's waist as he fixed her with a piercing glance that sent a shiver of fear down her spine. 'I do not want to see my wife upset.'

'Wife? You're married!' Patricia exclaimed. 'To him?' She waved a hand at Solo. 'I don't believe it.'

'Believe it!' Solo drawled. 'Penny and I were married last Monday in Italy, and I have to thank you, Patricia. If your family had not taken James on holiday, it might never have happened,' he ended with a mocking, cynical smile.

The sound of a car horn echoed in the fraught silence. 'Oh, damn—I have to go, they are waiting in the car.' Patricia frowned at Penny. 'But I'll talk to you later.' And, spinning on her heel, she left.

'You can let me go now,' Penny said bluntly. 'I think you made your point with Patricia.'

'Your friend is of no importance to me,' he opined in a flat, chilling voice, turning her to face him, his strong hands spanning her waist. 'But she obviously has a vast influence on you.'

'No, I hardly ever see her,' Penny said truthfully. The last thing she needed was to get into a discussion on Patricia. 'She lives in America.'

Solo's eyes rested thoughtfully on her taut face. 'Your ex-boyfriend Simon is her brother.' His lashes drooped, hiding any sign of emotion in his grey eyes. 'Cast your mind back, Penny—was she in England the first time we met?'

A hot tide of colour surged up into her face. 'She did visit to show her parents their first grandchild,' she said to somewhere over his left shoulder.

'And you listened to her gossip,' Solo prompted, jerking her closer, his hands tightening on her waist. 'What exactly did the woman tell you, *mia sposa*?' He kissed her angrily. Heaven knew what would have happened next if James hadn't appeared at the moment.

Penny had never been so grateful for an interruption in her life. James ran into the hall, his mouth covered in chocolate, and skidded to a halt at the sight of Solo.

'You let go of my Penny.' He stuck a sticky hand on Solo's jean-clad leg.

'What the devil—?' Suddenly Penny was free, and

Solo dropped gracefully down on his haunches. 'You must be James. I knew you when you were a baby, and I can't believe how big you have grown.'

'What you doing with my sister?' James asked, not to be deterred.

'Kissing her,' Solo grinned at the little boy. 'I know you love Penny very much, but I love your sister as well, and it is a lot for Penny to look after this big house and everything else, so I am going to live here and help you both.'

Penny was horrified. She had not thought how she would tell James she was married—she doubted he understood the concept—but she certainly would not have started with a lie. Solo did not love her. If only it were true, Penny thought with a stab of longing, staring down at the two dark heads so close together.

'Can you swim?' James asked with the single-mindedness of a child.

'Yes, and I have a house with its very own swimming pool where we can all go on holiday.'

'I've just been on holiday.' James grinned. 'And I can swim.'

'In that case we must build a swimming pool here, maybe in the basement, so you and I can practise swimming together—'

It was outright bribery. 'Hold on—' Penny cut in, but was stopped by James.

'Can we really have a pool?' James turned glowing eyes up at his sister, and she hadn't the heart to say no.

It was as inevitable as night follows day, Penny thought ruefully a few hours later, sharing a pot of tea in the kitchen with Brownie. James was completely captivated by Solo, and surprisingly Solo was extremely good with the little boy.

He had carefully explained he and Penny were married, husband and wife, as James's parents had been.
James had pondered for a while and then decided it was
okay. Which might have had something to do with discovering Solo had, not only a great car, but a boat and
plane as well. Penny glanced out of the window, and at
the moment Solo was showing James the engine of his
car.

'Alone at last,' Solo said as he walked into the bedroom,
just as Penny exited the bathroom wearing a blue towelling robe and nothing else. James had soaked her as
she had given him his bath and put him to bed, with
Solo looking on. She had left Solo reading James a
bedtime story, and had hoped to be washed and changed
before he had finished, but luck was not on her side.

'It is almost dinner time,' she said jerkily.

Solo, in a few lithe strides, crossed the room and
wrapped a hand around the back of her neck. 'I am sure
Brownie will not mind waiting. James is asleep.' His
voice dropped to a sibilant softness. 'And you and I are
going to have a talk, a long talk about what your so-
called friend Patricia told you four years ago.'

'I don't know what you're talking about.' Penny
looked straight at his broad chest, unable to meet his
shrewd gaze; she had been dreading this moment all
day. Solo was no fool, he must have guessed immediately after Patricia's unthinking outburst this morning
there was more to Penny's rejection of him years ago
than she had admitted at the time.

'You're a hopeless liar,' Solo taunted. 'Your pulse is
racing.' He drew her closer, and her nostrils flared
slightly at the familiar male scent of him. 'You're as

nervous as a mouse with a cat on its tail, and you know you really want to tell me.'

'I am not,' she snapped back, her green eyes flashing up to his. She did not appreciate being likened to a mouse. 'And I've forgotten anyway.' He held her gaze for a tense moment, and, although his expression did not alter, she sensed a hidden threat.

'Okay,' Solo said lightly. 'Then I'll ask your friend myself tomorrow.' She was lying and he had a damn good idea why. She had listened to the poisonous Patricia's gossip and stuck with young Simon. 'She's staying at the vicarage, I believe.' And he watched with savage satisfaction as colour flooded her skin.

'No... Yes. Oh...I don't want you upsetting my friends; I have to live here,' she said quickly.

There was a long moment of silence. 'Not necessarily,' Solo finally said coolly, and he allowed his hand to slip around the front of her throat and graze gently over the swell of her breast. 'We could live in Italy, James as well, of course.' His slate-grey eyes narrowed on her beautiful face, and he waited for her response, tension riding him.

Penny jerked back out of his reach, heat swirling within her, prickling through her breasts until the peaks pushed achingly against the cotton of her robe. Flustered and completely missing his point, she muttered, 'Then you get this house for your damn hotel. You must be joking.'

Solo's shoulders squared, his hard face an expressionless mask. Penny would not move an inch for him, never mind a country. Her friend must have done a real hatchet job on him, and he hated gossips almost as much as he hated liars. 'I never intended turning this house into a hotel. Architecturally it is a perfect gem, and I appreciate perfection. It would be a desecration to alter it. So if you really believed I wanted it for a hotel, then you're a fool.'

Struggling for composure, she looked at him, resentment fizzing inside her. 'No, otherwise you would have bought me out when I offered,' she had to concede. But he was so damn arrogant it would do him no harm to hear some home truths. Why not tell him? Deflate his enormous ego a notch or two.

'But I did believe once you wanted me so that you could get my house. Four years ago when I mentioned your name to Patricia as my boyfriend, she suggested I make sure you were not going out with me simply to get your hands on my home. You see, she recognised your name and told me all about you. A confirmed womaniser.' Penny was getting into her stride. 'You romanced a friend of hers, Lisa, for ages, then dumped her, by my reckoning a week after you met me.' She saw Solo's face darken like thunder but he made no attempt to deny her assumption—on the contrary.

'Lisa knew the score—it was mutually beneficial when I was in New York, nothing more, and it was over the day I met you.'

'For whom, I wonder?' Penny scorned. 'You broke the woman's heart. Jewellery was mentioned as a get-lost gift. Apparently that's a habit of yours.' She didn't see the angry narrowing of his eyes; she was on a roll.

'Never mind the fact you already had a long-time married mistress in Tina Jenson, who was the purchaser of the jewellery, as you obviously haven't got time between women to do it yourself,' Penny drawled sarcastically. 'If I remember correctly, Patricia's final comment was you were far too old for me.' Only then did she lift her eyes to his, and what she saw there made her take a step back.

'And you believed her?' He clasped her wrists, his fingers like manacles around them. '*Dio*, you had some opinion of me.' Fury did not begin to describe the flash of white fire in his eyes, but as quickly it vanished, his features becoming an iron mask.

'Are you saying she lied,' Penny prompted.

'Not exactly, but I'm a lot older than you. What did you expect—a blow-by-blow account of every woman I had before I met you?'

'No, I didn't, I don't,' she blurted, hating him for making her appear a naive young fool. 'I doubt if you could even remember them all.'

'Maybe not.' A cold, cynical smile curled his firm lips and he tightened his grasp on her wrists. 'But I do remember four years ago Patricia's brother was your so-called boyfriend. Did it never occur to you she might have had an ulterior motive in gossiping about me, to protect her brother's interest?'

'No.' She grimaced and tried to tug her hands free. 'Because he was never my boyfriend. He was just a convenient excuse at the time when I discovered what a rat you were, and you're hurting me.'

Solo saw red. His whole life he had been alone and fought for what he wanted. But the one brief moment he had allowed himself to consider a wife and family and reach out to Penny, idle gossip had destroyed it. Penny hadn't trusted him, and Simon had been nothing more than a decoy.

'Hurting,' Solo snarled. 'You don't know the meaning of the word. I would like to break your elegant neck.' Instead he pushed her away from him. 'I should have guessed.' He shook his dark head, his narrowed gaze raking over her contemptuously. 'No man could go out with you for years and not take you to bed; you're sex on legs.'

'He was a friend, I was crying on his shoulder when you turned up. He was in the right place at the right time,' Penny explained.

Solo smiled tightly. 'For whom, I wonder?' he drawled mockingly, quoting Penny's earlier comment about Lisa, and, tilting her chin with one elegant finger, he said softly, 'Not to worry, Penny, darling, we have each other—for a while.'

CHAPTER EIGHT

SINCE Solo had walked back into this house five weeks earlier, her life had changed dramatically. Penny stared sightlessly at the computer screen. James was fast asleep and she was in her old room trying to work, but her troubled mind would not let her. Solo was in New York and she missed him dreadfully. A sad smile twisted her lips, she loved him with every fibre of her being, but she could never tell him.

Solo had been great with James, and had managed to charm every one of her friends and acquaintances at the party they had held the weekend after they'd returned to England.

Luckily Patricia had returned to her husband in America before the party, but not before she had subjected Penny to a long and detailed questioning over the telephone, ending with the words, 'I hope you know what you are doing, Penny. It is bound to end in disaster.'

Well, her relationship with Solo hadn't. Yet! He was the perfect husband, to the rest of the household, and courtesy itself to Penny. It was only in the privacy of their bed at night he changed into a demon lover. A lover she could not resist. She was like a drug addict hungering for the taste of him, and the more she had, the more she wanted. Sometimes, lost in the wonder of his love-making, she could almost believe he cared, and other times she was filled with shame at her helpless response, her almost blind obedience to his mighty will.

After today it had to stop, she told herself adamantly; she had more to consider than herself now. Determinedly she focused on the screen; she was going to need her work and the money she could earn more than ever.

'So this is where you hide.' A deep, dark voice vibrated though the silence of the room.

Penny swung around in her chair, her startled gaze flashing to the tall, dark figure of Solo standing in the open door, and her heart lurched. 'You're back!' Simply the sight of him turned her on. He had shed his jacket and tie somewhere, his white shirt was open at the neck and his pleated trousers hung low on his lean hips. His black hair had escaped its usual sleek style to fall in wayward curls over his broad brow, and he looked dishevelled and less arrogantly assured than when she had last seen him. They had been married over a month and he had been away for the past four days.

'Miss me, did you?'

Yes—yes—yes! her heart cried. His face was taut, his silver eyes darkly shadowed as they captured hers. For the first time she noticed that his stunning features were tightly drawn and he actually looked tired. She had an incredible urge to simply throw herself into his arms, but instead, with her gaze remarkably level, she said, 'I thought you were away for a week.'

He gave an indolent shrug. 'I managed to finish my business quicker than expected.' He walked across to where she sat at her computer and slanted her a wickedly seductive smile. 'And decided to spend the night with my wife, so you can stop fooling around with the computer, and fool around with me.'

She clocked the time on her computer—it was almost midnight. Briefly she closed her eyes; she was tempted, very tempted. Involuntarily her tongue slipped out and ran over the fullness of her lower lip, but his arrogant assumption she should drop everything for him riled her no end. The past four days apart had made Penny take a long, hard look at herself and she did not like what she had become: a slave to her senses. 'How was your trip?' she asked stiffly.

His dark eyes gleamed with mocking cynicism. 'Polite convention at all cost.' His lips twisted sardonically and he let his gaze wander over her slender body. 'A little more wifely enthusiasm would not go amiss.' His eyes narrowed fractionally on the computer screen. 'What is that?'

Wifely enthusiasm! He made her sound like the little woman sitting at home, and it annoyed her. 'It is the draft of my latest children's book, the second of five I am contracted for,' she told him proudly. 'Contrary to what you think, I do not sit around waiting for some man to provide for me. I do work; I do have a career.'

'I know.' Hard hands caught hold of her arms and she gasped as he lifted her to her feet, and he chuckled. 'Poor Penny. James showed me weeks ago the book you had written. I was wondering how long it would take you to tell me yourself,' he admitted dryly.

Penny winced. 'Am I that transparent?'

'No, not at all,' he murmured wryly. 'You are like me in that respect, very good at hiding things. For instance, I came back tonight because I couldn't keep away from you a moment longer.'

Her green eyes widened in surprise on smouldering grey. It was not a declaration of love, but it was more than he had ever offered before, Penny thought wonderingly. Then his mouth closed over hers in a kiss of breathtaking hunger, his arms enfolding her, and she was left in no doubt he had missed her by the hard strength of him against her thighs.

'Hmm,' he drawled a long time later, giving her a scorching look. 'The master suite—or your childhood bed looks very tempting, and much nearer,' he opined with a husky groan.

Winding her arms around his neck, her whole body alive with excitement, she glanced teasingly up at him. 'The master suite,' she declared adamantly. 'You're a tough guy. I'm sure you can manage.'

'Remind me to exact due punishment later,' he threatened, swinging her up in his arms and carrying her from the room.

He did not need reminding—with deft hands he stripped her naked and laid her in the centre of the wide bed. 'Don't move,' he said in a deep, firm voice, and, standing up, he yanked off his shirt. 'I want to look at you.' He quickly stripped off the rest of his clothes, his heated gaze raking over her body the whole time.

Penny was transfixed; he was more beautiful, more magnificently male every time she saw him. Restlessly she moved her legs, her senses dizzy with desire.

'No.' He grasped her ankles and sat down on the side of the bed, his body angled towards her, and with tantalising slowness he pulled her closer. His silver eyes lingered over every inch of her, the lush, firm breasts, and flat stomach, until his strong hands curved the back of her thighs.

She sucked in a breath, her stomach clenching as he eased her leg over his lap and moved the other around his back, exposing her in every way. His heated gaze devoured her as his thumbs tracked her inner thigh and opened the velvet-soft flesh, brushing the throbbing centre of femininity. She groaned and his dark head swooped to lick and nip across the taut peaks of her breasts.

One hand reached for his shoulder and the other the tempting length of him against her thigh. 'No, not yet.' He slurred the words against her skin as he lavished kisses down over her stomach.

She was on fire, wild with excitement and yet shocked by the blatant eroticism of her position. She wanted to scream and beg him to stop, but her molten, shuddering body made a liar of her. Her back arched violently from the bed. Solo twisted and, grasping her ankles, placed them on his shoulders as he surged inside her already climaxing body. Grabbing her hips, he thrust deep and hard until he finally exploded, spilling his hot seed inside her.

They collapsed flat on the bed, satiated, and Solo murmured, '*Dio!* I needed that,' and, rolling onto his back, went out like a light.

Penny couldn't sleep. Her mind would not let her. He had forgotten the protection again, she realised, and sighed softly—not that it mattered any more... But Solo did not know that, and for a man as coolly controlled as Solo it was surprising. She had meant to tell him she was pregnant as soon as he returned—a visit to her GP yesterday had confirmed it—but one kiss from his beautiful lips and, as usual, sensation took over from sense.

Turning on one side, she gazed down at his sleeping form. He was flat on his back, one arm flung across the other side of the bed, the other above his head. Jet lag, probably. But even worn out he looked incredibly sexy. His hair rumpled, his thick black eyelashes resting on his bronzed cheeks, his sensuous mouth parted ever so slightly in sleep. The tiredness she had noticed earlier had gone, his striking features beautiful and younger somehow in repose.

Her gaze dropped lower, to his great nude body, and she groaned as her gaze moved slowly lower to where even at rest his magnificent sex tempted her touch. She swallowed hard, the memory of the incredible pleasure his body could bring her heating her blood all over again.

She lifted her hand towards his thigh and, with a stifled groan of shame, she flopped back down on the bed, and wriggled back into her nightdress, as if that would stop her wayward thoughts, and closed her eyes tight shut. When had she become such a sex addict she would actually contemplate waking a sleeping man?

Stop it, she ordered her erotic thoughts. Tomorrow she would tell Solo she was pregnant, she decided firmly. Their marriage might have been for all the wrong reasons, but that did not mean they could not make it a success.

Penny loved Solo, and he wanted her, he had come back early, and admitted as much, which was a good start, she told herself. In time he might love her, and in the meantime they would both love their baby. Solo would make a great father; one only had to watch him with James to see that. With her decision made, Penny fell into an exhausted sleep.

The distant ringing of a telephone echoed in Penny's head. She murmured and her eyelids flickered. She heard voices and slowly opened her eyes.

Her sleep-hazed glance slid across to the other side of the bed. It was empty and Solo was standing naked a foot away with a mobile phone in his hand.

For a moment she wallowed in the luxury of studying his tanned back and firm buttocks caught in the rays of the morning sun shining through the window. She stretched languorously and felt a tiny curl of heat ignite in her belly. Yes, today she would tell him they were going to be parents, and that she loved him...

Then she heard his voice. 'Yes, Tina, I know we only returned yesterday, but I want to go to Mexico. Under the circumstances I think it is necessary.'

Penny closed her eyes, ridiculously hoping to shut out the sound. Solo was talking to Tina and all of Penny's new-found determination of the night before to try and make her marriage work took a nosedive; jealousy, fierce and primitive, made the bile rise in her throat.

'Arrange the flight and get down here, as soon as possible. I'll be waiting for you. *Ciao, cara.*'

Penny squeezed back the sting of tears, the heat in her belly turning to nausea. Her eyes flew open. She knew enough Italian to know he had the gall to call Tina *darling* in front of her, and anger hot and swift flooded through her; she looked at him, her eyes on a level with his thighs.

The fiend was physically aroused! With a gasp of outrage she shot off the other side of the bed and dashed for the bathroom, locking the door behind her. She fell to her knees in front of the toilet bowl and was quietly, wretchedly sick. The strap of her nightgown cut into the flesh of her arm, and, shoving it back on her shoulder, she raised her head.

The door handle was turning. 'Penny, *cara*,' Solo drawled. He had the nerve to call her darling as well— the lying swine!

'Why have you locked the door? You can't still be shy.' She heard the amusement in his tone, and felt sick again. 'I need to talk to you. I have to leave soon.'

Rising to her feet, she crossed to the vanity basin and washed her mouth out before answering. 'I'll be out in a minute.' There was no way she was telling him she was pregnant now and, slipping on a towelling robe, she walked back into the bedroom.

He was still naked, but there was a subtle difference that didn't surprise her in the least. She looked up at him with hard green eyes. 'You wanted to say something.'

Solo's silver eyes roamed over Penny. She looked so small and sexy with her magnificent blonde hair falling around her shoulders, her slender body swamped in his robe. He wanted to sweep her into his arms and take her back to bed. But he had to leave soon. 'Yes, I have to go to Mexico on business. Some property I own needs checking. I'd ask you to go with me but I don't think you would enjoy the flight,' he teased.

Penny smiled back at him, a smile that never reached her gorgeous eyes. 'You've got that right. Have a nice trip. I have some work to do,' and she shoved past him and out of the room.

Solo stood frozen to the spot for a second, then, grabbing a towel from the bathroom, he dashed after her, wrapping the towel around his hips as he went. He caught her just before she reached her old bedroom, grasping her by the wrist and spinning her around to face him. 'Now, what the hell was that about?' he demanded angrily. 'Have a nice trip—I thought after last night—'

'You thought what?' Penny cut in. 'That you would indulge your enormous sexual appetite quickly before you left.' Or before Tina arrived, was what she should have said, but the thought angered her too much. 'Well, forget it, buster.'

'I am not going to stand here and argue with you in the hall,' Solo declared icily, straightening to his full commanding height, glacial grey eyes pinned to her flushed and furious face. 'I don't know what's got into you this morning.'

'Not you, that's for sure,' Penny snapped back, and before Solo could respond James came running out of his room.

'Is it time for breakie?'

Breakfast was a tense affair; only the childish chatter of James disguised the silence between the two adults. Then Solo disappeared into the study, and Penny thought things could not get much worse, but they did.

Feeling like death, dressed in jeans and an old blouse and with James at her heels, Penny answered the front door mid-morning to find Tina Jenson smiling down at her.

'Hi, Penny. Solo is expecting me.'

Elegant in a smart grey suit, the skirt ending inches above her knees and revealing her long legs to the best advantage, she walked past Penny.

'Hi,' Penny mouthed automatically in shock and, closing the door, turned to see Solo exit the study, smile at Tina and take the other woman in his arms and plant a kiss on her lips.

Penny stood frozen, her eyes burning in their sockets. She was horribly conscious of her own inadequacy in comparison to the stunning Tina. Her stomach cramped with nausea, which she was pretty sure had nothing to do with her pregnancy.

'Solo's kissing the lady,' James piped up. 'She his wife as well, Penny?'

Out of the mouths of babes, Penny thought bitterly,

glancing down at her brother, and murmuring under her breath, 'she is somebody's wife.'

'Penny.' Her name was a command. Penny jerked her head up, her startled gaze clashing with Solo's. 'I have to leave in an hour, and Tina and I have a lot to get through, so could you ask Brownie to serve coffee for two in the study?'

Bitterness turned to fury. Who the hell did he think he was talking to, the patronising pig? Grabbing James's hand, she opened the door. 'Sorry, darling, we are on our way to playschool and already late,' she lied. 'Have a good trip.'

Never in her life had she felt more hurt and humiliated, and, legs trembling, she almost dragged James outside. It was a beautiful June day, but it could have been raining cats and dogs for all Penny cared. She had never dreamt Solo could be so cruel as to bring Tina to her home, and kiss the woman in full view of her and James.

'Come on, James,' she said, tears welling up in her eyes. 'You and I are going for a walk.'

'Nice car.' James pointed to the blue sports car parked behind Solo's BMW.

Penny didn't have a violent bone in her body, but in an action totally out of character she kicked the car as she led James past it and wished it were Tina's bum or, better still, Solo's head...

Carrying a very tired James in her arms, Penny trudged back into the house five hours later.

'Where on earth have you been?' Brownie demanded. 'Poor Solo had to leave without being able to say goodbye. As it was he changed the time-slot for the take-off of his plane twice, but he could not wait any longer.'

Penny put James down on a chair, and then glanced

across the kitchen at Brownie. 'There is nothing poor about Solo,' she said. 'And we had lunch at the vicarage, but I could do with a coffee.'

'Sit down and I'll see to it, you look all in.' The concern in Brownie's eyes made Penny want to cry. 'Are you sure you are all right? I could put off going on holiday tomorrow, and wait until Solo returns if you need me.'

'No, no, I'm fine,' Penny said quickly. Religiously every year Brownie and her friend spent the last two weeks in June on holiday in the Lake District and Penny had no wish to spoil Brownie's pleasure. 'Don't worry, just make sure you're packed, and I'll make sure I get the pair of you to the railway station tomorrow to catch your train.'

Penny went up to bed that night, and, lying in the huge bed that not twenty-four hours ago she had shared with Solo, she did cry. The tears trickled down her cheeks. She buried her face in the pillow, but the faint scent of Solo lingered on the fabric and she sobbed all the more. She felt as if her heart would break. She missed him with every breath she took, and she despised herself for loving him, still wanting him, when he had made it plain he did not feel the same.

A long time later, all cried out and tossing and turning in the huge bed, going over every nuance of her relationship with her arrogant husband, she finally realised Solo didn't feel at all.

He was a self-declared loner. From an early age his emotions had been frozen in stone. He had never had anyone, and he didn't need anyone. He was a law unto himself. Wealth and power and striking good looks had enabled him to go through life taking his pick of anything, be it a work of art or a woman, and he cared no more for one than the other.

With that sobering realisation, she also conceded sadly he was not capable of love. Tina might be the nearest he ever got to the emotion, but even that was false. Because a man of his wealth could have arranged for Tina to be divorced and married her years ago if he had really wanted to. Penny could almost feel sorry for Tina—she had worked for him for years and been a convenient body in his bed. Probably still was.

So what did that say about her marriage? Solo had never pretended their marriage was to be a long-term arrangement, and Penny expected it to be over sooner rather than later. Tina was in Central America with him now…

Penny loved Solo, but, knowing him as she did, she realised once he knew she was pregnant he would never let her go. Given his upbringing, he would move heaven and earth to make sure any child of his had what Solo saw as the perfect family: two parents and the best money could buy. It would never enter his head that love was the most essential ingredient, because he had never known it, never felt it, and, as she recalled when he'd demanded she marry him, had freely admitted he did not believe love existed.

Could she stand being married to a man, bearing his child, living with him, loving him, and yet knowing he would never love her? Wondering if he was being unfaithful every moment they were apart…for ever.

No, Penny decided as the early rays of the morning sun slanted across the bedroom. Her stomach rolled and she lay a protective hand across her abdomen. She loved her unborn child and she had more than enough love for two.

Penny washed her mouth out—she had been sick—and looked in the mirror. God, she looked awful, her face was white as a sheet, and she wished she could turn the clock back, and go back to living her old life, the way it had been before Solo had forced her into this impossible position. With her books and only James to take care of, life had been so peaceful.

Maybe she could… The thought that had been festering in her mind all night took root. She was a strong-minded woman, with a growing career—it was time she claimed back her independence.

Penny pulled on a bathrobe and went downstairs. Glancing around the huge hall, she realised she didn't need this house, she didn't need a fortune. In fact, until Solo had made his outrageous proposal she'd been quite resigned to leaving Haversham Park. She was perfectly capable of looking after herself, her brother and her baby.

She must not think of her husband, soon to be her ex. She had made her mind up—she would divorce him for adultery, and to hell with agreements, or pre-nuptials. No more the honourable Penelope, she was going to join the modern, money-grabbing world with a vengeance, she told herself as she set about preparing breakfast for James and Brownie.

It was exactly the right time. As of today Brownie was on holiday. A quick call to Jane in London, and she had no doubt her friend would let her and James stay until she could find somewhere more permanent. As for her arrogant husband, if he tried to get in touch he would find the house empty. He could sweat it out in Mexico with his mistress as long as he liked, as far as Penny was concerned. The longer, the better—it would give her more time to settle into a new life. Solo was a ruthless bastard and she had to stop imagining she loved him.

CHAPTER NINE

SOLO slammed the receiver down, and glanced across the hotel room to where Tina sat sprawled in an armchair. 'Where the hell can she be?' He ran a hand through his hair, and paced the room. 'I've been calling all day every day since I arrived. I rang at night, knowing it was early morning in England, and sure I'd catch Penny before breakfast, or Brownie, even James—someone should have answered. I've called or had someone call for me every hour since, and nothing.'

'You have only been away three days. Why the panic?' Tina asked, watching Solo stride back and forward the length of the sitting room of his hotel suite. 'It's not like you to get ruffled over a lady, even if she is your wife,' Tina couldn't resist teasing him. Solo, her usually coolly controlled, stony-faced boss, now looked anything but. He was definitely cracking up and it had nothing to do with work.

For three days he had dealt with the result of a fire in a luxury block of apartments he owned. Luckily no one had been hurt, but the occupants had been evacuated. But Tina guessed his stress had everything to do with his very beautiful young wife, Penny.

'You don't understand.' Solo walked to the bar and poured a shot of whisky into a crystal glass, and, lifting it to his mouth, he downed it in one gulp, then threw himself down on the sofa. 'You saw how Penny and I parted—she would not even get us a cup of coffee,' he said flatly.

'She was taking her brother to school,' Tina prompted. She did not know Penny well, but she did know Solo had been a lot more hurt than he'd pretended when the girl had finished with him years ago. When she had seen Penny again in Solo's office a few weeks ago, she had been surprised and worried Penny might hurt Solo all over again. It seemed she'd been right.

'No. She didn't have to take James to school, that was just an excuse. Penny was mad at you and me,' Solo opined bluntly. 'Because I let her think we were having an affair. Why else would I kiss you on the lips when you arrived?'

'You what?' Tina jerked up in the chair. 'My husband would have something to say about that, never mind it would be incest. What on earth possessed you to let your wife think such a thing? Do you want to lose the girl?'

'No…I don't know.' Solo rubbed a weary hand across his eyes. 'Pride, jealousy, anger, or just plain stupidity, I guess.' He looked across at Tina. 'You might as well know it all. We didn't break up four years ago because Penny had another man in her life, but because a friend of hers that lived in New York had filled her head with gossip about me, and scared her off. Including the rumour you were my mistress.'

'My God!' Tina jumped to her feet. 'The poor girl thinks you have been having an affair with me for years.' Moving to sit on the sofa beside Solo, she reached for his hand, adding, 'You better tell me everything from the beginning.' And he did.

A long time later Tina looked at Solo. 'Let me get this straight. The first time you met Penny you decided to marry her because she would make the perfect wife. She said she loved you and then you got the hump when she dumped you because she was scared. The second time around you bullied her into marrying you by threatening her with bankruptcy. Yet the sex is great. That strikes me as odd, and maybe the girl still does care about you. Do you love her?'

Solo reared back. 'I don't believe...' He stopped and nodded. 'Yes.'

'Have you told her?'

'No.'

'And you wonder why she does not answer the phone.' Tina sighed. 'Really, Solo, if you want your marriage to work, if you want to keep Penny, you are going to have to show her you love her, and I don't mean with money or jewels, or even great sex. You have to open your heart, reveal your own pain and in-securities and trust her.'

'It is too late, she has obviously left me to go heaven knows where.' Solo sighed.

'You can appear to be a very cold, intimidating man with your private collection of art as your only com-pany. But a sculpture will not keep you warm in bed at night, and I know you're capable of great love. Find Penny and tell her.' Tina stood up. 'One thing you are not is a defeatist. I'll have the jet put on stand-by; get washed and get going. I can wrap up here.'

Solo stopped outside the vicarage and looked up at the house. There was still a light on. He didn't care if it was after midnight; he had checked out Haversham Park, and the house was empty—this was his only hope. The vicar's daughter was Penny's best friend and she lived in London. Solo wanted the address and telephone number.

He hammered on the door, and waited. The vicar

opened the door and Solo demanded to know where his wife, Brownie or any of his household was. The vicar insisted Solo have a drink, told him Brownie was on her annual holiday. As for Penny and James he had no idea, but refused to give him Jane's phone number at this time of night. Late-night calls were frightening to young women living on their own.

Solo had to mask a cynical smile. The vicar obviously was not part of the mobile-phone and text-message generation. He only parted with the address when Solo gave him his solemn promise he would wait until the morning before driving to London.

Solo returned to the house and the bedroom he had shared with Penny, and spent the early morning hours preparing what he would say to her, and wondering what he would do if Jane didn't know where Penny was and he never found her.

Penny heard the bell ringing, and rolled out of bed. She glanced at the sleeping James on his little camp-bed, and smiled. He thought leaving home was a great adventure, and today because it was Saturday they had planned with Jane to drive out to the zoo.

Slipping on a towelling robe, she tightened the belt and hurried past Jane's bedroom, downstairs and across the hall. It was probably the postman, maybe a parcel as it was Jane's birthday on Monday.

Penny opened the door. She closed her eyes, and opened them again, her heart hammering in her chest. Yes, it wasn't a dream; it was Solo.

'*You.*' she exclaimed, surveying him with wide-eyed amazement. She noted the feverish glitter in his pale eyes that seemed sunken in their sockets, with deep dark circles around them. His black hair fell in rumpled curls over his brow, and he badly needed a shave. His sartorial elegance had deserted him, apparently along with his voice. A tee shirt advertising a certain South American beer hung over his well-worn black jeans.

'What are you doing here?' Penny swallowed hard.

'I could ask you the same question,' Solo replied, and, stepping forward, he reached around her waist, propelling her backwards into the hall, and shut the door behind him. His face expressionless, he looked around the shabby hall. 'Not quite Haversham Park.' Suddenly all his practised speeches deserted him and he was angry. 'What do you think you are playing at? I've been trying to get in touch with you for four days. Where is James?'

Penny pulled free of his restraining arm, and determinedly tightened the belt of her robe. She told herself he was bound to find her sometime. She would have preferred later, rather than sooner. But it did not change her decision one bit. 'James is upstairs in bed, it is barely seven, and I've left you.' She stuck her hands into her pockets, curling them into fists, and lifted her chin. 'And I am not coming back—I want a divorce.' Penny expected him to explode in rage, but he didn't.

Solo's anger deserted him like a spent balloon. His worst fear was realised, and his heart ached as he looked at her. She was wearing a towelling robe, his robe, and it gave him a crumb of hope to know she had taken something of his with her. The over-large lapels were gaping open, revealing the soft swell of her firm breasts. Her magnificent hair was hanging in a tumbled mass down her back. She looked brave and beautiful and incredibly desirable.

His gaze fixed on her luscious mouth, he lifted a hand, and then, taking a deep breath, let it fall to his

side. Hauling her into his arms and ravishing her mouth
was not an option. She wanted to leave him again… He
had taken the one perfect thing in his life and destroyed
it, because of his stupid pride, his inability to show the
slightest sign of weakness towards anyone.

'Is there somewhere we can talk?' Solo demanded.
'We had an agreement and I deserve an explanation if
nothing else,' he said quietly.

Her green eyes narrowed on his. He looked serious,
and maybe telling him the truth would be the quickest
way to get rid of him. She could still feel the imprint
of his hand on her waist and she did not trust herself to
spend any length of time in his company without surrendering to his irresistible masculinity all over again.

'Okay, this way,' Penny said, taking charge and, turning, she led him into the little living room. 'You wanted
an explanation.' She spun around to face him. 'It is
really quite simple. I kept to our agreement, but you did
not.' The picture of Tina in his arms, his kissing the
other woman, was always there in her head to remind
her, and gave her the strength to carry on. 'I was prepared to try and make our marriage work, I gave it my
best shot, but when I find my husband kissing his mistress in my own home, even I am not that much of a
masochist—'

'No, you've got it wrong,' Solo cut in, reaching out
for her and capturing her shoulders. 'I've never been
unfaithful. Tina and—'

'No.' Penny flattened her palms on his chest. 'I am
not going to listen to any more of your lies.' Just hearing the woman's name on his tongue made her feel sick
with jealousy. 'I can't bear to live with a man who is
unfaithful.' She lifted glittering green eyes to his. 'Is

that clear enough for you?' She tried to shrug free of his hold, but his fingers tightened on her shoulders.

'You're going to listen, damn it,' Solo commanded. He was trying to be humble, but it wasn't easy. 'There is nothing between Tina and I, never has been.'

'Oh, don't give me that,' Penny shot back, her own temper rising. 'I saw you only the other morning on the telephone, and you were aroused simply talking to Tina.'

He stared at her as if she had gone mad; slowly, his mouth turning up in a smile, then a grin, then a chuckle, he shook his dark head. 'Oh, Penny, have you never heard of early-morning arousal in a man; especially this man who happened to be looking at his very lovely wife half naked on the bed? It had nothing to do with Tina.' He folded his arms around her, hauling her hard against his long body. 'And everything to do with you, can't you tell?' His dark head bent and he pressed a kiss to the curve of her neck and shoulder.

Her stomach lurched, the heat of his arousal was hard against her belly, and she shoved at his chest. 'So you say.' She blushed scarlet. 'But I'm not a fool, you are not getting me back with sex.'

Solo stiffened, his arms falling to his sides, and he stepped back, taking a deep, steadying breath. 'No.' His silver eyes captured hers. 'I swore to myself if I found you I would not touch you until I had told you the truth, and the best place to start is probably with Tina.' Penny scowled at the name she hated. 'I promised Tina I would never tell anyone, but there can be no more secrets between us. Tina is my half-sister.'

'Your sister!' Penny exclaimed, her green eyes widening to their fullest extent on his handsome face.

'Yes.' He spoke stiltedly. 'Apparently my mother had

a child before me, a baby girl. She sold the child to an Italian-American couple, strictly illegally. Tina's adoptive parents passed her off as their own. She only discovered the truth when she questioned them about the genetic family history when her and her husband discovered she could not have children, and they swore her to secrecy as they are pillars of the community in the small town where they live.'

Penny's head was reeling. The conversation she had heard under the window years ago suddenly made a different sense. Broad-minded about the unconventional family, and of course Solo would always love his half-sister, just as Penny would always love her half-brother. If only she had known! She kept her stunned gaze fixed on Solo's serious face and listened.

'Tina and her husband came to Naples looking for her birth mother, and found me. I was twenty-five at the time and agreed to keep the secret for the sake of her parents. But I can assure you she is very happily married, and enjoys her work.'

Solo lifted his hand and brushed a strand of hair from her cheek. 'I let you think we were lovers to make you jealous. That's how desperate I was, Penny.' His expression was bleak.

Penny cleared her throat. 'Desperate for what?' she made herself ask, the tiniest flame of hope igniting in her heart. Tina was his sister, not his lover. How much more had she got wrong? She owed it to herself to find out and this sombre man was like no Solo she recognised. She instinctively placed a hand on his chest to steady herself, her legs were shaking, and she could feel his erratic heartbeat beneath her palm.

'For you,' Solo said huskily. 'I don't want to lose you again, Penny.'

Penny stared up at him, her heart racing. The planes and angles of his face were taut with tension, he looked so hard, and yet so incredibly desirable to her foolish heart, and she despaired at her own weakness. 'You mean you don't want to lose the sex,' she prompted bitterly.

'That, too.' His eyes sparked with a trace of his old arrogance. 'But that is not what I meant. I am sick of all the pretence, all the time I have wasted,' Solo said, and she watched in growing wonder as his expression softened, his firm lips quirked at the corners in a wry smile. 'They say confession is good for the soul, and I promised Tina if I found you I would tell you the truth. Will you listen?'

Penny nodded and allowed him to lead her to the sofa. He sat down and pulled her down beside him. She was intrigued and made no objection when he slipped his arm along the back of the sofa, his hand resting lightly on her shoulder, and turned to face her. A vulnerable, unsure Solo was not something she had ever seen before.

'This isn't easy for me, Penny. I am not the sort of man to reveal my feelings to another person. In fact, until I met you I didn't think I had any. I much prefer inanimate objects to people—they are easier to deal with.'

'That is sad,' Penny murmured and was rewarded with a dry smile.

'No. To me it is…was normal. But—' his great body tensed '—to start at the beginning. Your friend Patricia was right about Lisa Brunton in a way. It was in her apartment some months before I met you that I saw a picture in a magazine of Veronica's wedding to your father. I recognised her because I had met her on a friend's yacht—she was his girlfriend. But I also saw you.

'Being a chauvinistic Neanderthal, or whatever you want to call it, I was intrigued by the difference. You looked so beautiful and innocent. You were my fantasy girl, everything a man could want in a perfect wife.'

A picture in a magazine! Penny was stunned, but realised sadly that was so like Solo—the inanimate object!

'Six months later when I bumped into your father and Veronica, I had no interest in doing business with them, but I wanted to meet you. When I walked into your home and saw you standing with baby James in your arms, I decided then and there to marry you. In my arrogance the first time I kissed you I knew I could make you want me, and buying a piece of land off your father was a small price to pay for a wife.'

Penny glanced at him. 'A bit medieval,' she opined, and he had the grace to look embarrassed.

'I asked your father's permission to marry you the last Saturday before we parted, and quite happily gave him more money as I thought he was going to be my father-in-law. I had to leave in a hurry before I could ask you, as you know.' He slanted her a wry glance. 'Six days later when I returned I signed the deed for half the house your father insisted on giving me while I waited for you to return home.'

'Oh, my God!' Penny sighed. 'I was so wrong. I came back that day after listening to Patricia's gossip,' she said honestly. 'But I was still determined to believe in you, Solo.' Penny did some confessing of her own. 'But I heard you talking to Tina from beneath the window. I heard you say you wanted a malleable wife, and to refurbish the house, and finally you loved her. I ran straight back to the vicarage and let Simon get me out of the mess I was in.'

'You overheard part of a conversation and judged me on that?' Solo shook his head in disgust. 'I didn't stand a chance.' He shot her an angry glance. 'You didn't trust me at all; no wonder you left me.'

'I'm sorry if you were upset,' she murmured.

'Upset didn't begin to cover it. I was gutted and furiously angry. I became half-owner of a house I didn't want and lost the girl I did,' Solo drawled cynically. 'My pride took a hell of a battering that day.'

'But you didn't love me,' Penny said flatly, and that was the bottom line. He had never loved her.

'No, at the time I did not believe in love,' he told her with brutal candour. 'But with hindsight I realise I do.'

'What are you trying to say?' Penny asked softly, holding her breath.

'For a long time I did not…would not admit I loved you.'

Solo had said he loved her, and she couldn't believe it. She studied his dark features, saw the strain in his silver eyes, and her heart swelled with love. 'You mean you…'

'Let me finish,' Solo commanded. 'I practised this all last night when I thought I might never see you again. If I don't say it now I might never have the nerve again.' His piercing gaze seemed to see right into her soul. 'I was angry when you finished with me, and thought it was a trick by you and your father to con money out of me.'

'Oh, no.' Penny cut in. 'I never knew anything about the money. I can't believe my dad could be so greedy.'

'Yes, well, to give your father his due he did get in

touch with me, and offered to give back part of the cash, but he also said he thought you were too young for marriage, and I should try again when you finished university.' His sensuous mouth tightened. 'Deep down I agreed with your father. You were very young, so I told him to keep the money, and decided to do just that in three years' time,' he vouched, almost talking to himself.

Penny stirred restlessly. 'So Dad wasn't really being deceitful,' she said softly.

'No.' Solo agreed. 'But I was, I fluctuated between thinking of your family as no better than thieves, and denying I loved you while hoping to get you back. I knew when you finished university and I was preparing to return to England to see you and find out if you were still with Simon.'

That was the second time he had suggested he loved her, and Penny was beginning to believe him. 'Why didn't you tell me all this when we met again?' What she really wanted to ask was why didn't he say he loved her, but she dared not. She had never known Solo to talk so long and openly and she did not want to miss a word.

Solo's hand tightened on her shoulder. 'I had made a big enough fool of myself once over you and I wasn't prepared to do it twice.' The look he gave her was full of self-mockery. 'When I heard of the death of Veronica and your father, I thought you must know I owned half the house—either your father would have told you or after the will was read. It gives me no pleasure to admit in a way I was glad. My ego had taken enough of a beating where you were concerned. Now I thought, Penelope Haversham will have to come to me,' he declared with some of his old arrogance. 'So I waited and waited for you to get in touch and, the longer I waited, the angrier I got.'

'Oh, Solo.' Penny was appalled by the bitterness in his tone.

But if he heard it he gave no sign. 'Until your solicitor finally got in touch with me, and set up a meeting. Then, the night before, I walked into the hotel bar where I was staying and there you were... *Dio*, Penny, the shock of seeing you in the hotel in a red dress—the innocent vision I had cherished in my mind had transformed into a sexy woman with acres of flesh on display.'

'I thought I felt someone watching me,' Penny recalled. 'But it wasn't my dress—it was Jane's and I was dying of embarrassment, and reeling with shock having just discovered your involvement in my home.' Instinctively she placed her hand over Solo's resting on his knee. 'That is not my style at all, believe me.'

Solo looked into her green eyes and what he saw there gave him hope and the strength to admit what he had been skirting around ever since he'd arrived. 'I know, Penny. Though you did look great, I felt sick.' He paused. 'Sick with love for you.'

'You love me.' Her voice trembled.

'*Dio mio*, I thought that was blatantly obvious.' He wrapped his arms around her, his silver eyes glittering down into hers. 'I love you to the depths of my soul now and for ever.' He bent his head, and gently rubbed his lips softly on hers before adding, 'You are my life, my love, and for a man who has never trusted anyone in his life, I am placing my heart in your hands.'

Elation flooded Penny's mind, and her mouth opened eagerly beneath his. His tongue flicked out to explore the moist, dark cavern of her mouth and hungrily she responded. She lifted her arms around his neck, her fingers streaked through his black curly hair, urgently clasping his skull as the kiss went on and on.

Finally they drew apart, needing to breathe. Solo, his silver eyes glittering with an intensity that touched Penny's heart, said, 'And if you will forgive me and come back to me, I swear I'll make you love me or spend the rest of my life trying.' A faint dark colour burnished his high cheekbones.

Penny could feel the tension in his body, and, although passion glazed her huge green eyes, she saw and recognised the vulnerability in Solo's face. He had told her he loved her, he trusted her, but he still wasn't sure of her.

'You won't have to try. I love you,' she admitted with a beautiful smile. Her heart cried for this perfect man, so alone in the world he had never known love. Her husband was a magnificent male animal, and yet he was afraid to reveal his feelings. 'I have loved you since the first moment I saw you,' she declared, and it was there for him to see in the jade eyes blazing into his. 'You have always had my heart, and I'll never doubt you again or leave you again.'

'I don't deserve you,' Solo husked, his silver eyes, suspiciously moist, fused with Penny's, and then he kissed her almost reverently.

A long moment later, curling her fingers in his silky black hair, Penny sighed happily. 'That red dress has a lot to answer for,' she quipped. 'I wish I had kept it, because it got you to admit you love me, and I seem to remember you came to my house the day after I wore it and seduced me.'

Solo slanted her a sardonic look. 'Not really—as I

remember you held out your hand and said, *"Come on"*.'

'You know I didn't mean it the way you took it,' Penny shot back, giving a quick tug on his silky curls. Her arrogant husband was back. It was too much to expect for Solo to stay humble for long, and if she was honest she preferred him his usual dynamic self.

'Ow. Woman, that hurt,' Solo said, his eyes glinting devilishly down into hers. 'But maybe you're right. By then I was so desperate to have you that nothing could have stopped me. Almost four years without a woman is hell on the old libido,' Solo husked, and lowered his head, stealing her mouth again in a kiss like no other they had shared before, a kiss of love and commitment freely given and a promise for the future.

'I…you…Solo…really?' She was filled with awe. 'You didn't…'

'Believe it.' He pressed her back against the sofa. 'I was waiting for you, no one else would do.' His mouth captured hers again as one hand slipped under the lapel of her robe, cupping her breast.

Immediately Penny was aching for him, but, breaking the kiss, she pulled his hand from her breast and, holding it in her own, she looked into his eyes. There was something more she needed to know. 'Then why after we made love the first time were you so cold, and demanded we marry on a temporary basis?'

'Because I dare not face another rejection.' The look he gave her was full of self-mockery and, lifting her hand to his mouth, he kissed the wedding band on her finger. 'I figured once I got you wearing my ring and in my bed, time was on my side. I thought I had succeeded on our honeymoon, but when we got back to England and I suggested we could travel together and you turned me down flat...' He let go of her hand and curved his own around the back of her neck, holding her face up to his, and looking deep into her green eyes. 'It felt like another rejection, Penny, and I couldn't take any more. I didn't know whether to love you or hate you, all I knew was that you loved that old house a hell of a lot more than me.'

She saw the flash of anguish in his eyes that he could not disguise, and her heart wept for him. This proud, wonderful man, so scared by his childhood, he didn't believe anyone could love him, she realised. 'So that was why you were in a temper. I wondered but I was afraid to ask, because I thought you were already tired of me.' Penny traced the outline of his lips with a loving finger, determined to let him know it was all right to be afraid by revealing her own doubts. Love was a scary emotion, but she had to show him how much she adored him. 'I loved our honeymoon and it was there on the tiny beach I realised I still loved you, Solo. I'd always loved you, and I did not want our marriage to ever end, still don't,' Penny admitted huskily.

Solo looked at her with brilliant eyes. 'You and I both,' he declared in a voice that was not quite steady. 'The last day at the cabin as we were leaving, you said you wanted to return one day. I looked at you, and wiped a tear from your cheek and said no problem, I would drive you across from England any time you wanted. But in my head I thought I would drive you to the ends of the earth if you asked. I was struck dumb. That was the moment, when I finally admitted to myself I loved you, and I was scared.'

Penny closed her arms around his neck and smiled up at him, her eyes shining with love and something else. 'I'm so happy I wasn't just bought and paid for.'

'Never.' Solo lowered his dark head, murmuring huskily, 'I love you as you love me.' He covered her face and throat with tiny kisses. 'And I'm never letting you go again,' he declared adamantly, pulling her onto his lap and kissing her thoroughly.

'I'm afraid you will have to,' Penny suddenly cried, and slid off his lap and dashed for the hall cloakroom.

'Penny, please.' Solo followed her. She couldn't leave him now; she couldn't change her mind. For a second he froze. She was leaning over the toilet bowl being violently sick. Oh, *Dio*! What had he done to her now? 'Penny, *cara*.' He leant over her, placing a supporting hand around her head and another around her waist. 'What's wrong?'

Penny straightened up, washed her mouth out at the vanity basin, and sank back against the hard length of his body. 'I'm fine now for the rest of the day—it only lasts for a couple of minutes.' She felt his arms wrap around her stomach, and smiled at his image in the mirror in front of her. Her stony-faced husband looked sicker than she felt, and she smiled. 'I'm pregnant, we are pregnant.' Suddenly she was lifted up in his arms and carried back to the living room.

'Oh, my God, you better lie down.' Solo deposited her on the sofa and knelt on the floor. 'You're sure?' His silver eyes glistened 'When, how?'

A mischievous smile parted her full lips and, rising up, she pulled Solo up onto the sofa beside her. No longer shy but all sensuous woman, with a slender hand she traced the outline of firm jaw, then trailed one finger down his strong throat and lower to scrape over a cotton-covered, hard male nipple, and she felt his body shudder.

'You know very well how, Solo.' A tiny grin flirted

around the edge of her mouth. 'As for the when, probably the first time we made love.'

Powerful hands burrowed under the towelling robe and pulled her close so her naked breast brushed his broad chest. Gleaming silver eyes burnt into hers. 'You have made me the happiest man alive, and the randiest right at this moment.' Solo groaned. His dark head dipped, and his mouth claimed hers as his hand cupped one firm breast.

'Solo, you're here! Are you coming to the zoo?' James asked.

A wave of frustration went through him. Solo quickly adjusted Penny's robe, and crossed his legs. He looked balefully at the little boy standing in the doorway. Then it hit him. Very soon he might have a son of his own. 'James.' He grinned broadly. 'Sorry, but I can't come to the zoo with you today.' Never one to miss a chance, as Jane walked in behind the boy he continued smoothly, 'Penny isn't feeling too well. So I am going to stay and look after her, while you and Jane go to the zoo.'

'Nice try, Solo,' Jane said with a glance at her friend's and her husband's flushed faces, and, guessing exactly what they had been doing, she was glad. 'But Penny is driving.' She grinned.

'No problem,' Solo drawled. 'I'll get the firm's limousine to take you both—it will be much safer that way, and you will have a man to help you around.' His grey eyes gleamed wickedly at Jane. 'The female staff are of the opinion the chauffeur is rather handsome and he's single, Jane, but make sure you bring him back. I'm taking Penny and James home tonight.'

Jane started to laugh. 'I can see why Penny loves you—you're a devil.'

*   *   *

'Alone at last,' Solo husked, walking towards Penny.

Breakfast over, Jane and James had left in the limousine for the zoo.

Penny, showered and dressed in a cotton print dress, was leaning against the kitchen sink having just finished washing the dishes.

'I thought they were never going to leave. Let's go upstairs.' Penny agreed.

'You really are devious.' Penny gasped as Solo slipped her dress down over her hips. 'I heard you tell the chauffeur not to come back until after six, and you'd pay him double.' She grinned up at him, her eyes shining with love and something more.

Solo laughed and pulled her into his arms. He had already stripped off, and his perfectly honed body gleamed golden in the daylight, his silver eyes sparked into hers. 'So I have a lot of time to make up for.'

'You're incorrigible.' Penny planted a kiss on his sensuous mouth, and nibbled on his bottom lip as his hands shaped her waist and thighs and slowly moved back up to remove her bra and cup her full breasts, his thumbs deliberately teasing the rigid, dusky peaks. Penny closed her eyes, breathing deeply as wave after wave of pleasure surged from her breasts to her thighs. Solo's husky-voiced, 'If I don't have you soon I'll die,' had her eyes flying open just as they tumbled back on the bed.

Solo looked into her eyes. He was breathing fast, his own eyes gleaming. 'I love you, Penny,' he said in a deep voice raw with feeling, then his mouth was on hers, hot, hard and insistent.

Penny was swept along on a great tidal wave of desire. They made love with a breathtaking, compelling, frantic urgency, an uninhibited passion that only two people who truly loved could claim. They possessed each other. As morning turned to afternoon the only sounds in the room were the murmured endearments, heavy breathing, the occasional laughter and the hoarse cries of completion.

Finally they clung together, sated and exhausted for the moment. Penny sighed. 'You really don't mind that I am pregnant?'

Solo leaned over her, tipped up her chin with a finger and kissed her, and it was some time later before he answered her question. He said unsteadily, 'I'm thrilled.'

'But how...how could it happen? How could they not know?' Solo demanded, looking tense and anxiously down into Penny's sparkling green eyes. 'The doctor, I mean... The hospital... I paid for the best...'

Propped up in the bed in the master bedroom of their Italian home, Penny bit her lip to stop from laughing. Ever since she had given birth suddenly twenty-four hours ago and three weeks early in this very bed, Solo had hardly left her except to pace to the two cribs and stare. His legendary cool control had completely deserted him.

'I seem to remember...' she lifted a slender hand and ran it teasingly up his long thigh '...it had something to do with a "come on" and you.'

'You know what I mean...' Solo began, and paused, catching her hand on his thigh and sinking down to sit on the bed, his handsome features relaxing in a wry, if tired smile. 'But twins, a boy and a girl, my darling, Paulo and Tina,' he husked in wonder.

He had flatly refused to call the boy Solo, but had

agreed to Paulo. In fact he had felt like Saul on the road to Damascus, redeemed by the love of Penny over the past seven months. She was his life. Solo rarely travelled on business any more; he delegated. They split their time between England and Italy. James was like a son to him, and now this…

'The best room was booked, I had it all arranged.' He still had trouble getting his head around it. The shock of seeing Penny in pain, and his housekeeper deliver the baby boy, had hurt and then awed him, his heart flooding with love for the tiny infant. But ten minutes later when the girl had appeared he had fainted. That the doctor had eventually arrived and declared everything was fine had done nothing to dispel his shock.

He lifted Penny's hand to his mouth and pressed kisses to her palm, and then raised his head and gave her a serious look. 'That's it; we are never doing this again,' he commanded forcibly. 'I can't bear to see you in pain.'

Penny felt the ripples of excitement in her palm, and grinned. 'No more sex, then.' She chuckled at the sudden flash of panic in his silver eyes.

'Witch.' His lips curved in a sensuous smile. 'You know what I mean.' Leaning forward, he captured her mouth in a deep, devouring kiss.

'Yes, all your money and planning gone to pot,' she teased when she had got her breath back. She was so happy she could burst. 'And I don't know what you are complaining about,' she added with a beaming smile, looking up into his incredible silver eyes. 'After all, you got the deal of the day. Two for the price of one!'

'I got the deal of a lifetime and beyond when I got you, Penny.' Solo blinked the moisture from his eyes, and gathered her into his arms. 'You have given me the greatest gift in our two perfect babies. I love you. You're my love, my wife, my life.'

With a heart brimming over with love and happiness, Penny stared at him, too full to speak, but she didn't need to. Glittering silver meshed with misty green and the look they exchanged said it all...

HIS CONVENIENT
MARRIAGE

by

Sara Craven

Sara Craven was born in South Devon and grew up surrounded by books, in a house by the sea. After leaving grammar school she worked as a local journalist, covering everything from flower shows to murders. She started writing for Mills & Boon in 1975. Apart from writing, her passions include films, music, cooking and eating in good restaurants. She now lives in Somerset.

Sara Craven has appeared as a contestant on the Channel Four game show *Fifteen to One* and is also the latest (and last ever) winn er of the 1997 *Mastermind of Great Britain* championship.

Don't miss Sara Craven's exciting new novel, *The Santangeli Marriage*, available in January 2009 from Mills & Boon® Modern™.

CHAPTER ONE

'CHESSIE—oh, Chess, you'll never guess what they're saying in the post office.'

Francesca Lloyd frowned slightly, but her attention didn't waver from her computer screen as her younger sister burst into the room.

'Jen, I've told you a hundred times, you're not supposed to come to this part of the house, and especially not during working hours.'

'Oh, nuts.' Jenny perched on a corner of the big desk, pushing aside some of the neat piles of paper to make room for herself. 'I simply had to see you. Anyway, The Ogre won't be back from London for hours yet,' she added airily. 'I checked that his car wasn't there before I came round.'

Chessie's lips tightened. 'Please don't call him that. It's neither kind nor fair.'

'Well, nor is he.' Jenny pulled a face. 'Besides, you may not need this job for much longer.' She took an excited breath. 'I heard Mrs Cummings telling the post mistress that she's had instructions to open Wenmore Court again. And that means that Alastair's coming back at last.'

Chessie's fingers stilled momentarily on the keyboard. For a moment her heart leapt, painfully—almost brutally.

She kept her voice even. 'Well, that's good news for the village. The house has been closed up for far too long. But it won't make much difference to us.'

'Oh, Chess, don't be silly.' Jenny gave an impatient sigh. 'It makes all the difference in the world. After all, you and Alastair were practically engaged.'

'No.' Chessie turned on her. 'We were *not*. And you've got to stop saying that.'

5

'Well, you would have been if his beastly father hadn't sent him to business school in the States,' Jenny retorted. 'Everyone knows that. You were crazy about each other.'

'And much younger, too.' Chessie began typing again. 'And a hell of a lot has happened since then. Nothing's the same.'

'Do you really think that would make any difference to Alastair?' Jenny demanded scornfully.

'I think it might.' It still hurt to remember how the weekly letters had dwindled to one a month, and then petered out altogether before the end of their first year apart.

Since then, her only contact had been a brief note of condolence following her father's death.

And if Alastair had known that Neville Lloyd had died, then he almost certainly knew the circumstances of his death, she thought, wincing.

'God, you can be a real drag sometimes,' Jenny accused. 'I thought you'd be thrilled. I ran all the way home to tell you.'

'Jen, we shouldn't make assumptions.' Chessie tried to speak gently. 'After all, it's been three years and a lot of water under the bridge. We're not the same people any more, Alastair and I.'

There'd been a time when she'd rejoiced in those three words, she thought sadly. When they'd had meaning—even a future...

She squared her shoulders. 'And now I've got to get on. Please don't let Mr Hunter come back and catch you here again.'

'Oh, all right.' Jenny slid mutinously off the desk. 'But how great it would be if Alastair asked you to marry him. Imagine being able to tell The Ogre what to do with his rotten job.'

Chessie stifled a sigh. 'It is not a rotten job,' she returned levelly. 'It's good, and well paid. It keeps food in our mouths, and a roof over our heads. And it allows us to go on living in our old home.'

'As servants,' Jenny said with intense bitterness. 'Big deal.' And she went out, slamming the door behind her.

Chessie sat very still for a moment, her face troubled. It was disturbing that even after all this time, Jenny had not been able to come to terms with the admittedly devastating change in their circumstances.

She could not seem to cope with the fact that Silvertrees House no longer belonged to them—or that the only part of it they were entitled to occupy was the former house-keeper's flat.

'Yet, why not?' Chessie asked herself, wryly. 'After all, that's what I am—the housekeeper.'

'I don't want, or need, a lot of staff,' Miles Hunter had told her at that first, fraught interview. 'I require the house to be run efficiently, and without fuss, plus secretarial sup-port.'

'Meaning what, precisely?' Chessie looked impassively back at her potential employer, trying to weigh him up. It wasn't easy. His clothes, casually elegant, were at odds with the harshly etched lines of his face, accentuated by the scar that ran from his cheekbone to the corner of his unsmiling mouth. The cool drawl gave nothing away, ei-ther.

'I use a very old portable typewriter, Miss Lloyd. I al-ways have, but my publishers now require my manuscripts on computerised disks. I presume you can handle that?'

She nodded wordlessly.

'Good. On the domestic side it will be up to you what additional assistance you require. I imagine you'll need a daily help at least. But I insist on peace and quiet while I'm writing. I also value my privacy.'

He paused. 'I'm aware this may be difficult for you. After all, you've lived at Silvertrees all your life, and you're used to having the free run of the place. That, I'm afraid, can't happen any more.'

'No,' Chessie said. 'I—I can see that.'

There was another brief silence. 'Of course,' he said,

'you may not wish to take the job on, but your lawyer felt it could solve a number of problems for both of us.'

The blue eyes were vivid against the deep tan of his thin face. 'So, how about it, Miss Lloyd? Are you prepared to sacrifice your pride, and accept my offer?'

She ignored the note of faint mockery in his voice. 'I can't afford pride, Mr Hunter. Not with a young sister to support, and educate. I'd be more than grateful for the job, and the accommodation.' She paused. 'And we'll try not to impinge on your seclusion.'

'Don't just try, Miss Lloyd. Succeed.' He drew the file on the desk in front of him towards him, signalling the interview was ending. As she rose he added, 'I'll get my lawyers to draw up the necessary lease, and contract of employment.'

'Is that really necessary?' There was dismay in her voice. 'It sounds a bit daunting. Couldn't we have some kind of—gentleman's agreement?'

His mouth seemed to twist harshly, or was it just the scar that gave that impression?

'I've never been a gentleman, Miss Lloyd,' he remarked. 'And appearances are against you, too. I think it better to put things on a businesslike footing from day one—don't you?'

And that, Chessie thought drearily, had been that. She was allowed to occupy the former housekeeper's flat, with Jenny, for a peppercorn rent, as long as she continued to work for Miles Hunter.

At the time, desperate as she had been, bleak with guilt and grief over her father, it had seemed a lifeline. Too good a proposition to turn down.

Now, with hindsight, she wondered if she should have refused. Taken Jenny and herself far away from old memories—old associations.

But that would have meant finding a new school for Jenny just before an important exam year, and she'd been loth to create any more disruption in her sister's life.

And at first it had seemed worth it. Jenny had done well, and was expected to go on to university in due course. She'd get a student loan, but it would still mean all kinds of extra expenditure.

So Chessie seemed contracted to several more years of transferring Miles Hunter's starkly exciting thrillers onto the computer, and keeping his home running like the clockwork he demanded.

It had not, she reflected, been the easiest of rides. As she'd suspected at that first meeting, he wasn't the easiest person in the world to work for. He expected consistently high standards, and could be icily sarcastic and unpleasant if these were not met, as several of the daily helps who'd come and gone could vouchsafe.

But while Chessie had adhered strictly to her own territory outside working hours, Jenny had not always been so scrupulous.

She'd made it plain she regarded Silvertrees' new owner as little more than an interloper in what was still her own home, and this had led to trouble, and almost confrontation, on more than one occasion. And this had led to her coining the resentful nickname 'The Ogre' for Miles Hunter.

Chessie pushed back her chair, and wandered over to the window, beset by sudden restlessness.

Jenny could be disturbingly intolerant at times, she thought ruefully. It was true that she'd found her father's disgrace and subsequent death traumatic in the extreme, but that was no longer a valid excuse. But her young sister bitterly resented the collapse of her comfortable, cushioned life.

She wanted things back the way they were—and that was never going to happen.

I've accepted it, Chessie thought sadly. Why can't she?

And now Alastair might be returning and Jenny had seized on this as a sign that their circumstances were about to change for the better in some miraculous way.

Chessie sighed under her breath. Oh, to be that young and optimistic again.

As she had been once—when she and Alastair had been together, and the world and the future had seemed to belong to them.

As a first love, she supposed, it had been pretty near idyllic. A summer of walks, and car rides; of swimming and playing tennis, and watching Alastair play cricket. Of kisses and breathless murmurs. And promises.

In retrospect, all very sweet. And absurdly innocent.

Alastair had wanted her. There was little doubt about that, and to this day she didn't know why she'd held back. Maybe it had been some unconscious reluctance to take the step that would have left her girlhood behind for ever, and made her a woman. Or, more prosaically, perhaps it had been the fear that it had only been her body that he'd really wanted. And that, having made the ultimate commitment, she would have lost him.

'A man will tell you anything, darling, if he's trying to get you into bed.' Linnet's husky voice, cloying as warm treacle, came back to haunt her. 'Don't make it too easy for him.'

Chessie had reacted with distaste at the time. But maybe the words had stuck just the same. Like so many of Linnet's little barbs, she reflected ruefully.

And if the Court really was being re-opened, that would mean that Linnet would be back too, proving that every silver lining had a black cloud hovering.

In a way, it had been Linnet who had unwittingly drawn Chessie and Alastair together originally.

Sir Robert Markham, like Chessie's father, had been a widower for several years. It had been popularly assumed in the village that if he remarried, his choice would be Gail Travis, who ran the local kennels, and whom he'd been escorting to local functions for the past year.

But one night at a charity ball he'd seen Linnet Arthur, an actress who, up to then, had made an erratic living from modelling, bit parts in soap operas, and playing hostess on daytime television game shows. Linnet, with her mane of blonde hair, perfect teeth, endless legs and frankly voluptuous body, had been decorating the tombola. And suddenly poor Mrs Travis had been history.

After an embarrassingly short courtship, Sir Robert had married Linnet, and brought her down to the Court.

The shock waves had still been reverberating when he'd given a garden party to introduce her to the neighbourhood. And Alastair, standing like a statue in the background, had clearly been the most shocked of all.

He'd disappeared during the course of the afternoon, and Chessie had found him sitting under a tree by the river, throwing stones into the water. She'd been about to creep away, convinced he'd wanted to be alone, but his face, white with outrage and misery, had stopped her in her tracks.

Over six feet tall, with chestnut hair, and good looks to die for, Alastair, three years her senior, had always been Chessie's god.

Somehow, she'd found the courage to say, 'Alastair, I'm so sorry.'

He glanced up at her, his brown eyes glazed with pain. 'How could he?' he burst out. 'How could he have put that—bimbo in my mother's place? God, Chessie, she even brings bimbos into disrepute.'

To her horror, Chessie found herself struggling not to laugh. Alastair noticed, and his own mouth twitched into a reluctant grin. After that Linnet was always referred to between them as 'The Wicked Stepmother', and they spent many enjoyable hours slagging off the time she devoted to her personal appearance, her horrendous schemes for redecorating the Court, firmly vetoed by Sir Robert, and her doomed attempts to establish herself as the lady of the manor.

After that, they devoted themselves to devising a range

of eventual fates for her more ghoulish and grisly than even the Brothers Grimm could have imagined.

'Thank God I'm going to university,' Alastair declared eventually, with scornful resignation. 'And I won't be coming back for vacations, if I can help it.'

Chessie missed him when he went, but she was soon absorbed in her school work, planning ahead for a career in her father's company.

It was three years before they encountered each other again. Chessie, newly returned from a month living as an au pair in France, had been asked to help on the white elephant stall at the church fête, held annually in the grounds of Wenmore Court, and one of the few village events with which the new Lady Markham sulkily allowed herself to be associated.

It was a blazingly hot afternoon, and Chessie was wondering when she could legitimately sneak off and go for a swim in the river, when Alastair halted beside the stall.

'My God, Chessie.' He was laughing, but there was another note in his voice too. 'I'd hardly have known you.'

But I, she thought, the breath catching in her throat, I would have known you anywhere. *Anywhere.*

It was as if all her life until then had been geared for this one brilliant, unforgettable moment.

They stood there, smiling at each other, almost foolishly. Momentarily oblivious to everything and everyone around them. Then Alastair said quietly, 'I'll call you,' and she nodded, jerkily, afraid of showing her delight too openly.

They were practically inseparable in those first weeks of reunion, talking endlessly. She'd just left school, and was preparing to join her father in the City the following September, initially as a junior dogsbody, styled personal assistant.

Alastair, they both presumed, would do the same—start learning the family electronics business from the bottom rung of the ladder.

The weather was hot, one perfect day spilling into another, and Chessie found herself spending a lot of time at the Court, where Linnet had managed to persuade her husband to install a swimming pool.

Until then, Chessie had been too insignificant for Lady Markham to notice, but she could hardly continue to ignore her when they were occupying adjoining sun loungers.

'Hi,' she drawled, eyes hidden behind designer sunglasses, and her spectacular figure displayed in a bikini one centimetre short of indecent. 'So you're Ally's little holiday romance. How nice.'

Chessie bit her lip. 'How do you do, Lady Markham?' she returned politely, touching the languidly extended fingers.

'Oh, Linnet—please.' The red mouth curled into a smile. 'After all, sweetie, we're practically the same age.'

Back to the Brothers Grimm, Chessie muttered under her breath as she turned away.

She'd have preferred to avoid Linnet altogether during her visits, but this proved impossible. To Chessie's embarrassment the older woman had immediately recognised the fact that she was still physically innocent, and enjoyed bombarding her with a constant stream of unwanted intimate advice, like poisoned darts.

But nothing Linnet could say or do had any real power to damage her happiness. Or her unspoken hopes for the future.

That came from a totally unexpected direction.

When Sir Robert announced that he was sending his son to business school in America, it was like a bolt from the blue. At first, Alastair seemed determined to fight his father's decision, but when Sir Robert remained adamant, his mood changed to coldly furious acceptance.

'Can't you make him listen?' Chessie pleaded.

'It's no use, darling.' Alastair's face was hard. 'You don't know my father when his mind's made up like this.'

It was true that Chessie had only ever seen the genial,

open-handed side of Sir Robert. This kind of arbitrary behaviour seemed totally out of character.

'But I'll be back, Chessie.' He stared into space, his face
set. 'This isn't the end of everything. I won't allow it to
be.'

And I believed him, thought Chessie.

She hoped it wasn't some subconscious conviction that
one day he'd return to claim her that had kept her here in
the village. Because common sense told her she was crying
for the moon.

If Alastair had been seriously interested in her, if it had
been more than a boy and girl thing, then he'd have asked
her to marry him before he'd gone to the States, or at least
begged her to wait for him. She'd made herself face that a
long time ago.

It had been obvious that everyone in the neighbourhood
had been expecting some kind of announcement. And even
more apparent that, once he'd departed, people had been
feeling sorry for her. The sting of their well-meant sympathy had only deepened her heartache and sense of iso-
lation.

As had the attitude of Sir Robert, who'd made it coldly
clear that he'd regarded it as a transient relationship, and
not to be taken seriously. While Linnet's derisive smile had
made Chessie feel quite sick.

She'd never realised before how much the other woman
disliked her.

She'd wondered since whether Sir Robert, a shrewd businessman, had divined something about her father's looming
financial troubles, and had decided to distance his family
from a potential scandal.

To widespread local astonishment, Sir Robert had announced his own early retirement, and the sale of his company to a European conglomerate. Following this, within a
few weeks of Alastair's departure, the Court had been
closed up, and the Markhams had gone to live in Spain.

'Joining the sangria set,' Mrs Hawkins the post mistress had remarked. 'She'll fit right in there.'

But now, it seemed, they were coming back, although that didn't necessarily mean that Alastair would be returning with them. That could be just wishful thinking on Jenny's part, she acknowledged.

And Chessie hadn't wanted to question her too closely about what she'd heard. For one thing, Jenny should not have been hanging round the post office eavesdropping on other people's conversations. For another, Chessie didn't want to give the impression she was too interested.

The burned child fears the fire, she thought wryly. She'd worn her heart on her sleeve once for Alastair already. This time, she would be more careful.

If there was a 'this time…'

'My God, Chessie, I'd hardly have known you.'

Was that what he'd say when—if—he saw her again?

Certainly, she bore little resemblance to the girl he'd known. The Chessie of that summer had had hair streaked with sunlight. Her honey-tanned skin had glowed with youth and health as well as happiness, and her hazel eyes had smiled with confidence at the world about her.

Now, she seemed like a tone poem in grey, she thought, picking at her unremarkable skirt and blouse. And it wasn't just her clothes. The reflection in the window looked drab—defeated.

Yet any kind of style or flamboyance had not seemed an option in those hideous weeks between her father's arrest for fraud and his fatal heart attack on remand.

She'd survived it all—the stories in the papers, the visits of the fraud squad, Jenny's descent into hysteria—by deliberately suppressing her identity and retreating behind a wall of anonymity. Something she'd maintained ever since.

She'd expected to find herself a kind of pariah, and yet, with a few exceptions, people in the village had been kind and tactful, making it easy for her to adopt this new muted version of her life.

And working for Miles Hunter had helped too, in some curious way. It had been a tough and exacting time with little opportunity for recriminations or brooding.

In the last few months, she'd even managed to reach some kind of emotional plateau just short of contentment.

Now, thanks to Jenny's news, she felt unsettled again.

She was about to turn back to her desk when she heard the sound of an engine. Craning her neck, she saw Miles Hunter's car sweep round the long curve of the drive and come to a halt in front of the main door.

A moment later, he emerged from the driver's seat. He stood for a moment, steadying himself, then reached for his cane and limped slowly towards the shallow flight of steps that led up to the door.

Chessie found she was biting her lip as she watched him. Her own current problems were just so minor compared to his, she thought, with a flicker of the compassion she'd never dared show since that first day she'd worked for him.

It was something she'd never forgotten—the way he'd stumbled slightly, getting out of his chair, and how, instinctively, she'd jumped up herself, her hands reaching out to him.

The blue eyes had been glacial, his whole face twisted in a snarl as he'd turned on her. 'Keep away. Don't touch me.'

'I'm so sorry.' She'd been stricken by the look, and the tone of his voice. 'I was just trying to help...'

'If I need it, I'll ask for it. And I certainly don't want pity. Remember that.'

She'd wanted to hand in her notice there and then, but she hadn't because she'd suddenly remembered a very different exchange.

'He had the world at his feet once,' Mr Jamieson, their family solicitor, had told her when he'd first mentioned the possibility of a job, and staying on at Silvertrees. 'Rugby blue—played squash for his county—award-winning journalist in newspaper and television. And then found himself in the wrong place at the wrong moment, when the convoy he was travelling with met a land-mine.'

He shook his head. 'His injuries were frightful. They thought he'd never walk again, and he had umpteen skin grafts. But while he was in hospital recovering, he wrote his first novel *The Bad Day*.'

'Since which, he's never looked back, of course.' Chessie spoke with a certain irony.

Mr Jamieson looked at her with quiet solemnity over the top of his glasses. 'Oh, no, my dear,' he said gently. 'I think it likely he looks back a good deal—don't you?'

And Francesca felt herself reproved.

She was back at her desk, working away, when Miles Hunter came in.

'I've just seen your sister,' he remarked without preamble. 'She nearly went into the car with that damned bike of hers. Doesn't it possess brakes?'

'Yes, of course,' Chessie said hurriedly, groaning inwardly. 'But she does ride it far too fast. I—I'll speak to her.'

Miles Hunter gave her a sardonic look. 'Will that do any good? She seems a law unto herself.'

'Well, I can try at least.'

'Hmm.' He gave her a considering look. 'She seemed stirred up about something, and so do you. Has she been upsetting you again?'

'Jenny does not upset me.' Chessie lifted her chin.

'Of course not,' he agreed affably, then sighed impatiently. 'Just who are you trying to fool, Francesca? You spend half your life making allowances for that girl—tiptoeing around her feelings as if you were treading on eggshells. I'm damned if she does half as much for you.'

Indignation warred inside her with shock that Miles Hunter, who invariably addressed her as Miss Lloyd, should suddenly have used her first name.

'It's been very difficult for her…' she began defensively.

'More than for you?'

'In some ways. You see, Jenny…' She realised she was about to say, Jenny was my father's favourite, but the words died on her lips. It was something she'd never admitted before, she realised, shocked. Something she'd never even allowed herself to examine. She found herself substituting lamely, 'Was very young when all this happened to us.'

'You don't think it's time she took on some responsibility for her own life, perhaps?' The dark face was quizzical.

'You're my employer, Mr Hunter,' Chessie said steadily. 'But that's all. You're not our guardian, and you have no right to judge. Jenny and I have a perfectly satisfactory relationship.'

'Well, she and I do not,' he said grimly. 'When I suggested, quite mildly, that she should look where she was going, she called back that soon I wouldn't have to bother about either of you. What did she mean by that?'

Chessie would have given a great deal to put her hands round Jenny's throat and choke her.

'I think perhaps you misheard her,' she said, cursing silently. 'What Jenny means is that she'll be going to university in the autumn and—'

'If her results are good enough.'

'There's no problem about that,' Chessie said stiffly. 'She's a very bright girl, and they expect her to do well.'

'Let's hope that their optimism is rewarded. I can't say that sharing a roof with her has been an unalloyed delight.'

Ouch. Chessie bit her lip. 'I'm sorry.'

'You haven't a thing to apologise for. You haven't the age or experience to cope with a temperamental adolescent. Wasn't there anyone else who could have helped?'

She wanted to tell him sharply that she didn't need help, thanks, but her intrinsic honesty prevailed. She said quietly, 'I have an aunt on my mother's side, but she didn't want her family involved—and who can blame her? Anyway, it doesn't matter.'

'Of course it matters,' he said. 'You're a human being, although you do your best, most of the time, to pretend you're some kind of robot.' He stopped abruptly. 'Oh, for God's sake, I didn't mean that.' He paused. 'Look, can I ask you something before I stumble into any more verbal disasters?'

'If you want.' *Robot*, she thought. *Grey robot.* That said it all.

'Would you have dinner with me this evening?'

For the first time in her life, Chessie felt her jaw drop. 'I—I don't understand.'

'It's quite simple. It may not seem like it, but I've had a really good day. My agent has actually sold *Maelstrom* to Evening Star Films, and they want me to write the first draft of the screenplay, so there's a slight chance of part of my original concept surviving.'

She saw his smile so seldom that she'd forgotten what a charge it could pack, lighting his whole face with charm, and turning his eyes to sapphire. Forcing her to startled acknowledgement of his attraction.

'I'd really like to celebrate,' he went on. 'And as *Maelstrom* was the first book you were involved with, I'd be honoured if you'd join me.'

She continued to stare at him.

Finally, he said, 'You do eat—don't you?'

'Yes—but…'

'But what?'

Chessie moved her hands defensively. 'It's a kind thought, but I don't think we should. After all, this is quite a small village.'

'I was asking you to dinner,' he said with studied patience. 'Not to bed. If you want, I'll put a notice to that effect in the parish magazine.'

Her face warmed. 'I'm sure you find it all very parochial and amusing,' she said. 'But I've managed to establish that ours is strictly a working relationship, which is important as we live under the same roof. If I'm seen having dinner

with you, people might assume—things have changed. And
that could embarrass both of us.'

And I've lived through one lot of gossip and scandal,
she added silently. I don't relish the thought of any more.

'I really don't embarrass that easily.' He sounded
amused. 'But I could always call in a builder, and have the
communicating door between your flat and the rest of the
house bricked up. That should silence the clacking
tongues.'

'I'm trying to be serious,' she protested.

'And, for once, I'm trying to be frivolous, not with any
conspicuous success,' he added drily. 'Can't you look on
the invitation as an expression of gratitude—an additional
bonus? Anyway—' he cast her a frowning but all-
encompassing glance '—you look as if you could do with
a square meal. You could rent out your collar-bones as salt-
cellars.'

'Thank you,' Chessie said with something of a snap. 'But
I don't think—'

'Precisely,' Miles interrupted flatly. 'Don't think. Do
something on impulse for a change. It's only a meal, for
heaven's sake.' He paused, his face hardening. 'Or do you
find my physical appearance distressing? Because I can assure you all the worst scars are hidden.'

'*No.*' Her flush deepened. 'That's a terrible thing to imply.'

'It happens,' he returned. 'I was living with someone
before the ill-fated assignment. We'd talked about marriage—made plans. When I came out of hospital and she
saw me without my clothes for the first time, she didn't
want to know any more.' He paused. 'And that is a matter
of pure fact—not a plea for sympathy.'

'You've made it more than clear that sympathy is the
last thing you want, Mr Hunter.' She hesitated. 'But I will
have dinner with you—if that's what you want.'

'Thank you,' he said quietly. 'Do you think you could
bend another rule, and call me Miles?'

Chessie felt suddenly confused. This, she thought, is not right, and I should put a stop to it, here and now.

Instead, she heard herself say awkwardly, 'Very well— Miles.'

He nodded gravely. 'Absolutely the right decision. I'll see you out by the car at eight.'

He limped across to the adjoining study and went in, closing the door behind him.

Chessie looked blankly at the computer. The screensaver had clicked on, and she was confronted by a series of coloured geometric patterns, endlessly changing shape as they whirled slowly in front of her.

I know, she thought, how they feel.

It was turning into a day for surprises, and she wasn't sure she cared for any of them. Particularly the latest one.

Had she really committed herself to going to dinner with Miles Hunter? she asked herself incredulously.

She thought, Well, it's too late to turn back now, and shivered as if she'd found herself on the edge of some nameless danger…

And that was a complete overreaction, she added flatly, probably brought on by reading too many thrillers by Miles Hunter. From now on, she'd switch to biographies about people who'd led very boring lives.

After all—and he'd said it himself—it was only a meal.

CHAPTER TWO

'THE Ogre's asked you out to dinner?' Jenny looked blank with disbelief. 'And you've actually accepted.' She shook her head. 'God, Chessie, you must be out of your tree.'

Chessie shrugged defensively. 'I don't see why. Something marvellous happened for him today, and he wants to celebrate.'

'Don't tell me,' Jenny said derisively. 'They've invented a mask for him to wear—like the Phantom of the Opera.'

Chessie stared at her, appalled. 'What an utterly foul thing to say,' she said slowly. 'Miles is my boss, and we owe him a great deal, yet you can't say one decent word to him, or about him.'

'Owe him?' Jenny's face reddened. 'What the hell do we owe him? He's taken our home away from us, and he's making us pay for it by treating us like drudges.'

'Really?' snapped Chessie. 'Well, I haven't noticed much drudgery from your direction. And if Miles hadn't bought this house, someone else would have done so, and we'd have been out on our ears. There was no way we could keep it. Why can't I get that through to you?'

Jenny looked mutinous. 'Well, I still think we could have done something. I saw this thing on television the other day about small country house hotels. It was really cool. I bet we could have made a bomb with Silvertrees.'

'In about twenty years, maybe,' Chessie said levelly. 'But Dad's creditors weren't prepared to wait that long for their money. And our present existence is like a holiday camp, compared with hotel-keeping. That's a twenty-four-hour job.'

Jenny sniffed. 'I still think it could have worked,' she said obstinately.

Chessie was suddenly caught between tears and laughter. Extraordinary how Jenny, so clever at school, could have such a tenuous hold on reality at other times.

She wondered what role her sister had pictured for herself in this make-believe ménage. Acting as receptionist, no doubt, and arranging a few flowers. Because she couldn't cook to save her life, and had never shown the slightest aptitude for housework either.

'And, anyway—' Jenny got down to the nitty-gritty of the situation '—if you're going out tonight, what am I going to eat? I bet The Ogre hasn't invited me.'

'No, he hasn't,' Chessie agreed. 'But you won't starve. There's some chicken casserole in the fridge. All you have to do is use the microwave.'

'Hardly on a level with being wined and dined.' Jenny pulled a face. 'And another thing—since when has The Ogre been "Miles" to you? I thought it was strictly, "Yes, Mr Hunter, sir."'

'So it was, and probably will be again tomorrow,' Chessie told her calmly. 'It's just a meal, that's all.'

I wonder how many times I'm going to say that before I convince even myself, she thought later as she reviewed the meagre contents of her wardrobe.

It had been a long time since she'd eaten in a restaurant. She'd been having lunch with her father, she remembered, hardly able to eat as she'd tried nervously to probe what had been going on in the company.

She could recall the uneasy questions she'd asked—the reassurances she'd sought.

Neville had patted her shoulder. 'Everything's going to be all right.' She could hear his voice now. 'There's nothing for my girl to worry about.'

He'd talked loudly, and laughed a lot. Drunk a lot too. He'd seen some former business associates across the restaurant, and had waved to them expansively, beckoning them over, but they hadn't come.

Even then that had seemed ominous, like the first crack in a dam, only she hadn't dared say so. Hadn't even wanted to acknowledge it could have been so. Longed for it all to have been her imagination.

She'd worn a plain cream linen shift, she remembered, with large gold buttons. That didn't exist any more, sadly, and she had little else that was suitable for dining out in.

Most of her clothes fell into two categories, she realised regretfully. There was working (ordinary) and working (slightly smarter). In the end, she opted for a plain black skirt reaching to mid-calf, and topped it with an ivory silk chainstore blouse. The gilt earrings and chains that Jenny had given her for her last birthday made the outfit seem a little more festive.

She was in her early twenties and she felt a hundred years old. There were little worry lines forming between her brows, and the curve of her mouth was beginning to look pinched.

She usually wore her light brown hair gathered for neatness into a rubber band at the nape of her neck, but decided to let it loose for once, its newly washed silkiness brushing her shoulders.

The only eye-shadow she possessed had formed into a sullen lump in the bottom of its little jar. Jenny had some make-up, she knew, purchased from her scanty and infrequent earnings delivering leaflets round the village, but, under the circumstances, a request for a loan would go down like a lead balloon, so she just used powder and her own dusky coral lipstick.

As a final touch, she unearthed her precious bottle of 'L'Air du Temps' from the back of her dressing-table drawer, and applied it to her throat and wrists. When it was gone, there would be no more, she thought, re-stoppering the bottle with care.

The salary she was paid was a good one, but there was little money left over for luxuries like scent.

Jenny had won a scholarship to the school in the neighbouring town where she was a day girl, so Chessie had no actual fees to find. But there was so much else. The only acceptable sports gear and trainers had to come with designer labels, and the school had a strict uniform code too, which had been a nightmare while Jenny was growing so rapidly.

But her sister was going to have exactly the same as all the other girls. She'd been determined about that from the first. No ridicule or snide remarks from her peers for Jenny.

But no one said it was easy, she thought, grimacing, as she picked up her all-purpose jacket and bag.

She paused to take a long critical look at herself in the mirror.

Did she really look the kind of girl a best-selling novelist would ask out? The answer to that was an unequivocal 'no', and she found herself wondering why he hadn't sought more congenial company.

Because, no matter what cruel comments Jenny might make, there was no doubt that Miles Hunter was an attractive and dynamic man, in spite of the scar on his face. And she wondered why it had taken her so long to realise this.

But then, she'd hardly regarded him in the light of a human being, she thought wryly. He was the man she worked for, and his initial rejection of her compassion had barred any personal rapport between them. He'd become a figurehead, she thought. A dark god who had to be constantly placated if she and Jenny were to survive.

She found herself thinking about the girl he'd told her about—the fiancée who'd ditched him because of his scars. Was he still embittered about this? Still carrying a torch for the woman who'd let him down when he'd most needed her support?

Could this be why, apart from the fan mail, which she dealt with herself, there were no phone calls or letters from women—apart from his sister, and his agent, who was in her late forties?

And could it also be why there was no love interest in his books—not the slightest leavening of romance?

He was a terrific writer, and the tension in his stories never slackened. Each book went straight into the best-seller lists after publication, yet if Chessie was honest she found his work oddly bleak, and even sterile.

But that's just my opinion, she told herself ruefully as she let herself out through the side door. The thriller-reading public who snapped him up had no such reservations.

Besides, she didn't know for sure that Miles had no women in his life. He was away a great deal in London, and other places. He could well be having a whole series of affairs without her being aware of it. Maybe he just liked to keep his personal life private—and away from the village.

He was waiting by the car. He was wearing beautifully cut casual trousers, which moulded his long legs, and a high-necked sweater in black cashmere. A sports jacket was slung across one shoulder.

He was staring at the ground, looking preoccupied and slightly cross, failing to notice her soft-footed approach.

He didn't seem to be looking forward to a pleasant evening, thought Chessie, wondering if he was regretting his impulsive invitation. If so, she was sure she would soon know, she told herself philosophically.

She found herself hoping that Jenny hadn't eaten the entire chicken casserole, because she might well be joining her.

She said, 'Good evening,' her voice shy and rather formal.

He looked up instantly, his eyes narrowing as if, for a moment, he had forgotten who she was. Then he nodded abruptly.

'Punctual as always,' he commented, opening the passenger door for her.

Well, what did he expect? Chessie wondered defensively as she struggled with her seat belt. She was hardly going to hang about coyly in the house, keeping him waiting.

As he joined her she caught a hint of his cologne, slightly musky and obviously expensive.

'I thought we'd try The White Hart,' Miles said as he started the engine. 'I hear the food's good there, if you don't mind the village pub.'

'Not at all.' Neither Chessie's clothes nor her confidence were up to a smart restaurant. 'Mrs Fewston's a marvellous cook. Before she and her husband took over the Hart, she used to cater for private dinner parties. In fact, I think she still does, sometimes.'

'I shall have to bear that in mind. It's time I did some entertaining.' He sent her a swift, sideways glance. 'Well, don't look so astonished. I can't go on accepting hospitality without returning it.'

'Er—no.' Chessie rallied. 'And Silvertrees is a great house for parties.'

'It's also a family house,' he said laconically. 'As my sister never fails to remind me.' He paused. 'I think that's a hint that I should invite her and her blasted kids to stay.'

'Don't you like children?'

He shrugged. 'I've never had much to do with them. Actually, Steffie's are great, although she calls them the monsters,' he added drily.

If it hadn't been for that land-mine, he might have been married with a family of his own by now, Chessie thought. She tried to imagine it, and failed.

But that was so unfair, she reproached herself. She was behaving just like Jenny. Because she'd never known the man he'd once been. The man who'd enjoyed everything life had to offer—who'd played sport, and laughed, and made love.

And the chances were she'd never have encountered him anyway.

Miles Hunter, the award-winning journalist and hard-hitting television reporter, would have been based in London. He wouldn't have been interested in a large, inconvenient house on the edge of a sleepy village. He'd have been where it was all happening—where he could pack a bag, and be off whenever a story broke.

He would probably never have contemplated becoming a novelist until circumstances had forced him to rethink his life completely.

Yet, here they both were. And together…

The White Hart was a pleasant timbered building, sited near the crossroads outside the village. A former coaching inn, it was always busy. Jim Fewston was as knowledgeable about wine as his wife was about cooking, and that kept the people coming. Tonight was no exception, and the car park was almost full when they arrived.

'Just as well I booked a table,' Miles commented as he slotted the car with expertise into one of the few available spaces. 'Although it would seem that not everyone's here for the food,' he added drily.

She followed his glance, and saw movement in a car parked on its own under the shelter of some trees. Glimpsed shadowy figures passionately entwined, and hurriedly looked away.

'What an odd place to choose.' She tried to match his tone.

'Not if you're having an illicit affair.' Miles shrugged. 'Presumably any corner will do.'

In the bar, Chessie drank an excellent dry sherry, and Miles a gin and tonic as they studied their menu cards.

Many of the people already there were local and known to her, and she'd been greeted cordially when she'd arrived, although a few of the greetings had been accompanied by slyly speculative glances.

But that was only to be expected, she thought as hunger drove out self-consciousness.

She chose watercress soup, and guinea fowl casseroled with shallots in red wine, while Miles opted for pâté, and steak cooked with Guinness and oysters.

'"Do you come here often?" is the usual opening gambit in this situation,' Miles commented sardonically as the waitress disappeared with their order. 'But I'm well aware that you don't, so what do you suggest as an alternative topic?'

'I'm not sure.' She played with the stem of her glass. 'I think my social graces are rusty with disuse.'

'And I doubt that I ever had any.' His mouth twisted in faint amusement. 'It promises to be a silent evening.'

'I'm quite used to that.' Tentatively, she returned his smile. 'Jenny spends most of her time in her room, studying for her exams, so I'm accustomed to my own company.'

'People tell me solitude is a luxury,' Miles said after a pause. 'But I'm not sure it works so well as a way of life.' He paused. 'What's your sister planning to do when she leaves school?'

'She's applied to read natural sciences, but I don't think she has any definite ideas about an ultimate career yet.' She thought she detected a faintly quizzical expression in the blue eyes, and hurried on defensively. 'But it's early days, and she doesn't have to make any hasty decisions.'

She leaned back against the comfortable red plush of the bench seat. 'I had to struggle every inch of the way at school, but learning seems to come easily to Jenny.'

'I'm glad to hear it,' Miles said politely, after another pause. 'There's a good St Emilion on the wine list, or would you prefer Burgundy?'

'No, the Bordeaux would be fine.' She remembered with a pang a holiday she'd once spent with her father, exploring the vineyards of south-west France. It had been a magical time for her, even though he'd constantly fussed about

Jenny left behind with her aunt's family, and made a point of phoning her each evening.

'There it is again,' Miles said quietly, and she looked at him in startled question.

'I'm sorry?'

'That expression of yours—like a child who's just heard Christmas has been abolished.'

'Oh, dear.' Chessie pantomimed dismay. 'How wimpish. I'll try and look more cheerful from now on.'

'Are all your memories so painful?'

She gave the pale liquid in her glass a fierce and concentrated stare. 'How did you know I was—remembering?'

'An educated guess—having attended the same school myself.' He finished his gin and tonic. 'Want to talk about it?'

She shook her head. 'What can anyone say? One minute you're riding high. The next, you're flat on your face in the mud, not knowing whether you'll ever get up again. That's my personal angle. The rest I'm sure you read in the newspapers at the time. They didn't leave many stones unturned.'

He said gently, 'It would have been difficult to miss.' He watched her for a moment. 'Well—aren't you going to say it?'

'Say what?'

'That your father was entirely innocent, and, but for his untimely death, he'd have cleared himself of all charges.'

Chessie slowly shook her head. She said bleakly, 'If he'd lived, I think he would still have been in jail. In many ways, his death was a mercy for him. He'd have hated—hated...'

She stopped, biting her lip. 'I'm sorry. I'm being very boring. This is supposed to be a celebration, not a wake.'

He said quietly, 'I would not have asked if I hadn't wanted to know, Francesca.'

But why did he want to know? she wondered as she drank some more sherry. Now that they were out of their working environment, maybe he felt he had to make conversation that didn't concern the current script or the purely domestic details either.

Yet he could have picked something less personal. Music, maybe, or cinema.

What did a man and a woman talk to each other about over dinner and a bottle of wine? She was so totally out of touch. And nervous.

She hadn't had a serious boyfriend since Alastair. The dates she'd gone out on in London had been totally casual and uncommitted. She couldn't think of one man out of all of them she'd wanted to see again, let alone know better.

And since London, of course, there'd been no one at all. Until tonight—which naturally didn't count, she reminded herself swiftly.

It was a relief when the waitress came to say their table was ready. The soup and pâté, when they arrived, were so good that it was really only necessary to make appreciative noises and eat.

So Chessie made appreciative noises, and ate.

She and Miles had been put in one of the smaller rooms off the main dining room. It was panelled and candlelit, and intimate, with all the tables set for two. Even the flower arrangements were small, presumably to allow diners to gaze unimpeded into each other's eyes.

The Fewstons must have a romantic streak, Chessie thought, buttering her bread roll, still warm from the oven. But it had led them severely astray this time.

She'd have settled for a wall of delphiniums and hollyhocks to shelter behind. Or even a privet hedge.

While their plates were being changed, Chessie hurried into speech, asking about the film script, and what would be involved in adapting the book.

It wasn't just an excuse to find an impersonal topic, she told herself. She was genuinely interested, and after all she was going to be closely involved in the project.

But what next? The weather? Would it be a hot summer, and was it really the greenhouse effect?

Brilliant, she thought. What a conversational ball of fire you are, Chessie, my dear.

'Am I really such a difficult companion?' Miles leaned back in his chair, the blue eyes hooded.

Rocked back on her heels, Chessie took a gulp of wine, feeling her face warm with sudden colour.

'No, of course not,' she managed. *Although he could be a mind-reader.*

'Perhaps I should have told you to bring a notebook, and dictated a few letters between courses,' he went on. 'You might have felt more at ease then.'

'I doubt it.' She put down her glass. 'I still don't understand what I'm doing here.'

'You're eating an excellent meal,' he said. 'Which you haven't had to prepare, cook, and wash up after.'

'And that's all there is to it?' She felt oddly breathless.

'No, but the rest can wait.' The cool face was enigmatic, the scar silver in the candlelight. 'May I refill your glass?'

'I don't think so.' Chessie covered it with a protective hand. 'Something tells me I need to keep a clear head.'

His smile mocked her. 'I haven't seduction in mind, if that's what you're thinking.'

'It never crossed my mind.'

'How incredibly pure of you,' he murmured. 'Considering the amount of time we spend alone together, have you really never wondered why I've never made a pass at you? Or do you think my scars have rendered me immune from the normal male urges?'

She bit her lip. 'I don't suppose that for a moment. But I took it for granted that passes were out because of our situation—the terms of my employment. And because...' She paused.

'Yes?' Miles prompted.

She swallowed. 'Because it would be—inappropriate behaviour, and tacky as well. The amorous boss and his secretary—that's a cliché, and you don't deal in clichés,' she added in a rush.

'Thank you—I think,' he remarked sardonically. 'Yet it was our—situation that I wanted to discuss with you.'

'Have you decided to sell the house?' Her last exquisite mouthful of guinea fowl turned to ashes in her mouth. Suddenly she was contemplating the prospect of being homeless and back on the job market at the same time.

It had always been a possibility, she supposed, yet just lately—stupidly—she'd allowed herself to feel settled. Safe even.

'Absolutely not.' He looked genuinely surprised. 'What gave you that idea? Didn't you hear me say I was planning to do some entertaining?'

'Yes—I'm sorry.' She hesitated. 'I suppose insecurity makes you paranoid.'

'I can appreciate that.' He put down his knife and fork, frowning slightly. 'That's part of the reason I want you to consider a change in your terms of employment.'

'A change?' Chessie was puzzled. Her contract with Miles had been carefully and meticulously defined. There were no obvious loopholes or room for manoeuvre. 'What kind of change?'

He drank some more wine, the blue eyes meditative as he studied her across the top of the glass.

He said, 'I thought we might get married.'

Chessie had a curious feeling that the entire world had come to a sudden halt, throwing her sideways. The subdued hum of conversation and laughter around them faded under the swift roar of blood in her ears.

Her whole body was rigid as she stared at him, lips parted in astonishment as she tried to make sense of what he'd just said.

'I'm sorry,' she said at last in a voice that seemed to have travelled vast distances across space and time. 'I don't think I quite understand.'

'It's perfectly simple. I've just proposed to you—asked you to become my wife.' He sounded totally cool about it—unbelievably matter-of-fact. 'Look on it, if you want, as a new kind of contract.'

He was mad, she thought dazedly. That was the answer. Completely and totally insane. Suffering some kind of delayed shell-shock.

Her lips moved. 'Marriage is—hardly a business arrangement.'

'I'd say that depends on the people involved.' His gaze was steady. 'Considering our individual circumstances and problems, marriage between us seems a sensible idea.'

He paused. 'You need more stability and security than you currently enjoy, and I'm going to require a hostess as well as a housekeeper. I think we could work out a perfectly satisfactory deal.'

'Just like that?' Her voice sounded faint. She still could not believe what was happening.

'No, of course not,' he said with a trace of impatience. 'I don't want an immediate answer. But I'd like you to give my proposal some coherent and rational thought before you reach any decision.'

Coherent? she thought. Rational—when applied to *this*? The words were meaningless.

'Judging by your reaction, this has been a bit of a thunderbolt,' he went on.

'Yes.' Chessie swallowed. 'You—could say that.' She spread her hands in an almost pleading gesture. 'I mean—we hardly know each other.'

'We work together every day, and we live in the same house. That's not exactly a casual acquaintance.'

'Yes—but…' She fought for the right words, and lost. 'Oh, you know exactly what I mean.'

'I think so.' His face was sardonic. 'You're still pondering the lack of amorous advances.'

'It's not that—or not totally, anyway.' She pushed her glass at him. 'I will have some more wine, please. I seem to need it.'

She watched him pour, his hand steady. He was completely calm, she thought incredulously. Detached, even. But how could that be, when he'd just turned her world upside down?

She hurried into speech again. 'There's never been anything remotely personal between us—not until now. Yes, we've seen each other every day, but we've never talked about anything but work, and problems to do with the house.' Mostly created by Jenny, she realised with a pang. Then—oh, God—Jenny.

'Has this shift in our relationship plunged you into some kind of trauma?' he drawled. 'I didn't intend that.'

'No—but it's all so sudden.' She stopped, grimacing. 'Hell, now I sound like the heroine of a bad historical novel.'

'And highly sensible of the honour I've just done you.' It was his turn to pull a face. 'Only I don't think you are, by any means. You look more winded than appreciative.'

'Being hit by a thunderbolt doesn't usually call for appreciation,' Chessie said with something of a snap. 'What did you expect—that I'd fall into your arms?'

'Hardly. You'd damage the crockery.' He was silent for a moment. 'If you're saying you'd have preferred a conventional courtship, then I can only apologise. But we've always had a reasonable working relationship, and our marriage would simply be an extension of this. So I thought the pragmatic approach would have more credence than hearts and flowers.'

Chessie said with difficulty, 'It doesn't—worry you that we're not in love with each other?'

'You forget I've been down that path once already. I can't speak for you, of course.' His face was expressionless. 'Is there anyone?'

She shook her head. 'No—not any more.' She kept her eyes fixed on the tablecloth. 'So it would be just a business arrangement—not a real marriage at all.'

'Yes,' he said. 'Initially, anyway.'

Her heart thudded in renewed shock. 'But later…?'

He shrugged. 'Who knows?' The blue eyes met hers directly. 'Ultimately, we might think again.' He paused. 'But any alteration in the terms would only be by mutual agreement.'

'I—I don't know what to say.'

'Then say nothing. Not yet. Just think about it, and take as long as you need. I promise I won't pressure you.'

She flicked the tip of her tongue round dry lips. 'And if I decide—no? Will I find myself out of a job?'

'Do I seem that vindictive?'

She reddened. 'No—no, of course not.' She took a deep breath. 'Very well. I'll—consider it.'

'Good.' His smile was swift, without a trace of mockery this time. 'Now shall I tell them to bring the dessert menu?'

'No, thanks.' Chessie doubted whether she could force another mouthful of food past her taut throat muscles. She pushed back her chair. 'Just coffee, please. And will you excuse me?'

The ladies' cloakroom was fortunately deserted. Chessie ran cool water over her wrists in a vain effort to quieten her hammering pulses.

She didn't look like someone who'd just been poleaxed, she thought, staring at her reflection, although her eyes were enormous, and there was more colour in her cheeks than usual.

But nor did she look like the future wife of Miles Hunter.

But then she wasn't really going to be a wife at all, she reminded herself, absently sifting her fingers through the bowl of pot pourri on the vanity unit, and savouring its fragrance.

Her present duties were being extended—that was all. Her change of status would permit her to sit at the opposite end of that beautiful oak dining table when there were guests, but little more.

She supposed he would expect her to move out of the flat, and live in the main house again.

She might even get her old bedroom back—for a while.

Initially. That was the word he'd used. But he'd also said *'ultimately'*, she thought, her heart beginning to pound unevenly. And what then?

She was shaking all over suddenly, her mind closing off in startled rejection.

'I can't,' she whispered. 'I couldn't. I'll have to tell him here and now that it's impossible.'

But she'd promised to consider his proposal, and she'd have to pretend to do so at least.

But she could not marry him. Not in a million years. Not even if Alastair never came back…

Chessie drew a deep, trembling sigh. There—she'd faced it at last. She'd allowed herself to admit the existence of the dream—the little foolish, groundless hope that had been growing inside her ever since she'd heard Jenny's news.

And how ironic that Miles should have chosen today of all days to present her with his own plan for her future.

'It never rains but it pours.' That was what Mrs Chubb, their current and longest-serving daily help would say.

Her little laugh turned into a groan. Once she'd told Miles her decision, it would be impossible for her to stay on at Silvertrees. In spite of his assurances, it would make things altogether too awkward.

There was a temping agency in the nearby town. She would make enquiries there, and then trawl through the letting bureaux for the cheapest possible flat.

Oh, *why* had Miles done this to her? she asked herself with something bordering on despair. Things had been fine as they were, and now everything was ruined again. And it wasn't as if he even *wanted* her.

Although that was something to be grateful for, at least. Because what would she have done if he had ever made a move on her?

Before she could stop herself, for one startled, stunned moment, she found she was imagining herself in Miles' arms, breathing the musky scent of his skin, feeling his mouth move on hers, coaxing her lips apart. His lean, long-fingered hand grazing her skin in a first caress…

Chessie came gasping back to reality, like a diver reaching the surface of some deep lake. Every inch of her body was tingling. Inside the silk shirt, her small breasts were burning, the nipples hardening helplessly.

Her eyes were green, like a drowsy cat's, she thought, gazing at herself in horror. Her lips, parted and trembling.

There was no way she could return to the table like this. Or he would know. And then she would be totally lost.

Oh, God, she thought frantically. What's happening to me? And what am I doing to myself?

And could find no answer that made any sense at all.

CHAPTER THREE

IF I don't go back to the table soon, thought Chessie, combing her hair for the umpteenth time, Miles will be sending out a search party.

Her skin no longer scorched her, but she was still shaking inside, and her hand felt too unsteady to renew her lipstick.

The cloakroom door opened, and two girls came in, giggling together. Chessie was aware of the curious glances they sent her as they passed by.

She thought, I cannot go on hiding like this.

As she walked reluctantly back towards the dining area, she was waylaid by Jim Fewston. 'Evening, Miss Lloyd. Hope you enjoyed your meal.'

'The food was delicious,' she assured him. *But as for enjoyment...*

'And how's that young sister of yours?' He shook his head. 'These days—they grow up before you know it.'

'Yes,' Chessie said. 'I suppose they do.'

'Sometimes,' he went on. 'they can be a little too grown-up for their own good.'

Suddenly, Chessie was uneasy. Up to then she'd thought Mr Fewston was just being the jovial landlord. Now, she wasn't so sure.

He lowered his voice confidentially. 'I hope she wasn't too put out the other night. In a strange pub, she might have got away with it, but I've known her all her life, as you might say, and I know she's not eighteen yet.'

He paused. 'The local police are down on under-age drinking like a ton of bricks, and I'm not prepared to risk my licence. I don't care for the lad she was with either, so when she started pushing her luck, and asking for vodka and tonic, I had to ask them to leave.'

He sighed. 'I'm sure you understand my position, and no hard feelings either way.'

'I don't think I understand much at all.' Chessie shook her head. 'Are you saying that Jenny has been in here trying to buy alcohol? I'm sorry, but you must be mistaken.'

'No mistake, Miss Lloyd.' His voice was kind, but firm. 'Why don't you ask her, my dear? Often a quiet word is all that's needed. I know it can't be easy raising a girl of that age when you're only a slip of a thing yourself, but this is something that wants nipping in the bud. And I'd keep an eye on her boyfriends, too,' he added with a touch of grimness.

'But Jenny has no boyfriends.' Chessie's protest was bewildered. 'She doesn't even go out at night. She's in her room, studying.'

'Not every night, Miss Lloyd, and other publicans will tell you the same. I suggest you make enquiries.' He gave her a polite nod, and went back into the bar.

She stood for a moment, staring after him dazedly, trying to assimilate what he'd told her. To make some sense of it. Jenny, she thought. *Jenny?*

As she made her way back to the table she saw that their waitress had brought the cafetière. But she didn't move away immediately. She was smiling and talking as she rearranged the cups and cream jug, bending over the table towards Miles as she did so. Fiddling with the collar of her blouse, Chessie realised, and pushing back her hair.

My God, she thought incredulously. She's coming on to him. She really is. And he's not exactly brushing her off either. He's leaning back in his chair, amused, but taking the whole thing in his stride.

It brought home to her once again just how little she really knew about the way in which Miles Hunter conducted his private life. In fact the entire evening had awoken all kinds of uncertainties she could well have done without.

She found herself moving forward more quickly, and the girl, noticing her approach, gave one last smile then hurried away.

As Chessie sank into her seat Miles glanced across at her, his brows snapping together interrogatively. 'What's wrong?'

'Not a thing.' Chessie summoned a smile of her own. 'I was just thinking how attentive the service is here.' She could hear the waspishness in her voice, and groaned inwardly. The last thing she wanted was to sound jealous or proprietorial in any way.

But Miles, fortunately, seemed oblivious to any undercurrents.

'Your friends run a smooth operation,' he returned. 'But that doesn't alter the fact that there's something the matter. What is it? Are you ill?'

'No—really.' She swallowed. 'But it's getting late. Would you mind if we just paid the bill and left?'

'Yes, I think I would,' he said unexpectedly. 'Whatever Jenny's been up to, it can wait until we've completed our first meal together in a civilised manner. In fact, I suggest you have a brandy. You look as if you need it.'

Indignation swamped her. 'Why should it be anything to do with Jenny?'

'Because that's what that stricken look of yours inevitably means.' His glance challenged her to deny it. 'Will you have that brandy?'

Biting her lip, she nodded silently.

'Good.' Miles gave her a faint smile as he signalled to the waitress. 'Rushing off in all directions won't solve a thing.'

'It's so easy for you,' she said bitterly. 'Jenny is not your responsibility.'

'Not at the moment, certainly.' He saw the swift colour flood her face, and his smile widened sardonically. 'Which,

I suppose, is your cue to tell me that you wouldn't have me if I came gift-wrapped.'

'No.' She didn't look at him. 'You asked me to think it over, and I will.' After all, she reasoned, she needed a breathing space to find a new job—a new flat. And she needn't feel too badly about it either. Judging by tonight's performance, he'd have little trouble finding a replacement when she turned him down.

'Hopefully it will have the added bonus of diverting your mind from Jenny, too.' He paused. 'I suppose you've discovered she isn't the saintly, single-minded scholar you took her for.'

'School used to mean everything to her.' Her voice was tired.

'I expect it did—while she was healing. It was safety—security, and she could use her studies to block out what was going on in the real world.' Miles shrugged. 'But the young recover fast, and now she's ready to rebel.'

He leaned forward. 'Face it, Francesca. Jenny's bright, but she's also spoiled, and brimming with resentment. Something had to give.' He smiled brief thanks at the blushing waitress as she put Chessie's brandy on the table, then reached for the cafetière. 'Cream and sugar?'

'Just black.' Desolation had her by the throat. 'I've failed her, haven't I?'

'Of course not. But you're not experienced enough to see the warning signs, and impose sanctions in time.' He handed over her cup. 'So, instead of revising, she was cavorting round the neighbourhood, right?'

'Apparently. The light was on in her room, and she used to play music all the time.' Chessie shook her head. 'It never occurred to me to check she was actually there. And, all the time, she was out, trying to con vodka and tonics out of unsuspecting landlords. With some fellow that Jim Fewston doesn't approve of.'

Miles raised his eyebrows. 'At least she's not drinking alone. It could be worse.'

She gave a small, wintry smile. 'I think it's about as bad as it gets.'

'Then you're being naïve.' He spoke gently. 'But I do understand that you need to see Jenny and talk to her about it, so, as soon as we've drunk our coffee, I'll take you home.'

'Thank you.' Her voice was subdued. 'I—I'm sorry that I've spoiled your celebration.'

'I promise that you haven't spoiled a thing.' He smiled at her. 'On the contrary.'

He thought she was going to accept his proposal, Chessie realised as she drank her coffee. And, on the face of it, she had every reason to do so. Marrying Miles would provide her with the kind of security she could dream about otherwise.

He obviously saw it as a practical solution to both their problems. The same cold-blooded approach he brought to his novels, she thought bitterly. And although you were swept along by the sheer force of the action, you were invariably left feeling slightly cheated at the end.

But I can't cheat him, she thought, swallowing. And I won't cheat myself either. We both deserve better from life. And we don't have to settle for second-best, just because we're both still hung up on other people.

She studied him covertly under her lashes, wondering what the girl he'd loved had been like. Attractive, if not actually beautiful, that was certain. A trail-blazer, probably, bright and sharp, with bags of energy, sexual as well as emotional. And demanding high standards in every aspect of her life, including the physical attraction of the man she'd chosen to share it. But ruthless when he'd failed to satisfy her criteria.

She jumped, startled, when he said softly, 'You're looking bereft again. I think we'd better go.'

While he was at the cash desk, dealing with the bill, Chessie wandered out into the reception area, and stood looking without seeing at the display of watercolour landscapes by local artists that were featured there.

It was the sudden wave of fragrance in the air—half forgotten, but haunting—commingling the scent of some heavy sweet perfume and Sobranie cigarettes that alerted her to the fact that she was no longer alone. And that the newcomer was known to her.

She half turned, arranging her face into polite pleasure, expecting to greet an acquaintance, and stopped dead, staring with incredulity at the woman framed in the archway that led to the bar.

She was eye-catching enough, her lush figure wrapped in a silky leopard-skin print dress, and a black pashmina thrown carelessly over her arm.

Violet eyes under extravagantly darkened lashes swept Chessie from head to toe in an inspection bordering on insolence. Full red lips parted in a smile that combined mockery with a hint of malice.

'Well, well,' Linnet Markham said softly. 'If it isn't the little Francesca. Now, who *would* have thought it?'

'Lady Markham.' Chessie swallowed. 'Linnet. So you're back.'

'Don't sound so surprised,' Linnet drawled. 'I'm sure the local grapevine has been working overtime.' She strolled forward. 'But I'm astonished to find that you're still around. I'd expected you to have made a fresh start somewhere a long way from here—where you're not known.'

Chessie flushed. 'Fortunately not everyone agrees with you. And I needed to provide stability for my sister.'

'Ah, yes.' Linnet said reflectively. 'The sister. She was the pretty one, if my memory serves.'

'Indeed,' Chessie agreed quietly. 'And with brains, too. In fact, you'd hardly credit that we were related.' She paused. 'Is Sir Robert here with you?'

Linnet's smile developed a slight rigidity. 'No, he's still in London. I came down ahead to oversee arrangements at the house. You simply can't rely on staff,' she added, dismissing the faithful Mrs Cummings with a wave of her hand. 'I've booked into a hotel for a couple of nights. I just popped into the Hart for a drink for old times' sake.'

'I didn't realise it was a place you visited.'

Linnet shrugged. 'Oh, it's always been a good place to see people, and be seen.' She paused. 'But I'd have thought it way above your means,' she added, eyeing Chessie's blouse and skirt. 'Or are you working here as a waitress? You never really trained for much, did you? And you wouldn't have any real references either—working for your father.' Her brow furrowed. 'Nor anywhere decent to live. I presume Silvertrees House had to be sold.'

This, Chessie thought detachedly, was quite definitely the evening from hell. She lifted her chin. 'Yes, of course, but I happen to work for the new owner, and we still live there. I keep house for him, and do his secretarial work.'

'Well, that sounds a cosy little arrangement,' Linnet purred. 'You've certainly fallen on your feet. So, who is this paragon who's taken you on?'

Chessie hesitated. 'I work for Miles Hunter, the thriller writer,' she said reluctantly.

'Hunter?' The violet eyes sharpened. 'But he's a best-seller, isn't he? You see his books everywhere. He must be worth an absolute fortune.'

'He's very successful,' Chessie agreed, wincing inwardly at the older woman's crudity.

'And charitable to waifs and strays too, it seems.' Linnet's voice was cream spiced with acid. 'How did you manage it?'

Chessie shrugged, trying to control the temper boiling up inside her.

'He needed someone to run things for him,' she returned shortly. 'I was available.'

'I'm sure you were.' Linnet gave a small, tinkling laugh. 'However, I don't advise you to start getting any foolish ideas this time. No girlie crushes. Because not everyone's as understanding as Alastair.'

Chessie felt her whole body jolt with shock as if she'd been physically struck. Her nails curled into the palms of her hands. Over Linnet's shoulder, she saw Miles emerging from the dining room, pausing to lean on his cane as he slotted his wallet back into his jacket.

She said, 'Thanks for the warning, Linnet, but it really isn't necessary.'

She went to Miles, sliding her arm through his with deliberate possessiveness, and giving him a radiant smile.

'Darling, may I introduce Lady Markham, who's just come back to live at Wenmore Court? Linnet, this is Miles Hunter.' She paused quite deliberately. 'My fiancé.'

Miles did not move, but the sudden tension in his body hit her like an electric charge.

Later she would hate herself, and she knew it, but now the expressions chasing themselves across Linnet's face made it all worthwhile. Or nearly.

Linnet, however, made a lightning recovery. 'Congratulations.' She held out her hand to Miles, along with a smile that lingered appraisingly, and frankly approved.

My God, Chessie thought bleakly. First the waitress, now Linnet. Am I the only woman in Britain not to have registered his attraction on some personal Richter scale?

'So, when did all this happen?' Linnet went on.

'Tonight,' Miles returned, his face impassive. 'We've been having a celebratory dinner. You're the first to know.'

'How marvellous,' Linnet approved fulsomely. 'I'm sure you'll both be fabulously happy.' She paused. 'When's the big day? I suppose you'll marry locally?'

'We haven't decided yet,' Chessie intervened hastily. 'Miles has a book to finish, and a film deal, so he's incredibly busy just now.'

'How very unromantic you make me sound, my darling,' Miles said lightly. 'Actually, I think we should be married as soon as possible, although the honeymoon might have to wait for a while.'

He drew Chessie closer. Allowed his lips to graze her

hair. He said softly, 'I think it's time we went, don't you? So we can continue our celebration at home.'

Helpless colour warmed her face. She murmured something unintelligible, and moved forward, her arm still trapped in his.

He turned to Linnet, smiling. 'Goodnight, Lady Markham. It's been a pleasure. I hope we meet again soon.'

'Oh…' Linnet sent him a blinding look under her lashes '…you can count on that.'

They walked to the car in a silence that Chessie dared not break. Miles opened the passenger door for her, and she shot in like a fugitive seeking sanctuary.

He took his place beside her, and sat for a moment, staring straight ahead into the darkness.

Eventually, he said quietly, 'I take it that was a matter of expediency rather than a final answer.' He turned his head and looked at her. 'Well?'

Chessie bent her head, pressing her hands to her burning face. 'God, I'm so sorry,' she mumbled. 'That was a dreadful—an appalling thing to do. I—I don't know what you must think.'

'I think you needed to score points.' His voice was dry. 'And I can understand that, even if I don't applaud the means you employed.'

Chessie's voice shook. 'She thought I was a bloody waitress.'

'I doubt that very much,' he said sardonically. 'As you commented, the staff were attentive to a fault. Too much so, perhaps. No one could ever say that about you.'

Oh, *hell*, thought Chessie dismally. He knew exactly what I was getting at. And I want to die.

After a brief silence, he went on levelly, 'However, thanks to Lady Markham's intervention, we are now to all intents and purposes engaged to each other, and we'll behave accordingly.'

'Must we?' She stared at him beseechingly.

'Of course.' His scar looked silver in the moonlight.

Carved from stone. 'Any kind of volte-face at this stage would simply make us both look ridiculous, and I won't permit that.'

'Thank you.' Her voice quivered. 'You—you're very kind.'

He said quietly, 'Don't kid yourself, Francesca. At this moment, I feel a number of things, and kindness, believe me, is not one of them. Now I'll take you home.'

They completed the journey in another, to Chessie, unnerving silence.

Miles brought the car smoothly to a halt beside the flight of steps that led up to the housekeeper's flat.

Hunched in her seat, Chessie was aware that he'd turned his head, and was studying her.

Oh, what now? she thought, her skin tingling in sudden apprehension. And if he—reached for her, what would she do? How should she react? In the space of a few hours, her entire life had shifted on its axis, and she was floundering.

Instead: 'Would you like me to come in with you?' The offer was polite, no more. And he didn't move an inch.

She shook her head, weak with relief. 'I think it's better if I deal with this on my own. But—thank you, anyway,' she added stiltedly.

'One day, I'll have to teach you to show your gratitude more positively,' he murmured. 'Goodnight, Francesca. I'm sorry the evening was such a disaster for you. I'll see you in the morning.'

She stood in the moonlight, watching him drive away to the front of the house. He might have proposed marriage, but the protocol between boss and employee was still being maintained, she thought as she went slowly up the steps. Not that she'd have it any other way, of course.

She sighed, and switched her attention resolutely to her most immediate problem.

She had no idea what she was going to say to Jenny, or even how to approach the problem, although she could possibly begin with a pointed reference to the cost of electricity, she thought as she stepped into the narrow hall to find lights blazing everywhere.

As she took off her jacket the sitting-room door opened, and Jenny appeared wreathed in smiles. 'Chessie—at last. I've got the most wonderful surprise for you.'

'I think I've had all the surprises I can handle for one day,' Chessie told her grimly. 'We need to talk, young lady.'

'Oh, that can wait,' Jenny said in gleeful dismissal, and stood aside so that Chessie could precede her into the sitting room.

For a moment the whole world seemed to stop as she stared in total disbelief at the tall figure rising from the sofa to greet her.

Her heart lurched painfully. Her voice was barely a shaky whisper as she said, 'Alastair...?'

'No one else.' He walked across to her, and put his hands on her shoulders, smiling down into her startled eyes. 'Aren't you going to say "Welcome home"?'

'Yes—yes, of course.' She drew a deep, steadying breath. 'It—it's great to see you again. I just didn't expect...'

His look was quizzical. 'It can't be that much of a shock. Jenny says she told you we were reopening the Court.'

'Yes,' she said. 'Yes, she did.'

'And anyway...' his voice sank to a whisper '...you knew I'd be back one day—didn't you?'

No, she thought, with an odd detachment. I knew nothing of the sort. You disappeared from my life, and it felt like for ever.

She said, 'I—I assumed you'd decided to stay in America.'

'Well, it was tempting,' he conceded. 'And I wasn't short of offers. But when this merchant bank in the City came up with a job, it seemed too good to turn down. So, here I am.'

His smile widened. 'And aren't you the tiniest bit pleased to see me?'

'Of course I am.'

It was like Christmas, she thought, and her birthday. And having her most private and secret dream miraculously come true. But, like all dreams, there was still that touch of unreality about the whole thing—almost like a warning.

'Then show me,' he whispered, and bent his head to kiss her. But her body felt rigid in his arms, and her lips were numb, unresponsive as he tried to coax them apart.

'Is that all the welcome I get?' He sounded amused and slightly irritated at the same time as he let her go.

'I think I'm still in shock.' She tried to smile. 'How did you know where to find me—us?'

'I dropped my stuff off at the house,' he said. 'And Joyce Cummings filled me in on everything that's happened. With Jenny supplying the details, of course.'

'I can imagine,' Chessie said ruefully. She looked round. 'Where is she, anyway?'

'A tactful withdrawal, I'd guess, on the pretext of making more coffee.'

There were used cups on the fireside table, she saw, and a half-empty bottle of wine and two glasses. Her brows drew together.

'So I rush to your side,' Alastair went on. 'Only to find you're out, sampling the bright lights with your boss. Except Jenny made it sound like an act of charity. She tells me the guy's hideous with a disposition to match.'

Chessie bit her lip. 'Jenny could do with employing a little charity herself.'

'Oh, come on, love. You can hardly expect her to enjoy the situation. It's a hell of a comedown, after all.'

He paused. 'But never mind all that. This is hardly the reception I was anticipating.'

He sounded almost reproachful, she realised. He'd been expecting her to fall ecstatically into his arms—and why wasn't she doing exactly that? Because she'd imagined this moment—had longed for it so often. Had cried into her pillow as she'd wondered where he'd been, and what he'd been doing, and if he'd ever thought of her. And now he was here and she felt—blank.

She stepped backwards, shrugging off her jacket and tossing it across the arm of the sofa. 'Alastair, be reasonable. You disappear from our lives for years on end, then walk in, expecting everything to be just the same. Only, it doesn't work like that.' She couldn't believe how cool she sounded. How controlled.

'Are you cross with me because I didn't keep in touch?' His smile reached to her, coaxed her. 'I blame myself totally, believe me. But it's not easy from that distance. And I've never been much of a letter writer.'

There are telephones, Chessie thought. There is email. If I'd been the one to leave, I'd have kept the relationship going somehow.

'No,' she said. 'I appreciate that. And life has a habit of moving on.'

'But I'm back now,' he went on eagerly. 'And I'll make up for everything.' He shook his head remorsefully. 'Poor sweet, what a terrible time you've had. And having to live here, little better than a servant. It must be a nightmare.'

'Don't believe all Jenny's sob stories,' Chessie said quietly. 'The situation has its plus side as well.' She paused. 'I saw your stepmother earlier. She was in The White Hart having a drink.'

There was a small, odd silence, then he said, 'Yes, I gathered she was planning a visit. I'd hoped to get on with the alterations at the Court without interference.'

'Alterations?'

'Nothing too drastic.' He shrugged. 'We'll be converting a couple of the downstairs rooms in the West Wing—installing ramps—that kind of thing.'

Chessie frowned. 'I don't understand…'

'Didn't Linnet tell you—about my father?'

'She simply said he was still in London.'

'That's perfectly true,' Alastair said stonily. 'Out of sight, out of mind, apparently. She might also have mentioned he's in a private clinic, having tests after a stroke.'

Chessie gasped. 'Oh, Alastair, no. How dreadful. When did it happen?'

'A few weeks ago while they were still in Spain.' His face was hard. 'He was flown home five days ago. There's some paralysis, so he'll have to use a wheelchair for a while, and his speech has been affected, but the doctors are optimistic. They think he could recover well with therapy and proper care.' He was silent for a moment. 'I just hope that's true.'

'Oh, dear God.' Chessie remembered Sir Robert's tall, robust presence, his brisk stride, and the commanding power of his voice. She couldn't imagine him sick—diminished in any way. 'I'm so sorry.' She hesitated. 'In a way, it's fortunate you decided to take this job in London.'

'Yes, I suppose so.' He gave a brief, almost bitter sigh. 'Hell, what a mess.'

'But why didn't Linnet mention it to me?'

'Who knows why Linnet does anything?' Alastair said with a slight snap. 'After all, it's hardly something that can be kept under wraps, however much she might wish it.'

'Perhaps she feels your father needs rest and quiet when he comes down here, and wants to discourage visitors,' Chessie suggested.

'You're joking, of course.' His tone was derisive. 'She regards his condition as a temporary inconvenience. I gather she's even planning to revive the Midsummer Party. Mark her return in style.'

'But surely...' Chessie stopped herself right there. If Linnet couldn't see that was inappropriate, it was no concern of hers.

'It's so good to be back here,' Alastair said softly. 'Know that there's someone on my side again.'

She thought, But I'm in no position to take sides—even if I wanted to—which is by no means certain.

She felt guiltily relieved when she heard Jenny coming noisily along the passage with the fresh coffee. The whole evening had been too intense—too bewildering, she thought. She needed time and space to think. To come to terms with everything that had happened. Not least with Alastair's sudden reappearance.

She should have been giddy with delight and relief. Jenny had clearly thought she'd find them wrapped round each other. Instead, she simply felt—stunned.

I have to adjust, that's all, she told herself defensively.

And her talk with Jenny would have to be postponed, too, which maybe wasn't such a bad thing. It would give her time to prepare, to work out a reasoned argument, instead of steaming in with all guns blazing, which had rarely succeeded in the past. She would have to be understanding, she thought glumly. Speak to Jenny woman to woman.

But what will I do if she won't listen? she asked herself unhappily as she drank more coffee she didn't want and her sister chattered away to Alastair.

'And I've got this wicked CD in my room,' Jenny was saying. 'I'll get it, so we can listen to it while we're finishing off the wine.'

'I don't think so,' Chessie intervened, feeling like someone's Victorian granny. 'It's getting late, and Alastair has to go. You have school tomorrow, and I must work.'

Jenny's scowl was immediate. 'Oh, for God's sake, Chess, don't be so wet,' she exclaimed impatiently. 'Tell The Ogre that his beastly meal gave you food poisoning, and you're having the day off. Don't you realise? Alastair's *back*.'

'Nice try, honey.' He grinned at her. 'But Chessie's quite right. Tomorrow's a working day for all of us. And there'll be plenty of other evenings—now that I'm back.' And he allowed his hand to rest briefly but significantly on Chessie's.

'You haven't a clue how to deal with men,' Jenny accused when he'd gone. 'I was going to put the music on, and leave you alone with him.'

'Not very subtle.' Chessie piled crockery and glasses onto the tray. *And what made you suddenly such an expert on men?* she wanted to ask, but didn't.

'Well, who needs subtlety—especially when you haven't seen each other for yonks?' Jenny sniffed. 'You were just sitting there like a stuffed dummy. No wonder he pushed off to the States if this is how you used to treat him.'

Chessie sighed. 'Love, I don't want to argue at this time of night. We're both tired. But I need to deal with Alastair in my own way. And at the moment, I feel really confused.'

Now, she thought, would certainly not be a good time to introduce the topic of Miles' extraordinary proposal. And, as far as Jenny was concerned, there would probably never be an optimum moment.

Besides, when the time came, she could always make up some story about feeling in a rut to explain why they were moving. So there was no real need to mention it ever to her volatile sister.

Because she was turning Miles down, and the sooner the better. She knew that, and she was comfortable in her decision.

Which did not explain why she spent much of the remaining night tossing and turning in her bed. And it wasn't Alastair's easy charm and smiling brown eyes that were keeping her from sleep, but a man with a scarred face and premature winter in his gaze.

And that, she told herself firmly, was ridiculous.

CHAPTER FOUR

CHESSIE felt edgy and out of sorts as she made her way to the small room adjoining Miles' study that she used as an office.

She'd cleared her desk the previous afternoon, so she was surprised to find a substantial pile of new script awaiting her attention.

Apparently, she wasn't the only one to have had a restless night, she thought, biting her lip.

She sat down with a sigh, and switched on the computer. Jenny had been irrepressible at breakfast, Alastair's name never off her lips. She plainly saw him as the romantic knight on the white charger who was going to solve all their problems and carry Chessie off to eternal bliss as a bonus, and Chessie had longed to put her aching head in her hands, and beg her to stop.

'I'll be a bit late this evening,' Jenny said as she grabbed her school bag and headed for the door. 'Choir practice.'

But Chessie, newly suspicious and hating it, saw that her sister did not look at her directly, and her heart sank.

She couldn't put off the inevitable confrontation for much longer, she reflected unhappily.

The distant bang of the back door alerted her to the arrival of Mrs Chubb, the daily help. And no prizes for guessing what would be her prime topic of conversation, Chessie thought as she made her way to the kitchen.

'You'll have heard, then.' Mrs Chubb, resplendent in a flowered overall, had already switched on the kettle for her first cup of tea of the day. She tutted. 'Poor Sir Robert. Who'd have thought it? Mind you, I always said he should never have gone to a hot place like Spain,' she added ominously. 'You should leave the Tropics for those who've been bred there. They can stand it.'

Chessie, contemplating Spain's new geographic status, murmured something neutral as she began to assemble Miles' coffee tray.

'And that means we'll have her ladyship back, coming the high and mighty,' Mrs Chubb went on. '"Call me madam," was what she told us all in the village.' She snorted. 'And a right madam she's turned out to be. Sir Robert at death's door, and her wanting Chubb to mark out the tennis court.'

'Actually, Sir Robert is expected to make a good recovery,' Chessie said, trying not to relish Mrs Chubb's unflattering remarks about Linnet.

Mrs Chubb sniffed. 'Not with her nursing him, he won't. Suffer a relapse, I shouldn't wonder. Make her a rich widow, and suit her just fine.'

'Mrs Chubb—you really mustn't…'

'I,' Mrs Chubb said magnificently, 'speak as I find. Chubb loves those gardens at the Court, and he'd never leave, but I'm not going back there to clean, not even if she doubled my hours and my money—which she won't.'

She poured boiling water onto her tea bag, compressing it until the water turned black, then added a splash of milk, and two spoonfuls of sugar.

'Proper tea, that is,' she remarked with satisfaction. 'Not like that scented muck that Madam drinks. Used to fair turn my stomach, that did.' She sipped with deep appreciation and nodded. 'Now I must get on,' she added, as if Chessie had been deliberately detaining her. 'The master left a note asking me to do out the spare room, so he must be expecting visitors. And about time, too. This old place could do with cheering up.' And she departed purposefully, mug in hand.

'The old place is not alone in that,' Chessie muttered as she spooned the rich Colombian blend that Miles favoured into the percolator.

While she was waiting for it to brew, she collected the mail from the box by the front door. Dealing with it was a simple process. All junk mail in the bin, all invitations to speaking engagements declined, all business correspondence opened and date stamped, and any personal letters placed unopened on Miles' desk.

Normally she hardly spared these a second glance, but today she found herself noticing that one of them came in an expensive cream envelope, with unmistakably female handwriting. And recalling that a similar item had arrived the previous week…

Oh, for heaven's sake, she adjured herself irritably. Anyone would think I were genuinely engaged to the man. Whereas nothing has changed. There is no personal relationship, and absolutely no reason for me to be in the least curious. And certainly not jealous.

And she added the cream envelope to the neat pile on the tray.

When the coffee was ready, Chessie carried the tray to the study and tapped lightly on the door. But there was no sound at all, not even the clatter of typewriter keys, so, after waiting a puzzled moment, she opened the door and went in.

The room had changed a great deal from her father's time, and she had never ceased to be glad of that. When the house had gone on the market, most of its contents had already been sold, leaving only the bare essentials. Miles had brought his own furniture, and had had Silvertrees redecorated too.

That, Chessie recalled wryly, had been one of the early bones of contention with Jenny, who couldn't be mollified even by the total refurbishment of their own accommodation.

But she herself had felt it right that the new owner should cut as many links with the past as possible. Stamp his mark on his new home.

The room was much lighter and more workmanlike these

days. Different books stood on the shelves that lined the walls, and that also held his stereo system and CD collection. A massive leather Chesterfield occupied pride of place in front of the fireplace.

The big imposing desk had gone, and Miles worked instead at a very ordinary table set by the window. His chair, however, had been specially made for him, with extra support for his spine.

Normally, he was at work by now, busy at the small portable typewriter that had accompanied him to so many places in the world.

'I thought you'd have had the latest thing in laptops,' she'd said once in the early days.

His mouth twisted. 'And how do you recharge batteries, Miss Lloyd, when there is no electricity?' He ran his fingers over the sturdy frame of the portable in a curiously caressing movement. 'This once belonged to my father, and he gave it to me when I got my first job in journalism. And I'll go on using it until the last spare part and the last ribbon have vanished from the earth. It's been my lucky talisman.'

'Not always lucky,' she said slowly, thinking of the mined road.

He shrugged, the blue eyes cool and meditative. 'We both survived, didn't we?'

But this morning, the chair was empty, and the typewriter hidden under its cover. Chessie set the tray down on the table, feeling bewildered. She organised Miles' appointments diary, and there was nothing that would have taken him away from the house at this hour.

Perhaps he was ill, she thought apprehensively, remembering Jenny's comment about food poisoning. But, if so, surely he'd have asked her to send for a doctor.

The room was very still, bathed in early summer sun, but the quality of its stillness told Chessie suddenly that she wasn't alone.

She trod quietly across the room and looked over the

high back of the Chesterfield. Miles was stretched out on its cushions, eyes closed, and his breathing soft and regular.

Well, Chessie thought, astonished. Another first.

She tiptoed round the sofa, and stood watching him for a moment. He was wearing the same clothes that he'd worn the previous night, indicating that he hadn't been to bed at all.

He looked much younger asleep, she realised with an odd pang, and almost vulnerable. The harsh dynamism of his features was softened and relaxed, the hard mouth gentler. The scarred side of his face was hidden, and his dark lashes, longer than she'd ever noticed, curled on his tanned cheek.

Chessie stood there feeling confused, and almost helpless. This situation had never cropped up before. So, what did she do now? Wake him, or leave him to the rest he obviously needed?

'Well, make your mind up, Francesca. The suspense is killing me.'

The softly drawled words nearly made her jump out of her skin, and she clamped her lips tightly on a yowl of surprise.

'You're awake.'

'I'm a light sleeper.' He sat up slowly, suppressing a grimace of discomfort. 'I learned a long time ago that it's better to know and be alert when someone's creeping up on you.'

'I was not creeping anywhere,' Chessie denied with dignity. 'I simply brought in your coffee and the post, as usual. And if you knew I was there, why did you let me go on standing about?' she added crossly, feeling a fool.

The sardonic smile flicked her. 'Perhaps I was hoping you'd wake me with a kiss.'

Chessie decided it was wiser to ignore that. 'Have you been up all night?' she asked, her brow furrowed.

He shrugged as he got to his feet, and stretched. 'It's something I do on occasion. I wasn't particularly tired last night, and I had a lot on my mind, so I went into the garden and sat for a while, then took a walk.' He paused. 'I gather you had a visitor.'

'Why—yes.' To her vexation, Chessie felt her face flood with colour. 'It's not against the rules, is it? And why were you spying on me?'

'I wasn't,' he said mildly. 'But like any householder, I'm interested in the identity of a stranger leaving my grounds after midnight.' He limped over to the table, and poured himself some coffee. 'I hope he didn't cause you any problems.'

'Problems,' Chessie echoed. 'Why should he?' *And what difference would one more make among so many, anyway?*

'I assumed,' he said, 'that he was Jenny's unsuitable boyfriend—the one you were so concerned about at dinner.'

'Oh,' she said. 'Oh, no. That was Alastair Markham—an old friend.'

'Markham?' Miles brows rose sharply. 'You mean he's connected to the spectacular lady we encountered last night?'

'Yes.' Chessie bit her lip. 'He's her stepson. His father's had a stroke, very sadly, so they've had to come back from Spain. And Alastair's come down from London to make Wenmore Court more—wheelchair-friendly.'

'And renew some old acquaintances.'

'Well, yes. Naturally.' Chessie lifted her chin. 'There's no harm in that, surely.'

'I think,' Miles said gently, 'that might depend on the acquaintance.'

'Are you claiming exclusive rights to my company on the basis of this—pseudo-engagement?' Her voice shook slightly.

'I'm not claiming anything at the moment.' Miles drained his cup, and replaced it on the tray. 'But when I do, you'll be in no doubt,' he added pleasantly.

He allowed her to assimilate that for a moment, then:

'How did your talk with Jenny go, by the way? Did you resolve anything?'

She could hardly tell him to mind his own business when she'd confided in him so readily twelve hours before.

'It wasn't a good time,' she said shortly. 'I'm going to take things up with her tonight.'

'Unless any more old friends drop by,' he murmured. 'You know, Francesca—'

His voice halted abruptly. Glancing across at him in surprise, Chessie saw that he'd picked up the cream envelope and was staring at it, his face suddenly taut.

'Is something the matter?' If he can spy, she thought, then I can ask questions.

It was a moment before he answered, and when he looked at her Chessie had the odd impression that he wasn't really seeing her. That he'd been away somewhere else, and his journey had not been a happy one.

'Not a thing,' he said coolly. 'Except that I need to shower, and get a shave and a change of clothes. And you, of course, have work to do.'

'Yes,' she said, and summoned a brief smile. 'Your walk in the garden must have been—stimulating.'

'It was,' he returned. 'Very. It happens like that, sometimes.'

She walked past him to the communicating door on the other side of the room that led into her office. She paused in the doorway, and looked back, just in time to see Miles slipping the cream envelope into the pocket of his trousers, his face cold and abstracted.

Clearly, it was something he needed to deal with in real privacy, she thought as she closed the door quietly, and sat down at the computer.

And, as she so badly needed to remember, it was no concern of hers.

Chessie found it irritatingly difficult to concentrate that morning. She faltered over the names of some of the

Eastern European characters in the story, although they should have been perfectly familiar to her by now. Also, the plot had reached a high point of drama and crisis, and some of the scenes were correspondingly tough and violent, which disturbed her as it had never done in the past.

I must be feeling ultra-sensitive today, she thought, crossly deleting another mistake.

She was almost glad when the last page was transcribed, saved to disk and printed off to join the mounting pile of manuscript in her out-tray.

She was dealing with the correspondence when Mrs Chubb popped her head round the door.

'Visitor,' she announced in a stage whisper.

'Oh.' Chessie got up from her chair. 'I forgot to ask him about that. Is the room ready?'

'Not that one.' Mrs Chubb flapped a dismissive hand. 'Madam's come calling. Strolled up the drive while I was doing the brasses, and asked for Mr Hunter. They're in the drawing room, and he wants you too.'

As she reached the drawing-room door, Chessie paused, smoothing back her hair with her fingers and taking a deep breath. Then, teeth gritted, she went in.

Miles, casually dressed in jeans and a white shirt, was standing by the empty fireplace, leaning against the mantel shelf.

Linnet, decorative in honey-coloured silk, was draped across one of the sofas that flanked the hearth.

'Such a bore, but no one was prepared to help at all,' she was saying, gesturing helplessly with one crimson-tipped hand. 'In the end I had to call one of the London nursing agencies, and they have someone who can start almost at once, thank heaven.'

'It must be a weight off your mind,' Miles agreed gravely. He looked across at Chessie, his expression giving nothing away. 'Hello, darling. I hope we can offer Lady Markham some lunch.'

'As long as it's not too inconvenient,' Linnet fluttered.

'I'm sure I must be disrupting your latest *oeuvre*.' She turned to survey Chessie, absorbing her simple blue chambray shift dress. 'In housekeeper mode today, sweetie?'

'That's what I'm paid for,' Chessie said lightly. 'Would soup and omelettes do?'

'I'd really prefer eggs Benedict,' Linnet said sunnily. 'But whatever you can manage will be fine, Chessie, dear.'

'Great,' Chessie returned with equal cheerfulness. 'Omelettes it is, then.'

The contents of the freezer in the storeroom adjoining the big kitchen were looking depleted. It looked to Chessie, hunting out the last carton of her home-made vegetable soup, as if she had a weekend of intensive cooking ahead of her.

She put the soup on the stove to heat through gently, set a bottle of Chablis to chill, then dashed to the dining room with the bleached linen place mats and napkins, and a handful of cutlery.

Back in the kitchen, she diced ham, grated cheese and chopped peppers, onions, tomatoes and salad potatoes to spice up the omelettes.

'Everything under control?' Miles appeared in the doorway behind her as she was whisking the eggs in a large bowl.

'The food certainly is,' she said crisply. 'I can't vouch for my temper.'

He leaned a shoulder against the doorframe. 'Then consider this your baptism of fire.'

'I prefer to remain unscorched.' She drew a steadying breath. 'I'm sure you'll excuse me if I don't join the lunch party. I'll have a sandwich in my office.'

'Then think again,' he said calmly. 'And lay a place for yourself in the dining room. I told you that I'd expect my future wife to help me entertain my guests.'

She said between her teeth, 'I am not your future wife.'

'Lady Markham thinks you are,' he said softly. 'Because you told her so, Francesca. And, as I've made clear, you'll behave accordingly until I decide otherwise. So it's lunch for three, and no arguments.'

She gave him a defiant glance. 'Is that an order—sir?'

He had the audacity to grin at her. 'Yes, ma'am.' He limped forward and perched on the edge of the table beside her. 'I'm seeing a totally new side to you, Chessie,' he remarked. 'All these months, you've behaved like a polite, efficient mouse. Yet now...'

'Overnight I've turned into a rat?' She glared at him.

Miles laughed. 'I was thinking of something altogether more feline—a tigress, maybe.'

Chessie looked down at the froth of eggs in her bowl. There was something about this turn in the conversation— a note in his voice perhaps—that disturbed her. That, and his proximity.

She said crisply, 'Now you're being absurd. And if you want me to feed your guest, I'd better get on.'

'Presently,' he said, and his voice was soft, the blue eyes narrowed in speculation. 'I've seen your claws, Chessie. But now I'm wondering if I might just make you purr.'

The egg whisk dropped from her hand, clattering to the tiled floor as he reached for her, pulling her into his arms with a stark purpose that defied resistance. She was held against him, trapped between the hard muscularity of his thighs. One arm lay across her back like a band of steel. His other hand shaped the slender curve of her hip as he smiled into her eyes.

Her lips parted to protest—perhaps even to plead—but the words were stifled by his mouth. At first it was a quest—a slow, controlled exploration. Firm but tender. Serious and teasing.

So many sensations—emotions—building inside her as he quietly and deliberately ravished her mouth. She hung in his arms, her limbs turning to water, tiny sparks of light dancing behind her closed eyelids. And her hands, braced against his chest in a vain attempt to push him away, crept upwards to fasten on his shoulders.

And everything changed. He pulled her closer still, kissing her deeply, hungrily, making no more concessions to her relative inexperience, or the fact that it was still the first intimate contact between them.

Ruthlessly, her lips were pressured apart so that he could plunder all the inner sweetness of her mouth. There was no gentleness in him now. No coolness either. Just a fierce need driving him beyond tenderness, beyond consideration.

The high dam of his reserve had been breached, and she was caught in the torrent. Drowning now in unguessed-at desires of her own, her aroused nipples blooming against the wall of his chest, her fingers biting frantically into his shoulders.

Gasping, tasting him, breathing him, drawing the male scent of him deep into her lungs as the world spun dizzily around her. The warmth of his skin blazed through her thin dress. She felt the sudden clamour of her pulses, the surge of the dark, heavy blood through her veins.

And then, as if a light had been switched off, it was over, and she was free. Taking a shaky step backwards, then another. Staring at him with ever-widening eyes. Lifting a mechanical hand to touch her swollen mouth. Hearing nothing but the raggedness of her own breathing. And his. In a silence that seemed to go on for ever.

When at last he spoke, his mocking drawl scored her senses like a sharp blade. 'Well—that was—instructive.'

Her breasts were aching against the cling of her dress, her nipples white-hot pinnacles of excitement. And he could see that. Would know…

She crossed her arms across her body, hiding the evidence of her self-betrayal from his cynical scrutiny.

'Why?' she whispered hoarsely. 'Why did you do that? How did you dare…?'

'Because we were both curious,' he said. 'And now we know.' His smile was suddenly mocking. 'Besides, our betrothal needed a little local colour, if only to prevent the worldly wise Lady Markham becoming suspicious.'

'What are you talking about?' There were tears not far away, constricting her throat, burning her eyes.

'Most newly engaged couples can't keep their hands off each other.' Miles' shrug was almost casual. 'Your transparent innocence was doing my street cred no good at all.' He gave her a measuring glance. 'At least you look now as if you know you're a woman.'

'And is that supposed to be your excuse—your rationale for—for *assaulting* me.' Her legs were weak, shaking under her. Her mouth was throbbing, and she was trembling wildly inside, ashamed of her own response. Of the destruction of her defences. And wanting to hit back.

His brows lifted over blue eyes turned suddenly cold. 'Is that how you see it? Just remember, my sweet hypocrite, that I was the one who called a halt. And if we didn't have a guest, and a cleaner roaming the house,' he added softly, 'I would not have stopped, and you wouldn't have wanted me to.'

He allowed her to digest that, then sent her a smile, swift and impersonal. 'Now, I'll leave you to get on with lunch.'

Alone, Chessie slumped against the kitchen table, her hands pressed to her hot cheeks. The temptation to sweep the entire preparations for the meal into the bin, then pack her bags and walk out was almost overwhelming. But she couldn't do that because she'd signed a contract, which required a minimum of a month's notice. And there seemed little doubt that Miles would enforce it, if necessary.

So, she had four weeks to endure before she could legitimately make her escape.

She groaned softly. Twenty-four hours ago, she'd been settled. Not ecstatically happy, perhaps, but resigned—even contented. Now her life was in chaos, and heading for meltdown.

And the worst of it was that Miles' final jibe had been no more than the truth, she thought unhappily. For the first time in her life, she had wanted everything that a man had to give—and more. And she would have offered her entire self in return.

If he had allowed it, she realised, wincing.

Well, she would never let him get so near her again. For her remaining time in his house, she would revert to being the calm, efficient employee. She would fill the freezer, run the house, and finish transcribing the new book. And she would ensure a smooth transition for her replacement.

She retrieved the egg whisk from the floor and washed it, wiping the small pool of beaten egg from the tiles. There was a smear on her dress, too, and she didn't have time to change, but what the hell? Her appearance was immaterial after all, she thought with a faint shrug. Although she would have to comb her dishevelled hair, and disguise the more obvious signs of Miles' kisses.

She made a salad from mixed leaves, heated a French stick in the oven, then poured the steaming soup into pottery bowls and carried them through to the dining room.

'This is actually quite good,' Linnet approved as she tasted it. 'I'd no idea you could cook, Chessie.'

'I had to learn,' Chessie returned. 'And fast.'

'Of course you did,' Linnet said in a tone of such gentle understanding that Chessie longed to slap her senseless. 'And to have to do all this cleaning as well, when you'd always had a housekeeper of your own in the past.' She tutted. 'You must be absolutely worn out.'

Chessie raised her eyebrows innocently, 'Oh, didn't you notice Mrs Chubb on your way in? She's the real treasure round here.'

'Well, I wouldn't describe her in those terms,' Linnet said with a touch of tartness. 'And I'd have got rid of her surly brute of a husband too, only Robert wouldn't allow it for some reason.'

'Probably because Mr Chubb is one of the top gardeners in the county, and his family has worked for the Markhams for generations,' Chessie commented pensively. 'You're really lucky to have him. More bread?'

But Linnet was not finished yet. 'All the same, it must have been hard on you, having to take a subservient position in your old home. Although everything seems to be working out for you now.

'What a pity your poor father couldn't say the same.' She sighed. 'It's all such a tragedy, although Robert predicted it years ago, of course. He was so shrewd about these things. But somehow one felt that your father might just get away with it. He seemed to have a gift for survival.'

She turned to Miles, leaving Chessie flushed but mute with fury. 'So, how do you come to be in Wenmore Abbas? Don't you find it the most frightful backwater?'

'No, I was looking for peace and quiet, and some space,' Miles responded with cool courtesy. 'Silvertrees seemed to fill the bill.'

'All this and a domestic goddess thrown in.' Linnet's smile was honeyed. 'I have to admit, alas, that if it weren't for poor Robert's mishap, I wouldn't have come back here ever. But the prospect of anything else seemed to agitate him so dreadfully, I gave way.' She gave a little trill of laughter. 'But at least we've returned to find a congenial neighbour for a change. And a famous writer too. So exciting.'

'Francesca would be the first to tell you that I lead a very dull life,' he drawled. 'Although, occasionally, it has its moments.'

Chessie, aware of the lightning glance of amusement that he'd thrown her, felt her hands curl into impotent fists in her lap.

She was thankful that Linnet seemed to be tired of her as a topic, and had turned instead to her husband's illness, her reaction to it, and her determination to see that he had the best of care.

She makes herself sound like an amalgam of Florence Nightingale and Mother Teresa, Chessie thought wearily as she removed the soup bowls and prepared to cook her omelette.

Linnet was fulsome in her praise for this too. 'I wish I'd known Chessie was available,' she sighed. 'Or I might have snaffled her from you. But I suppose it's too late now. Rather a drastic step,' she added. 'To propose marriage in order to keep your staff, but I can appreciate that you wouldn't want to lose her.'

Miles' smile was silky. 'Fortunately Chessie has other talents apart from the purely domestic,' he said softly.

'I'm sure she has.' Linnet leaned confidentially towards him. 'I hope I'm not telling tales out of school, but Chessie was involved with my stepson years ago. She was little more than a child, of course, but *so* precocious.' She paused. 'You haven't met Alastair yet, of course.'

'No,' Miles said meditatively. 'But, apparently, I caught a glimpse of him last night.'

Linnet's fork clattered onto her plate. She picked up her napkin and dabbed at her lips. 'Really? I don't see…'

'He was paying a visit on Chessie and her sister,' Miles went on. 'I happened to be around when he was leaving.'

Linnet's smile was rather pinched. 'Well, he hasn't wasted much time.' She put her hand on Miles' arm. 'I'd tie Chessie down without delay. From what I remember, she used to be very smitten with him. When do you plan to announce your engagement?'

'We don't.' The words were out before Chessie could stop them. She saw Linnet's arched brows lift, and groaned inwardly.

'What Chessie means is that we prefer to keep the whole thing private,' Miles said smoothly. 'Inform only the people we want to know about it.'

'But you are going to buy her a ring. Call me old-fashioned, but I do think it's a convention that should be observed.'

Linnet's own 'convention' was a diamond cluster reaching to her knuckle. Chessie had always been surprised she didn't list to port under its weight.

'I couldn't agree more,' Miles said affably. 'I'd planned

to take Chessie into town this afternoon and rectify the omission. I've asked Atterbournes to have a selection of rings for us to look at, darling,' he added.

Chessie didn't trust herself to look at him. She said stiffly, 'I'd hoped there wouldn't be a lot of fuss.'

'I'll buy the smallest stone available,' he promised instantly.

Linnet made a fuss about pushing back her chair. 'Then I must leave you in peace to go shopping,' she exclaimed. 'No dessert, thank you, Chessie, dear, although fresh fruit is always so tempting. And goodbye for now, Miles.' She took his hand and clasped it. 'Although I'm sure we'll meet again very soon.'

'I think it more than probable,' he agreed impassively.

'I'll see you out,' Chessie said, trying not to sound too eager.

As they reached the front door Linnet turned on her. 'Take my advice,' she said brusquely. 'Get what you can out of him while it's on offer. Because it won't last. He's come down here to put the Sandie Wells thing behind him, but you're only a stopgap. Very soon he's going to realise that a few scars and a walking stick haven't reduced his pulling power by any noticeable amount, and he'll be looking elsewhere.'

Chessie lifted her chin. 'I bow to your expert knowledge,' she said scornfully. 'Goodbye, Linnet.'

She closed the door and leaned against it, struggling to control her temper, and the odd wave of misery that had attacked her suddenly from nowhere.

Linnet was a Class A bitch, and always had been, and she was stupid to let her remarks get to her.

None of this is real, so why should I care what she thinks? she thought. And wished she could find an answer to that that made any sense at all.

CHAPTER FIVE

CHESSIE marched back to the dining room, expecting confrontation, but was disconcerted to find it deserted.

So, I may as well revert to housekeeper mode, she thought, tight-lipped, as she began to clear the table. She carried the dirty crockery into the kitchen and started to load the dishwasher.

She still felt dazed at the way events seemed to have snowballed in the last twenty-four hours, but about one thing she was very clear. She was going to leave Silvertrees at the earliest opportunity. She no longer had any choice in the matter. Or reason to delay her decision.

As she worked she kept glancing over her shoulder, expecting to see Miles appear in the doorway at any moment. And what would she do when—if it happened? How would she react? That was what she found impossible to figure out. And that was why she knew she had to go.

She switched on the dishwasher, and stood for a moment, staring out of the kitchen window at the view she'd known all her life. It would be a wrench to leave it, but she had no choice. Things were spiralling out of control, and she was frightened—scared stiff of how Miles could make her feel, and what he might make her do.

What was the name Linnet had mentioned? Sandie—Sandie Wells? It sounded familiar, but she didn't know why. How strange, she thought, that she should have worked for Miles all this time, yet had only recently learned he'd once been in a serious relationship, and the name of the girl he'd loved.

Sighing, she walked out of the kitchen and back to her office. She sat down at her desk, drafted her resignation, and printed it. She folded the sheet of paper and put it in an envelope. She would leave it on Miles' table for him to find when he returned. He might have gone for a walk, as he sometimes did after lunch, or disappeared down to the cellar, which he'd had fitted out as a gym, for a workout. Or he might simply have decided to go up to his room for a rest.

She had not, however, expected to find him in the study, also gazing out of the window.

'Oh.' She checked in surprise. 'I didn't realise…'

'Is there a problem?'

'No—not really. I…' She looked down at the envelope she was clutching. Simply handing it to him in person had not been part of the plan at all.

'Is that for me?' He held out his hand. 'What is it?'

'Four weeks' notice,' she said, and swallowed. 'As specified in the terms of my contract.'

He opened the envelope and read the contents, his face expressionless. 'May I ask why?'

'Oh.' Chessie shrugged awkwardly. 'So many reasons.'

'I hope what happened between us earlier isn't one of them.' He spoke gravely.

'No.' Then: 'Well, yes—a little, perhaps.'

'You've been kissed before.' His tone was dry.

'Of course.' *But not like that. Never like that.* 'All the same, it was something that shouldn't have happened.'

'If you're waiting for me to apologise, or even express a word of regret, then you'll wait a long time,' he said. He paused. 'You have another job to go to?' He spoke with courteous interest—no more.

'Not yet.' Chessie kept her own voice steady. 'But I will.'

'Naturally.' His mouth twisted. 'You're an excellent worker.'

Was that really all he had to say? she asked herself in bewilderment.

She said, 'Do you want me to draw up an ad for my replacement?'

'I think I'll use an agency instead.' He was silent for a moment, looking down at the paper in his hand. Then his eyes met hers. He was smiling faintly. 'Is this an oblique way of telling me you won't marry me?'

Chessie bit her lip. 'That was never going to happen. You must have known.'

He shrugged. 'It seemed to make a lot of sense. I hoped you'd think so too.'

'I'm sorry.' She shook her head. 'But I don't see marriage as an expedient.'

'Ah,' he said softly. 'Love or nothing. Is that it, Francesca?'

'You don't think that's possible?'

'I think it might well depend on where you went looking for love.' He spoke crisply, glancing at his watch.

Clearly, the interview was at an end. Her resignation accepted and confined to history, thought Chessie, feeling oddly deflated.

She lifted her chin. 'I'm sorry. Am I keeping you from something?'

'Our appointment at Atterbournes is in an hour's time.' He sounded matter of fact. 'I thought you might have things you want to do first.'

'Atterbournes,' Chessie echoed, staring at him. 'But I don't understand.'

'We're going to buy an engagement ring. I mentioned it at lunch.'

'Yes.' Her head was spinning. 'But I didn't think you meant it.'

'I rarely say what I don't mean. I thought you'd have realised that by now.'

She said wildly, 'But I'm leaving. You know that—you've agreed. Under the circumstances, you can't mean us to go on with this ridiculous pretence.'

'Oh, but I do,' Miles said gently. 'And when the four

weeks are up, we can stage a spectacular quarrel, or simply cite irreconcilable differences and part in a civilised manner. The choice is yours.'

She gave him an inimical look. 'I choose to stop now.'

He shrugged. 'Not on offer, darling. Besides, you'll be job-hunting soon, and you're going to need a reference,' he added silkily. 'So, you'll work out your notice on my terms. And I require the current arrangement to continue.'

'That's blackmail.' Her voice shook.

Miles tutted reprovingly. 'Think of it as pragmatism. A simple and practical exchange of favours.'

If she'd only had herself to consider, she'd have wished him to hell and back, and walked out, but there was Jenny, who had important exams coming up. She couldn't afford to make them both homeless.

She bent her head. 'Very well.' Her voice was colourless.

'Cheer up, Francesca.' His tone was mocking. 'Only four weeks to endure. You'll take it in your efficient stride.'

Will I? she thought. *Will I?*

She said, 'But I won't wear a ring.'

'Not negotiable, I'm afraid,' Miles drawled. 'I think it's wise—with all these old friends around. But I'll make sure it's the smallest stone available, if that makes you feel better,' he added, his mouth twisting.

She said fiercely, 'I am not your property. You cannot—mark me.'

He threw back his head, and the blue eyes burned into hers. 'I could,' he said. 'And we both know it. Or do you require further proof?'

Chessie was the first to look away. 'No.' Her voice was barely audible.

'Another sensible decision. You see how easy it all becomes?'

All I see, Chessie thought as she went back to the flat to change, is that I could be heading for the four most difficult weeks of my life.

*   *   *

Atterbournes was an old-fashioned family jewellers, occupying double-fronted premises in the High Street. There
was a thick Turkey carpet on the floor, and several highly
polished tables, with comfortable chairs, set at discreet distances from each other, where negotiations could take place
in appropriately hushed tones.

Chessie's first pair of earrings had been bought there,
and the string of real pearls her father had given her for
her eighteenth birthday, she remembered with nostalgia as
she lingered for a moment, scanning one of the window
displays.

I wonder what happened to it all, she thought regretfully
as the shop bell tinkled their arrival.

She felt absurdly self-conscious as the current Mr
Atterbourne advanced, smiling, to welcome them and lead
them to a table where a velvet cloth had already been
spread.

'Miss Lloyd, how very good to see you again, and on
such a joyous occasion.'

She murmured, 'Thank you', and sat down, aware of the
ironic look Miles had flicked at her.

A flat leather case was brought and ceremoniously
opened, and Chessie almost blinked at the coruscating array
of stones thus revealed.

My God, she thought. Even the least of them must be
worth several thousand pounds. Is Miles completely crazy?

'Now this,' Mr Atterbourne was saying, 'is a particularly
fine solitaire.'

She was all set to protest, then remembered just in time
that she'd agreed to go on with this farce. So, she held out
her hand in mute resignation, and allowed the ring to be
slipped onto her finger.

One by one, she tried them on, solitaires, marquises,
three- and five-stone bands and clusters, listening to Mr
Atterbourne murmuring about carats, and colour, and the
various cuts that had been used. And she could see that
they were beautiful, but they did nothing for her particu-

larly. She felt it was like gazing into an ocean of frozen tears.

'Not seen anything you like yet, darling?' Miles prompted. 'What about this one?' He was holding out a cluster of diamonds, so large and magnificent that it made Linnet's ring look puny.

She looked at him indignantly, scathing words forming on her lips, and realised that although his face was solemn, the blue eyes were dancing with unholy amusement, and challenge.

It was not funny, and she knew it. There was no aspect of her current situation that was even remotely laughable, but she could feel her mouth twitching in response, and an uninhibited giggle welling up irrepressibly inside her. And Miles joined in, his shoulders shaking.

Mr Atterbourne looked surprised, then indulgent. 'Perhaps Miss Lloyd would prefer coloured stones,' he suggested. 'I have some good sapphires, and an especially beautiful ruby.'

Chessie pulled herself together. How could he have done that? she asked herself in total bewilderment. After all he's putting me through, how on earth can he make me laugh like that? And could find no answer.

'It's just so—difficult,' she said, and meant it. She sent Miles an appealing glance. 'Do we have to decide today—darling?'

'Yes, my love,' Miles returned softly, a warning note in his voice that only she could hear. 'We do.'

'Or we could make up a ring, perhaps, if Miss Lloyd has a preferred stone…' Mr Atterbourne was trying hard.

'Yes,' she said slowly. 'Actually I do have a favourite.' She paused. 'There was a ring I saw in the window just now. A square aquamarine, with diamonds on each side of it. Could I try that?'

Miles' eyebrows lifted. 'Aquamarines?' he queried. 'Aren't they semi-precious stones?'

'At one time they were considered so,' said Mr

Atterbourne, rising to his feet. 'But they are becoming increasingly rare, and consequently more valuable. The ring
in question is part of our antique collection, and very
lovely.' He beamed at them both, and hurried off.

The ring slid over her knuckle, and settled on her slender
finger as if it had been born there. The aquamarine looked
cool and pure in contrast to the fire of the diamonds that
flanked it. Two pairs of them, set one above the other, she
saw, as if they were guarding the central stone.

'The colour is deeper than many of its modern counter-
parts,' Mr Atterbourne told them almost reverently. 'It's a
very good piece.'

Miles studied it, frowning slightly. 'Surely it's more a
dress ring?'

'It's an unconventional choice for an engagement, perhaps,' the jeweller admitted cautiously.

'You wanted me to decide,' Chessie said steadily. Her
gaze locked with Miles in challenge. 'If I have to wear it,
this is my choice, and no other.'

He looked back at her, his mouth twisting in wry acknowledgement. He said, 'Then we'll take it.'

She watched it placed in a satin-lined box, and then in one
of Atterbournes' distinctive suede bags. Mr Atterbourne
clearly expected it to be presented to her later in some romantic ceremonial, she thought ruefully, accompanied by
flowers, candles and champagne.

Whereas the only likely accompaniment was going to be
one hell of a scene from Jenny, who couldn't be kept in
the dark any longer.

She stifled a sigh, sneaking a sideways glance at her
companion. His face was harsh, and set, his mouth a hard
line. She found herself wondering if he was realising he'd
just made a very expensive mistake, and was searching for
a way to call the whole thing off.

Please, she wanted to say. We don't have to do this. I
can tell people that I played a joke on you, and it backfired.
And that I'm getting another job because I'm embarrassed.

But inside the car, he took the ring from its package, and turned to her. 'Give me your hand.'

Now—*now* was the time to speak. To offer him a way out.

Yet no words would come. Instead, she found she was obeying reluctantly, trying not to shiver as his fingers touched hers. As the gold band slid over her skin. She looked down at the clear blue sheen of the stone. Touched it, as if it were some kind of talisman that would keep her safe. Four weeks, she thought. Only four weeks.

'So,' he said. 'Why this ring?'

She shrugged. 'It caught my eye. And aquamarines are my birthstone, so I've always loved them. I had a pendant once...' She stopped abruptly, aware that she was giving too much away. 'Also, it's very beautiful,' she went on swiftly. 'And it's been worn by other women, so it has a history.' She didn't look at him. 'Besides, antique jewellery holds its value. You shouldn't lose out too badly when you come to re-sell it.'

'You're all consideration.' His tone was sardonic. 'But actually I'd prefer you to keep it.'

'But I couldn't possibly,' Chessie began, remembering with dismay how much it had cost.

'Look on it as a souvenir,' he said. 'Or even a reward for suffering, bravely borne.' He paused. 'Are you going to tell me what happened to your pendant?'

Nothing could have been further from her mind, yet, somehow, her lips were already shaping a reply.

'It was sold,' she said. 'They took everything. Left us with the bare essentials.' She hunched a shoulder. 'You saw how the house was.'

'I did.' He spoke gravely. 'And I'm sorry. That was a bad time for you.'

'Yes,' she said. She smoothed the aquamarine again with a gentle finger. 'But, strangely, it wasn't the jewellery that hurt most, or even the furniture.'

'What, then?'

'They took my old rocking-horse from the attic.' Her voice was bleak. 'I saw them carrying it out, and I wanted to shout at them to bring it back. Because one day my own children were going to ride it, and I needed it.' Her laugh cracked in the middle. 'I couldn't believe they'd actually take toys. Things that we'd loved so much. That had no value for anyone else.'

He said quietly, 'It's not a merciful process.' And started the car.

I've never told anyone that before, she thought, startled. Not even Jenny. Haven't let myself think about it. So, why now?

But she didn't want to go down that road, she told herself with determination. She couldn't afford to. Besides, she had more pressing problems to consider.

They were almost back at the house when he observed, 'You've been very quiet.' He paused. 'I hope I haven't resurrected too many sad memories.'

She said ruefully, 'I was more concerned about the immediate future, and how to tell Jenny.' She shook her head. 'Or even what to tell her. She's not exactly the soul of discretion.'

'Then tell her anything,' he said. 'Except the truth.'

She stiffened. 'I don't make a habit of lying to her.'

'What a pity she doesn't treat you with equal candour.'

There was no answer to that, so she sent him a fulminating glance instead.

'Tell her that you've accepted me on purely economic grounds,' he went on. 'Then later you can admit that you can't bear to go through with it, and you're pulling out completely. She'll believe you. After all,' he added, almost casually, 'why should any woman agree to marry an ogre?'

'Oh, God.' Chessie bent her head as the car drew up in front of the house. 'You know about—that.' Her face was burning, and she couldn't look at him.

'I certainly knew she had a rock-bottom opinion of me.'

Miles shrugged slightly. 'But the nickname was news to me, until recently.'

He must, she thought wretchedly, have overheard them talking at some point. How many times had she begged Jenny to control her wayward tongue?

'I'm sorry. I—I don't know what to say.' She paused. 'She's very young in some ways, and she hates what's happened to us so much. And I think you've become a symbol of that.' She swallowed. 'Although that's no excuse.'

'Don't worry about it.' His mouth twisted. 'She'll have even more reason to slag me off when she hears I'm going to be her brother-in-law.'

Please let me wake up, Chessie pleaded silently as she undid her seat belt. Let me wake up and find this has all been some terrible dream.

'And just to add to your list of worries,' Miles added as she got out of the car, 'my sister is coming for the weekend.'

'Mrs Chubb mentioned there was to be a guest.' Chessie bit her lip. 'Is she bringing her family too?'

'Not this time. Robert is taking the children to stay with his parents. So we'll have Steffie's undivided attention.'

Chessie stared at him, appalled. 'What on earth is she going to think?'

'She'll think I proposed to you, and was accepted. That was Plan A, if you remember.' He gave her a brief, ironic smile. 'She's looking forward to meeting you,' he added, and drove off.

Chessie made her despondent way indoors, and went to her office. There were two calls on his answering machine. One was from his agent, but on the second, the caller had rung off without leaving a message.

I really hate that, Chessie thought. If it's a wrong number, why can't they have the decency to apologise? She wrote Vinnie Baxter's request for Miles to call her back on the memo pad on his desk, then took herself off to the flat.

As she entered she heard a chair being pushed back, and Jenny appeared in the kitchen doorway, white with temper.

'It's not true. Tell me she's lying, and it's not true.'

Chessie's heart sank. So much for breaking the news gently, she thought, sighing inwardly. She temporised. 'You're early. I thought you had choir practice.'

'What?' Jenny stared at her in bewilderment, then flushed. 'Oh—it was cancelled. And don't change the subject, Chess,' she added heatedly. 'What's going on?'

'Just calm down, please.' Chessie lifted her chin. 'Who is supposed to be lying—and about what?'

'You—and that bastard you work for. I've been told you're going to marry him.'

'Who told you?'

'Lady Markham—Linnet. I was at the bus stop in Hurstleigh, and she stopped and gave me a lift. She said you were engaged to Miles Hunter. She talked as if I should know all about it. I told her she must be mistaken, but she just laughed.' Jenny's voice shook. 'Tell me she's got it all wrong.'

'No,' Chessie returned with an assumption of calm. 'I can't do that. I am engaged to Miles. We've just been in Hurstleigh ourselves, buying the ring. But I'd like to know what you were doing there,' she added coldly. 'Why didn't you come straight home from school, if choir practice was cancelled, as you're supposed to do?'

'My God, will you listen to yourself?' Jenny rolled her eyes to heaven, temporarily diverted. 'I'm not a small child. I can go into town, if I want.' She shook her head. 'I can't believe you, Chessie. How could you do this? It's obscene.'

'How dare you say that?' Chessie said furiously.

'Because it's the truth. How can you marry anyone when you're in love with Alastair? It's crazy—horrible. And especially when it's The Ogre.' She shuddered. 'Then it becomes revolting.'

'Stop that right now.' There was a note in Chessie's

voice that shocked them both. 'You will never talk like that about Miles again, understand? I won't allow it.'

'Chessie!'

'I mean it. Your attitude to him has been a disgrace from the start.' The words were tumbling over each other. 'He's kind and generous, and he wants to take care of us both, so, from now on, you start being civil at least.'

'But Alastair's back,' Jenny wailed. 'Why didn't you wait for him?'

'Because he didn't ask me to,' Chessie said steadily, steeling herself against the pang of remembered pain.

'But you can't be in love with Miles Hunter. You just can't.'

'I didn't say that.' Chessie dipped her toe into deep waters. 'But we have—an understanding, and our relationship will be based on that—not on some silly romantic dream.'

'I can't believe you've just said that.' Jenny sounded genuinely horrified. 'You must have let him brainwash you.'

'No,' Chessie returned. 'I'm just facing up to reality.'

'Then Linnet was right. She said you just wanted his money, and he was looking for a nurse. Oh, Chess, how can you?' She ended on a little wail of distress.

'Come and sit down.' Chessie led her firmly into the kitchen, and placed her at the table. 'Miles and I are engaged, but not for any of the reasons you think.' She took a deep breath. 'We're going to try and build a relationship together, that's all. See if we can make it work.'

'And if it doesn't?' Jenny's eyes were fixed on her painfully.

Chessie shrugged. 'Then we part friends,' she returned with an insouciance she was far from feeling.

'Friends,' Jenny said bitterly. 'When was he ever our friend? He'd never get anyone to work as hard as you do for the money, and he wants to tie you down so that you don't leave and make a life for yourself. You're just going to—*moulder* here with him. And he's an ice man. He has no feelings.'

For one burning, tingling moment, Chessie remembered the feel—the taste—of Miles' mouth on hers. The hunger in his lean body that had ignited her own crazy response. *No feelings?*

She swallowed. 'Well—we're not married yet. And I'm certainly old enough to make my own decisions. And while I'm doing so, you will behave,' she added sternly. 'So— no more of these secret pub crawls of yours.'

Jenny's flushed face wore an expression of mingled guilt and anger. 'I suppose *he* told you. He's always hanging round the garden at all hours being spooky.'

'Well, it's his garden,' Chessie reminded her levelly. 'And it wasn't Miles, anyway. Jim Fewston tipped me off.' She hesitated. 'He also told me you were seeing someone. Why didn't you tell me, Jen? You know I'm always glad to meet your friends.'

'For tea on Sunday, I suppose,' Jenny returned rudely. 'Do me a favour. Anyway, it's not a big thing, so don't fuss.'

'Has he at least got a name?'

'Zak,' Jenny conceded reluctantly. 'Zak Woods. He works in the garage on the bypass.'

'Oh.' Chessie tried to conceal her dismay. She'd assumed he would be a sixth former at the local boys' school. 'How did you meet him?' she asked carefully.

Jenny looked down at the table. 'It was at that disco,' she said. 'The one I went to with Linda.'

But that was weeks ago, Chessie realised with alarm. And Jenny presumably had been seeing this Zak secretly all this time.

She steeled herself. 'Jenny, darling,' she said gently. 'You're going to take your exams in a week or two, and so much depends on them. Please don't do anything silly— that could affect the rest of your life.'

Jenny got to her feet. 'I call that rich coming from you,

Chessie. Sort your own life out before you start handing
out good advice, why don't you? Because from where I'm
standing, you're a complete mess.'

And she flounced out of the room and slammed the door.

Well done me, Chessie thought, wincing. I made a really
good job of that.

And she couldn't really argue with Jenny's parting shot
either. She was in total chaos, lost in a kind of limbo, and
uncertain what to do next.

The thought of how different it all might have been could
never be far from her mind, of course. If only Alastair had
returned a week—even a day earlier. If he'd never gone
away in the first place, she thought sadly, and been there
for her to turn to when her life collapsed around her.

Linnet was bound to have told him about her engagement
by now. She seemed hell-bent on spreading the news far
and wide, and would have particular malicious pleasure in
telling Alastair, as the tensions between them had clearly
not abated.

And this time Chessie would not be able to act as buffer
between them.

But it was little use sitting here, tormenting herself with
what might have been. She might be wearing Miles' ring,
but that meant nothing. It was still a working day, and she
was his employee.

As she came back into the main part of the house, she
saw a battered leather travel bag by the front door. She
gave it a frowning glance, then continued into Miles' study.
He was there, over by his table. He'd changed, she noticed
at once, into more formal clothing—dark trousers, and a
jacket with a shirt and tie, and he was packing papers into
his briefcase.

Chessie checked, staring at him. 'Are you going somewhere?'

'I called Vinnie back,' Miles returned, without pausing
in his task. 'She wants to discuss my schedule once the

current book is in. So, I said I'd go up to London for a couple of days.'

'A couple of days,' she repeated. 'You mean you're going to stay up there?'

His glance was faintly derisive. 'You catch on fast, darling.'

'But you never do that. Where will you stay?'

'At the flat. That's what it's there for, after all.'

The flat, she thought, swallowing, that he'd once shared with Sandie Wells. That must have its memories. So why had he chosen this particular moment to return to it?

'You said once you were going to sell it.'

'And then I changed my mind.' He shrugged, and fastened his briefcase. 'At times like this, it's convenient.'

'Isn't this rather a sudden decision—to simply take off like this?'

'I used to be famous for it.' His voice was dry. 'But Vinnie's call seemed—opportune. It occurred to me that you've been under a lot of pressure, and that maybe you could do with some time and space to think about things. So, I'm letting you do just that.'

She stood very still, watching from the other side of the room, while a small frantic voice in her head whispered, Don't go. Don't leave me—please. Or—take me with you.

For a moment, she thought she had spoken aloud, and shock tightened her chest. Along with denial.

She said huskily, 'Are—are you getting the train?'

'No, I'm taking the car this time.'

'But it's late, and you've had a long day. You'll be tired…'

His brows lifted ironically. 'Why, Chessie, we seem to have skipped a bit. You sound just like a wife.'

She bit her lip. 'I'm sorry,' she said stiffly. 'Of course it's none of my business.'

'And you look a little fraught,' he went on. 'Surely it can't simply be concern for my welfare.'

'I've just been talking to Jenny,' Chessie admitted. 'I'm afraid I didn't handle it very well.'

'I suppose she told you she wasn't a child any more.'

'Something like that,' she agreed ruefully.

'In which she's perfectly correct, of course.'

'What do you mean?'

He said with faint impatience, 'You have to let her go, Francesca. If she passes these examinations of hers, she'll be off to college, and you won't be able to go with her to coddle her, and give way to her every whim.'

'I don't…'

'No? Yet she has the best that money can buy, and you look as if you dress from a second-hand stall.'

She drew a quivering breath. 'How dare you?'

'I dare because it's the truth, however unpalatable.' His tone was dispassionate. 'You spend your time endlessly making up to Jenny for something that wasn't your fault in the first place. But it's time you pushed her out of the nest, and started taking care of yourself instead. Or else find someone who'll do it for you.

'But what you can't do is live her life, and make her choices for her. She has to be able to make her own mistakes, and you have to let her.'

She stiffened defensively. 'And what makes you such an expert?'

'Personal experience,' Miles said drily. 'I can remember stretching parental tolerance to the limits, and Steffie was even worse. Jenny isn't the first girl to find an unsuitable boyfriend. I presume he's one of the stumbling blocks.'

'She met him at a disco on St Patrick's Night, and she's kept quiet about him all this time. And it's not even one of her fellow students. He's a garage mechanic, called Zak.'

'So, he can afford to take her to places like The White Hart. That will be part of the attraction, of course. And the fact that you'd disapprove, as you've just demonstrated, which makes him forbidden fruit, and all the sweeter.' He shrugged. 'All perfectly normal, so far.'

She said, 'I thought Jenny and I had a different relationship.'

'She's striking out for herself,' he said. 'And giving you the opportunity to do the same.' He paused. 'How did she take our engagement?'

'Not well.'

His mouth twisted. 'Hardly a surprise either. But maybe my absence will help there, too. Give her a chance to accustom herself. Let you build a few bridges.'

She said, 'But your sister's coming to visit.'

'I haven't forgotten. In fact, I shall be bringing her back with me.'

She followed him into the hall, feeling oddly lost. 'Is there anything special you'd like me to cook?'

'I leave it to your good judgement. But don't work too hard. Take a break, and relax a little. Regard it as a bonus,' he added drily. He paused. 'You don't have to cook on Saturday night, by the way. Your friend Lady Markham rang just now, and asked us up to the Court.' He sent her a brief, taut smile. 'Something for you to look forward to.'

'Oh,' she said. And: 'Yes.'

'I should be back about mid-afternoon on Friday,' he went on. 'But I don't foresee any problems during my absence.'

Except, she thought bleakly, that I *really* don't want you to go. And that scares me.

She stood at the top of the steps, watching him drive away, then turned slowly and went back into the house.

Emptiness closed round her. And silence.

She thought, I'm just so used to him being here. He's become part of everything I do. And now he's gone.

And realised she wanted very badly to burst into tears.

CHAPTER SIX

CHESSIE sat on the bottom stair, arms wrapped tightly round her body as she struggled to regain control of her emotions. She was frightened and bewildered. Unable to make sense of her own reactions.

But the simple truth was that watching Miles drive off had been like a wound in the heart. Something she could neither understand nor explain.

When Alastair had left, she had cried into her pillow, but it had never occurred to her to swallow her pride and beg him to stay. Yet that was what she'd been tempted to do only minutes before.

I'd have pleaded with him, she thought, astonished, if it would have done any good.

He had kissed her until she'd melted in his arms, bought her a ring, and walked away from her, and she was at a loss to explain any of it. Especially her own sense of desolation now that he'd gone.

He'd offered her space, and now she was standing in the middle of a vast and echoing wilderness.

She got slowly to her feet. There was no point in sitting here brooding. He'd gone, and he would not be back until Friday.

Three nights, two whole days, and a morning before she saw him again.

The precision of her calculation made her shiver. I must, she thought, be going mad. Cracking up. Because *this is not me*.

I should be using this time—his absence—to prepare for my future. For the day when I walk through that door, and don't look back. Or come back.

Of course, Miles himself might not come back. Maybe he'd decided that he didn't want to deal with her problems, or go on with this charade, even on a temporary basis, and planned to stay away until the month was up.

He was not, she thought, someone who would be good at saying goodbye.

He'd told her not to work—to relax, and treat his absence as a holiday—but that was impossible. She felt as if she were strung up on wires.

Besides, there was always something to do when Miles was busy with a book. He was tough on himself, drafting and re-drafting, then doing a final hard edit on the transcript she produced for him. She would see what there was in the alterations folder, and have the new pages awaiting his return.

She wandered into the study, and stood looking round her for a moment, at this place that was so definitely his domain.

It had always been very much easier to insist to herself that he was just a stranger. A man for whom she happened to work. And that when she went into her flat each evening and closed the door, he somehow ceased to exist.

But she knew now she'd just been fooling herself. Because, working with him so closely each day, she'd become quite intimately acquainted with him.

She knew, for instance, what food he liked, and that he preferred the linen sheets on his bed to be changed every three days. She knew that he favoured mellow earth tones over pastels, and natural fibres over man-made.

She knew that when he was thinking, he liked to walk round the room. That when he was putting his thoughts down on paper, he liked to play music. And that his only real superstition was the little portable typewriter sitting forlornly on his table.

If he'd left his lucky charm behind, then he must be coming back.

'He wouldn't go without you,' she said under her breath,

touching the yellowing keys. And what was she doing talking to inanimate objects?

She'd learned also to gauge his moods, to judge if and when his work could be safely interrupted, and by whom. And to know when he was in pain. Which were the good days for him, and which the bad.

And the past twenty-four hours would probably not get any gold awards. He'd asked her to marry him, for God's sake, and all she'd done was turn his proposal against him in order to score points off Linnet.

And the fact that she now wished the words unsaid a hundred times over made no difference at all.

There were only about twenty pages in the alterations folder. They wouldn't keep her occupied for long, she thought with a sigh. And she needed to stay busy.

As she turned away she noticed some torn scraps of paper in his waste basket, which she might as well empty now rather than wait for Mrs Chubb in the morning.

As she picked up the metal bin, she realised its contents were the tiny fragments of the cream envelope that had arrived that morning. For a moment, she stood very still, remembering his reaction to it. The way he'd slipped it into his pocket. And her own conviction that it was from a woman.

Was this the reason for his sudden decision to go to London? Could it be?

Despising herself, she sifted through the pieces, making sure that it was only the envelope that he'd thrown away, then shamefacedly dropped the bits back in the bin.

She had never in her life done such a thing before. She'd always regarded herself as discreet and honourable. Not someone who snooped and pried.

And if the letter had been ripped up and thrown away too, would she have got down on her knees on the carpet and pieced it together to satisfy her curiosity? Had she really sunk so low?

And was she simply curious, or was there a more fundamental emotion driving her on? Was it—could it be possible that she was actually jealous?

A shiver ran through her. She thought, I don't know who I am any more.

She needed to feel better about herself, and quickly too. Maybe she'd make a start on building one of those bridges with Jenny that Miles had mentioned. See if she could capture their lost rapport.

She left the bin and what it contained beside his table, and took the folder through to her office, then went back to the flat.

Jenny was on the phone when she went in. 'No, that's fine,' she was saying eagerly. 'I'll cycle over. See you later.' She replaced the receiver and turned to face her sister, her expression defiant.

She said, 'That was Linda. She wants us to get together this evening, and do some revision, and for me to sleep over. I said it was all right.' She indicated the phone. 'But feel free to call her mother, and check that it's really happening.'

Chessie bit her lip. 'Does it have to be tonight? I thought we might go into Hurstleigh, and go to the pizza place. Rent a video for afterwards.'

Jenny shook her head. 'I'd better go to Linda's. She's offered to go over a couple of things with me, and, as you keep reminding me, the exams are almost here.'

Which indicated that Jenny had been missing classes in order to meet with Zak, Chessie thought wearily. But this was probably not the time to make an issue of it.

'Anyway,' Jenny went on with a toss of her head, 'I wouldn't want to separate you from your lover. You have a relationship to invent. I'll see you tomorrow night,' she added over her shoulder as she went off to her room to pack.

Feeling oddly deflated, Chessie trailed into the kitchen and put the kettle on. Getting back on terms with Jenny was going to be more difficult than she'd envisaged, she thought, spooning coffee granules into a mug. And it was just as well her engagement to Miles wasn't the genuine article, or her sister's inimical attitude could have caused real problems. In fact she might even have been forced at some point to choose between them.

Although that was no contest. Jenny, after all, was her own flesh and blood, and needed her. She would always take priority.

But did Jenny necessarily feel the same about her?

The sheer disloyalty of the thought brought her up with a gasp of shock. That was Miles' fault, she upbraided herself, with all that talk of Jenny making her own life—moving away and moving on.

But perhaps it was wrong to rely too heavily on her sister always being around. Because clearly that wasn't going to happen. And tonight was a case in point.

She thought, I'm going to be alone here for the first time.

She supposed it was a step in the right direction. After all, if Miles was right, she was going to have to get used to the concept of being on her own. Of having only herself to rely on.

An evening, besides, when she could do exactly what she wanted, she reminded herself. When there would be no arguments about television programmes, or how loud Jenny's music should be. Or even the appropriate bedtime for a school night. That was for Linda's mother to deal with.

And Chessie was off the hook.

But once Jenny had departed, with the usual shouted goodbye and slammed door, the silence seemed to close round her.

Be positive, she adjured herself. Keep busy.

She got supper out of the way first. She didn't feel particularly hungry, so she made toast, and heated a tin of beans. While she ate her unexciting meal, she cheered herself up, making notes about far more adventurous menus for the weekend ahead, and beyond.

Without the car, she wouldn't be able to get to the supermarket on the other side of Hurstleigh, but Miles preferred her to use the smaller local shops anyway, and had opened accounts at most of them. So, all she had to do was to hand in an order, and the meat, groceries and vegetables would be delivered to the house later the same day.

Which would leave her time to do a little shopping on her own account, she thought. Miles' acid comment about her wardrobe might have rankled, but she couldn't deny its justice. She rarely bought herself any new clothes, and when she did she was attracted by hard-wearing qualities rather than fashion.

But if she had to compete in the market-place for a new job with good pay and some prospects, she'd need to pay some attention to her appearance.

And that was the route she had to take, or she'd be in danger of making an abject fool of herself. She needed to distance herself from Miles Hunter as quickly and completely as possible. Today's events had convinced her of that. And she needed to cling to that conviction.

Supper over and cleared away, Chessie took a long and leisurely bath, revelling in the fact that there was no Jenny banging on the door demanding admittance. She washed and dried her hair, slathered moisturiser on her face, then, wrapped in her elderly towelling robe, gave herself a manicure, watching a thriller she'd missed at the cinema.

Missing it might have been a good move, she decided restively halfway through. Even though it was brilliantly acted, it was too dark and violent for her taste, and not the wisest choice to watch alone.

She switched it off, and, to cheer herself up, decided to paint her toenails as well with the soft coral polish she'd purloined from Jenny's dressing table.

But with that task completed—what?

She tried reading her library book, but the story failed to grip her attention. She turned on the radio, and station-hopped, in an unavailing attempt to find some music she liked.

Oh, this is ridiculous, she thought crossly. I have all this time to do whatever I like, yet there's nothing I want to do.

Perhaps she'd just have an early night. After she'd been round the house, and checked it was secure. Something that Miles normally did himself, of course. The ground floor doors and windows were all locked, but she decided to go upstairs and make sure Miles had closed his bedroom window before he left. He had a habit of forgetting it, as Mrs Chubb often pointed out.

And this time was no exception. The thick carpet was soft under her bare feet as she went to the window and fastened the latch. As she turned she glimpsed a movement and froze, only to realise she'd seen herself, like a pale ghost, in the wall mirror.

She gave a nervous giggle, and stayed where she was for a moment, waiting for her heart to stop racing.

It was a very masculine room, she thought. When her father had used it, there'd been ornaments—pictures on the wall. After her mother had died, he hadn't changed a thing.

But now, the room was as bleak as a monastic cell. No softening touches at all—rather like his writing, she decided rather sadly. Except, she supposed, for the wide bed with its dark green quilt. That was definitely an indulgence.

Obeying an impulse she barely understood, she walked across the room and stood beside it, remembering how he looked when he was asleep. Imagining his dark head on the pillow now.

She bent, smoothing the already immaculate pillowcase with her hand, and the faint, familiar scent of his cologne reached her. She stepped back abruptly, with a little gasp. Because, in that moment, she'd been aware of him so vividly, it was as if his hand had clasped hers and drawn her down into the bed beside him.

But that was nonsense, she told herself vehemently. For

Miles was a long way from here, in another bed, in a room she'd never seen. And perhaps not even alone...

The breath caught sharply in her throat. It was time she got back to where she belonged, and stopped letting her stupid imagination run away with her.

Whoever shared his bed, in London or here, it would not be her. And that was her decision. Her choice.

Except for this one night, when she was alone, and so lonely, so isolated in this big house that she wanted to moan with the pain of it. And where to sleep where he slept might bring a kind of comfort.

No one, she thought, will ever know.

She loosened the belt of her robe, and let it fall to the floor, then lifted the edge of the quilt, and slipped beneath it, burying her face in his pillow, and breathing the scent of him into her starved lungs.

The linen felt cool against her skin as she sank weight-lessly into the mattress, and gradually the tension and the trembling seeped away, leaving a strange peace in its place.

She should not be here, and she knew it, yet there was nowhere she would rather be.

And as her eyes closed, and she began to drift away, Chessie heard herself whisper his name.

When she awoke, the sun was streaming in through the window. For a moment, she lay, stretching languidly, to-tally disorientated, wondering who had opened her curtains, then she remembered where she was, and sat up with a gasp of alarm.

One glance at the clock on the night table told her that it was late, and that she'd overslept.

'Oh, no,' she groaned, stumbling out of bed and grabbing up her robe. Supposing Jenny had decided to come back last night, and found her missing—or Mrs Chubb had ar-rived early. What possible explanation could she offer for her extraordinary behaviour?

She didn't even understand it herself, but, at the same

time, she couldn't deny she'd had her best night's sleep in months, she thought breathlessly as she straightened the bed, erasing any tell-tale signs of her occupancy.

Back at the flat, she showered quickly and dressed in a navy cotton skirt and white blouse. Before leaving her room, she took off the aquamarine ring and put it back in its box, hiding it in a drawer.

Mrs Chubb would spot it in an instant, she thought ruefully, and she couldn't face the kind of eager interrogation that would follow, or the nine days' wonder that the good woman would set off in the village.

By the time Mrs Chubb arrived, Chessie had made the coffee, and was able to greet her with a semblance of composure.

'Off to London, is he?' Mrs Chubb said comfortably. 'Well, a gentleman needs to enjoy himself from time to time.' She nodded. 'Perhaps I'll give that room of his a good turn out. Make it nice for him to come back to.'

She shook her head. 'Not like poor Sir Robert. Chubb says there's wheelchair ramps everywhere at the Court, now. They're bringing him back by ambulance tomorrow, and a trained nurse with him.' She sniffed. 'And all Madam can think of is the parties she's going to give.'

'I'm sure she's very concerned about him,' Chessie said without any real conviction. 'Besides, it will probably cheer Sir Robert up to have company in the house,' she added more positively. 'It would be awful if he thought people were avoiding him because he's ill.'

'Well,' Mrs Chubb said tolerantly, 'you were always one to think the best of people. You just be careful you're not taken in, that's all.' And she collected her polish and dusters, and departed with a portentous nod of the head.

Chessie picked up a plastic bin liner, and headed back to begin the arduous task of sorting out her clothes. She was determined to be ruthless. A symbolic clear-out, she told herself with determination. Off with the old life, and on with the new. And in future she would not be trying to turn herself into the invisible woman either, she added silently, ramming a handful of washed-out tee shirts into her sack.

There was a daunting amount of space in her wardrobe when she'd finished. She would have to dip into her carefully garnered savings, and maybe use the credit card she'd been keeping for emergencies only.

Well, so what? Chessie thought, shrugging mentally. I've tried to be cautious and sensible, and look where it's got me. I'm just a confused mess. But by this evening, at least I'll be a better-dressed confused mess.

It clouded over during the afternoon, and when Chessie emerged from the last boutique she found it had begun to rain a little.

She grimaced faintly as she looked up at the sky, wishing she'd remembered her umbrella. But a little drizzle wouldn't kill her, and there was a bus due in ten minutes.

She'd forgotten how enjoyable a few hours of pure self-indulgence could be, she thought as she made her way along High Street. She'd concentrated on work clothes, and her first and most expensive purchase had been a smart black jacket. She'd chosen a couple of skirts, one in black, the other in grey check, and a handful of contrasting tops. Finally, she'd added a pair of black medium-heeled pumps, and a matching leather bag.

In addition she'd treated herself to several pairs of casual cotton trousers, some cheap tee shirts in clear, cool colours, and even a couple of summer dresses. She'd also replenished her underwear drawer.

That was the plus side, she thought. On the minus side, the first jobs agency she'd visited had told her with polite regret that they could already fill any temporary posts with the staff already on their books, and the second hadn't held out any great hopes either.

The prices being charged for rental property in the area had made her whistle too.

But it was still early days, she told herself. And something would turn up eventually.

Her carrier bags were weighing heavy by the time she arrived at the stop, and joined the end of the queue. The rain was heavier now, and she was beginning to feel damp and chilly.

The bus was late too, she realised with exasperation, transferring her bags from one hand to the other.

A car going past on the other side of the road slowed, then stopped, and someone called out her name. She glanced across, and saw Alastair beckoning to her. With a sigh of relief, she heaved up her bags and started across the road, where he was waiting with the boot open.

'Thank you,' she gasped.

'It's lucky I saw you,' he returned. He looked at the names on the carriers, and his brows lifted. 'Shopping for your trousseau?'

The query had a bite to it, and Chessie flushed. 'No, I just needed some new clothes.'

Alastair switched on the engine, then sat, watching the rhythmic swish of the windscreen wipers, but making no attempt to move off.

'So you're going to marry Miles Hunter,' he remarked eventually. 'Well, that should solve a whole lot of problems for you.' He turned and looked at her reproachfully. 'Why didn't you say something the other night, Chess? Why did you let me ramble on like that?'

She said quietly, 'Because I hadn't told anyone, least of all Jenny.'

'Linnet knew.' His sense of grievance was strong in his tone.

She bit her lip. 'Well—that was a mistake. It just— slipped out.'

'It's an odd feeling,' he said slowly. 'To come back, and find your girl's engaged to someone else.'

'Your girl?' Chessie echoed. She shook her head. 'After all this time without a word? You can't be serious.'

'But I'm back now,' he argued. 'Surely that changes things? I know I should have kept in touch, but you can't have forgotten how happy we were together.'

She said slowly, 'That was a long time ago, Alastair. Things have changed. *We've* changed.'

There was a silence, then he said in a low voice, 'Why are you doing this, Chess? You can't love him, and it's odds on that he's not in love with you.'

She lifted her chin. 'How can you possibly know what we feel about each other?'

He said gently, 'Chessie, you're a lovely girl, but he was living with Sandie Wells, for heaven's sake. They were a huge item.'

'So I keep hearing.' She frowned. 'Am I supposed to know who she is?'

He sighed. 'You must have heard of her. She was a top model before she turned to acting. She was in that film about jewel thieves, and she's done loads of television, too. Amazingly beautiful girl,' he added. 'With legs up to her forehead.'

'I really don't remember,' Chessie said quietly. 'But I have had other things on my mind.'

'Well, she dumped your fiancé pretty brutally, I understand, but rumour says he's still hung up on her, even though she's been married to some electronics millionaire for the past year.'

'She's moved on,' Chessie countered. 'Perhaps Miles feels it's time he did, too.'

He grimaced. 'Come off it, sweetheart. If he thought there was a chance of getting her back, he wouldn't give you a second thought.'

She drew a swift, uneven breath. 'May we change the subject, please?'

He gave her a surprised look. 'Yes, of course. I just thought you should know the score, that's all.' He paused. 'After all, I wouldn't want you to get hurt. And you could.'

That was true, she thought. Because she was hurting already, a knife twisting slowly deep within her.

The car moved off, and Chessie sat silently, looking down at her hands clasped in her lap. If she'd been harbouring any illusions about Miles' reasons for proposing to her, they'd have been shattered for ever. Every time he looked at her, she thought painfully, he would be drawing comparisons between her and the amazing beauty he'd lost. And when he touched her…

Her mind closed off in rejection. She could never allow that to happen again, she told herself starkly. Never permit herself to forget everything in his arms, under the subtle torment of his mouth. From now on, that was the forbidden zone.

It wouldn't be easy. Miles was an experienced man who knew perfectly well what he was doing. And he'd set out, deliberately and cynically, to expose the depth of that blind, unthinking need that she hadn't realised existed until his lips took hers. A need that would not—*could not* ever be satisfied.

And I shall have to learn to live with that, she thought. Somehow.

'I'm running low on petrol. I'd better get some.' Alastair's voice broke abruptly across her unhappy reverie.

'Yes,' she returned mechanically. 'Of course.'

It was only when he'd filled his tank and gone off to pay that Chessie realised they were at the garage on the bypass. She wound down her window, allowing a rush of cool damp air to enter the car, and looked around her.

It was a busy place, selling new and used cars as well as offering repairs, and there were mechanics in dark blue overalls everywhere. But one in particular caught her attention—tall, and coarsely good-looking, with his dark hair caught back in a pony-tail. There was a dragon tattooed on his arm beneath the rolled-up sleeve, and he wore a silver earring, and a nose stud.

As if aware of her scrutiny, he glanced towards the car, his expression one of surly indifference.

Chessie's heart skipped a sudden, alarmed beat, as her premonition sharpened. She thought, Oh, no. Please, no. Not him. It can't be...

Only to hear a voice call 'Zak' and see him look back over his shoulder, mouthing some obscenity.

Her hand crept up and touched her throat, all her worst fears confirmed.

'Are you all right?' Alastair swung himself back into the driving seat. 'You're as white as a ghost. What's happened?'

'Nothing,' she said quickly. 'It was just a bit stuffy in the car, that's all.'

'Do you want the air-conditioning on?'

'No, it's fine.' Closing the window, she summoned a smile, trying to ignore the churning in her stomach. *Jenny*, she thought. *Oh, God, Jenny*. 'Anyway, we'll be home soon.'

'Come back to the Court, and have some tea,' he invited. 'Linnet's not there. She's gone up to London to bring my father down.'

'Oh, how is he?' Chessie was thankful to focus on something else.

'No different, I gather.' He shook his head. 'I can't imagine why he's so set on being at the Court, anyway. The medical facilities in Spain were first class. And keeping the place up is a hell of a drain on his finances.'

'But it's his home,' Chessie said. 'And your inheritance.'

'I'm not sure I relish being saddled with a great barn of a place like that.' His tone was moody as he pulled off the forecourt, and waited for a gap in the traffic. 'I plan to be based in London. Or I might even go back to America if there's a suitable opportunity.'

She was aware of the faintly challenging look he sent her, and suspected it was her cue to react with distress. Beg him to reconsider. And for a brief moment, she was tempted. This was Alastair, after all, on whom all her girl-hood hopes and longings had been centred. She'd cared for him once. Maybe she would again, once she'd rid herself of the distraction of Miles.

Alastair, after all, showed every sign of wanting to renew their relationship, and perhaps she was a fool to hold back when he could well be the substance in her life, and Miles only the shadow. Time alone would show—only she didn't have that much time…

She wondered why she hadn't confided in him when he'd asked—expressed her fears for Jenny, and the feelings of instinctive revulsion that Zak had inspired in her. After all, Alastair had known her sister since she was a child, and who better to advise her?

Because she had to do something. And it wasn't just Zak's appearance that made her uneasy. Tattoos were fashionable, and so was body piercing. And she could see that his raffish good looks might have an effect on an impressionable girl.

No, there was something about him—some element in his body language or his attitude that chilled her, and it was pointless telling herself that she was being over-imaginative, and that Zak was probably kind to animals and good to his mother.

Because kindness was not in him, and she knew it.

'Am I invited in?' Alastair asked when they reached Silvertrees. 'I'd like to congratulate the bridegroom.'

'He's rather busy, I'm afraid.' Which was an evasion, Chessie told herself, and not a downright lie. Again, she had no real idea why she'd concealed the fact that Miles was away. Except that instinct told her that he would not appreciate her entertaining Alastair during his absence.

'Besides, we'll see you on Saturday evening,' she went on. 'Your stepmother has asked us to dinner.'

'Has she?' His surprise was genuine. 'It's the first I've heard of it.'

'Unless, of course, you think visitors would be too much for your father.'

His grimace was painful. 'To be honest, I don't know whether it will register with him that strongly. He's in a bad way, Chessie. And now, just when I need you, you belong to someone else.'

She said drily, 'How times change. A week ago, I didn't seem necessary to anyone in particular. I'm not used to being so much in demand.'

He took her hand, his eyes moody and faintly brooding. 'Just remember this, my sweet. If you change your mind, I'll be waiting.' He pressed a light kiss to her palm. 'Now, go in, before he gets suspicious.'

She found she wanted to snatch her hand away, but she made herself wait for him reluctantly to relinquish it. Then, with a murmur of thanks for the lift, collected her shopping and went into the house.

She only wished Miles were there, suspicious or not.

He was the one she could tell about Jenny. He would understand.

She needed to hear his voice, she realised suddenly. Wanted him to reassure her that the repulsive Zak was simply part of Jenny's belated adolescent rebellion. Her first foray into the adult world, even if it was with the wrong companion.

She badly needed to hear that it was an infatuation that would end as swiftly as it had begun, with her sister older and wiser, but with no real harm done. And that it would all come right in the end.

And she could talk to him about it, she thought. She could call him at the flat, and tell him what had happened. Pour out her fears and forebodings, and be comforted.

Even if he told her she was being a fool, it would help in some strange way.

She went into the study, found the number and dialled. Of course, he might not be there, she thought as she heard the ringing tone. He might be at Vinnie's office in the

Haymarket, and, if so, she would leave a message asking him to call her back, preferably this evening.

She heard the receiver lifted, and was about to rush into speech when she heard a woman's voice say, 'Hello?'

She thought, I must have got the wrong number. She wanted to say something—to apologise and ring off, and be more careful next time. But she couldn't speak. Because her heart was beating frantically, and a hand seemed to be tightening round her throat.

'Hello?' the voice repeated, more forcefully. Then: 'Miles—there's no one there.'

And Chessie found herself letting the receiver drop back onto its rest as if it had suddenly become red hot and burned her fingers to the bone.

She realised she was kneeling on the floor, bent double, gasping for breath, her arms wrapped protectively round her body. While all the time a small, desperate voice in her head was whispering, What shall I do? Oh, God, what shall I do?

CHAPTER SEVEN

WELL, what had she really expected? Chessie asked herself wearily, peeling onions as if her life depended on it. Miles was a man, and, as she knew only too well, possessed of all the usual male instincts. And to be fair, he had never indicated that he was celibate.

And, anyway, it was none of her business, whatever she might have suspected.

It was something she'd repeated to herself at intervals during the course of the previous day, and two restless nights, until the words seemed to hammer at her brain.

But, she'd discovered, suspicion was one thing. Having it so openly confirmed was quite another, and she was still reeling under the impact. Still at a loss to know how to deal with the situation when he returned.

The letter in the cream envelope had, of course, been from the woman in his life, arranging an assignation. And one that he was keen to enjoy to the full, judging by the haste of his departure, she thought, biting her lip.

But if there is someone in his life, Chessie argued with herself, all over again, then why did he ask me to marry him? It makes no sense. Unless his unknown lady can't cook or use a computer, and he thinks I'm a better economic proposition.

She rinsed her hands, and wiped her streaming eyes on a piece of kitchen towel. At least she had an excuse for weeping this time, she thought wryly. She couldn't say the same for the tears she'd shed over the past twenty-four hours.

They'd been nothing but the purest self-indulgence, and she was disgusted with herself. Scared, too, because, in spite of all the traumas she'd gone through in the past, she'd never experienced such anguish in her life before.

Yet how could that be possible? And why was she beating herself up like this? After all, the rules of the game hadn't changed.

Because Miles' original offer had been a business proposition, and nothing more. He wanted her to go on running his house, and take on the additional role of his hostess.

And even if sex at some stage hadn't been entirely ruled out, it certainly hadn't been uppermost in his mind.

As indeed why should it be, when he had his London lady to fulfil his needs already?

He never at any time said he was in love with me, she reminded herself. And, anyway, I've turned down his proposal, and very soon I'll be out of his house, and his life altogether. So, it's ludicrous for me to behave as if there's been some kind of betrayal involved here. As if I have the right to be hurt by anything he does. Because Miles is a totally free agent, and so am I.

And I cannot—*cannot*—allow myself to care—even if he has a mistress for every day of the week.

Yet, knowing all this, how can it still matter so much—and so bitterly?

She heated oil in a pan, and began to fry chunks of steak. She'd been cooking all morning, concentrating almost grimly on the task in hand, whereas usually she found it a relaxation. She was now making a rich beef stew for dinner that night, to welcome his sister.

In a way, she was dreading meeting the unknown Steffie because it was inevitably going to mean more deception in the short term. On the other hand, her presence would curb any reckless bid by Chessie to venture into forbidden territory, and ask questions that were none of her concern. Which she had to admit would have been a danger otherwise.

She'd worked hard, trying to blank out the thoughts still reeling in her head. The house was full of flowers, the dining-room table was already gleaming with silver and crystal, and candles in tall holders waiting to be lit, and the scent of lavender and beeswax hung in the air thanks to Mrs Chubb's ministrations.

Chessie was determined that Miles would have nothing to complain of in the time before she left his employment. She would fulfil each and every one of her duties to the letter—including playing the part of his fiancée, if that was what he still wanted.

She would make sure she took glowing references to her next job.

Not that she was having much luck in that connection, she admitted, grimacing. She'd gone through the advertisements in the local paper, and rung the few secretarial posts on offer, only to be told they were already filled. She'd enquired after a position as a receptionist too, but the money was barely a quarter of what she was earning at the moment, and she'd hardly be able to keep herself in a bedsit, let alone contribute towards Jenny's student career.

It might be better to forget about working in an office altogether, she thought with a sigh, and find another residential post as a cook-housekeeper—only this time she'd ensure her employer was an elderly lady.

'Something smells good.' Mrs Chubb came bustling in. 'It'll be nice to have some company here for a change. I was saying to Chubb, it seems dead quiet here without Mr Hunter, even though he generally keeps himself to himself.'

But not always, thought Chessie with a pang, lifting the browned meat into a casserole dish.

She said, 'Mrs Chubb—do you know a Zak Woods?'

Mrs Chubb sniffed. 'Know of him,' she said. 'And not much good either,' she added ominously. She gave Chessie a curious look. 'Why do you ask?'

Chessie shrugged. 'Oh, someone mentioned his name.' She paused. 'He's a mechanic, isn't he?'

'So they say. Trouble-maker, more likely. Been one step

ahead of the law since he could walk. I wouldn't take any motor of mine near him.'

Who said things can only get better? Chessie wondered wearily when the good woman had departed.

She'd put her own problems aside the previous evening, and attempted, gently, to question Jenny a little. She hadn't mentioned that she'd seen Zak, and had tried to keep her questions friendly, concealing her instinctive anxieties about the relationship. But it had been no good. Jenny had made it angrily clear that she'd regarded Chessie as invading her privacy.

I'm out of my depth here, Chessie had thought tiredly as her sister had banged out of the room.

Now, as she poured wine into her casserole, it occurred to her that perhaps she'd been too protective of Jenny, and by doing so had driven her to break out, and seek an extreme like Zak.

What can she see in him? she wondered, then checked herself hastily, realising that she probably wouldn't like the answer, so it might be better not to know.

She could only suppose that Jenny had genuinely fallen in love with him, and love was said to be blind. Even so, surely she must sense the malevolence in him that Chessie had spotted in one brief moment? Or, in some ghastly way, was that part of his attraction?

She knew she had to tread carefully. Jenny was above the age of consent, and she could get married among other crazy things.

Maybe I've just got to be patient, and wait for this madness to run its course, she thought as she transferred her casserole to the oven.

And perhaps that's how I'll get over Miles too, she added bleakly.

She was waiting edgily at the open front door as Miles' car came round the curve of the drive and stopped on the gravel with a soft whisper of tyres.

Unobtrusively, Chessie blotted damp palms on her jean-clad hips, and composed her face into a smile.

Steffie Barnes was nearly as tall as her brother, and had the same blue eyes, but her hair was fairer, and she had a merry face and a warm, low-pitched voice.

'So you're Francesca,' she said, destroying Chessie's last frail hope that maybe she'd been the one answering the telephone in her brother's flat two days earlier. Her hand clasp was firm, and her gaze friendly. 'I began to wonder if I was ever going to meet you, or if you were just a figment of my dear brother's fertile imagination.' She turned, lifting a wry eyebrow in his direction.

'Oh, she exists.' Miles' drawl held amusement and something less easy to define. The blue eyes were cool and searching as they scanned her. 'Don't I get a welcome too, Chessie?'

Flushing, Chessie stepped forward, offering her cheek awkwardly. But Miles captured her chin, and turned her face to receive his kiss, swift and sensuous, on her lips. He did not release her at once.

'You've got shadows under your eyes.' He spoke softly, but he wore a faint frown. 'I hope they're because you've been missing me.'

'Why else?' Her smile was beginning to feel as if it had been glued there, but at last he let her go. She turned to Steffie. 'Would you like to see your room, and then have tea?'

'That would be fine,' Steffie accepted. 'Or I could always make myself scarce in the garden, and let you and Miles have a proper reunion.'

Miles laughed. 'We can wait. Give Steffie the guided tour, darling, while I check through the mail.'

As they went upstairs Steffie said abruptly, 'I owe you a vote of thanks. I was terrified that Miles was going to turn into a real recluse. Writing's a solitary occupation at the best of times, but he seemed to have no incentive to lead any kind of life outside working hours.' She gave a gleeful grin. 'Yet now here you are engaged to each other. And I couldn't be happier.'

Chessie flushed again. She said constrictedly, 'It's all happened so fast. I'm not really used to it yet.'

'I've been married for ten years,' Steffie said. 'And I still sometimes look at the face on the pillow next to me, and think, Who's that?' She gave a gasp of pure pleasure as Chessie opened a door onto late afternoon sunlight billowing off primrose walls. 'What a lovely room.'

'I've always loved it,' Chessie agreed quietly, putting Steffie's case on the bed.

Steffie gave her a quick glance. 'Was this your room—before? Miles filled me in on some of the background. I hope you don't mind.'

'Of course not.' Chessie made herself speak lightly. 'And—yes—this was mine.'

'Oh, dear,' Steffie said, then brightened. 'But it isn't as if I've turned you out or anything.'

'No. And the housekeeper's flat is really comfortable.'

'The flat?' Steffie was clearly surprised. 'You're not over there, surely?' She shrugged. 'I mean—you and Miles are going to be married. I assumed you'd be sharing more than a roof.'

'I live with my younger sister.' Chessie was suddenly floundering. Burning all over, too. 'It makes things—difficult.'

'I thought she was all grown-up with a love life of her own.' Steffie shrugged. 'But you know best. Or I hope you do.'

She opened her case and pulled out a dress, shaking out the creases. 'I appreciate this is something of a crash course in getting acquainted, but you don't have any reservations about Miles—his injuries?' She gave Chessie a straight glance. 'Because he's been down that road already, and it wasn't good.'

'Yes.' Chessie swallowed. 'He—he was very frank about it.' She glanced round the room. 'I hope you have everything you need.' She gestured awkwardly. 'I—I'll leave you to unpack while I go and talk to Miles.'

'You do that,' Steffie replied cheerfully. 'I'll make sure I sing loudly on my way downstairs.'

Chessie paused outside the study, bracing herself physically and mentally before she went in. Miles was standing by the window, looking out at the garden. He turned slightly as she came in, and smiled at her.

'It's good to be back.'

His smile wrenched at her heart until she could have cried out with the anguish of it. She stiffened slightly, defensively. 'I came to ask whether you wanted tea in the drawing room or the garden.'

'You decide,' he said. He paused, eyeing her meditatively. 'And for the duration of Steffie's visit, could you be primarily my future wife, rather than the paid employee?'

'I don't find it easy,' she said. 'Being a hypocrite.'

'Implying that I do?' The smile had gone. 'If you recall, I asked you to marry me, Chessie—not take part in a charade, which you set in motion.' He paused, allowing her to digest that. 'At least you're wearing your ring.'

She lifted her chin. 'I presumed you'd wish me to.'

'I hoped you'd want to,' he came back at her sharply, then sighed. 'Oh, God, Chessie, this is not what I'd planned. May we start again, please?'

'Perhaps we'd better.' She forced a smile. 'Your sister's very nice.'

'I think so too.' His mouth twisted. 'You must be relieved to find that I'm the only bastard in the family.'

He looked tired, she thought, his eyes shadowed, his facial muscles taut. But then there was an excellent reason for his weariness, and she felt her hands curl into fists at her sides as that swift, uncontrollable pain slashed at her again.

She found herself saying stiltedly, 'Did you enjoy your—time in London?' And waiting, scarcely breathing, for his answer.

'The meetings with Vinnie and the publishers went well.' His tone was matter-of-fact. No guilty look, or sign of evasion. But then—why should there be? Miles had never offered her fidelity, she thought, sinking her teeth into her lower lip. No promise had been broken.

No promise. The thought was an unwanted intruder, invading her mind. *Just my heart...*

'The next three years of my life are certainly spoken for,' he added, while Chessie stood rigid, aghast at this moment of self-revelation. Fighting for a semblance of composure.

She managed to say, over-brightly, 'Your new secretary is going to be kept busy.'

'I'm sure she'll cope.' He was watching her again, his eyes narrowed. He took a step towards her, and she fell back a pace, the wary defiance in her eyes meeting the incredulity in his.

For a few seconds the tension in the silence between them made her nerve-endings jangle.

Then Miles limped across to the Chesterfield and sat down. He said, quietly, 'I'd like you to come here, please, and tell me what's wrong, because clearly there's something. You look like your own ghost.' The cool drawl sharpened in warning. 'And don't put me to the trouble of fetching you, Francesca.'

Chessie complied reluctantly, huddling into the opposite corner, as far away from him as she could manage. She could see from the tightening of his mouth that this wasn't lost on him either, but she couldn't allow herself to worry about it. She was battling for self-preservation here.

'Well?' The blue gaze was piercing.

She said, 'I've seen Jenny's boyfriend.'

'He came here?' His brows rose.

'Oh, no. He was at work—at the big garage on the by-pass.'

He stared at her. 'Are you telling me you walked all that way just to take a look at him?'

'No.' She hesitated. 'As it happens, Alastair was giving

me a lift back from Hurstleigh. I—I'd been shopping, and it came on to rain.'

'How good of him,' Miles said softly. 'But then he is an old friend.'

'He needed petrol,' she went on. 'And that's when I saw him—Zak Woods, I mean.'

'And?'

'Think of your worst nightmare,' Chessie said. 'Then double it.' She raised anguished eyes to his. 'According to Mrs Chubb he's lucky not to have a police record.' She shook her head. 'There's something horrible about him. I don't know how Jenny can bear it.'

'It might just be the attraction of opposites,' he said. 'Or it could be a punishment.'

'Who is she punishing?'

He shrugged. 'Herself, you, the whole world. Who knows?'

'She's going to ruin her life,' Chessie said wretchedly.

'I doubt that. The one good thing about nightmares is that you wake up from them eventually. Or so I've always believed,' he added drily. Then paused. 'So—what else is the matter?'

'I don't know what you mean.' Chessie shook her head, allowing a soft swathe of hair to fall across her suddenly flushed face. Her physical awareness of him—of his nearness—was acute. She was shaking inside, her mouth dry, an unfamiliar ache grinding deep within her.

'I think you do.' He was silent again, and she was aware of his gaze measuring her—lingering...

'I also think,' he went on, a wry twist to his mouth, 'that offering you a breathing space may not have been such a wise move, after all. I—really shouldn't have left you on your own.'

She drew a quick breath. 'That—that's nonsense. And I'd better go,' she added quickly. 'I have things to do— your sister's tea to get.'

Miles shook his head slowly. 'Steffie will wait, I promise. But I can't.'

She was starting to get to her feet as he reached for her. Caught off balance and vulnerable, Chessie found herself pulled backwards, his arms closing round her, so that she fell against him.

Gasping, she tried to struggle, but it was too late. Miles lifted her as if she were a featherweight, settling her, helpless and imprisoned, across his thighs.

'Much better,' he approved softly, smiling down into her outraged face as he lowered his mouth to hers.

She tried to fight him. To deny the hammer of her heart, and the quicksilver heat pulsing in her bloodstream. But she'd forgotten—or tried to forget—the deliberate beguilement of his lips, coaxing her mouth to open for him. And then—the warm, honeyed glide of his tongue against hers.

Her lashes swept down to her flushed cheeks. Her head fell back against his encircling arm as her body arched towards him, mutely, involuntarily.

'My love,' he whispered against her skin. 'My sweet love.'

He kissed her again, deepening his demand, compelling a reciprocation that she was powerless to deny, feeding the hunger he had incited with his first touch.

His lips pressed tiny kisses to her forehead, her cheeks, her eyelids, and the corners of her eager mouth. His hand soothed her throat, moving down to her shoulder, then down again to the first of the pearl buttons that fastened her white shirt.

He released them slowly, kissing her softly and sensuously as he did so, murmuring words of reassurance against her lips as if he recognised the swift, shocked hammer of her heart and sought to allay any last vestige of uncertainty.

The last button undone, Miles pushed the shirt off her shoulder, and looked down at her, his blue eyes slumbrous as they regarded the scraps of white lace that hid her breasts.

'Pretty,' he approved softly, then slid a questing finger under one narrow strap, slipping it down her arm.

'And exquisite,' he added huskily, brushing the loosened cup away from her rose-tipped breast, baring it for his caress.

His hand cupped her as if she had been made to fit his palm, his thumb stroking her nipple with a delicate, rhythmic intensity that brought a small, choked whimper from her throat.

Her body was slackening in his arms, turning boneless as tiny rivers of fire lapped at her nerve-endings, sapping any last thought of resistance.

He bent his head, and she felt the moist flame of his mouth against her inflamed skin, encompassing her, laving the aroused peak to new heights of sensation.

When his lips returned to hers, she welcomed him with passionate eagerness, her arm sliding up round his neck, her hand entwining in his hair to hold him closer yet.

His fingers fondled the curve of her hip, then glided downwards, and she was aware of a sudden, scalding rush of heat between her thighs as her startled flesh responded to the sureness of his touch.

His hand went to the fastening of her jeans, and paused...

He lifted his head, staring down at her, the blue eyes dazed and smoky, his breathing as ragged as her own.

'God, Chessie.' The words were slurred, dragged from his throat. 'What are you doing to me?' He shook his head in a kind of self-derision. 'All the times we've been alone together in this house—and I have to choose now—when my sister could walk in on us at any moment.'

It was reality with a vengeance. And it awoke Chessie to the horrified realisation of exactly what she'd invited.

Gasping, she jerked upright, hands shaking as she tried unavailingly to remedy the disarray in her clothing, and crawl away from him at the same time.

'Let me...'

'No.' She choked the word. 'Don't touch me. Don't dare…'

There was an incredulous silence, then, to her eternal mortification, Miles began to laugh softly.

'Why, Francesca,' he mocked, 'and you said you weren't a hypocrite.'

He got slowly to his feet, and stood, leaning against the arm of the Chesterfield as he watched her.

Knowing that he was nowhere as cool as he looked was no consolation for the total shamelessness of her behaviour either.

And she'd wanted him to go on, Chessie thought wildly as she dragged the edges of her shirt together. Wanted to be naked in his arms, and to give him whatever he asked.

Only that was impossible. Because, no matter how deep her need, the time would soon come when she would have to walk away. And she wanted to be able to do that with her head high, and her pride undamaged.

So, while she remained here in this house, even the slightest physical contact between them had to be strictly taboo from now on.

He said quite gently, 'I'm sorry.'

'I should hope you are,' she flung at him. 'You had no right…'

'You don't understand.' He cut across her. 'I'm sorry only for starting something I didn't finish. That was wrong of me.'

'Everything that happened here was wrong.' Her voice was suffocated. 'But it will never happen again—do you hear me? Otherwise I'm leaving, and to hell with four weeks' notice.'

His brows lifted. 'Do you really need to play the outraged virgin?' he drawled coldly. 'I can't be the first—'

He stopped abruptly, his eyes narrowing suddenly as they studied her flushed embarrassment. Her averted gaze.

He said in a different voice, 'But I am the first, aren't I,

Francesca? So how can that be when you spent a summer with Alastair Markham?'

She lifted her chin. 'Perhaps he had too much respect for me to involve me in casual sex.'

'Is that what you think I was doing just now?' His smile was sardonic. 'Lady, believe me, I was in deadly earnest. And I still am. Because some time soon, despite all your protests, I intend to take you to bed.'

'You flatter me.' Her voice shook, mainly with anger, and that was good. She needed to sustain that anger, use it as a shield against him. Against the knowledge that if he crooked his little finger, she would walk over red-hot coals to him.

And that in spite of the fact that less than twelve hours ago he'd been making love to another woman. Oh, God, how pathetic was it possible to get? And how had she dared censure Jenny when she was equally bad?

She lifted her chin. 'However, I do not intend to be another notch on the bedpost in your—sexual rehabilitation.'

'Meaning?' She'd expected an angry, even explosive response, yet Miles sounded almost amused.

She said with emphasis, 'Meaning—I—will—not sleep with you.'

'Ah,' he said softly. 'But who mentioned sleeping?' He looked at her, and smiled, and for one shocked moment she felt as if he'd stripped all the clothes from her body.

Then he turned and went back to his table, and picked up the sheaf of correspondence lying there.

He said, without looking at her, 'If you're back to being the housekeeper, Chessie, then perhaps you should serve tea.'

She said between her teeth, 'Very well,' and marched to the door. She managed not to slam it behind her, then stood for a moment, leaning weakly against the sturdy panels, her mind reeling.

Why, she asked herself in total bewilderment, had it taken her all this time to realise she was in love with him?

Because it was no sudden thing, and she knew it. Even though she would have probably denied it with her last breath, he had been necessary to her for a long time. And she had hidden behind the barrier of their working relationship, and told herself it was enough.

But I lied, she thought desolately. And now there's nothing left for me but to go on lying.

As she straightened she looked down at herself in sudden dismay, recommencing the struggle to force her shirt buttons back into the relevant holes. She heard a faint noise, and, looking up, saw Steffie poised halfway down the stairs.

'Oh, no,' Chessie moaned under her breath as embarrassed heat swamped her again, and her already clumsy fingers turned into thumbs.

'Oh, dear,' Steffie commented with unabashed amusement. 'I quite forgot to sing.' And, her smile widening, she launched herself into a soft contralto rendering of Marvin Gaye's 'Sexual Healing'.

While Chessie swallowed back the tears threatening to engulf her, nailed on a smile of her own—and tried very hard to share the joke.

CHAPTER EIGHT

ENCOUNTERING Steffie had probably been the best thing that could have happened to her, Chessie decided that night, when she could at last escape to her own part of the house. Otherwise, she would probably have served tea with very red eyes, thus alerting Miles to her emotional state. Which was the last thing she wanted.

On the other hand, Miles' sister was so friendly, and genuinely eager to welcome her to the family, that Chessie felt even more guilty over the deception she was perpetrating.

But guilt was probably easier to deal with than her agony of confusion over Miles.

No matter how professional she'd intended their relationship to be, and how aloof she'd vowed to remain, there had always been pitfalls to living in the same house with a man as dynamic as Miles Hunter. It hadn't been easy, because he could be tricky, but it had never been less than fascinating, throwing up new challenges all the time.

Proximity, she thought wearily, has a lot to answer for.

And, maybe, at the beginning, gratitude had played its part too. Because there was no denying he'd provided her with a roof, a livelihood, and a form of security, even if it was for his own convenience.

There was also, she supposed, the glamour of his status as a best-selling writer, although she knew in her heart it had always been Miles the man she'd been drawn to—and not for purely intellectual reasons either. Because if she'd merely glimpsed him at some social gathering, with no idea who he was, she knew she would have looked—and looked again.

No amount of scarring could diminish his physical attraction in the least, she thought, and Sandie Wells had been worse than an idiot to walk away from him.

All of this an undeniably potent mix for a girl who had as little experience of men as herself.

And small wonder she was lying awake again, wondering what to do next and failing to come up with any answers.

Oh, if I could just turn the clock back, she thought unhappily. I'd have been happy to go on typing and cooking, and never asked for more.

Yet now it was as if someone had opened a door in a high wall, and shown her paradise, and there was no going back to her earlier innocence. Not when she knew what it was to be in Miles' arms and to discover the ravishment of his hands and lips on her body.

Just the memory of that was enough to send a shiver of longing rippling through her senses.

But it could not reconcile her to the prospect of a marriage without real love in it, she thought sadly. And that was all he'd offered, however practised he might be in the art of giving physical pleasure.

She didn't know what he'd been like before his accident, but now there seemed to be a cold core in Miles that she could not reach, and which might explain why romance had no place in his novels.

He doesn't think it matters, she told herself, and that applies to his life as well as his literature. But it matters to me.

He'd called her his 'sweet love', but that was only the language of seduction. He wanted to take her to bed. He'd said so quite openly. It went no deeper than that and perhaps Linnet's cynical advice years ago hadn't been so far off the mark after all.

She turned over, burying her face in her pillow. It would be easier tomorrow, she thought. Miles was taking Steffie sightseeing for the day, and although she'd been invited to go with them she'd refused, inventing an endless list of weekend chores. Miles had given her a thoughtful look, but he hadn't pressed her.

And in the evening, she had the ordeal of dinner at the Court to face, and that was something she couldn't get out of.

Steffie had mentioned it over the evening meal. 'Who are these Markhams, love?' she'd asked Miles. 'And will I like them?'

He'd shrugged, his face inscrutable. 'You'd better ask Francesca,' he commented indifferently. 'They're her friends, rather than mine. I've only just made their acquaintance. And I've never met Sir Robert Markham, or his son, come to that. At least, not officially.'

'I doubt that you'll meet Sir Robert tomorrow either,' Chessie said, biting her lip. 'He's had a severe stroke,' she added to Steffie. 'And he's now in a wheelchair. I don't think he'll be well enough to see people, or that he'd even want to.'

There was an odd, rather strained silence. Then Steffie said quietly, 'I see. How terrible for him, poor man. And for his family, of course.'

Miles' smile was a little remote. 'I think Lady Markham is bearing up in spite of everything—don't you, darling?'

'She has great strength of character,' Chessie agreed evenly. *And not a great deal of choice*, she added under her breath. She reached for the serving dish. 'Would anyone like any more beef?'

Looking back, she was faintly bewildered by the exchange. Did Steffie think she'd been tactless, referring to Sir Robert's physical disability in front of Miles? Had she unwittingly revived bitter memories of the way he used to be?

Surely there was no comparison between their two situations, she thought. Miles might use a walking stick, but he could walk wherever he wanted, drive a car—and make love to any woman who took his fancy, it seemed. Whereas Sir Robert was paralysed, and might remain so.

Besides, Miles could always have refused Linnet's invitation.

Oh, how I wish he had, she thought. For all kinds of reasons.

She was still wishing the same thing the following evening as she changed into one of the new dresses she'd bought in Hurstleigh. It was in a fine silky fabric, patterned with tiny cream daisies on a dark green background, sleeveless and round-necked, with a brief swirl of a skirt falling to just below her knee.

It was the first completely frivolous thing she'd bought in a long time, and she hardly recognised herself as she circled slowly in front of the mirror. But it wasn't just the dress, she thought. Suddenly, she was a girl with secrets in her eyes.

In the back of the wardrobe she found some cream strappy sandals and a matching bag. Relics of her former life. And from the bottom of a drawer, she unearthed a cream shawl with a long fringe, and draped it round her shoulders.

Ready, she told herself, for anything the next few hours might throw at her.

'You look lovely,' Steffie approved, herself elegant in black, when she joined brother and sister in the drawing room. 'Doesn't she, Miles?'

'Quite breathtaking. Have I seen that dress before?'

Chessie shook her head. 'I bought it the other day,' she said. 'In Hurstleigh'

'An eventful trip.' His smile did not reach his eyes.

'And clearly a successful one,' Steffie contributed cheerfully. 'There are no decent clothes shops where I live. When I need something I have to trail up to London.'

She carried on the same line of insouciant chatter on the short drive to the Court, and Chessie was glad of it as she sat silently beside Miles, acutely, almost shamingly aware of him.

The big house was lit up like a Christmas tree. They were admitted by Mrs Cummings, wearing the smart navy uniform that Linnet had always insisted on. And the lady of the house was waiting in the doorway of the drawing room, all smiles. She was wearing another of her figure-hugging dresses in deep crimson jersey, with lips and nails to match.

She looked, Chessie decided dispassionately, like some exotic jungle flower. One of the poisonous variety.

'Miles—so wonderful to see you.' The words poured out like warm treacle. 'And this is your sister, Mrs Barnes? Except that's so formal. Do let's make it Stephanie and Linnet. Oh, Chessie,' she added as an afterthought. 'Good evening. If you're looking for Alastair, he's with his father.'

I wasn't, Chessie thought indignantly. Aloud, she said quietly, 'How is Sir Robert?'

'I'm told he's making progress.' Linnet shrugged. 'I can't see any sign of it, myself. But his nurse seems very good.' She turned to the others. 'The big problem is he's incapable of dealing with his affairs at the moment, and there's no power of attorney. The lawyers are having to set up some emergency procedure, but it takes time, and it's so inconvenient.'

She might have been talking about the cancellation of a hairdressing appointment, Chessie reflected with distaste.

Linnet was targeting her again. 'Why don't you run over to the West Wing, sweetie, and tell Alastair the guests are here? After all, you know the way. You'll find him in the Blue Room.'

Which immediately established her in the same bracket as Mrs Cummings, whose task it should have been, Chessie realised with shock. For her hostess, her smart new dress and the ring on her finger counted for nothing. She was primarily Miles' housekeeper.

She said in a small stony voice, 'Yes—of course.' And left the room.

She was quivering with temper as she went towards the Blue Room, but she made herself calm down. She'd read somewhere that stroke patients needed a tranquil atmosphere, so she didn't want to carry her resentment of Linnet's cavalier behaviour into Sir Robert's sick room.

As she reached the door it opened, and a middle-aged woman in a nurse's uniform emerged carrying a tray covered by a white cloth. She checked when she saw Chessie. 'Can I help you?' She spoke briskly, her eyes shrewd behind her glasses.

'I'm Francesca Lloyd,' Chessie said quietly. 'A—a friend of the family. Lady Markham sent me to fetch her stepson.'

'Chessie?' Alastair's voice was raised questioningly. 'Come in.'

She drew a deep breath, and obeyed.

She was prepared for a shock, but she hadn't bargained for the ruined figure slumped in his wheelchair that confronted her. He was, she thought, barely recognisable, and for a moment dismay halted her, then she made herself smile and walk forward.

'Father.' Alastair bent over him. 'Here's Chessie to see you—Chessie Lloyd.'

She said quietly, 'Good evening, Sir Robert. I don't know if you remember me?'

The sunken eyes stared up at her with puzzled fierceness, then a spark of recognition seemed to dawn, and the sagging mouth struggled to utter a few guttural sounds. Chessie pulled forward a chair and sat down, putting a hand gently over Sir Robert's flaccid fingers. 'It's good to have you back. The village has missed you.'

She launched into a flow of gentle, almost inconsequential chat about what had been going on locally while he'd been in Spain, aware that his eyes were fixed on her face painfully, almost angrily.

Eventually Alastair broke in, a note of impatience in his tone. 'Isn't it time we were going in to dinner, Chessie?'

She glanced up, a little startled. 'Well, yes, but...'

'But Nurse Taylor is waiting to settle my father down

for the night. Besides, he doesn't understand a word you're saying,' he added with a shrug.

'You can't know that,' Chessie objected. She turned back to Sir Robert, and squeezed his hand. 'I hope you'll let me come back and see you again very soon,' she told him softly.

As she followed Alastair to the door she turned back, lifting her hand in farewell, and realised the sick man's gaze was still fixed on her, almost as if he was silently pleading with her. Or was she just being fanciful?

She smiled at Nurse Taylor who was waiting impassively. 'I'm sorry if I've interrupted your routine.'

'Please don't apologise. I'm sure it's done him good,' the older woman returned. She lowered her voice. 'And you're quite right. He understands far more than people credit,' she added, casting a significant glance at Alastair's retreating figure.

As Chessie joined him Alastair sent her a faintly derisive look. 'I never took you for Florence Nightingale, my sweet. Is this something you've learned from coping with your fiancé?'

She stared at him with frank distaste. 'That's a thoroughly unpleasant suggestion. What on earth's happening to you, Alastair?'

He shrugged defensively. 'Sorry, Chess, I'm just a bit wound up. To be honest, bringing Dad back here isn't working—for any of us.'

'But I thought this was where he wanted to be.'

'That was before he had the second stroke.'

'Oh.' Chessie shook her head. 'I didn't realise there'd been more than one.' She halted, gesturing round her. 'But surely being in his own environment again—back in the house he loves…'

'I'm not convinced he knows where he is, whatever that nurse says,' Alastair said moodily. 'After all, it's her job to boost his chances. Where there's life, there's hope and all that.'

'But people do make amazing recoveries...'

'Yes, but at what cost?' he demanded, impatient again. 'This house is a dinosaur. It eats money. And Dad's had so many chances to sell it, even before he went to Spain. A hotel chain were after it, and one of the private health companies, as well as property developers. It has to go, and as far as I'm concerned it should be sooner rather than later. Just as soon as I get control of my father's affairs, in fact.'

'But it's your family home,' Chessie protested. 'There have been Markhams here for generations.'

'Well, here's a Markham that has very different plans.' He saw her white face, the sudden tears in her eyes, and softened his tone. 'Chessie, my father would be far better off in a good nursing home. You must see that.'

'Would he?' she asked bitterly. 'All I can think about is how he'd hate to know these decisions were being made for him. In spite of him, even.' There was a choke in her voice. 'I remember what he was like—before. The way he'd stride about, giving his orders. He was so strong, so full of life, and now he's totally helpless in that ghastly chair—and it's so *awful*,' she added passionately. 'I—I can't bear seeing him like that.'

Alastair put his arms around her, drawing her forward to lean against his shoulder. 'Poor Chess,' he muttered. 'But it's terrible for me, too, you know. And I have to decide what's best for everyone.'

For everyone? Chessie wondered. Or for yourself—and Linnet...

Distressed as she was, she experienced a sudden uneasy prickle of awareness. Looking round, she saw Miles standing at the end of the corridor, leaning on his cane. He was watching them, his face expressionless.

'Oh.' She detached herself hurriedly, aware that she was blushing. 'Alastair—you haven't actually met my fiancé, Miles Hunter.' Her words seemed to tumble over themselves. 'Miles, this is Alastair Markham.'

Miles limped forward, extending his hand. 'How do you

do?' he said with cool politeness. 'Lady Markham wanted you to know that dinner is served.'

'Oh, dear. Have we kept you all waiting?' Alastair smiled with easy charm. 'But Chessie and I had things to talk over.' He gave her a swift, almost caressing smile. 'I'd better go and grovel to Stepmother.'

He disappeared, leaving Chessie and Miles alone together.

There was a taut silence. Then: 'That,' Chessie said in a fierce whisper, 'was *not* what you think.'

'Unless you've become a mind-reader,' Miles drawled scornfully, 'you can't possibly know what I think.'

'I can make an educated guess,' she flung back at him. 'But you're wrong. His father's in a bad way, almost completely paralysed, and I was upset, that's all.' She dragged a hand across her damp cheeks. 'I just wasn't prepared—not when I remember how things used to be...' she added in a muffled voice.

'I'm sorry,' Miles said quietly, after a lengthy pause. 'It can't be easy for you.'

'I'll survive.' She lifted her chin, forcing a smile. 'Now I'd better do something about my face.' And she walked quickly away.

The meal that followed did little to raise her spirits. Linnet dominated the conversation, talking with open discontent about the wonderful life she'd been forced to abandon in Spain, and how she couldn't wait to return.

Which would happen, Chessie supposed bitterly, when Wenmore Court was sold to the highest bidder, and Sir Robert was safely hidden away in some private facility.

She sighed quietly, then looked up to find Miles' reflective gaze fixed on her. She offered him a tentative smile, but it was not returned. Instead he turned to Linnet with some bread and butter question about the Spanish property market.

She bit her lip, then switched her attention to Alastair. 'Is the Midsummer Party still going ahead?'

He offered her more wine, and, when she declined, filled his own glass. 'We thought we'd give it a whirl,' he agreed carelessly. 'Go out on a high note. There isn't time to organise the usual full-scale fête, of course. So it will just be the evening party.'

To which I was never invited, Chessie thought.

'Which reminds me,' Linnet broke in. She gave Miles a seductive smile, making great play with her eyelashes. 'As the party's for charity, I thought it would be fun to have a celebrity speaker during supper. Just ten minutes' light chat about past career and future plans, you know the kind of thing. And you'd be ideal.' She put a coaxing hand on his arm. 'So you will be a darling, and help us out, won't you?'

'I'm afraid not,' Miles returned, unmoved. 'I'll gladly make a donation, but I don't do public appearances.'

'But you've no need to feel self-conscious,' Linnet purred. 'And nearly everyone there will be local, so they'll understand, anyway.'

Chessie found she was holding her breath, but Miles was imperturbable.

'Thank you for being so reassuring,' he said, 'but my answer still has to be "no".' He paused. 'For one thing, I'm not sure what my plans will be around that time.'

'Oh, well.' Linnet gave a fatalistic shrug. 'I'll have to think of something else. Unless of course you were sweet enough to change your mind,' she added with another dazzling smile. 'But I suppose that's too much to hope for.'

'I'm convinced of it,' Miles said gently, and changed the subject.

Leaving Chessie to ponder exactly what those plans he'd referred to might be…

'Did you say these people were friends of yours?' Steffie enquired caustically.

Dinner was over, and Linnet had swept both her female guests up to her bedroom 'to freshen up' as she'd coyly put it. She'd left them there to their own devices, merely telling them that there would be coffee in the drawing room when they came down.

Chessie fiddled with her lipstick. 'Not exactly,' she returned reluctantly. 'The summer I left school, I spent some time with Alastair, that's all.'

Steffie's brows lifted. 'Really? Was it serious?'

'I thought so then. But it was just a boy/girl thing. It petered out when his father sent him to business school in America.' She hesitated. 'I don't actually think Sir Robert approved, anyway.'

'I see.' Steffie dabbed scent on her wrists. Her voice was level. 'And is that why you were gone for such ages before dinner—because you were catching up on old times?'

'No, of course not. I was trying to talk to Sir Robert.' She shook her head. 'He seemed to know who I was, but it wasn't easy. He can't move—or speak.'

Steffie was silent for a long moment, then she said quietly, 'That—does not bear thinking about. Poor man.'

She sighed abruptly, then determinedly took herself in hand. 'So what about the glamorous Lady Markham, then?' She glanced round her surroundings with unholy appreciation. 'I suppose this is what they mean by a boudoir. I love the curtained bed and fluffy rugs—just like an old-fashioned Hollywood film set. I keep expecting someone to shout "Camera! Action!"' She chuckled. 'The tub for two in the *en suite* bathroom is fairly special, as well.' She paused, thoughtfully. 'I wonder who shares it with her.'

'I suppose Sir Robert used to.' Chessie tried to visualise this, and failed. In fact, she couldn't imagine him forging a path through the bedroom's floating draperies either.

Steffie put her scent back in her bag, and closed it. 'Did you tell Miles how bad he was?' Her tone was over-casual.

'I didn't really have a choice. He could see I was upset.' Chessie gave her a puzzled look. 'Why do you ask?'

Steffie sighed again. 'It's just that it could have stirred up a hornet's nest for him.' She hesitated. 'Has he told you why he still walks with a limp?'

'He rarely mentions any of it.'

'After the incident, they had to operate to remove steel fragments, and the X-rays showed one piece embedded near his spine.' Steffie's face relived the nightmare. 'He was told that removing it was not going to be easy, and that even if they succeeded there was a fifty-fifty chance that he'd be left paralysed.'

She shuddered. 'It was a ghastly possibility, and he was emotionally shattered anyway, while Sandie was having hysterics all over the place, so—he told them not to risk it.' She gave Chessie a wan smile. 'But it's still a sensitive topic.'

'Yes,' Chessie said slowly. 'I—I can see it would be. I'm glad you told me.'

'However, it's well in the past,' Steffie continued more robustly. 'And now he has the future to look forward to— with you. So no need to raise it, really—unless he does.'

No, Chessie thought as she followed her downstairs. No need at all.

She couldn't wait for the evening to be over, but it seemed to drag on for ever. In the drawing room, she found that Linnet had stationed herself next to Miles on one of the sofas, and embarked on the kind of murmured conversation that required her to lean intimately towards him, and touch his arm a lot.

Alastair, looking moody, was fiddling with the small pile of sheet music on top of the grand piano.

'Chessie—do you remember this?' He'd picked up one of the pieces, and was beckoning to her. Reluctantly she went over to him. 'It's that duet we used to play.' He smiled at her coaxingly. 'Shall we try it out again?'

'Oh, no,' she protested. 'I—I haven't played the piano in years. I really can't...'

'Of course you can.' He was arranging the music on the stand, placing the piano stool correctly. 'Come on, it'll be fun.'

'Yes, why not?' Steffie urged, smiling. 'Did you know your fiancée could play the piano, Miles?'

His smile was cool, almost cynical. 'No, but then Chessie has so many little secrets.'

Biting her lip, she joined Alastair on the piano stool. It was the kind of bravura piece that sounded more difficult than it actually was, and after a nervous start she acquitted herself well.

'There you are.' Alastair gave her a lingering smile as the others applauded. 'Perfect harmony.'

Chessie wanted to scream.

'Well, that was a barrel of laughs,' Steffie observed as the car made its way down the drive at last. 'Lady Markham was paying you a lot of attention, brother dear. Practising for when she's a merry widow?'

'I don't think she needs to.' Miles' tone was sardonic. 'I'd say her plans are already made.'

When they reached Silvertrees, Steffie excused herself almost immediately, and went to bed. 'Too much excitement is bad for me,' she explained.

'And what about you, Francesca?' Miles said softly when she'd gone. 'Are you going to be too excited to sleep tonight?'

'Why should I be?'

He shrugged. 'You had quite an eventful time. That was—a virtuoso performance you gave.'

'My piano playing has never been more than mediocre,' she denied curtly.

'Ah,' he said. 'But perhaps I wasn't talking about the duet.'

'Then say what you really mean.' Chessie rounded on him with sudden fierceness. 'Because I've had it up to here tonight. I was snubbed by that bitch,' she went on hotly. 'I had to watch someone I once respected suffering and helpless. And to cap it all, the Court's going to be sold off—

as ghastly flats or something—and—and they're all going to leave…'

And, to her own surprise, she burst into tears.

Miles said wearily, 'Oh, dear God.' He led her over to a sofa, made her sit, pressed an immaculate handkerchief into her hand, and brought her a glass of brandy as she sat, hiccuping, her eyes streaming.

'No, drink it,' he directed as she tried to demur.

She wanted him to sit beside her so that she could throw herself into his arms and weep all down his shirt, but he took a seat on the sofa opposite instead.

After a while, he said, 'You really care, don't you?'

'I didn't think so.' She drank some of the brandy. 'But I suppose I must.'

How can I explain, she thought, that Sir Robert's face doesn't belong to him any more, and his clothes all seem too big as if he's shrunk? And instead of being the master in his own house, he's just a nuisance that they'll shunt into a home and forget, because Linnet wants to go back to Spain, and Alastair's got a job in the City, and they're both vile and shallow.

And, worst of all, how I keep thinking that it could be you in that wheelchair, unable to move. You—my dear love…

And that is the unbearable thing. Which I cannot tell you because I'm not supposed to know.

She put down the glass. 'I'm sorry. I've behaved like an idiot. I—I'll go to bed now.'

She rose, and Miles got to his feet too.

He said, 'Goodnight, Francesca. I hope you sleep well.'

She looked across at him, and everything she felt for him—all that she longed for and desired to give—roared through her suddenly like a flood-tide. Carrying her away…

And she heard her own voice saying, 'May I sleep with you tonight?'

There was a silence, then he said quietly, 'No, that wouldn't be a good idea.'

She tried to smile, but it turned into a grimace instead. 'Don't you—want me?'

'Yes,' he said. 'Far too much, indeed, to offer you the kind of comfort you seem to need tonight.'

'It isn't that…'

'No?' His brows lifted. 'Frankly, I don't think you know how you feel.' He paused. 'I'm not a saint, Francesca, nor am I in the mood for the initiation of an inexperienced girl. My needs, this evening, are very different. I don't think I could handle the inevitable aftermath, either,' he added drily. 'Believe me, things are best left as they are.'

'Yes,' she said. 'I—I'm sorry.' His handkerchief was a damp ball, crushed in her hand. She felt numb now, but soon the pain would begin, and for that she needed to be alone. Because she could not let him see…

She looked at him, her lips moving in a small, meaningless smile. 'Well—goodnight.'

I have to get out of here, she thought. *I have to get out before I fall on my knees and beg him to take me, here on the floor.*

'Chessie.' His voice was suddenly husky. 'Listen—I want you to understand…'

'I do,' she said. 'Really. You don't need to explain any more. And I'll try not to embarrass you again.'

Walking away was easy, she discovered. Just a matter of putting one foot in front of another until, somehow, she reached the door, and could close it behind her.

And then, one clenched fist bruising her lips, she ran.

CHAPTER NINE

ON ANY normal Sunday, Chessie could have avoided Miles, of course, because it was part of her jealously guarded free time. But Steffie's presence changed everything. So, she would have to come out of hiding, and make coffee, and cook lunch, and say goodbye at some point in the afternoon—and pretend all the while that she weren't dying inside.

She had no idea how she was going to face Miles, as she would soon have to do. She had fled from him the previous night, humiliated beyond belief, and had spent much of the night pacing round her small sitting room, trying to come to terms with what had happened.

In a strange way, it was his kindness that had hit her the hardest. He had obviously been trying to let her down gently.

But would it really have made her feel any better if he'd told her with brutal honesty that his sexual needs were being satisfied elsewhere by an infinitely more sophisticated partner?

Just the thought was enough to send her anguished mind wincing into limbo.

But before she'd allowed her tired body and reeling mind to sleep last night, she'd managed to make a few big decisions.

And the first and most important was that she would never make such a fool of herself again. Never again be a suppliant to a man who had nothing to give. In that way, she might be able to salvage a few rags of pride.

In addition, whatever job she took would only be temporary, she told herself. As soon as Jenny started college, she would start again too. Go right away somewhere—maybe abroad, and forge a whole new life for herself.

And teach herself to forget the old one.

It would not be easy. Every time she walked past a book-stand anywhere in the world, she'd probably see Miles Hunter's name emblazoned there. And memory of this brief time would claw at her again.

But slowly—gradually—she would become accustomed. Even hardened. And then one day, far in the future, she would cease to care at all.

She dusted and vacuumed the flat, then showered and changed into her navy skirt and a matching short-sleeved top. She pulled her newly washed hair back from her face, and confined it at the nape of her neck with a silver clasp.

This was the image she would present from now on—businesslike and practical. And aloof.

When she reached the main house, she found the study door was firmly shut, and from behind it she heard the staccato rattle of typewriter keys.

Steffie was stretched out on one of the drawing room sofas with the Sunday papers spread around her.

'I thought Sunday was supposed to be a day of rest,' she complained languidly. 'Yet my dear brother was down here at dawn, giving that machine of his serious grief.'

'He's at a critical point in the book,' Chessie offered rather lamely.

'Really?' Steffie's smile was catlike. 'Now I'd attributed it to a totally different cause.' She gave Chessie a shrewd look. 'Did you two have a fight last night?'

Chessie bit her lip. 'Absolutely not.'

'You didn't take exception to Miss Deadly Nightshade 1980 coming on to him last night? And he didn't comment on the amount of attention the boy tycoon was paying you in return?' Steffie cast her eyes to the ceiling. 'I thought there'd be blood on the carpet this morning.'

'I've known the Markhams a long time,' Chessie said. 'And Miles—understands that.'

'Does he?' Steffie's voice was tart. 'Then he must have developed powers of tolerance that I've never suspected.'

'Well, we all change.' Chessie gave her a brief, brittle smile. 'Would you like your coffee served in here?'

'In other words—mind my own business.' Steffie swung her legs off the sofa. 'But I'll come along to the kitchen, if that's all right. The amazingly understanding Miles doesn't wish to be disturbed, and I can lend a hand with lunch.'

She gave Chessie a companionable pat on the shoulder. 'And don't look so worried, sugar. The inquisition is over for the day.'

She was as good as her word. In the kitchen, she was deft and competent, chatting about recipes, and the problems of cooking for a family none of whom seemed to like the same food.

'I'm not in the way, am I?' she broke off at one point to enquire.

'No—really.' Chessie hastened to assure her. She smiled. 'It's such a novelty, having someone to chat with while I'm cooking.'

'Not your sister?'

'Heavens, no.' Chessie pulled a face. 'You'd never find Jenny within a mile of a stove.' She shook her head. 'I don't know how she'll cope when she goes to college.'

'I have news for you,' Steffie told her solemnly. 'Very few students die of starvation—even in the first year.' She paused. 'Isn't she joining us for lunch?'

'She's gone to a friend's house for some last-ditch revision. Her exams start tomorrow.' At least that was what Chessie hoped she was doing. Any mention of Zak Woods had become taboo.

It would be good to confide in Steffie and ask her advice, but also pointless as they were unlikely to meet again.

Life could be very unfair, Chessie thought ruefully, scraping carrots. Just as she'd found a woman she'd have liked as a friend, she was about to lose her again.

'Well, I think a glass of sherry is called for,' Steffie commented with satisfaction as lunchtime approached.

'Not for me, thanks,' Chessie said quickly. 'Perhaps you'd tell Miles that everything's ready while I dish up.'

She'd made a creamy cauliflower soup, to be followed by roast beef and Yorkshire pudding, and a lemon meringue pie was waiting on its serving dish. It all looked and smelled wonderful, and she wouldn't care if another morsel of food never passed her lips.

From the doorway, Miles said softly, 'Running away again, Francesca?'

She did not look round. Her voice taut, she said, 'I'm serving lunch. That's what happens when you have a guest. And I am the housekeeper.'

'To hell with lunch. We need to talk.'

'About last night?' She concentrated fiercely on stirring the soup. 'There's nothing to discuss.'

'I think there is.' His voice gentled. 'I want to explain…'

'No.' She almost slammed down the spoon. 'I don't want your explanations—or your sympathy. I'm not the first person to find herself in love with the wrong man. It happens.' She shrugged. 'I'll get over it.'

'You do realise, then, that it can't work?' He sounded almost surprised. 'You've accepted that—in spite of everything?'

'Yes, of course.' She took a bowl from the warming oven, and poured the soup into it. 'But last night had nothing to do with it. I—found out some time ago.'

'I was afraid you'd be hurt,' he said quietly. 'And you are. I shall always regret that. But remember this, Francesca, you need never settle for second-best.'

'Advice to treasure.' She turned a brief glittering smile on him. 'Now perhaps you'd take Steffie into the dining room. Unless you have any more worldly wisdom to pass on, of course?'

Miles took a step towards her, and for a frantic moment she thought he was going to touch her, and knew that the

mere brush of his hand would be enough to destroy her—
to smash her into small, bleak fragments.

She said hoarsely, *'No'* and recoiled, her white face daring him to come any closer.

He stopped instantly, staring at her, his lips parting in shock and disbelief.

He looked, she realised, almost haggard, and for a moment her heart lurched. Then she was back in control, loading the steaming bowl and the soup plates onto a tray.

In a voice that seemed to belong to someone else, she said, 'If you'll take Stephanie into the dining room—please...'

Without another word, he turned and limped away, leaving her to follow with the tray.

It was going to be one of the worst meals of her life, she thought apprehensively as she ladled out the soup. Miles' face looked as if it had been carved from granite. And she herself felt as if she were balanced on a knife-edge.

She saw Stephanie give both of them a quick glance, then launch airily into a series of reminiscences about her working days. She too had been a journalist, Chessie discovered, but on various magazines rather than a newspaper, and her verbal portraits of some of the celebrities she'd interviewed were wickedly funny.

Even Miles' set expression had relaxed into a faint smile, although he took little part in the conversation himself. But then, under normal circumstances, he wouldn't have come to lunch at all when he was working, Chessie reflected. Instead, he'd have asked her to slice off some of the beef and put it in a sandwich he could eat in his study.

She forced herself to eat, to offer second helpings, and accept praise for her cooking. While inside she felt cold and numb.

Because, presently, Steffie would be gone, and she would be alone with Miles again.

And, as if on cue, Steffie glanced at her watch. 'It's time

I was leaving for the station, brother, dear, or my family will think I've been abducted by aliens.'

At the front door, she gave Chessie a fierce hug. 'I've told Miles, he must bring you to stay—meet the monsters on their home territory.' She paused, lowering her voice. 'And don't worry. Everything will work out, you'll see.'

Chessie stood in the doorway, waving goodbye as Miles' car moved down the drive, her face aching with the effort to smile.

Once the door was shut, she flew into action, clearing the table and loading the dishwasher. Tidying the dining room and returning the drawing room to its usual pristine elegance.

I have to be out of the house before Miles comes back. Have to…

The words ran in her head like some feverish mantra.

The clearing-up done, Chessie changed swiftly into jeans and a sweatshirt, and went quickly and quietly out of the rear gate, and up into the birch woods behind the house.

The sun glinted down on her through the slender branches, and she could hear the throaty murmurings of woodpigeons as she walked briskly, hands in pockets.

At the top of the rise, she turned and looked back, and saw the roof of the house through the sheltering trees.

There had been a time when to leave it behind would have been an unbearable wrench. Now, she could not wait to get away.

If only, she thought, her memories could so easily be left behind. But, like this ache in her heart, they would be with her always. Even, she realised with a kind of helpless desolation, if she went to the ends of the earth.

'They've had valuation people round at the Court.' Mrs Chubb wagged her head. 'Looks like Madam's planning to sell up.' She snorted. 'Scandalous, I call it. If Sir Robert had his health and strength, he'd soon give them their marching orders.'

'But he is getting better,' Chessie protested. 'Now that he's having regular physiotherapy, he's got movement back in his hand and arm. Only it's a slow process.'

'Too slow to save the Court, I reckon,' Mrs Chubb said ominously. 'And not everyone there is glad to see the gentleman improve either.'

'Mrs Chubb,' Chessie said uncomfortably, 'you really mustn't…'

'Mark my words,' the lady returned magisterially. 'That Nurse Taylor was saying the other day, he'd be hard up for visitors, his own flesh and blood included, but for you—and Mr Hunter, of course.'

Chessie, who was making coffee, nearly spilled boiling water on the stove. 'Miles visits Sir Robert?' she exclaimed, and could have kicked herself for betraying her astonishment.

Mrs Chubb nodded with satisfaction. 'Almost as regular as yourself. Reads the paper to him, and such.' She gave Chessie a shrewd look. 'He hasn't told you, then.'

Chessie put the coffee-pot on its stand. She said coolly, 'He probably mentioned it. But he doesn't have to account to me for every minute of his day, Mrs Chubb.'

Nor did he, she thought unhappily as she carried his coffee to the study a little while later.

They were right back to the early days of their working relationship, with Miles behind a barrier of aloof courtesy she found it impossible to breach. And telling herself over and over again that this was for the best did nothing to assuage the pain of it.

She sometimes wondered if the events of the past weeks had simply been a preposterous dream. But the ring that she still wore, at his brusque insistence, told her differently. And so did the ache in her heart.

Not that she was allowed a great deal of time for introspection, she admitted almost gratefully.

Miles was driving himself harder than ever to finish the current book—almost as if he were out to break some kind of record. And he was being incredibly tough on himself, too, making constant alterations and revisions. For the first time since she'd started working for him, Chessie was pushed to keep up.

But it wasn't all graft, she reminded herself with difficulty. Miles had paid another two visits to London, each time remaining overnight. So he was allowing himself some rest and recreation at least, even if she was left in sleepless torment, at the mercy of her too-vivid imagination.

As she reached the hall the front door bell sounded imperiously. She put the tray down on a side table and went to answer its summons. She was frankly taken aback to find Linnet waiting.

'Is Miles at home?' The older woman walked past her. 'Ah, I can see he is,' she added, spotting the coffee-pot and cups. 'Why don't I kill two birds with one stone and take this in for you?'

'But he's working,' Chessie intervened desperately. 'He really can't be interrupted.'

'Nonsense,' Linnet said lightly. 'You must try to be less possessive, my sweet.' And she opened the study door, and carried in the tray, Chessie trailing behind her apprehensively.

'Darling Miles...' Linnet's voice and smile were appealing '...Chessie seemed to think you were too busy to see me. Surely not.'

'I'm honoured.' Miles rose awkwardly, reaching for his cane. 'Bring another cup, will you, Francesca?'

'There are two on the tray,' Chessie said quietly. 'I'll have my coffee later.'

'Don't go, Chessie.' Linnet disposed herself gracefully on the Chesterfield. 'This concerns you too.' She produced a large square envelope from her bag, and handed it to Miles with a flourish. 'Your invitation to the summer party.'

'Thank you.' His brows lifted. 'Is the post office on strike?'

'Oh, I wanted to bring it in person—to make sure you're going to accept. I was saying to my stepson how little we've seen of you over the past couple of weeks. I hope you're not becoming a recluse.'

'On the contrary, I've been out a great deal—much of the time at the Court,' Miles returned silkily. 'However we seem to keep missing each other.'

For one joyous moment, Chessie saw Linnet actually disconcerted, but she soon recovered. 'What a shame, but of course I'm frantically busy with the arrangements for the party. Dashing here, there and everywhere. I've decided to have tombola during supper—but with more interesting prizes than the usual cans and bottles.'

She gave Miles an arch look. 'I hope I can persuade you to contribute this time. A signed copy of your latest book, perhaps?'

'Willingly. Would you like it now?' Miles returned courteously. He walked over to the shelf, and took down one of the hardbacks, scribbling his name on the flyleaf.

'Perfect.' Linnet gave him a honeyed smile as she accepted it. 'All I need now is someone fabulous to run the tombola for me.' She paused. 'And I was wondering about Sandie Wells.'

His face expressionless, Miles poured out the coffee and handed her a cup. 'It's your party,' he said. 'Do as you think best.'

Linnet sighed. 'I haven't seen her in ages, of course. I suppose she'll be trying to get her career back on track, poor sweet, now that her marriage is on the rocks.' She gave him a limpid look. 'Could you ask her for me, darling?'

Chessie realised she was holding her breath, her eyes fixed painfully on Miles' impassive face.

He said quietly, 'I think it would be far better if you approached Sandie through Jerry Constant, her agent.'

Linnet sighed again. 'Well—perhaps. But I haven't finally decided to ask her, of course. I may run the tombola myself, along with everything else.'

She pulled a little face. 'I'd forgotten what a chore this party is to organise,' she confided. 'And Mrs Cummings isn't being as helpful as she could be either.

'Which brings me to you, Chessie,' she went on, smiling. 'I was wondering if you'd lend me your housekeeping skills for the party, and take over some of the catering. Nothing too onerous, of course—mostly buffet fodder. I'll be able to give you the numbers in a couple of days.'

'I think you forget,' Miles said gently. 'Chessie is in my full-time employment.'

She twinkled charmingly. 'But she can't have all that much to do,' she objected. 'Because a little bird tells me she can't keep away from the Court either. So, if you could just loan her to me for a few hours…'

'Quite impossible, I'm afraid. If Chessie wishes to attend the party, it will be with me, as my fiancée.' He looked at Chessie, his brows lifting, a challenge in his blue eyes. 'Well, darling? Do you want to go?'

'Of course,' Chessie said quietly. 'I wouldn't miss it.' *Especially if Sandie Wells is going to be there…*

Linnet was simply mischief-making. She was sure of it. And although Miles had given nothing away, it must have had some effect on him.

Was it news to him that his former love had ended her marriage—or had he known already?

Suddenly, Chessie found herself remembering those mysterious letters. The woman's voice on the phone at the London flat.

Was it—could it be possible that Sandie Wells was back in Miles' life again? And was he the reason Sandie's marriage was over?

However desperate she was to find out, Chessie knew she could never ask. And jealousy, dark and despicable, twisted inside her like the blade of a poisoned knife.

'Maybe the landlady at The White Hart could help out with the food instead,' Miles was suggesting blandly.

'At her prices?' Linnet asked with something of a snap. 'I don't think so. Our other expenses are incredibly heavy, now, with the fees these agency nurses charge, and all this physiotherapy that does no good at all.'

'I gather Nurse Taylor wouldn't agree with you,' Miles said drily. 'She's delighted with the progress your husband is making. And she should know,' he added. 'She's worked with Sir Philip Jacks at the Kensington Foundation, which deals with whole numbers of stroke patients in addition to its other services.'

There were angry spots of colour in Linnet's cheeks. 'Oh, she's highly qualified, no doubt. I just don't want her giving my poor Robert false hope.'

'No,' Miles said quietly. 'I agree that would be cruel. But I'd say she prefers to deal in even chances.' He paused. 'Was there anything else? Would you like some more coffee?'

'Oh, please don't let me keep you.' Linnet drained her cup, and put it down. 'I have a thousand things to do. See you next week at the party,' she added brightly.

Miles was studying the elaborately engraved card when Chessie returned having seen their unwanted guest off the premises.

He said, 'What exactly have we let ourselves in for?'

'Not a great deal.' Chessie bit her lip. 'It used to be a much more elaborate affair, with all the local organisations running stalls and sideshows in the grounds during the afternoon. But this time, it's just drinks and dancing in a marquee on the lawn, and supper, of course.'

'Which will not be provided by you.'

'No.' She hesitated. 'I wouldn't have minded helping, you know.'

'I think we've done quite enough for charity with the cost of this ticket.' He tossed it onto his table, then paused. 'Don't sell yourself short, Francesca,' he added curtly.

'You're not cheap labour.' He paused, giving her a meditative glance. 'How's the job hunt going, by the way?'

'Oh, there are a few possibilities,' Chessie said, waiting for her nose to grow six inches. 'It's just a question of choosing the one with the best prospects.'

She'd applied to two agencies offering residential posts only to be told categorically that she was far too young. The latest rejection letter had arrived that morning.

'I'm sure it is.' Miles spoke abstractedly. He was already sitting at his table, feeding a sheet of paper into the typewriter, his attention clearly elsewhere.

But was he thinking solely about work, or had more personal matters intruded?

Whatever, she could consider herself dismissed, she thought flatly as she removed the tray.

At the door, she paused, a thousand questions milling in her head.

As if aware of her gaze, he glanced round. 'Yes?' The question was curt—almost as if he was warning her off. Forbidding her to probe too deeply.

She found herself saying, 'I—I didn't realise you were visiting Sir Robert as well.'

'Why should you? I went originally to pay my respects, which I signally failed to do when we were there for dinner,' he added, his mouth tightening. 'It was time for the nurse's break, but no one turned up to relieve her, so I filled in.' He looked at her, brows raised. 'Is it a problem for you?'

'No,' she said. 'On the contrary.' *Considering what Steffie told me, I thought you might be the one having the difficulty.* 'It—it's kind of you.'

His lip curled. 'Well, don't sound so surprised, Francesca. I am capable of the odd selfless action. I even gave your sister a lift home from school yesterday.'

'She didn't mention it.' Chessie looked at him with misgiving. 'Was she all right?'

'She was preoccupied but polite. Something of an advance, you'll agree.'

'Yes.' She paused, brow furrowed. 'I don't think her exams are going too well.'

'And when they're over, is she going to revert to snarling and sulking?'

'I hope not,' Chessie said, encouraged by the fact he was smiling faintly. 'But I can't guarantee a thing.'

Back in the hall, she leaned against the door panels for a moment, waiting for her heartbeat to settle down again before she took the tray to the kitchen.

She was thankful he would never know how deeply she yearned to have the right to touch him—to kiss the tiredness from his eyes. And—the sadness too. That, she thought, most of all.

And how she wanted quite desperately to beg him not to go away again.

But that, she thought, would be crying for the moon. And, anyway, she would be the next to leave—if she could just find somewhere to go.

Leaving him free to do exactly as he wished, she thought, and felt the knifeblade turn again.

'I can't believe you've done this.' Jenny glared at her accusingly. 'You've actually made us homeless?'

'Not exactly.' Chessie tried to make the impossible sound reasonable. 'I've managed to find a bedsit in Hurstleigh. It's big enough for us both, but not very glamorous. But the landlady says she'll let us do some redecorating at our own expense.'

'Well, yippee.' Her sister's voice dripped with sarcasm. 'And how do we afford that—as you're giving up your job as well?'

Chessie hesitated. 'I'm going to be working at The White Hart on a temporary basis,' she said. 'The Fewstons need help with food preparation, and I'll do some waiting on tables as well.' She pinned on a smile. 'We'll manage.'

'Manage?' Jenny echoed derisively. 'Baby, you're out of your tree.'

No, thought Chessie with great weariness. Just at the end of my tether.

Aloud, she said, 'Jenny—it's all I could get. But it's not for ever.'

'You had this.' Jenny gestured round the flat. 'And you had The Ogre too. You were going to marry him, for God's sake. What's happened?'

Chessie hesitated. 'We—decided to call it off. So—I need to move on.'

A few terse words to encompass all the anguish, betrayal and heart-searching that had really gone on, she thought sadly.

'In other words, he's throwing us out. And just when I was beginning to think he might be semi-human after all,' Jenny said bitterly. 'But no. Lo and behold—he's a bastard.'

'No, he isn't.' Chessie was fierce. 'And I won't have you say that. It—it's a mutual decision. And you've always hated being here, anyway.'

'It's better than some slum in Hurstleigh, with you slaving in a pub for peanuts,' Jenny hit back. 'Well, don't expect me to go with you, Chess. I'm going to ask Linda's parents if I can stay with them. Linda's going to work, packing boxes at her father's factory during the holidays, and there's a job for me too if I want. I'm going to ring now, and tell them yes.'

And left Chessie sitting limply at the kitchen table with the sound of a slammed door ringing in her ears.

She got tiredly to her feet, and began to make herself some coffee. She'd always known that there'd be uproar when she finally told Jenny about the change in their circumstances, but there was simply no way she could conceal it any longer. Her time at Silvertrees was running out like the sand through an hourglass.

All this, she thought, and Linnet's damned party too.

She glanced through the kitchen window at the relentlessly blue sky, and wondered why it was that weather never seemed to reflect one's mood—or wishes. She'd prayed fervently for a monsoon, that would threaten to flood the giant marquee and force the whole thing to be called off. And, more importantly, ensure that she would not have to make her final public appearance as Miles' fiancée.

Her only consolation was the news, gleaned from Mrs Chubb, that their local MP's pretty red-haired daughter was running the tombola. So Sandie Wells was still just a few scraps of paper and a disembodied voice.

Maybe it would be better to see her face to face, she thought. Know your enemy.

She didn't have a clue what she was going to wear tonight. She supposed it would have to be the flowered dress again, although it wasn't really smart enough. And no doubt Linnet would recognise it instantly, and make some bitchy remark.

But that, she thought unhappily, was the least of her troubles.

Sandie Wells might not be present at the party, but Chessie was sure she was never far from Miles' thoughts. He'd been more than usually preoccupied during the last week, and it wasn't just the end of the book that was absorbing his attention. Clearly there were big decisions to be made—and ones he was not prepared to share with her.

Even the coffee tasted bitter today, and, grimacing, she poured it away and braced herself for the rest of the day.

She'd expected Miles to be working, finalising and refining the last chapter, but he was standing by the study window, deep in thought again, when she entered.

She said, 'I've brought the mail.'

'Leave it on the table.' He didn't look round. 'I'll deal with it later.'

She hesitated. 'You haven't forgotten it's the party at the Court tonight.'

Say you can't go, she willed him silently. Tell me you've still got too much work on the manuscript.

'On the contrary.' He dashed her hopes. 'I wouldn't miss it for the world either. And I have something for you.' He bent awkwardly, retrieving a large flat box that had been hidden behind his table.

'For me?' Chessie received it, startled. 'Do I open it?'

'Only if you want to see what's inside.'

Biting her lip, Chessie complied. Hidden inside the folds of tissue was a drift of creamy silk. She shook it free, and held it up, gasping a little. It was a dress, with narrow shoulder straps supporting a straight-cut bodice, which flowed down into a full-length gracefully fluted skirt. There was a matching jacket too, slender and reaching to her hips.

Miles said, 'It is your size. I checked with Jenny.'

For a long moment, she stared at the lovely thing, feeling her throat tighten uncontrollably, then quietly she replaced it in its sheltering tissue.

'You don't like it?'

She said in a low voice, 'It's beautiful—but I can't accept it.'

'Why not? Your notice hasn't run out yet, so we're still officially engaged, and we're making a very public appearance together tonight.' He shrugged. 'I thought your courage might need a boost. Or regard it as a uniform if that makes it easier.' His voice hardened. 'But you will wear it for me, Francesca, even if I have to dress you with my own hands, and that's an order.'

Her eyes snapped to his dark face in outrage—and sudden pleading. But there was no softening in the blue eyes.

'An order,' he repeated softly.

She replaced the lid on the box, and stepped back, tucking it under her arm.

'Very well—' her voice bit '—sir.' She paused. 'May I go now, please?'

He said grimly, 'I think you'd better—before you make me really angry. In fact, take the rest of the day off.' He limped to his table, and sat down. 'But be ready in the hall at eight, please,' he flung over his shoulder. 'And smile, darling, this evening. After all, you won't have many more of them to endure in my company.'

'No.' Chessie lifted her chin defiantly, hurting and wanting to hurt in return. 'And the sure and certain knowledge of that is all that makes—any of this—remotely bearable. Believe me, I'm counting the days.'

And she whirled, and almost ran from the study, banging the door behind her as she went.

CHAPTER TEN

TO CHESSIE'S frustration, the dress looked even better when she was wearing it. She'd half-hoped it would either swim on her slender body, or be tight enough to rip, but it fitted perfectly, the skirt rippling round her ankles as she moved.

The only drawback was that its design forbade her to wear a bra, and, while this wasn't obvious, the cling of the bodice to her bare breasts made her feel absurdly self-conscious, and glad of the concealing jacket.

Earlier in the day, she'd rung the hairdresser in Hurstleigh where she went for her monthly trim, and arranged to have her hair highlighted, courtesy of a last-minute cancellation. She'd recklessly plunged on some new cosmetics too.

No one would think she looked like a robot tonight, she thought. She was all living, breathing woman. Although the wisdom of that was questionable.

She lingered for a moment in front of the mirror. The pale dress made her look almost bridal. And she fitted the old rhyme too. Her sandals were something old, and the dress something new. Blue, for the aquamarine on her finger. And borrowed—well, that was her remaining time with Miles.

But I'm going to a party, she reminded herself, shaking off the sudden feeling of bleakness that had assailed her. Probably my first and last for some time. And I intend to enjoy myself tonight—whatever the ultimate cost...

She gave herself a final, resolute smile, then left her room.

Jenny's door was ajar, but the room was empty, and a selection of her clothes, books and tapes was also missing.

It seemed she'd meant what she'd said, Chessie thought, biting her lip.

Her first impulse had been to take a taxi to Linda's house and insist that Jenny come home, but on second thoughts she'd decided it was best to let the situation calm down a little.

She would have to talk to Linda's mother, of course, if only to make sure that Jenny was really there, she thought, an unwanted image of Zak Woods imprinting itself on her mind. But, principally, she needed to know if the other woman was prepared to house Jenny for the time being, and, if so, offer to pay for her sister's keep until the packing job materialised. If it ever did.

It wasn't eight o'clock, yet Miles was already waiting, immaculate in dinner jacket and black tie. She'd never seen him in this kind of formal attire before, and her heart missed a beat.

She stood mutely, her face warming as his blue eyes performed a leisurely and detailed assessment of her in turn, from the glowing lights in her hair to the fluted hem of the skirt drifting round her ankles. Lingering, she was sure, on the thrust of her untrammelled breasts.

He said, quietly, 'You look—very lovely.'

The faint huskiness in his voice betrayed him, and her body responded with the swift flutter of her pulses, and the burgeoning, deep within her, of a soft, trembling ache.

For an endless moment, they stood, locked together in shaken, unacknowledged urgency. The space that separated them charged and tingling.

It was Miles who broke the spell.

He said, almost grimly, 'We'd better go.'

'Yes.' Her voice was barely a whisper. He'd remembered just in time, she thought as she followed him out of the house into the evening sunlight, why all connection between them had to be severed.

But she could understand why he'd insisted on maintaining the charade of their engagement. It was excellent camouflage while Sandie was obtaining her divorce.

It was all so simple when you worked it out. And Chessie had expended a lot of time and unhappiness in doing precisely that.

She sat beside him, in silence, her hands tightly clenched round her bag, telling herself it would be better—easier—when there were more people around them. That it was being alone with him that inflicted the lasting damage.

The lights in the huge marquee were already lit, and the sound of music drifted across the lawns as they approached.

Chessie found she was already bracing herself for her first encounter with Linnet, who was waiting at the entrance of the marquee to greet her arriving guests, handing out smiles like over-sweet bon-bons.

Tonight, she was sinuous in a strapless black satin creation that barely covered her full breasts, and flowed over every other inch of her like a second skin.

Chessie felt her eyes widening, and was needled to see that her companion was surveying his hostess with frank and totally male appreciation.

'Miles, darling, you're here at last,' she cooed. 'And Chessie. Still looking so virginal after all this time. How very sweet—and unexpected.'

Miles took Chessie's arm firmly and drew her away while she was still struggling to frame a suitable response.

'Yes, she's the arch bitch of the western world,' he said softly. 'But you don't have to join her in a slanging match. Regard what she said as a compliment. After all, I doubt if it's ever been used as an adjective about her.'

'Not in that dress at any rate,' Chessie, still smarting, said with something of snap. 'Not just no bra. No anything else, by the look of it.'

'And just how much more are you wearing, darling?' Miles murmured, his hand sliding down from her hip in a lightning exploration that forced a stunned gasp of outrage from her. 'A few inches of lace doesn't confer any moral superiority. In fact it can be even more enticing—under the right circumstances.' He smiled into her shocked eyes. 'Now come and have some champagne.'

'I bet no one ever applied ''virgin'' to you either,' Chessie said between her teeth as they walked to the bar set up along one side of the tent.

'Certainly not after the age of fifteen anyway,' he agreed without shame. 'Besides, wouldn't you rather go to bed with someone who knew what he was doing?'

Whatever she replied to that, she was on unsafe ground, and she knew it.

She said coldly, 'May we change the subject, please?'

'For now,' Miles told her pleasantly. 'But not for ever.'

Why? she thought. Why did he say things like that to her when he knew he didn't mean it? Why couldn't he limit the pretence to when other people were with them?

The chilled champagne felt wonderful against the dryness of her mouth, and she drank it far too quickly. Miles had her glass refilled, but chose mineral water for himself this time around.

'Don't you like champagne?' Chessie sipped the second glass with determined circumspection.

'Very much,' he said. 'But I'm driving.'

'We could always walk home,' she pointed out.

'I also want to keep a clear head.' He frowned slightly. 'I scent trouble.'

'You mean a fight?' Chessie tried for lightness, looking around her and shaking her head. 'I hardly think so. A lot of the top people in the county are here tonight.'

'Not that kind of trouble. I used to get bad vibes before certain assignments, always for good reason, warning me that something was wrong. And I have them now.'

Chessie stared into her glass. 'Did you get them before—that last one?'

He said softly, 'Oh, yes.'

'But you still went ahead with it?'

'Of course.'

'That,' Chessie said, 'was either extremely brave, or totally mad.'

'One doesn't necessarily rule out the other.' He paused. 'Someone's trying to catch your eye.'

Chessie glanced in the direction indicated, and stiffened. 'Heavens—Mrs Rankin. But she hasn't spoken to me since—well—in years...'

'Well, she seems determined to speak to you now,' Miles commented. 'She's coming over.'

And Mrs Rankin and her meek husband were only the first of many. Everyone suddenly wished to remember themselves to Chessie, and to meet her future husband, and, to her embarrassment, she found she was the centre of attention.

Although it was Miles they actually wanted to talk to, rather than herself, she reminded herself with cool realism. When word went round that she was no longer engaged to him, she would be consigned to oblivion again. Especially when it was discovered that she was waitressing at The White Hart.

When the disco started, there was almost a queue of men eager to ask her to dance. For a moment, she was hesitant, glancing at Miles, wondering how he would feel about her joining in an activity in which he could have no part.

But he only smiled and said lightly, 'Go for it, Chessie.'

She loved to dance, feeling the rhythm of the music in her bones. As she moved she was aware of Miles watching her from the edge of the floor, felt the intensity of his blue gaze like a hand on her bare skin. And she looked back at him, unable to disguise her longing for him, her lips trembling into a pantomime of a kiss. Only to see him turn away, and disappear into the crowd.

Her impulse was to run after him, but she managed to check herself. Why expose herself to further rejection? she thought bitterly. Far better to go on dancing with men who did want her company. And she smiled, and flirted, and let her body move seductively in the pale silk dress, and looked as if she didn't have a care in the world.

Her last partner, however, was more energetic than skilled, jigging around, red-faced as she swayed in front of him.

'Sorry, Greg.' Alastair appeared from nowhere. 'I'm cutting in, old man.'

Chessie did not return the masterful smile he gave her as Greg disappeared ruefully. 'That was rude,' she commented.

'Well, how else was I supposed to get near you?' he countered. 'You seem to be the belle of the ball, my sweet.' His smiling scrutiny made her feel oddly uncomfortable. 'That's an amazing dress.'

'Thank you,' Chessie said politely. 'Miles bought it for me.'

'Did he now?' His smile widened as the music changed, slowing romantically, and he put his arms round her, drawing her much closer than she wished. 'How very generous of him. But are you equally liberal in return, my sweet? Because you never used to be.'

She said coldly, 'I think that's entirely my own business.' She tried to extricate herself unobtrusively from his tight embrace, but failed. She tried another tack. 'How is your father this evening? I feel I've neglected him this week, but Miles has almost finished the book, and I've been really busy.'

'He's safely tucked up in his corner, I imagine, with Wonder Woman.' His face was suddenly moody. 'She says he's regaining more movement in his right hand every day.'

'Miles told me he's learning to write his name again.'

'Yes,' he said. 'At the most inconvenient possible moment, too.'

She stared at him in disbelief. 'Because he can prevent you selling the Court? Is that it?'

He nodded. 'Among other things.'

'Sometimes,' she said, quietly, 'I feel as if I've never really known you at all.'

'I thought you of all people would understand. After all, you know what it's like to have everything you want—only to see it snatched away from you.'

'Yes,' she said bleakly. 'I know about that all right.' She paused. 'But the Court will belong to you—one day. You just have to be patient.'

'I don't do patience very well. And I'm a bad loser. Besides, seeing you with Hunter drives me crazy.' He looked at her with narrowed eyes. 'I keep wondering how it might have been if I'd come back even a week earlier. Or if my father hadn't made me go to the States in the first place.'

What do I say to that? thought Chessie. Should I be brutally honest, and say it wouldn't have made an atom of difference? That I've known for a long time that we were wrong for each other, and tonight has confirmed it.

She said stiltedly, 'I hope we'll always be friends.' And wasn't even sure that was true any more.

'Is that all you can say?' His voice sank to a whisper. 'You could be my salvation, Chess.'

She was disturbed by the note in his voice, the way he was holding her. She was also aware that people were beginning to send them curious glances.

She said quietly and coldly, 'That's enough. Let go of me now, Alastair.' She pulled herself from his slackened grasp, and walked away.

She'd no idea where Miles had gone, but he was certainly not in the marquee, nor could she spot him in any of the groups standing on the moonlit lawn.

She went into the house, and stood looking round her irresolutely. He couldn't simply have vanished. Sir Robert, she thought, with sudden inspiration. That's where Miles might be.

But when she reached the West Wing, Nurse Taylor told her regretfully that she'd missed him. 'Mrs Cummings

came for him, Miss Lloyd. He was wanted on the tele
phone, apparently. And I'm about to settle Sir Robert fo:
the night now.'

'I see,' said Chessie, who saw nothing. Why on eartl
should anyone call Miles here? she asked herself in tota
bewilderment as she trailed back down the corridor. Who
would even know where he was this evening?

Back in the main part of the house, the supper was bein;
laid out in the dining room by members of the loca
Women's Institute, under the supervision of a harassed Mr:
Cummings. When she spotted Chessie, she came dartin;
over. 'Oh, Miss Lloyd, Mr Hunter asked me to tell you
he's sorry, but he's been called away, and he'll be back
later to take you home.'

'Called away?' Chessie echoed. 'By whom?'

'I couldn't say, miss.' The housekeeper shook her head
'There was a young lady on the telephone for him, sound
ing agitated. And then he gave me the message for you
and went off.' She looked round. 'No, no, Mrs Hancock
dear, the desserts on the long table, please.'

Chessie, realising she was underfoot, retreated back intc
the hall. She could hear the distant noise of the party, and
knew that she hadn't the slightest wish to rejoin it. She had
no idea what kind of emergency could have made Mile:
rush off like that, but the fact that the summons had come
from a girl fuelled all sorts of disturbing ideas.

Well, she didn't want to hang round here, waiting and
wondering, she told herself flatly. She'd fetch her wrap, and
go home, even if it meant burdening Mrs Cummings with
another message.

One of the guest bedrooms was being used as a ladies
cloakroom. Chessie retrieved her shawl from the pile on
the bed, and went out into the corridor, heading for the
stairs.

'Have you gone stark, raving mad?' It was Alastair':
voice, low-pitched and furious, and so close at hand tha

Chessie jumped involuntarily, wondering momentarily if he were talking to her. 'Why have you got me here?'

Then she heard a familiar laugh, and froze. 'Why, darling,' Linnet purred. 'There was a time, not so long ago, when you couldn't wait to be alone with me.'

'Oh, for God's sake. That's all over. It's got to be. My father's getting better, can't you understand that? That damned consultant says he'll be perfectly capable of controlling his own affairs again, and you know what that means—divorce for you, and disinheritance for me. His lawyer's coming down next week.'

Chessie knew that she was eavesdropping, and common decency demanded that she should walk on immediately, and try to forget what she'd heard. But her feet seemed weighted down, trapping her outside Linnet's bedroom, and its half-closed door.

'But that's what we've always wanted—to be together.' There was a note in Linnet's voice that Chessie had never heard before. Fear.

'Oh, get real,' Alastair said roughly. 'We have been together—here—London—Spain. Things could have gone on exactly as they were, if you'd been discreet. He was just suspicious when he sent me off to America. But he didn't have proof, and now he does, thanks to your stupidity. You told me you always burned my letters.'

'I did—I thought I had.'

'Really?' Alastair sneered. 'Are you quite sure of that? Or did you make a unilateral decision to force the confrontation you've been pestering me about for long enough? You got your way, baby, and he's finished with the pair of us. We're out.'

'And if it was intentional, do you blame me?' Linnet hissed. 'I'm sick of pretending—of you telling me it's not the right time.'

'So you let him find out,' he said slowly. 'And it was nearly the death of him.' His voice rose. 'My God, do you realise what you did?'

'How was I supposed to know?' She sounded almost hysterical. 'He'd always been as strong as a horse. I'll never forget his face—how he keeled over…'

'Well, you're going to have plenty of time to remember it,' he said. 'But not with me. We're through, Linnet.'

'You don't mean it.' Her voice cracked.

'Yes,' he said. 'I do. I have other plans for my future. And with you out of the picture, I may even be able to talk Dad round at some point.' He paused. 'Especially if I'm married to someone he approves of,' he added significantly.

She said venomously, 'I suppose that was why you were wrapped round that little Lloyd bitch earlier. Although you didn't seem to be getting very far.'

'I'll talk her round,' he said confidently. 'When she realises Hunter is simply stringing her along, she'll be glad to turn to me again. And now we have a houseful of guests who'll be wondering where we are.'

Any minute now, Chessie thought wildly, one or the other of them was going to come out of Linnet's bedroom and catch her there. She couldn't make it to the stairs in time, so she turned, diving back into the room she'd just left.

She sank down on the edge of the bed, and stayed there, shaking from head to foot, trying to come to terms with what she'd just heard. Linnet and Alastair—secret lovers— even during that summer when she'd thought he'd belonged to her. And ever since.

She felt, shuddering, as if she'd been touched by slime. Was that all there was in the world—infidelity and betrayal? And Sir Robert too—what he must have suffered.

Oh, why wasn't Miles here, when she needed him so badly?

She froze as she realised what she was saying. Because Miles was just as bad. He didn't want her. He was using her to divert attention from his own affair. What had Alastair said—that he was just stringing her along? Had she been the last to realise this?

She got up slowly, stiffly. Outside everything was quiet, Linnet's door closed. The coast, it seemed, was clear, and she went down the stairs and out into the night like a fugitive seeking sanctuary.

The house was in total darkness when she got back, so Miles was evidently still occupied somewhere with his mystery caller. But he couldn't have gone to London, she argued as she let herself into the flat. Not if he'd said he'd return to the party for her.

I can't think any more, she told herself wearily. I'd go to bed, if I thought for one minute I'd sleep.

But sleep seemed beyond her. There was no rest for her reeling mind, so, instead, she trailed into the kitchen and switched on the kettle. She wasn't thirsty, but it was something to do. Something to fill the time.

Her coffee made, she took it into the sitting room and, curling up on the sofa, tried to watch some late-night television. But the horror film on offer failed to distract her, apart from making her wish that the sinister vampire at its centre would bite the entire cast.

Eventually, in spite of everything, she fell into a light doze.

She was awoken suddenly an hour later by the sound of the flat door opening, and voices. Sitting up, and pushing the hair back from her face, she was astonished to see Jenny walk in with Miles close behind her.

She said, 'Jen—you're back.' Then, seeing her sister's white face, and tear-filled eyes, 'What's happened?'

As she got to her feet Jenny ran forward, flinging herself at her. 'Oh, Chessie.' Her voice broke, and she began crying. 'I've been under arrest.'

'Arrest?' Chessie repeated with stupefaction. She looked at Miles who was waiting in the doorway, his face grave. 'Is it true?'

'No,' he said instantly. 'Although she has been at Hurstleigh police station, answering questions. But I swear to you, she's in the clear. No charges are going to be brought.' He hesitated. 'At least not against her.'

Chessie coaxed Jenny to sit down. She took her hands, clasping them firmly. She said, 'Darling, has this got something to do with this man you've been seeing?'

There was a pause, then Jenny nodded in reluctant assent, before hurrying into speech, 'Chess, I swear I didn't know what he was doing—not until tonight. Linda and I went out to meet him at the Millennium club. He had these tablets with him—and he wanted us to take them. Linda said she would, but I stopped her, and Zak and I had this terrible row. He was cursing me, calling me names—dreadful things. In the end, I walked out. I meant to go home with Linda, but I went back to the club instead.' Her face was pinched. 'I wanted to see him—reason with him. Only the police were there, and they were taking him away in handcuffs.' She choked. 'Because he'd sold one of those tablets to a girl, and she'd collapsed and been taken to hospital.

'And someone told them that I was his girlfriend—that I'd been with him earlier in the evening, so they said they wanted to talk to me too. And they took me to the police station, and I didn't know what to do, so I phoned the Court and asked for Miles. And he came and stayed with me while I answered their questions, and then they let me go,' she added with a little wail.

'Oh, God.' Chessie was appalled. 'And you really had no idea what he was doing?'

Jenny pulled away. 'Of course not. What do you take me for? I'd never—never…'

'But the poor girl in hospital—what's happened to her?'

'She's in intensive care,' Miles said quietly. 'But expected to make a full recovery.'

Jenny was sobbing again, and Chessie stroked her hair, whispering soothingly.

Miles said gently, 'I think a warm drink and bed might be advisable.'

Chessie looked up at him. 'I don't like to leave her...'

He said, 'I'm here, Francesca. She'll be all right.'

She relinquished Jenny to him, and went into the kitchen, pouring milk into a pan and finding the tin of chocolate to mix with it. When she returned, Jenny had calmed a little, and was sitting with Miles' handkerchief clutched in her hand.

She gave her sister a watery smile as she accepted the beaker of hot chocolate. 'Chessie—I'm so sorry—about everything,' she added, stealing a contrite look at Miles.

'It's all right, darling,' Chessie said quietly. 'Love makes fools of us all.'

Jenny was silent for a moment. 'I may not have done very well in my exams. What am I going to do?'

'We'll worry about that when the time comes.' Chessie tried to sound upbeat, but it wasn't easy. She had taken it for granted that Jenny's future was settled, and she only had herself to worry about.

Her sister finished her chocolate, and said wanly that perhaps she would like to go to bed.

Chessie went with her to her room. 'Is there anything I can do?'

'No.' Jenny was staring around her as if she were in a foreign country. 'I—I'll be fine. Goodnight, Chess.'

She's hurting so much, Chessie thought soberly as she returned to the sitting room. And I can't make it better.

Miles was occupying the corner of the sofa, long legs stretched out in front of him. He'd discarded his jacket and tie, and unfastened the top of his dress shirt. He turned to look at her as she entered. 'Well?'

'Not good.' Chessie shook her head. There was space beside him, but she chose the small armchair at the fireside instead. In spite of her concern about Jenny, she was aware of a small fierce tingle through her nerve-endings at the sight of him, and knew it had to be resisted.

'Well, don't worry too much,' he said quietly. 'She's had

a very bad shock, and it's made her question her own judgement.' He smiled faintly. 'She'll bounce back.'

'But if she really cared about him…'

Miles shook his head. 'I think she'd already begun to have second thoughts. She may not have known exactly what he was up to, but she knew there was something wrong, and it frightened her.'

'Will she have to give evidence against him?'

'Possibly, although they seem to have enough to convict him several times over. Apparently he made a habit of targeting girls like Jenny, so that he could meet their friends and open up new markets.'

Chessie shivered. 'That's—horrible.' She was quiet for a moment, then she said, 'Tell me something—why did she send for you tonight, and not me?'

'Because I told her she could—that day I gave her a lift from school.' His tone was matter-of-fact. 'I said that if she ever really messed up, and didn't want to worry you about it, she could turn to me.' He paused. 'I got the impression then that all was not well.' He added drily, 'I'm still not her brother-in-law of choice, but at least I'm not The Ogre any more.'

'No.' She spoke with constraint.

'Another thing,' he went on. 'I think she could do with a period of stability, so it would be better if you stayed on here. Gave up your plans to be a waitress and went on working for me.'

She stared at him. 'But I'll have to move on eventually,' she said at last. 'Isn't that just delaying the inevitable?'

'Perhaps,' he agreed. 'But it will also give you more time to think about what you want for the future. The White Hart's a stopgap, Chessie. You need to consider the whole of your life.' He studied her for a moment. 'Are you even dead set on remaining in this area?'

Mutely, she shook her head. Although the other side of the world wouldn't be far enough away, if she had to live with the knowledge that he was here with Sandie Wells.

'Then I think you should allow yourself this breathing space.' He paused. 'There'll be no pressure from me. I shall be in London for the next few weeks.'

She sank her teeth into her lower lip. 'That's—very kind.' *And at the same time so bitterly, endlessly cruel.*

'That's settled, then.' There was another silence, then he said, 'I'm sorry to have left you in the lurch at the party.'

'It didn't matter.' She looked down at her hands, twisting the aquamarine ring on her finger, struggling to keep her voice level and hide the agony of emotion inside her. 'Your instinct for trouble was quite right, it seems.'

He frowned. 'But I thought it would concern the Court, not Jenny.'

'It did.' She swallowed. 'I discovered tonight that Alastair and Linnet have been having an affair for years.'

'Ah,' he said, softly. 'So that's come out at last.'

She stared at him. 'You—*knew*?'

He nodded. 'Remember the night I took you to dinner at The White Hart?'

'Yes.' She didn't just remember. Every detail was etched in her mind for ever.

'And the couple wrapped round each other in that parked car? When I met Lady Markham, I realised at once that she was the woman involved, and that she was desperate to know if I'd seen enough to identify her—and the boyfriend. When I recognised him, I became—interested.' He gave her a level look. 'So what happened? Did Alastair make a full confession in the moonlight before he proposed to you?'

She looked down at her hands. 'There was—no proposal.'

'You amaze me,' Miles said sardonically. 'I'd assumed you'd be the path back to his father's favour. So—how did you find out?'

She bit her lip. 'I—overheard something I shouldn't have done.'

'Poor Chessie,' he said. 'It's been a night of unwelcome revelations, hasn't it? Does it hurt very much?'

'Hurt?' She looked up, suddenly incredulous. 'Heavens, no. I got over Alastair a long time ago.'

Although I didn't know it, she thought, *until he kissed me that night, and I wished it were you…*

'It's just that I always thought they hated each other.' She shook her head. 'I feel such a fool.'

'They're the foolish ones.' He shrugged. 'They may get to spend the rest of their lives together.'

She said in a low voice, 'I don't think so.'

His lip curled. 'You mean he's decided to dump her? Could he be having conscience problems at last?'

'Yes,' she said quietly. 'Because his father found out, and that's what triggered his stroke.'

'Proving that honesty is not always the best policy.' He was silent for a moment. 'What about you, Francesca? Do you believe there's a place for secrets—or do you prefer everything laid on the line—publish and be damned?'

'That might depend on the secret.' *Oh, God*, she thought, *he's going to tell me about Sandie Wells—that their love affair is on again—and I can't bear it. I can't…*

He said, 'There's something I need to tell you, Chessie.'

She flung up a defensive hand, trying to laugh. 'Oh, no—not another unwelcome revelation, please.'

'As you wish.' His tone was level. 'Then, let's talk about something else. You're a wonderful dancer—did you know that? All inhibitions flown when the music starts.'

She flushed. 'You didn't watch me for very long.'

'No,' he said. 'I found it more disturbing than I'd bargained for. Dancing is one of the things I can't do—like playing football with the children I hope to have one day, or carrying my wife upstairs to bed. I jog along most of the time, then, just occasionally, reality bites hard.'

Her mind winced away from the images he'd created. She said falteringly, 'You have your books—a career a lot of people would envy…' *The woman you've always wanted.*

'And that should satisfy me?' he asked ironically. He

shook his head. 'It doesn't work like that, Francesca. But you really don't want to hear my plans, do you?'

'Well—it is rather late.' She got clumsily to her feet. 'And we've both had a difficult evening. You look tired.'

'Do I?' He watched her from half-closed eyes, a faint smile playing about his mouth. 'Yet sleep's the last thing on my mind.'

'All the same, perhaps you should go.' Chessie was aware she was trembling, unable to take her eyes from him. 'But before you do, I have to thank you—for what you did for Jenny, and...' She hesitated.

'And?' Miles prompted.

'And for this dress.' She looked down at herself. 'I don't think I've ever worn anything so lovely—even if it was only for half an evening. I—I'm so grateful.'

'You made it beautiful,' he said quietly.

Her voice broke. 'Please—you mustn't...'

'Why not?'

She said passionately, 'Because it isn't right—it isn't fair.'

Miles got slowly to his feet. 'You said you were grateful,' he reminded her softly as he began to walk towards her. 'Isn't it time you offered some proof?'

She said his name in a small, frightened voice, but it didn't stop him.

'All evening,' he said, 'I've dreamed of this moment.' He reached her, and his arms went round her, pulling her hard against his body. 'Chessie.' His voice was suddenly harsh, passionately urgent. 'Don't send me away. Not tonight.'

She knew that she should. But the stark, trembling yearning within her would not be denied any longer.

If this one night was all he could offer, she thought, then she would take it. Give herself this solitary memory of the few hours when he'd been hers alone to comfort her in the desert of loneliness that awaited her.

Then his mouth came down hard on hers, and all thinking ceased.

CHAPTER ELEVEN

CHESSIE'S bedroom was full of shadows, a small bedside lamp providing the sole illumination. She watched Miles close the door and come towards her, and knew that, no matter how much she wanted him, now that the moment had come she felt absurdly shy.

'You're trembling,' he said softly as he drew her towards him. He framed her face with his hands, looking searchingly into her eyes. 'Am I really so scary?'

'No. It's just that...'

'That in all the best stories, the virgin ends up with the prince, not the ogre?' He was smiling faintly, but there was a question in his eyes.

'Don't—don't ever use that word again,' she said passionately. 'Miles—I never did—I swear it...' *And you were always the prince—only I was too blind to realise.*

'I was teasing you,' he whispered. 'Isn't that allowed?'

He kissed her again, his mouth moving warmly and sensuously on hers, and she surrendered helplessly to the pleasure of it, her arms sliding up round his neck to hold him closer still.

His hand stroked her hair, and the nape of her neck, then moved downwards to release the tiny hook at the back of her dress, and, unhurriedly, to lower the zip.

Eyes closed, she stood motionless, listening to the heavy thud of her heartbeat, reassured by the gentleness of his touch.

She caught her lower lip between her teeth, tensing as he slid the straps of the dress from her shoulders, and she felt the silky fabric glide down her body, and pool round her feet.

Her hands went up automatically to cover her bared breasts, but he caught her wrists, forestalling her.

He said huskily, 'Darling—please. I—need to look at you. To remember you like this always.'

Her lashes lifted wonderingly, and for a breathless moment she studied him. In the lamplight, he seemed almost haggard, deep hollows beneath his cheekbones, and the scar a livid slash as the burn of his gaze travelled over her.

He said softly, remotely, '"But beauty's self she is..."'

That strange note in his voice sent alarm signals through her senses. Because it sounded almost like regret—as if he planned, even at this moment, to step back.

Instinct came to her aid. Chessie lifted her hands, pushing back her hair in a deliberately languorous gesture, while the smile that curved her mouth beckoned and promised.

She whispered, 'Just a few inches of lace.'

She heard the harsh catch of his breath, saw the stark yearning in his face, and then she moved, taking his hand, and leading him to the bed.

They lay facing each other. He stroked the curve of her face with his hand, then kissed her softly, fleetingly on her mouth, her eyes, her throat, and the hollow beneath her ear.

But even as her body sighed with pleasure she was conscious that Miles was still fully dressed while she was almost naked. She reached shyly to unfasten his shirt, but he captured her hand and kissed it, whispering, 'Later.'

'I don't understand...'

'Don't try,' he murmured against her mouth. 'This is all just for you.'

He kissed her, his lips parting hers in sensuous mastery, and she surrendered her inner sweetness to the invasion of his tongue, her arms sliding up round his neck, her hands tangling in his hair as she responded.

He was touching her now, his fingers tracing tiny patterns on her skin, the lightest brush of his hand making her pulses leap and throb.

The blue eyes were fixed on her face, observing every

slight intake of breath between her parted lips, the dilation of her pupils, the play of colour in her cheeks.

Each thrill of response seemed to swell and intensify, and when, at last, his hand moulded her breast, the warm, rounded flesh blossomed against his palm, her nipple hardening irresistibly under the exquisite teasing of his fingers. He bent his head, taking each rosy peak in turn between his lips, and suckling it gently.

The caressing hand moved downwards, exploring every curve and hollow, and she heard herself moan softly in mingled surprise and delight as her body moved restlessly in a growing fever of arousal and need.

His mouth covered hers, kissing her deeply and sensually in unequivocal demand as his hand pushed aside the scrap of lace and found the molten velvet heat of her.

Chessie gasped, her body arching against the intimate glide of his fingers as he stroked the core of her womanhood, exploring and inciting. Circling her tiny vibrant peak with languorous insistence as his mouth moved down to her breast.

His tongue flickering against her nipple echoed the friction of his touch against her secret heated bud. She could scarcely breathe, all her senses suspended in some limbo of anticipation. And, just as she thought she could bear no more, she was pierced by a pleasure so sudden and so fierce it was almost anguish, and she cried out as shivers of rapture convulsed her entire being.

Afterwards there were tears on her face, and he brushed them away with his lips.

'Still scared?' he whispered.

She shook her head slowly. 'Only of myself.' The thought of what he could make her do—how he could make her feel—frankly terrified her. Yet at the same time, she could feel excitement building again inside her.

He laughed softly, and switched off the lamp.

In the darkness, she heard the rustle of his clothes as he removed them. Felt the warmth of his naked skin caressing hers as he pulled her back into his arms, the points of her breasts grazing his chest, his thighs hard against her softness.

As they kissed Miles took her hand, guiding her to him, so that she could experience the stark strength of his male arousal.

'I'm not made of glass,' he murmured as his lips began a leisurely traverse of her throat.

'I'm afraid of hurting you.' For the first time in her life, she found herself cursing her lack of experience. Her total uncertainty that she could please him on this one night they would spend together.

She felt his smile against her skin. 'If you do, I promise I'll scream.' Then, with his voice thickening suddenly, 'Oh, God, yes—*yes...*'

His mouth and hands were warm and sure as they moved on her, and she felt an answering heat building inside her as she caressed him. So that when his hands slid under her hips, lifting her gently towards him for his full possession, she was not merely acceptant, but eager for this last mystery to be revealed. As he filled her, completed her in a way she had never dreamed of, she felt the breath catch in her throat.

Instantly, he paused. 'Are you all right?' His voice was shaken—urgent. 'Darling, I'm scared I'll hurt you too.'

Instinct came to her aid again. She moved, slowly and luxuriously, beneath him, hearing him gasp. 'Only if you stop,' she whispered.

At first he was gentle, murmuring endearments—reassurance—against her lips, then as she began to respond more boldly the rhythm of his mastery changed—strengthened. And she was carried with him, swept away on the flood-tide of his passion, her body as insistent—as driven, both of them aware of nothing but the rasp of their breathing, and each silken, burning thrust taking them inexorably towards their goal.

As the pleasure overtook her, overwhelmed her, she felt

herself screaming silently as each glorious spasm tore into her, wrenching her apart, tossing her like glittering fragments into a dark universe where there was only his voice, groaning her name like a prayer.

When the maelstrom receded, she lay, drained and spent, in his arms, her head pillowed on his chest. She could have remained there for ever, but she was suddenly aware that he did not share her total relaxation. That she could feel the tension radiating through him like an electric current. That he was trying to move, slowly and gingerly, his teeth gritted to hold back a groan.

She sat up. 'Miles—darling—what is it?'

'Nothing.' His voice was curt with pain. 'I'll be fine.'

'Oh, God, it's your back, isn't it?' She was suddenly frantic. 'I didn't think—didn't realise. You must be in agony.'

'A little.' There was faint laughter in his voice as his hand stroked her face. 'But the pleasure of you was well worth any torment, believe me.'

'I'll get you something—a drink—painkillers.' She reached for the lamp and switched it on.

He shifted position quickly, pulling the sheet up to cover him. 'No—I don't need anything. And turn the light off—please.'

For a moment, she was bewildered, and then she remembered the hidden scarring. The dream of happiness it had so brutally ended for him. And knew what she had to do.

She said gently, 'Miles—you've seen me naked. It's only fair if I claim the same privilege.'

His face was ashen, slicked with sweat. 'You don't understand…'

'Yes.' She bent over him, kissing his mouth. 'Yes, I do.'

Her lips moved down over his shoulder, licking the salt from his skin, and across to the hair-roughened plane of his chest, teasing the flat male nipples with the tip of her tongue.

'Nice?' She lifted her head, smiling at him.

His voice was taut. 'For a girl who lives with a writer, you have a lousy vocabulary. Chessie—are you quite sure about this?'

'Certain.' She pushed the concealing sheet down further, and stroked her fingertips across his stomach, feeling the muscles contract.

He had a wonderful body, she thought detachedly, lean, firm and smooth. Her exploring hand reached his hip and encountered the first puckering of scar tissue.

'Chessie…'

'Hush,' she whispered, touching a quietening finger to his lips. She took the edge of the sheet, and turned it back, revealing him completely. Disclosing the jagged purple lines that criss-crossed down to his thigh.

She could feel the tension in him as he waited for her reaction. For even the slightest hesitation.

She ran a caressing hand over the ugly marks, then bent her head and begin to kiss each one, her mouth soft and deliberate as it followed each twisted track.

Miles did not speak, but as her mouth and tongue became ever more adventurous she felt him relaxing.

At last he said, almost conversationally, 'Chessie, I warn you, if you go on like this, your act of compassion is going to turn into something very different.'

'So I've noticed.' Her voice quivered with laughter. 'And it's not compassion. I'm enjoying myself. But hasn't your poor back taken enough punishment tonight?'

'Probably,' he said solemnly. 'So this time I thought I'd just lie back and think of England—if that's all right with you?'

She said softly, 'Oh, I'll try to give satisfaction—sir.' And let her mouth drift gently over his hip, and down.

When she woke the next morning, she was conscious of a feeling of total well-being that was entirely new to her. For a moment, she lay still, eyes closed, letting herself luxuriate in it, dreaming a little of the day ahead, then she turned her head slowly to regard the adjoining pillow, and see if Miles was awake too.

But the bed beside her was empty. Miles had gone. His clothes were missing too, so at some point, while she'd been asleep, he'd dressed and left her quietly enough not to waken her.

Perhaps he'd decided he would be more comfortable in his own room, or maybe he thought Jenny's new acceptance of him might be tested by finding him in her sister's bed, but Chessie felt absurdly disappointed just the same.

Last night, she'd fallen asleep in Miles' arms, her sated body reduced to blissful exhaustion. Her final memory, his voice whispering to her with passionate tenderness. Surely, she'd rated a word of goodbye?

However it was Sunday, sweet Sunday, she thought, rallying her spirits. And there was nothing to stop her going over to the house and cooking him the breakfast of his lifetime.

She stretched, acknowledging the faint wincing of her muscles, then got out of bed and put on her dressing gown. Her dress was still in a crumpled heap on the floor, and she shook it out and placed it on a hanger, a little reminiscent smile playing mischievously round the corners of her mouth.

She went into the kitchen, put on the kettle, and slipped a couple of slices of bread into the toaster.

A minute later she was joined by a yawning Jenny. Her sister still looked pale, but she seemed slightly less subdued than the previous evening as she sank into a chair by the kitchen table.

'How did you sleep?'

'All right, but I had horrible dreams.' Jenny looked at her almost blankly. 'I suppose last night couldn't be one of them—please?'

Chessie patted her shoulder as she took down the coffee jar. 'I'm afraid not, honey. It was a ghastly thing to happen, but let's hope it's behind you.'

'I just feel so stupid.' For a second Jenny's lip trembled. 'I really thought he cared about me. But he just wanted me to sell his beastly drugs to my friends.'

'But you didn't.' Chessie made the coffee and handed Jenny a beaker. 'That's what you have to remember.'

'That's what Miles said.' Jenny glanced round her. 'Where is he, anyway?'

'In his own part of the house, I presume.' Chessie put the hot toast on a plate, trying to look and sound casual. 'Why do you ask?'

'Oh, no reason.' Jenny helped herself to butter, eyeing her sister. 'I didn't hear him leave last night, that's all.'

Nor did I, Chessie thought ruefully. Aloud, she said, 'Well, he's certainly not here now.' And hoped it was sufficiently ambiguous.

'He wants me to stay on for a while—go on working for him,' she continued. 'So we don't have to move out after all.'

'Well, that's one relief.' Jenny bit into her toast, and chewed in reflective silence. 'Chess,' she said at last. 'If you and Miles are getting it together, I shan't make waves. I've been a real bitch about him, I know, but that's all over, I promise.'

Chessie bit her lip. 'It's not like that. He's going away, and he needs me to act as caretaker until he gets back.'

'Oh,' Jenny said, sounding depressed. 'Is that all.'

No, Chessie thought, drinking her own coffee. But it's all I can bear to contemplate for now.

It occurred to her that one reason for Miles' absence could be that he was suffering from a massive flare-up of regret, and even guilt, having belatedly remembered he belonged to someone else.

If so, she needed to see him—put a brave face on things—assure him there would be no recriminations.

Although there might be repercussions, she thought, sinking her teeth into her bottom lip. But she couldn't allow herself to worry about that now.

An hour later, showered and dressed, she made her way into the main house. She'd half expected Miles to be in the study, but the room was deserted, and there was no sign that he'd even come downstairs yet. She went soft-footed up to his bedroom and tapped on the door. There was no reply, so she turned the handle and went in, rehearsing a teasing remark about his need for sleep.

But the wide bed was unoccupied and totally unruffled.

Chessie wheeled and ran downstairs, calling his name, only to hear her voice echo into silence.

Stop panicking, she thought. He's probably gone out for a walk, to clear his head. After all, it's a beautiful morning.

And while she was waiting, she might as well see if he'd left any work for her.

There was indeed a small pile of script waiting on the table in the study. But his portable typewriter—his talisman—had vanished with him, she realised with sudden numbness. He'd never taken it out of the house before. And that suggested with chilling emphasis that he had no plans to return for the foreseeable future.

Numbly, she picked up the script and scanned through it. He'd finished the book, but as she'd expected there was no happy ending this time either.

And then she saw the envelope lying beside it, addressed to her.

She reached for it, looking down at it, knowing with total clarity that she did not want to read what was in it. But that she had no choice. She took a deep breath, then slit the envelope open. The letter ran:

Dear Chessie,

As the book is finished, I have decided to leave for London earlier than planned. When you've finished transcribing it please send a hard copy and disk to Vinnie direct. She's expecting it.

As my plans are fluid, I've left some money for general expenses in your desk, also a letter of authorisation for the bank, if you need more.

Forgive me for last night, if you can. It should never have happened, but I can't bring myself to regret one moment. I'll remember it always.

It ended with his signature.

The sheet fell from her suddenly nerveless hand, and fluttered to the carpet. Chessie followed it, sinking to her knees and resting her head against the side of the table.

Well, she could not pretend she hadn't been warned, she thought desolately. But that was no comfort—no comfort at all.

And burying her face in her hands, she began to weep.

'Cleared out,' said Mrs Chubb. 'Gone off without a word to anyone. Well, good riddance to bad rubbish, I say.'

Chessie felt as if she'd been punched in the face. Her voice shook. 'Mrs Chubb, how dare you say that? You have no right—'

'I thought you'd be pleased.' A note of offence sounded in the good woman's voice. 'Never thought you were one of Madam's admirers.'

Chessie stared at her, open-mouthed. 'You mean—Linnet—Lady Markham has disappeared?'

'Didn't I just say so?' She gave Chessie a severe look. 'You don't seem as if you're with it, mind,' she added critically. 'White as a teacup. Are you going down with one of those nasty viruses?'

'No.' Chessie lifted her chin. Forced a smile. 'Does no one know where Lady Markham's gone?'

'Seemingly not. They were worried about telling Sir Robert, but Chubb reckons he took it in his stride. Mr Alastair hasn't had much to say either. Probably glad to see the back of her too.'

'Yes,' Chessie said slowly. 'I think you're right.' She pulled herself together. 'Mr Hunter's away for a few days, so I thought maybe we'd take the opportunity to give the study a good clean.'

'I'll lend a hand as soon as I get back from posting his script.'

It was a relief to get out of the house. She'd spent the rest of Sunday completing the typing of Miles' book, and trying to evade Jenny's questions about his sudden absence.

'Did you have a fight with Miles about something?' her sister had demanded.

'Of course not.' That at least was the truth. 'He'd told me he had to go away—a combined business and research trip.' She shrugged. 'No big deal.'

'Why didn't you go with him, then?'

Chessie bit her lip. 'Because I have things to do here,' she returned. 'Besides, I could hardly leave you here on your own.'

'Yes.' Jenny gave her a level look. 'Actually, you could.' Her smile was wintry. 'Chessie—I'm not a child any more. I can cope.'

She paused. 'And you should be with Miles. I tell you, if I was in your shoes, I wouldn't let him out of my sight.'

To which, of course, there was no answer, Chessie thought now, pursuing her listless way to the village post office.

She'd seen the heavy Jiffy bag safely on its way, and was just emerging into the sunlight when she heard a voice say, 'Miss Lloyd?'

Turning, she saw Nurse Taylor smiling at her. 'Beautiful morning,' she went on with enthusiasm. 'And I'm glad to see you out and about, keeping occupied. It doesn't do to brood.'

Is she a mind-reader as well as a nurse? Chessie wondered wearily.

She was just about to enquire about Sir Robert, but the older woman forestalled her.

'Sir Robert is very concerned, of course,' she said. 'Have you heard yet when it's going to happen?'

'I'm sorry.' Chessie shook her head in bewilderment. 'I don't think I follow you.'

Nurse Taylor stared at her. 'But I meant the operation on Mr Hunter's back, of course. I understood it was to be this week.'

The familiar village street seemed to sway and dissolve. Chessie felt herself thrust down onto the post office step, and told firmly to put her head between her knees.

When she recovered, she found herself being helped to her feet by Nurse Taylor and conducted into the tearooms next door.

As Chessie was sipping with distaste the cup of sweet tea that had been ordered for her Nurse Taylor said in a matter-of-fact voice, 'I take it you didn't know.'

'No—no, of course not.' Chessie set down her cup. 'It's such a dangerous operation—I know that. Oh, how could he take such a risk?'

The older woman said levelly, 'Because it offers him the chance of regaining normal mobility, which has clearly become important to him. I'm sure you understand why.'

Yes, Chessie thought in agony. Because of Sandie Wells, that's why. Because that's the condition she imposed for resuming their relationship. And if the operation fails and leaves him helpless, she'll simply walk away. She's done it once, she can do it again.

'Why?' she whispered. 'Why—after all this time?'

'Because there's a new procedure they're going to try. My former boss at the Kensington Foundation was testing it last year, and I happened to mention it to Mr Hunter during one of his visits.' Nurse Taylor paused. 'He went up to London, and talked to Sir Philip, who agreed to operate.' She looked doubtfully at Chessie. 'I was sure he'd have discussed it with you first.'

'No,' Chessie said quietly. 'But he'll as sure as hell discuss it with me as soon as I get to London.' She took a deep breath. 'Because he shouldn't have to do this. He deserves to be loved for himself—just as he is.' *The way I love him...*

She paused. 'And I'm going to tell him so—before it's too late.'

She was sorely tempted to call at the flat on her way to the Kensington Foundation, and give Sandie Wells the tongue-lashing of her life, but she decided it was more important to get to the clinic and stop Miles taking this potentially disastrous step. Besides, if Sandie Wells had an atom of decency she'd be at the clinic too.

And I can kill two birds with one well-aimed brick, she told herself, biting her lip.

She found the Foundation's expensive receptionist frosty, and determined to protect the privacy of its patients, but she unbent slightly when Chessie told her that she was Miles Hunter's fiancée, and wasn't leaving until she saw him.

'He is scheduled for surgery with Sir Philip later today,' she was informed. 'But I'm sure you can see him for five minutes before his pre-med.'

A very junior nurse was summoned and told to conduct Chessie to Miles' private room. He was lying on top of the bed in his hospital gown, reading the paper, which he lowered to regard Chessie with frowning incredulity.

'Visitor, Mr Hunter,' the nurse announced, beaming, and withdrew, leaving them together.

Miles broke the silence, his eyes watchful. 'If you've brought me some grapes, I'm not allowed to eat anything.'

Chessie looked round the room. Miles' portable typewriter was reposing on a table in the corner, and she found the sight of it oddly reassuring. Though there was nothing else to comfort her.

'You're alone?' she demanded accusingly. 'She can't even be here for you when you're putting your life—your entire well-being on the line for her?'

'What are you talking about?' His voice was rough. 'And more to the point—what are you doing here?'

'I met Nurse Taylor in the village. She told me what you were planning.' She brushed that aside impatiently. 'And I'm talking about Sandie Wells. It's for her sake you're taking this insane risk.'

'Is it?' There was an odd note in his voice. 'I thought it was for you.'

She said desperately, 'Please don't play games because this is too serious. I know that you've been seeing her again. That she's been at your flat. And if you still want her that badly, then you must have her. I—I won't stand in your way, I swear it.

'But don't have this operation. It's too dangerous. Steffie told me what the consequences might be, and why you'd rejected it the first time. Tell this surgeon you've changed your mind. It's not too late. And if she really loves you, she'll take you as you are.'

There was a long silence, then Miles said softly, 'We need to get a few things straight. Firstly—Sandie has indeed been staying at the flat, but not with me. Some friends of mine have let me use their spare room. Secondly, she and I are not in love with each other. She and her husband have been having problems, because he wants her to be a full-time wife, and she'd like to build her career. She wanted somewhere quiet to stay while she got her head together, so I let her use the flat for old times' sake. The upshot is that she and her man have now agreed on some kind of compromise, and are giving the marriage another go. They left this morning for a second honeymoon in the Bahamas.'

He paused. 'And even if that wasn't so—if she was occupying the place for the foreseeable future, it would be inconvenient but not fatal. Because whatever we had was dead and buried a long time ago, and we both know it.

'Whereas you, my sweet prickly Francesca, are the girl I love, and the only wife I'll ever want. And I need to be your husband in the fullest sense of the word. And that's why I'm here.

'And if you love me back, now might be a good time to say so,' he added.

'I do love you—I do,' she said huskily. 'I think I've loved you always, but I wouldn't let myself accept it. And that's why I'm here to tell you that you don't need to do this awful thing—not for me...'

He patted the bed. 'Sit down and listen to me, my darling. When we first met, I was still feeling pretty sorry for myself, and bloody uptight. But then I looked at you, and I saw the saddest, most frightened eyes I'd ever seen in my life. And all I wanted to do was pick you up in my arms and keep you safe for ever. Only, I couldn't, and, just to rub salt into the wound, you tried to help me instead.' He shook his head. 'Not my best moment.'

She said, 'I remember.'

His mouth curled slightly. 'I imagine you might. But that's not the only thing. I'm so sick of it all. Sick of being in pain so much of the time, and feeling I'm only half a man.'

Her laugh cracked in the middle. 'We both know that isn't true.'

'It may not be logical,' he said. 'But it's a fact.' He took her hands in his. 'I told you, my love. I want to kick a ball with our children, and carry you up to bed. And make love to you all night long, when we get there. And for that, any risk is worth the taking.' He raised her hands to his lips. 'Besides, Sir Philip assures me the odds on my making a full recovery are much improved now.'

'You're not going to let me talk you out of this.' There were tears on her face. 'Then hear this, Miles Hunter. Whatever the outcome, I'm going to be your wife, and love you in sickness and in health—for as long as we both shall live. And nothing can change that.'

His arms went round her, and he drew her to him, kissing

her passionately. He said, softly, 'Will you be here when I wake up?'

'Yes,' she said. 'And tomorrow. And the day after for as long as it takes.'

He nodded. 'You'll find the keys for the flat in the locker drawer.'

As she found them the door opened and a nurse came in. 'Time for your pre-med, Mr Hunter.' She smiled at Chessie. 'I'm afraid you'll have to go to the visitors' room now, madam.'

'Yes.' Chessie pushed the keys into her pocket, then bent to kiss Miles, her mouth warm and sure as it lingered on his.

She whispered, 'I'll be waiting.' Then went out without looking back.

The visitors' room was comfortable, with armchairs and an array of newspapers and magazines, and she was its only occupant during an endless afternoon. Members of staff kept appearing with offers of tea, coffee and sandwiches, but she refused them all.

Each time she heard a step in the corridor outside she looked up in painful hope, and eventually the door opened and a tall grey-haired man came in, still wearing his green theatre gown.

He said pleasantly, 'Miss Lloyd—I'm Philip Jacks. I'm afraid you've had an anxious time, but it's over now, and I'm happy to say everything's gone well, and Mr Hunter will make a complete recovery.'

There were tears running suddenly down her pale face. 'You—you promise me?'

He smiled and held up a hand. 'Word of honour. He's young and tough enough to come through most things. And, of course, he has the perfect incentive,' he added drily.

'Can I see him?'

'Not for a little while. But I'll be happy to take a message. May I?'

'Yes,' Chessie said. 'Tell him I'm going out to buy a football.'

His brows rose. 'Is that all?'

'No,' she said, laughing through her tears. 'Believe me—that's only the beginning.'

A CONVENIENT WIFE

by

Sara Wood

Childhood in Portsmouth meant grubby knees, flying pigtails and happiness for **Sara Wood.** Poverty drove her from typist and seaside landlady to teacher till writing finally gave her the freedom her Romany blood craved. Happily married, she has two handsome sons: Richard is married, calm, dependable, drives tankers; Simon is a roamer – silversmith, roofer, welder, always with beautiful girls. Sara lives in the Cornish countryside. Her glamorous writing life alternates with her passion for gardening, which allows her to be carefree and grubby again!

CHAPTER ONE

THE shock silenced him. In the dimly lit room he heard nothing but his thundering heartbeat. And the voices in his head saying, it isn't true. *Can't* be!

Blake fought the red mist that clouded his brain. Generations of his ancestors must have been born, slept and finally died in the opulent surroundings of this vast bedroom. Yet he doubted that any of them had ever heard such a devastating outburst as this.

You are not the legitimate heir. You are...my love-child.

His mother's words spun around his head, destroying his ability to reason. It took a supreme effort of will for him to recover his senses. Seconds more before he realised there was a logical explanation. Her mind must be confused from the intensive course of medication.

Deeply distressed for her and with his concern for her uppermost in his thoughts, he masked his own chaotic feelings and sought to calm her. 'I've tired you with our chatting, Mother. I think you should sleep,' he advised gently.

Kay Bellamie's eyes blazed with anger, the only living sign in the once-beautiful face that was now a putty-coloured mask of imminent death.

'Don't treat me as if I'm mad!' she croaked. 'I'm perfectly sane. You are *not* a Bellamie! I want you to know that!'

'Mother!' Blake winced at her insistence, and at the destruction of her lyrical, fluting voice.

'It's the truth! You have *no right* to the inheritance. Look at yourself!' she flared. 'Do you think you have Bellamie blood? Where is your blond hair? Your fat gut? Your

5

bulbous nose? I *know* who fathered you. It was my lover, I tell you!'

He couldn't bring himself to humour her. This was too painful and must be stopped. 'Take it easy,' he cautioned. 'Perhaps you've been dreaming—'

'No!' Her skeletal hand clutched at his, its bony fingers a series of white claws against his healthily tanned skin. 'Do you know why I refused to allow you to be called after a Bellamie ancestor? I broke with tradition because I was desperate to keep something of your father. A name that linked you with him—'

'*Blake?*' He frowned, his inky brows two uncomprehending angles.

His mother looked at him as if she saw someone else and he felt fear clutch at his stomach with a scouring ferocity. No, he thought in silent horror. Don't let it be true!

'No, I daren't use his name. Blake means dark.' For a brief moment her eyes closed and he felt a pang to see the blue pallor of her lids. 'You've seen your baby photos,' she grated. 'You know you were born with masses of raven hair. Like my lover's.' A far-away smile lifted her thin lips for a moment. 'Dear God, Blake!' she went on vehemently. 'I know this is hard but, for your own sake, accept what I'm telling you! My mind is crystal clear. I've carried this secret all your life and I *must* unburden myself before I die. For the last time, you are not the son of Darcy Bellamie!'

Exhausted, she let her hand fall away to lie limply at her side. Slowly, reluctantly, his gaze flickered in the direction of the oil painting of his father over the baroque mantelpiece. A chill settled deep within his spine and spread to his entire body till he felt as if he'd been carved from ice. How many people had commented on the total lack of resemblance?

Every ounce of his strength seemed to leave him. Once

again, rational thought had become suspended. Utterly motionless, he sat like a zombie beside her rumpled bed, feeling as if he'd been poleaxed.

What was she saying? Why? his brain screamed. But he held back his raging emotion, crushing it remorselessly as he'd been instructed every day of his childhood until he had become adept at hiding his tempestuous feelings.

Frustration gripped him. It was impossible to know why she was exerting all her meagre energy to make such an astonishing claim.

Unless it was true.

Shuddering, he sought denial because acceptance would destroy him. Tenderly he stroked her hot forehead.

'Mother. The drugs you've been prescribed are powerful sedatives and they—'

'I haven't taken any for days. I needed to think. I'm speaking the truth, I swear on my grandson's head,' she cried in desperation.

That rocked him. He sucked in a long breath to fill his crumpled lungs. Defiantly his fists clenched. Preposterous—surely? All his life he had been groomed and trained and guided by his parents, governesses, fencing masters, riding instructors and stewards in preparation for his future as the Bellamie heir.

He'd been twenty when his elderly father, Darcy, had died. From that day he'd been catapulted into a position of authority where his decisions affected the lives of many. Consequently, he had made them with great care. After eight years of such unnerving responsibility he had become supremely confident in the role which would be his until he died and his son took over.

Confident…yes. And yet, admittedly, sometimes he felt restless and increasingly resentful of the constant pressures of duty. Occasionally he just longed to be free.

The hairs rose on the back of his neck. Had he inherited

that restlessness from his true father? The stolid and conventional Bellamie men had reputedly always been content with their lot of wealth and privilege. Maybe there *wasn't* a drop of their blood in him!

But of one thing he was certain. He loved every inch of Cranford Hall, every blade of grass on the vast estate—even the handful of estate workers' cottages spilling into the adjoining village of Great Aston.

And now his mother claimed that none of this belonged to him, after all! If this was true she'd just ripped apart the very fabric of his life.

God. He couldn't handle that. He'd spent twenty-eight years living a lie. Pretending to be someone else. When he was just his mother's by-blow. Base born. Illegitimate. *A bastard!*

A sudden pain made his stomach muscles tighten. He looked at his mother, who loved him, and saw the truth written there in her pleading eyes. She was perfectly lucid, her gaze steady and focused as she fumbled with the gold locket around her neck and opened it.

He swallowed. A photograph. Fearing what he'd see, nevertheless he leant forward to peer at the miniature heart-shaped snapshot.

A young man. Dark-skinned, vital and bursting with life, with black hair that curled defiantly, exactly like his, and laughing black eyes—the mirror of his. Same bone structure. Same fire. Two peas in a pod.

'Your father,' she whispered and lovingly stroked the photograph with a shaky finger.

'No!' But he could see it was. And his heart seemed to stop with shock.

'Look at him,' she said tenderly. 'You and he are so alike.' She sighed. 'He possessed me, body and soul. I almost abandoned everything for him. But he had nothing—and I'd known poverty only too well. I wanted this for you!' she cried, flinging out a quivering arm to encompass the room and its priceless contents.

Hardly breathing at all, he sank heavily back into the chair. It was as if he'd been cast adrift on the open sea. *His father.* A whirlwind of emotions rampaged through him: anger, despair and finally a hunger for this unknown father's love, which brought a lump to his throat and the pricking of tears to his haunted eyes.

A limp blue-veined hand lifted from the raw silk coverlet and covered his. 'Blake, you know I love you,' she said with a heartbreaking tenderness. 'I've devoted my life to you. I vowed that the son of my lover must one day inherit Cranford—'

'Inherit? How? You've made my position here impossible!' he cried more harshly than he'd meant.

But he was fighting a maelstrom that seethed inside him and the words had stubbornly stuck in his throat. He didn't want to do the honourable thing and give up Cranford because he wanted to forget this conversation had ever happened. To deny that dark-eyed laughing man. To remain what he was—Blake Bellamie, master of all he surveyed, proud of his heritage.

'Why?' she whimpered.

Impatiently he began to stride about the room, trying to resist the wicked urge to remain silent and to keep his mother's secret. He and his son and Cranford were inextricably linked. They had been his whole life, his entire reason for existing.

Yet the truth hammered at him relentlessly. Searing anguish shredded his guts. Shock and fear of the future weakened the muscles of his legs, turning them to mush. He'd never known such violent feelings.

Staggering a little, he leant heavily against a chinoiserie chest making the Satsuma vases on its racks rattle alarmingly. Sick to the stomach, he knew what he must do. God, he was shaking from that decision! Never in his entire gold-plated life had he felt so ill, so diminished. So…empty and alone.

Bleak-faced, he allowed his hooded black eyes to rest moodily on his panic-stricken mother, a pathetic figure almost devoured by the huge Jacobean four-poster.

Which wasn't his. *Nothing* was his. Nothing that he'd imagined he'd inherited. Only that morning he'd ridden across *his* land, spoken to *his* tenants, walked into the pub and discussed renovations with *his* builder and carpenter over a pint of local ale. Now everything belonged to someone else. His whole life had been a sham.

And destitute, it seemed, he and his six-year-old son. Throwing his head back, he inwardly groaned. What would he tell Josef? His child, his beloved son, light of his life since his wife had left…

He covered his face with his hands and groaned. But he couldn't hide from the truth. He had to start anew. And find the man who'd sired him.

'My…real father. Where is he?' he said jerkily, appalled by his need.

'Gone. Vanished into thin air.' Tears sprang from his mother's pale eyes. 'I told him to go, said that I didn't love him even though I would have laid down my life for him, I loved him so much. Still do…'

In deep shock, he stared at the desolation expressed in her face. Never had he known his mother so fervent. Within that cool, emotionless exterior there had been a passionate woman who had sacrificed everything for him. Including her own happiness

And, rattled by his own emotional reaction, he was beginning to understand. All his life she'd drummed it into his head that showing passion was unseemly for a gentleman.

Every excessive display of his had been relentlessly

crushed until he'd realised that his innocent, natural responses of joy and sorrow and anger weren't acceptable. Whenever he'd lost his temper or had become over-exuberant he'd been punished severely.

A bitter anger swept through him. Because she'd wanted him to behave like a Bellamie he'd been denied his own personality!

There had been times when he'd felt like exploding from suppressed fire and energy within him but had been forced to control himself. That was when he rode till the wind tore at him, the speed and ferocity of his riding easing the heat from his body.

So he had inherited passion and a lust for life. What else? The restlessness, the urge to feel the wind on his face, his hatred of being cooped up indoors for hours on end?

Bitterly, he realised that it didn't matter. He must leave Cranford and start a new life. It was the right thing to do. He blanched at the burden she had placed on him and suddenly knew the name of his father.

'He was called Josef, wasn't he?' he shot and at her soft smile of acknowledgement he felt his chest tighten.

The same name as his own son. Chosen by his mother who'd claimed it had been the name of her Hungarian grandfather.

Feeling light-headed, he realised he'd been holding his breath. Letting it out in a despairing exhalation, he clung to the remnants of his self-respect. Dying inside, every word an effort, he said tightly, 'I have to find the true heir. The legitimate descendant—'

'*No*! Not Giles. Not your father's cousin!' she wailed.

'If he's the rightful heir then I am duty bound to find him,' he vowed, tearing the words out of his body one by one because they didn't want to emerge at all.

She bit her lip then, looking desperate, she blurted out

wildly, 'And inflict hell on everyone here? Giles is...' She gulped, her voice wavering. 'He's...evil, Blake!' It seemed she was struggling for words to convince him, to change the doubting frown on his face. 'Giles was a drunk! You can't turn Cranford over to him!' she sobbed. 'You have your own son to think of now!' Her hands raked at him in desperation. 'I beg you, my darling! Don't let me die knowing that my whole life, my sacrifice, has been in vain!'

His heart twisted, loving her so much that it hurt him deeply to see her distress. He listened to her hesitant and stumbling description of Giles's habits. And was sickened by the man's degrading behaviour.

Stroking his mother's deeply lined forehead, he managed to soothe her. Gave her a pill. Waited till she slept. Then with heavy steps, his tall, lean body bowed under an impossible weight, he crossed to the full length window, seeing everything with different eyes. A stranger's eyes.

Not his. *Not his.* He swayed, crushed by the cruel pain of knowing.

What should he do? The right thing? Or what would be best for the majority of people? Including himself. He groaned. How could he be objective about this?

Josef appeared. Solemnly sitting on his new pony, chatting happily to Susie, the groom. Love swelled in his heart. And, when Blake swept his dark and troubled gaze over the parkland and wooded hills beyond, he felt a visceral tug of belonging that could never be expunged from his system.

Giles was an evil man. The estate, the business, the tenants—all would suffer in his hands. Blake knew this was no longer a decision based on his own desires but the cold, hard fact that Giles would go through the Bellamie millions like a knife through butter.

He had no choice. For the sake of everyone who depended on him he would keep the secret.

Even so, his life would never be the same. Already he felt a fraud. Shadows had already begun to darken his life, to weigh down his heart. He wondered with a bleak fury if he could ever be truly happy again.

CHAPTER TWO

'I SUPPOSE you're wondering why I've invited you to a meal just three weeks after my father's death.'

Despite the almost defiant set of her chic blonde head Nicole Vaseux was aware that the tremor in her voice had betrayed how she really felt. Forcing a feeble cover-up smile, she studied her guests who were seated around the long table beneath a rampaging grape vine. There was sympathy in her friends' faces for the death of her father, Giles, and they were making small, encouraging noises for her to continue.

Reaching out with her long fingers, she fiddled nervously with her cutlery making the silver bangles on her wrist jangle noisily. Almost certainly her friends would try to stop her leaving the country, thinking she was in no fit state to transport herself and a seven-week-old baby to England. They'd be right, of course.

Her mouth, as crimson and as lavish as her flowing dress, became tight with tension. After the blows that life had dealt her lately she felt as if she'd been hit by a pile-driver and all but driven into the ground.

'It's a kind of temporary goodbye,' she ventured, as casually as possible.

There was a sudden silence, knives and forks being suspended in mid-air. They were used to her unpredictability but they obviously sensed that even she felt in two minds about her forthcoming announcement. Here goes, she thought.

'I'm driving to England tomorrow.' Her chin lifted in a show of bravado. 'I don't know how long I'll be away.'

Eyes widened. Mouths dropped open. Edgily she pushed away her untouched plate and braced herself for the protests. She didn't have long to wait.

'*Chérie!* It is too soon. You have a tiny baby—!'

'But he's an angel. Look how peacefully he sleeps!' she said, her husky voice low and loving. And she felt hearts soften around her.

They all looked towards the Moses basket beneath the olive tree where the fair-haired Luc slept and Nicole took advantage of their doting smiles, launching with, 'It'll be easier to go now than when he's more active.'

Adjusting the bootlace strap that had slid from her slender shoulder, she took a deep breath. For a moment she was distracted from the matter in hand when the gazes of the men in the party zoomed in like Exocet missiles on the deep ravine between her swelling breasts. There was a sudden chill emanating from the women. Startled by the unexpected sexiness of her post-baby body, she placed her arms strategically before concentrating her bombshell.

'I must go,' she insisted. 'I have no choice. Father asked me to scatter his ashes in an English churchyard.'

'*Mon Dieu!*'

There was a buzz of chatter around the table. Their surprise almost equalled hers—and she'd been stunned by the request.

'But Nicole, you were born in the Dordogne!'

'With dual nationality—'

'And an English *mother*—'

'Surely your father was French—Giles Bellamie... A French name, yes? And you, so chic, so…artistic…'

'I know.' She sighed, the unconsciously elegant shrug of her shoulders expressing her utter mystification. 'But he was actually born in a village called Great Aston. In the Cotswolds.' She stumbled a little over the unfamiliar name.

Voices clamoured. She barely heard them. Her head ached with the thinking she'd done recently, with the trauma of her divorce, the birth of her child, the death of her father. Too much for anyone to bear, even a fatalist like herself. And now this, out of the blue.

Her father had been utterly French in style and outlook, though they'd always spoken English in the house. Even her mother—long divorced from her father and now living in New York with her new husband—knew nothing of the British passport tucked in the back of the locked desk drawer.

In a state of shock, Nicole had found the village on a map. It lay in an area called the Cotswolds, a rural part of England.

She had recognised the name of Stratford-upon-Avon which was to the north since that was Shakespeare country, and the city of Bath to the south-west. Close to Great Aston was Broadway, the mecca for tourists seeking a quaint, historical English village.

It must be lovely there, she'd thought. And had felt less resentful of the need to make the trip.

'It's an interesting area. I thought I'd make it a holiday,' she announced into the babble of English and French. 'I need one, badly.' She rolled her eyes, making fun of her troubles, and took a sip of her mineral water.

'I'll take you,' announced Louis.

'No, I will. I know England!' insisted Leon.

Nicole had noticed how their eyes had darkened speculatively as their gazes had strayed yet again to the honey-eyed mounds above the silk slip dress which hugged her newly curvaceous body. She sighed. Men! The last thing she needed was a sexual interlude right now. Her libido was non-existent. She had other priorities now.

'Thanks, but no.' There was a noticeable relaxation amongst the women. Nicole deeply regretted the change in her friends' attitude towards her. She felt suddenly very alone, a different person now she was no longer married. And, apparently, a dangerous woman. 'I need time to grieve,' she explained. 'It will be what the Americans call "closure". And then I can play the tourist, come home and fling myself into life again.'

They nodded in agreement, several of the men reminding her to make sure she came back.

'Why would I ever want to live anywhere else?' Her graceful artist's hand indicated the million-dollar view from her father's—no, *her*—cottage. The fruit trees were laden with blossom. The scent of herbs permeated the air. Bees darted busily among the unusual flowers her father had planted.

She went pale and the deep blue of her eyes took on a grey hue as a chill slid like cubes of ice down her spine. This was an English style garden. Like the many English ex-pats in the Dordogne he'd been recreating a little patch of England in a foreign country.

Forgetting her guests, she stared blankly at the tumbling roses, the lilies, the sweetly perfumed lilac. Her troubled mind resounded with the word *why*?

Why had he never told her his secret, when they'd been so close? Why had he never left France during her lifetime? Had he hated his birthplace—or was there another darker reason why he'd turned his back on his country?

Despite the warm evening she shivered. It was a secret she must unravel. However long it took.

'There's a lady chucking dust about in the graveyard! And she's got a hunchback on her tummy!'

An unusually excited Josef came hurtling into the church and down the nave as if he'd been shot from a gun. Still in his Sunday best—though decidedly grubbier than when he'd set out for church an hour earlier—the sparkling-eyed Josef skidded to a halt in front of his sombre-faced father who was indulging in a convivial after-service coffee in the nave.

Almost two weeks had passed since Blake had learnt he had no right to control Cranford. But he'd promised his mother that he wouldn't act hastily. His days and nights had been filled with questions, his conscience had crucified him every time he'd taken a decision concerning the estate.

Only Josef had given him heart. He smiled at his son, reflecting that he was well used to Josef's novel way with words. There'd be a rational explanation—there always was. A woman in her late pregnancy, perhaps. Though, he mused ruefully, Josef knew all about pregnant women and could identify them with ear-piercing certainty.

Politely excusing himself, Blake put down his coffee cup to deal with his son's latest misunderstanding, conscious that everyone there was indulgently watching his much-adored son whose joyous attack on life caused more smiles than offence.

'Why do you think she's doing that?' he asked, unable to stop himself from curving his palm lovingly around Josef's eager face. In a flash he knew why his mother had sacrificed so much for *him*. Of course you did. Your children held your sanity, your heart and brain in their tiny hands. You would go through hell for them. Sacrifice whatever you must to ensure their survival. It was a biological drive that ensured you defended your child, the future of the human race, against all harm.

''Cos she's mad,' Josef declared. 'She's talking rubbish to herself, like she's saying spells. And crying.'

'Crying?' Blake frowned and exchanged a concerned glance with the Reverend Thomas. 'Paul, I think I'd better see what I can do to help.'

Reaching for his son's hand he loped off, his long legs

covering the ground so quickly that Josef was obliged to trot.

No one questioned his authority. The small group clustered together for refreshments after Sunday worship had always deferred to the Bellamies. As had their ancestors, willingly and unwillingly, for more than five hundred years—though this particular Bellamie, everyone agreed, was an absolute gem.

Emerging from the church where countless Bellamie forebears lay peacefully beneath stone effigies and bold brass inscriptions, he couldn't help but catch his breath in awe, despite the familiarity of the view. Behind the small churchyard were the higgledy-piggledy roofs of the old weavers' cottages, the sun turning the Cotswold stone slabs to gold. Glorious parkland spread out in the valley beyond them, green and lush and merging with the petticoat of woods at the foot of Cranford Hill.

Blake knew that he owed this beauty, this precious heritage, to the fact that for hundreds of years the Cotswolds had produced the finest wool in Europe. He beamed with pride.

The Sunday silence was sweetly pierced by the sound of birdsong and the gentle hum of honey bees. He felt a pang of unutterable love. This place had become a part of him—body, soul, heart, mind. It was his and he was it. Legitimate or not, he was its temporary warden, dedicated to its welfare and its preservation until his son inherited—

'She's gone, Daddy! Has she magicked herself invillible?'

'Invisible,' he corrected automatically. 'Let's see.'

'But you can't *see* invillible!' argued his son.

He laughed. 'True! Perhaps there'll be some mystical sign?'

Amused, he began to walk around the ancient church in

search of her with Josef crushing his hand nervously and taking exaggerated tiptoe steps. Blake's heart glowed with love and he wondered if all parents were so hugely entertained by the funny things their children did.

They saw the woman just beyond the thousand-year-old yew, its ancient branches so massive and heavy that its limbs had been supported in the eighteenth century with sturdy props.

Slim and with curves in all the right places, she was crouching on her haunches by a gravestone so he couldn't see the alleged hunchback. For a moment he caught a glimpse of her face when she looked to one side and he estimated her age as somewhere around twenty-four or five.

Her clothes were unusual—a softly flowing long skirt in what his mother would have called eau-de-nil, teamed with a figure-hugging cotton top that exposed a good two inches or more of a golden-skinned back. And yet she looked stylish. Perhaps it was the trailing silk scarf, elegantly draped around her long neck.

Her pale blonde hair had been expensively cut, the silken strands swinging gently forward in a glistening arc as her slender and tapering fingers moved slowly over the lichen-covered stone. Not your average madwoman, he thought, intrigued by her sophistication, her chic.

'She's *feelin'* the grave!' his son whispered. 'Bet she's blind, too!'

Worrying about Josef's startling ability to put both feet in his mouth, Blake adopted a stern expression.

'Hush. Don't say a *word*. Understand? Leave this to me.'

He watched Josef's mouth adopt a comical zipped-up shape and suppressed a faint smile. How he loved his eager, caring son! He was doing the right thing in retaining the inheritance. He felt sure. And crushed the little voice within his innermost soul which disagreed.

They walked towards her, the warm April sunshine caressing his back and the scent of lilac from the rectory garden pleasing his senses with its fragrance.

Blake knew that he would serve Cranford better than the evil Giles. He had earned his right to the inheritance. Even though that insistently nagging voice kept ripping through his guts by saying, *Impostor. Charlatan. Liar.*

Nicole groaned. Here was yet another indecipherable grave! She felt close to despair and wondered if she would ever find evidence of her late father's family. Still clutching the now-empty jar of his ashes, she crouched down beside the next gravestone and tried to see if it bore the name Bellamie. But that, too, was badly weathered and the fresh disappointment hit her hard.

Ever since she'd arrived in Great Aston she had felt a passionate need to find her roots in this lovely English village. Its peace and serenity had folded around her aching heart as if reaching out to comfort her.

The entire village had seemed to be drowsing in the silent Sunday morning, the stone of its picturesque cottages a pleasing honeyed shade in the warm sunshine. The palette of colours ranged through golds, greens and whites, enhanced by the soft pastels of spring flowers. The gentle hues had a soothing effect on her travel-weary mind.

It was all very English. Fallen magnolia petals littered the road from a tree which leaned over a mellow stone wall. Opposite the church drowsed a timbered pub with a quaintly thatched post office right next to it. Just beyond, she could see a small village green, complete with pond and ducks and a crumbling market cross.

On the way to the small church she'd felt the overwhelming sense that she was walking in her father's footsteps. As a child, she felt sure he must have wandered these lanes. He had been here. Skipping along, laughing with friends...

The knowledge stirred her in a way she'd never known before. It was almost a feeling of being welcomed back by loving arms after a long time away. For the first time she understood the wonderful completeness in knowing your roots, your past.

She frowned. Why her father had left such a lovely place remained a nagging mystery. Still, whatever the truth, she had done as he'd asked. Returned his ashes to the foot of the great yew tree.

And now she was on her second quest, searching for evidence of her father's relatives. But not one solitary person in this graveyard had been called Bellamie!

Depressed by her lack of success and choked by her farewell to her father, she let out a sigh. *'Papa! Quelle trahison!'* she mourned, her forehead resting against the weathered stone. What a betrayal of their closeness!

Then she stiffened. Something made her turn her head, though she'd heard no sound. Through a fine veil of tears she saw the figures of a tall dark man and a tousle-haired child a few yards away, anxiously staring at her.

Knowing how odd she must have looked, Nicole blushed and instantly scrambled to her feet, her arms cradling the weight slung around her chest.

The man's dark, sparkling eyes suddenly crinkled with laughter. Eyes so deep and glittering that she felt disorientated for a moment, as if she'd slipped into the black void of unconsciousness. But one that was warm, velvety, thrilling...

'A baby! Josef, the lady has a baby in a sling!' The man whispered to the goggle-eyed boy beside him and the child's crimped-up mouth unravelled.

'I fought it was a hunchback. Hunchtummy,' he announced, then hastily folded his lips in again.

Nicole swam back from the velvet pit and came back to reality. *'Comment?'* she cried, not realising in her confusion that she was still speaking French.

'Une bossue,' the man solemnly explained and a little giggle of surprise flew unexpectedly from her lips. A hunchback! How funny! Her soft blue gaze regarded the man who had turned to his son, gently admonishing him with, 'And it's *thought*, Josef, not "fought".' His hypnotic liquid eyes met hers again. *'Bonjour, Madame. Je m'appele Blake…'*

'Good morning, Blake!' she said hastily, impressed by his knowledge of French. She smiled. 'I do speak English. My mother came from London and we used English most of the time. I'm Nicole Vaseux,' she offered. 'And my hunchtummy is called Luc,' she informed Josef in amusement, captivated by the child's enormous black eyes. 'He's seven weeks old.'

To Nicole's surprise the little boy's tousled dark head tilted to one side and he looked deeply upset. 'Oh, dear! Did you bring him here 'cos he's dead?' he enquired unhappily.

'Josef!'

Suppressing more giggles, Nicole calmed the man's horrified gasp of protest with a pacifying shake of her head that sent her blonde hair bouncing. 'No! Look. He's fine. Just asleep.' Crouching down again in a lithe, easy movement, she let the little boy inspect her son for signs of life.

'He's breathin'!'

She nodded, enchanted by Josef's delight and relief. With her face soft and adoring, she joined him in gazing in wonder at the little scrap of flesh and blood that was her son. Huge waves of love welled up inside her and she gently kissed Luc's peachy little cheek. He was her life. His welfare would come above everything else.

'Mon chou,' she murmured.

'Is that a magic spell?' gasped Josef, backing away hastily.

Her eyes twinkled at his awe-struck face. 'Do I look like a witch?'

'You could be in disguise,' he replied cautiously.

'I'm not. This is how I am,' she said, merrily gesturing at herself. 'I was speaking French, that's all. It means my pet, my darling,' she explained and, seeing the little boy's contented grin, she stood up again, suddenly becoming aware that Blake had been watching her intently.

A *frisson* shivered through her body. He was extraordinary in every way. *Different*, though she couldn't quite decide how. He was certainly the first man ever to scramble her brains!

Tall and immaculately dressed in a soft grey suit whose quality and cut she immediately appreciated, he had opted for individuality by teaming it with a Lake Blue shirt and violet tie. With a wilting daisy in his buttonhole. She smiled, suspecting that was the child's doing.

The face above was anything but formal—tanned, outdoor and healthy, his wide mouth and strong nose and brows forming a face of immense character. The hair, too, was unconventional. Inky black like a raven's wing, it tumbled in well-groomed waves to a length far beyond that which she'd imagined any English country gentleman might favour. It gave him a raffish air which she rather liked.

The intense quality of his liquid brown eyes seemed to note everything about her. Suddenly she was conscious of her travel-creased skirt and tear-stained face. She was a mess! And, having been brought up as a Frenchwoman, she minded dreadfully.

Nicole set about bringing order to her appearance, dabbing at her eyes with a soft linen handkerchief and smoothing her hands over her hips to ease any creases.

'I'm sorry,' he said gently as she replaced her handkerchief. 'Forgive me for intruding. I thought you might be—'

'Mad,' Josef provided with great enthusiasm. Blake's glare was met with an innocent protest. 'Well, what about her chuckin'—?'

'*Throwing* would be a better choice,' his father said. 'Joe, I think you'd better see if you can help the vicar and his ladies to clear away the coffee things. There might be a chocolate biscuit left for your reward.'

'He wants me to go,' the boy explained with a 'tut' and a heavy 'adults are so transparent' sigh. Nicole wanted to laugh and for the first time in days her spirits lifted. The child took a few steps towards the church then turned. 'But you'll tell me why she chu...*threw* that dust, won't you, Daddy?'

'Go!' Blake thundered. And turned to Nicole who was having difficulty keeping a straight face. He seemed to think she was wincing because he frowned. 'I can only apologise again,' he said quietly. 'Tact isn't in his vocabulary, but I am persevering and thinking of tattooing the word on to his forehead. What do you think?'

She noticed how his eyes glowed with sincerity and warmth. A likeable man, one to be trusted.

'A losing battle!' she said with a little laugh.

Blake sighed. 'I think you're right. Sorry.'

'It's all right. In fact, I was very sad and he's brightened my day.'

The most beatific smile lit his face, his even teeth a dazzling white against the Caribbean tan.

'Sometimes I think it's his purpose in life,' he said fondly.

She liked him even more. He evidently adored his son and had never crushed the child's wonderful spirit. Having been brought up unconventionally, she valued that immensely.

'You adore him,' she murmured.

The radiance of his expression shook her. 'With all my heart,' he confessed. And he laughed. 'Is it so obvious?'

She laughed too. 'Transparent. But it's understandable.' Her hand caressed her baby's head. To her astonishment she found herself saying to this complete stranger, 'When Luc was born I learnt what it means to love someone with my whole mind, with every beat of my heart. I loved my father, but this—'

'I know,' he said softly. 'I'm besotted too. Hopeless, aren't we?'

They both laughed at their mutual captivation.

'I think I should explain my behaviour here,' she said.

'I am intrigued,' he admitted.

Her eyes grew sombre. 'I came here to spread my father's ashes on the ground. It was his dying wish.'

The smile vanished, his face softening into lines of sympathy. 'I see.'

Churned up anew after her emotional goodbyes to her father, she said croakily, 'Maybe I should have asked the vicar, but the church service was on and I didn't want to disturb anyone—'

'It's fine,' he said, the tender understanding in his voice making her eyes briefly film with tears again. 'I wouldn't have intruded but Josef dashed in to say the lady was crying outside and I was concerned.'

'Not only that—' she suggested wryly '—you were curious about the hunchtummy!'

He grinned, dazzling her with the radiance of his smile. 'Guilty!'

'I was...talking to my father. Saying a prayer and...' She broke off. The stranger didn't need to know that she had spilled her heart out, asking her father *why*?

Sadly she surveyed the wild flowers beneath the yew tree where she had scattered his ashes and felt a huge sense of loss roll through her. There was a silence but it seemed friendly and encouraging and she found herself confessing, 'I wish I didn't have to leave him here. So alone. Far from home.'

'It was what he wanted,' came the quiet and consoling reply.

'I know, but...' White and even, her teeth bit hard into her lower lip. 'I suppose I'm being selfish. Because I'll be going home soon. And he'll be here, in a foreign land...'

'Where he longed to be.' The strong and calming tones washed over her, steadying her a little. 'I can understand that this must be hard for you, though. You think you're abandoning him and his memories. But you've done what he asked and he must have had a good reason.'

Oh, Father! What reason? she agonised. Again Blake's sympathy brought the tears pricking the backs of her eyes and she struggled to overcome them. Riven with sadness she gloomily watched a yellow butterfly dancing from flower to flower. *Citron* had been her father's favourite colour. He'd always worn yellow shirts, she thought mournfully.

'I'll miss him so much. We were very close, as I was his only child,' she murmured, following the dancing butterfly as it fluttered up to the soft blue sky and disappeared.

'Then you and he were very lucky.'

'Yes, we were,' she agreed and felt comforted.

There was a moment's silence then he added with great gentleness, 'Maybe it will help a little if I tell you of an experience I had, long ago when my grandmother died. I was only seven and I found the idea of death quite terrible. It gave me nightmares. But my mother told me of an old legend—' He hesitated, looking doubtful. 'You might find this fanciful...' His voice tailed away.

Nicole was very still, her huge eyes fixed on his.

Already a sensation of calm was stealing over her. 'Go on,' she said, longing to be consoled.

Blake's face softened. 'I was reminded of the legend,' he reflected, 'when the Brimstone—the yellow butterfly—appeared just now. It's unusually early this year, which is why I noticed it. My mother told me that robins and butterflies are said to appear to people who've lost a loved one, people who are inconsolable with grief. She said it was a sign that the soul is eternal and never dies.'

She smiled. True or not, the legend had eased the weight of sorrow that had filled her heart. 'Thank you for telling me,' she said gratefully. And quivered at the warm smile he bestowed on her. 'What about you?' she asked, confused by her disturbed feelings and desperately seeking normality. 'Did the legend come true for you?'

'Not to begin with,' he replied amiably, 'though I kept looking. Then ten days later I saw a robin on grandma's favourite seat in the garden. I felt as if she'd tried to comfort me.' He frowned for a moment and continued slowly, 'Even if...' He paused and then continued. 'If I hadn't been related to her I believe she would have reached out in some way because of the love between us. I firmly believe love never dies and that a spiritual thread has continued to link us. So I believe that there will always be a thread connecting you and your father, Nicole.'

Enormously soothed by his huskily spoken words, she looked at him with deep gratitude, her lashes spiky around her huge, misted eyes. How fortunate she was to have met such a kind person at this time. Without him—and his son—the whole episode would have been traumatic.

'That's a lovely thought. I'll remember that. Thank you,' she said simply, the limpid depths of her eyes telling him more than she could say.

For a moment he stared at her as if in a trance, then snapped himself out of it with a brisk, 'Look, I don't know what you'll think of our very English coffee, but we can offer a cup of instant in the church—or you could have proper coffee, even something a little stronger, in my house if you need fortifying. You and your husband are welcome—'

'I don't have a husband at all,' she broke in, lowering her eyes to gaze at Luc's small, vulnerable head. 'I'm on my own,' she said jerkily.

The nightmare of Jean-Paul's betrayal still had the power to hurt her. How could she ever forget such pain? It had been like walking into a brick wall when, three months pregnant, she'd found Jean-Paul in bed with her supposed best friend. Nicole winced, her face wrenching with a spasm of anguish. According to him, it had been her fault. Luc had not been planned and, although she'd been thrilled, Jean-Paul had been appalled. He'd never wanted her to have a child. He'd hated her pregnancy and the way her figure had disappeared.

Stupidly, mindful of the child she carried, she'd forgiven him. And two weeks later she had returned early from work feeling horribly sick, only to discover her husband and her 'friend' in bed again.

It was then that her love for Jean-Paul Vaseux had died. Her father had warned her about love. Enjoy sex, he'd advised her. But don't mistake it for love. Love comes but rarely. And it hurts. He was right. It did. And how appropriate, she thought with a flash of waspishness, that *vaseux* meant slimy, seedy, spineless!

She noticed that Blake was looking at her baby with sadness and she felt the wave of compassion reaching out to her. And suddenly his offer was doubly welcome. She craved human company for a while, someone who was caring and who could calm her jagged nerves. The last hour had tested her reserves to the limit.

Her hand went to her brow. She felt bone-weary from

it all. Sheer physical exhaustion was taking its toll. Hours of driving, feeding Luc, missing meals and precious sleep…

'You look all in,' he said in concern. 'Please come and rest for a while, if only for your baby's sake.'

'You're very kind.' She pushed her hair back behind her ears, managing a small smile for her saviour. 'A good Samaritan. Coffee of any sort would be wonderful. I seem to have been driving for ever—'

'From France? With a baby?' he enquired, lifting a thick eyebrow in a perfectly shaped and somehow appealingly devilish V.

'I travelled over several days.'

'Heaving baby stuff in and out of your car and into hotels en route?'

Her eyes kindled. He was one of those people who found no difficulty in putting himself in other people's shoes.

'It was a nightmare,' she confessed. 'There is a bonus, though. I could lift weights for France if I ever need a new career.' She faked a weightlifter's snatch and lift then remembered she didn't have any French blood in her veins. How odd. She was English through and through. It took a bit of getting used to.

Blake was laughing, his handsome face sparkling with vitality. His amusement was so infectious that she began to grin too and her momentary pang soon passed.

'That's certainly a plus,' he conceded, chuckling. 'But it must have been tough travelling on your own.'

Her nose wrinkled. 'Not one of the best times in my life. Apart from Luc and hotel concierges, I didn't speak to a living soul the entire time.'

Though she'd felt lonely even before that. Her father's Bohemian—and sometimes raucous—friends had ceased to visit the cottage. As far as her own friends were concerned, initially she'd been swamped by loving concern, but either they were single men who looked ready to make a move on her or they were part of a doting couple whose affection towards one another pointed up her own failed relationship. Gradually there had been that shift in the attitude of all her female friends now that she was divorced, available and still potentially sexually active. It seemed that she'd gone from being everyone's best mate to a dangerous *femme fatale*. The ripening of her body didn't help, of course. She'd always been skinny before...

'Where have you come from?' Blake asked, interrupting her thoughts.

An image of the cottage came to mind. Her father on the terrace, a glass of wine in his hand, his voice slurred with alcohol as he told her he had a short time to live. Impatiently she roused herself from this maudlin diversion. 'I live in the Dordogne.'

'Ah. That explains it. The land of English ex-pats.'

'Except... I always thought my father was French!' she blurted out on impulse. 'I never knew he had any English connections till I saw his British passport,' she cried. 'He was born here. I didn't have any idea till he...'

Her voice faltered and he stepped forward in concern, slipping his hands beneath her elbows for support. Something peculiar happened. It started in her breast and shot in milliseconds down to her womb. Almost as if he'd electrified the whole of her nervous system.

'Gently, gently. It's all right,' he soothed, but that wasn't true at all.

Her emotions were going into overdrive. She wanted to burst into tears again. And have him hold her, stroke her into quiescence, murmur to her in that honey-gold voice that seemed to seep into her bones and melt them. *Quelle folie!* How vulnerable grief had made her to a kind word and gesture!

'Excuse me,' she mumbled, pink with embarrassment. Dashing her hands across her eyes she squared her shoulders in determination. 'I'm being so stupid—'

'I don't think so. Your father. A new baby. The long journey,' he began, warming her heart with his consideration and understanding.

'Yes,' she agreed. And little did he know that there was so much more to cope with! She had to find her father's family. Suddenly her stomach grumbled in complaint and she clutched at her bare midriff, realising how hungry she was. 'As you can hear from the sound effects—' she said with an apologetic smile '—I'm in desperate need of food! I think I'd better find somewhere to eat. And he'll need feeding soon, too.' Her hand curved lovingly around baby Luc's head, enjoying its silky warmth. 'I feel odd. Woozy, as my fa-father used to say.' She managed a brave smile. 'My blood sugar level is probably non-existent,' she explained softly. 'I missed breakfast and—'

'Right. In that case, come.'

His authority was so compelling that she was being guided along the path before she knew what was happening. He strode with an ease that suggested a dangerous, feral prowl, a liquid-limbed lion lording it over the entire jungle.

And that weird fizzing sensation was attacking her again. It was like being hooked up to a pylon. Odd, how the combination of lack of food and a handsome charmer could make your head reel. She pulled away, unnerved that a stranger could be making such a dramatic impact on her. None of her male friends had made the slightest dent in her armour-clad libido.

But her defences had been weakened by events, she knew that. If she wasn't careful, she'd be flinging herself weeping into his welcoming arms and making a right fool of herself. Despite her longing for someone to cuddle her, it was time to make a run for it while her dignity was still intact!

'I don't want to take up any more of your time. I'll go to the pub,' she said, quite appalled that she felt grumpy about meeting his wife and having her romantic illusions of Blake's feral nature tainted by domesticity. 'There's one in the village. And you must be wondering where your son is—'

'In the church. Being petted and indulged. I'll tell him I'm leaving. No doubt he'll come home under escort with a stomach bulging with chocolate biscuits and his head full of misunderstandings which I'll have to unravel when he repeats them.' Blake's eyes twinkled. 'The ladies adore him. They'll probably all insist on accompanying him home so they can regale me with the funny things he's said.'

'I'm sure. All the more reason to refuse your kind offer,' she said reluctantly, liking him far too much—his ready smile, his kindness, his increasingly compelling sexiness. When had she ever met a man who was compassionate, gorgeous and not the slightest bit self-centred? And, she thought shakily, who electrified her. With difficulty, she forced herself to say a half-truth. 'I'd like to eat in the pub, anyway. It'll be fun.'

He stopped and she felt ridiculously flattered that he looked disappointed. 'As you wish. If you're sure you'll be all right on your own.'

'I have to get used to that,' she replied gravely.

'That's true. Nevertheless, I admire your strength.'

Their eyes locked and there was, indeed, admiration in his glance. It seemed to heat her through and through, coiling like a fiery cognac into her veins and quickening her pulses.

The light-headed sensation came back and she knew she had to eat before she fainted from lack of food and a surfeit of charisma. Yet she hesitated. This was, after all, a golden opportunity. A caring man, anxious to help her.

'Blake... There *is* something you can do for me before I go,' she ventured. Her heart thudded.

He looked inordinately pleased. 'Name it.'

For a moment she thought from the simmer in his eyes that he was flirting with her. Then her sense of reality returned. This was human kindness, nothing more. A man who smiled with his entire being and projected an embracing warmth without even knowing he did so.

He'd do his best to help her. Hope glowed in her eyes. She'd solve the mystery and go home content. She took a steadying breath, feeling quite excited. 'I'm trying to discover why my father wanted me to come here with his ashes,' she explained. 'You live locally, do you?'

He gave a wry smile as if thinking of a sweet-sour secret. 'I was born here. And...my parents and grandparents before me.'

Her face lit up with unconfined joy. 'Then you might be just the person I've been looking for!'

'Might I?' he murmured.

Initially, his response took her aback. Again there was that subtle shift in his expression. A deeper meaning in his eyes that made her insides turn to water. But after she'd blinked she saw that she'd been mistaken and his face showed merely a polite interest.

Oh, Nicole! she thought in reproach. How badly you need to be loved! Time she filled up with a good steak and fries. *After* she'd pumped her knight in shining armour for information.

'Yes,' she said, managing to sound brisk instead of lovelorn. 'The fact is that I've been searching the gravestones to see if any of my father's family were buried here. But they aren't, as far as I can tell. It's impossible to read many of the stones because of the...er...the...'

'Lichen,' he supplied genially, realising she was search-ing for the word. 'I'm afraid the frost has damaged most of the older inscriptions, too.'

He thrust his hands into his trouser pockets and smiled again. Nicole tried not to let her attraction for him show. But he was the most electrifying man she'd ever met and she wasn't very successful.

'So,' he murmured when she stood staring hazily at him. She blushed, realising that many women had probably looked at him with the same doe-eyed adoration. He'd probably dealt with them all by adopting that shuttered look. 'If you're searching for the name Vaseux,' he said, 'then I'm afraid I don't know of—'

'Oh, no!' she broke in hastily. 'My father's name wasn't Vaseux.'

'No?'

Picking up the cue, he looked at her hand and frowned because it was bare of any rings. But in her eagerness she didn't pause to explain that she'd hurled her wedding ring at Jean-Paul in fury. Tense with hope she took a deep breath, willing him to know something, anything, about her family.

'No.' She stared up at him, taut with hope. 'It was Bellamie,' she cried.

'Bellamie?'

She cringed, bewildered by his reaction. The smile had been wiped from his face and replaced by an expression of sheer alarm.

'Ye-e-es...why?'

'Bellamie!'

Nicole felt horribly sick. In a perfectly kind and cour-teous man, her father's surname had provoked a horrified response. Her senses reeled. Why, why? She knew with a feeling of utter dread that it was because of something awful that had happened.

She let out a small groan. If she could have taken back her request for help she would. It had been a mistake to probe into the past. She should have scattered the ashes and gone home, none the wiser. Now her father's memory was about to be sullied with some awful revelation. And she didn't want to hear it.

CHAPTER THREE

WHEN Luc began to cry she didn't know whether to be glad or sorry. His yells seared into her brain, making her incapable of coherent thought. Shaken immeasurably by Blake's reaction, she did her best to soothe her baby but his hysterical cries only grew louder and her own agitation increased till she felt like screaming herself.

It was no use. She'd have to feed him. And she needed to sit down before she collapsed anyway. Her whole body had begun to tremble with a terror of the unknown.

'Excuse me,' she squeaked in panic, searching around desperately for a convenient place to sit. She jerked out unnecessarily, 'He needs feeding.'

'There's a bench over here.' The tone was curt and laced with a steely hardness. This time the guiding hand beneath her elbow seemed to push her along without ceremony.

She could hardly collect her thoughts, they were churning so furiously in her head. He must see how shallow her breath was, how swiftly her chest rose and fell. And there were two prominent red spots of heat that she knew must stain her cheeks, together with the tenseness of her muscles which were so taut that she trembled as if she had the ague.

Thankfully she sank to the wooden seat beneath a bower of pear blossom. Such a pretty spot. Ironically, such a nightmare moment.

Not daring to look at Blake, she concentrated on extricating the yelling Luc from the sling and sliding it off, taking twice as long as usual because her fingers had become suddenly clumsy in her panic.

Father, what have you done?

In distress she bent her head, hoping Blake would go
but he remained firmly planted in front of her as if on
guard. Perhaps he thought she was a danger to society?
she thought hysterically. It amazed her that she could feel
his hostility as if it were a living thing, the power of his
seething presence overwhelming her.

Quivering from the onslaught of his—as yet—unspoken
disapproval, she shrank into the seat, the hard slats digging
painfully into her back.

Desperately pleading with Luc to be calm, she fumbled
awkwardly with the buttons of her shirt. Normally she felt
no qualms about discreetly feeding her baby in public. But
there was something so rawly masculine about Blake that
she felt intensely aware of her body. And he wouldn't stop
staring at her. Those diamond glinting eyes would examine
every move she made, assess the curves of her breast...
She quivered.

Luc yelled on. Modesty, she thought frantically, must
be thrown to the winds. Defiantly she shot Blake a glare
from under her lashes, as if to remind him of common
decency. His expression of intense fury left her breathless,
every scrap of air rushing from her lungs.

'Let's get this straight. You call yourself Vaseux but you
are a Bellamie?' he ground out, utterly disregarding her
need for some peace and privacy.

'Yes!' she yelled over Luc's piercing cries with a defiant
toss of her head. 'And proud of it!'

That told him, she thought grimly. And, not caring if
Blake saw her breast or not, she undid her buttons and let
Luc's rosebud lips brush her engorged nipple. After a moment or two of fussing around Luc latched on to her and
his whimpers died away. There came the familiar tugging
which normally relaxed her into a state of blissful pleasure.
But not this time.

Not with the tall and menacing Blake looming over her,

his very stance a calculated threat as if he might be an avenging angel, determined to make her suffer because she bore her father's name.

Papa, you must have known this would happen! she mourned silently to herself. Why put me through this when you loved me?

Unhappily she cradled her child. Even the sight of Luc contentedly feeding, with all his red, screwed-up anger vanished and replaced by utter satisfaction, did nothing to ease her agitation. Something terrible was about to happen. Feeling nausea rise to her throat she choked it back. Bent her head and found refuge in kissing the pale silk of her son's white-blond hair.

But a relentless force dragged her gaze back, up to the scowling Blake. No, she thought, taken aback. Not scowling—riven with horror. Her tongue slipped nervously over her dry lips. If her hands had been free she would have put them over her ears to shut out anything he might say.

It was the sheer contrast of Blake's former pleasantness and this dreadful loathing that shocked her so much. Blake wasn't the vindictive sort. She'd instantly felt a bond with him. The kind that could, in other circumstances, have developed into a wonderful relationship.

And yet—

'I need to establish one or two facts,' he said, all ice and steel.

Unable to speak for the massive lump which sat resolutely in her throat, she clutched Luc more tightly as if he were her lifeline. What had her father done to deserve this? Why had the mention of his surname produced such a reaction?

'Like what?' she asked in a strangled kind of croak.

'Your father's full name.'

She trembled. 'Giles. Giles Bellamie.'

He inhaled sharply and she knew he recognised the

name because his face became drawn and his eyes darker than ever.

'And he is dead,' he stated bluntly, as if needing confirmation.

She winced. 'You know he is! I've scattered his ashes, haven't I?' she replied, feeling hysterical.

Why did he want to rub it in when he'd been so thoughtful before? She made an effort to even out her breathing. It was all over the place. She must stay calm for Luc's sake.

'Do you often interrogate women when they're breast-feeding?' she flung and had some satisfaction in seeing the colour flare across his high cheekbones.

'These are unusual circumstances.'

'Are they?' Her caustic glance swept across his uncompromising face.

'You want to trace your family?'

She narrowed her eyes. He sounded more under control now. But cold. So horribly cold in his manner.

'Depends,' she fended warily.

It seemed that he was considering various options. She watched him as he turned away and stared in the direction of the beautiful parkland beyond the drystone walls of the churchyard. The expansion of his back and the high carriage of his broad shoulders suggested that a conflict raged within him. Knots of sick anxiety twisted in her stomach. This was unbearable. Better to know everything than to carry this terrible suspicion about her father within her.

'Tell me what's wrong!' she demanded, her low voice vibrating with urgency. 'You know my father—'

He turned then, his expression haunted. '*Of* him.'

'And?' She could hardly breathe.

Slowly his glacial gaze devoured her, from the top of her shining blonde head to the tip of her chartreuse green pumps peeping from the gentle folds of her skirt. His mouth thinned in what she thought must be disapproval.

'You're very young,' he mused, his manner tight and shuttered as if he was repressing strong emotions. She thought he'd muttered, 'Too young,' under his breath but she wasn't sure.

'Twenty-five!' she supplied, a little indignant. 'Are you so old?'

'Twenty-eight,' he said in a clipped voice. 'And Luc is your own son, your own blood?'

Her mouth gaped. What was this? 'Of course! Do you think I carry another woman's baby around and feed him?' she flared, stung into fury by his inexplicable behaviour.

'I have to know!' he rasped.

The frostiness of Blake's expression—this man she'd instantly liked, whose son she'd thought so adorable—made her blurt out in self-pitying misery, 'Luc is all I have in the whole world, now!'

Immediately she wished she hadn't said that. It had sounded pathetic, as if she wanted to soften Blake up by appealing to him by means of her child.

True, there had been a tremor in his mouth as he'd briefly surveyed the swell of her breast and the blissful infant suckling there. But then his jaw had turned to concrete again and now his eyes were brooding on her—hooded, secretive, wary.

As if, she thought wildly, she might leap up and bite him and turn him into a vampire or worse.

'Your mother's dead?' he shot.

'Remarried, living in America and too busy living the high life to be bothered...' Irritably she checked her explanation and pruned in her mouth. 'What the hell has it got to do with you?'

'Everything.' He surveyed her for a moment then his head angled to one side speculatively. 'The name you used. Vaseux. Was that something your father adopted as a false identity?'

She shrank with horror, her eyes huge as her mind ticked off the reasons he'd think that. Crime. Fraud. Bigamy... Oh, this was ridiculous! There'd be a simple explanation. A misunderstanding.

'He was always Bellamie. It was my name too,' she muttered, still too shell-shocked to say any more.

'But...' He frowned. 'You said you weren't married,' he growled.

'No, I didn't. I said I didn't have a husband and I haven't,' she replied flatly. 'Not any more. I'm divorced.'

His head fell back in a gesture of despair. When he looked at her again she saw his teeth were clenched tightly together in an angry grimace.

'Does that mean that your husband was Luc's father?' he asked tightly.

Rage made her eyes glint with steely lights. What kind of person did he think she was? Maybe her life had been freer than that of most people she knew but she'd never been promiscuous or sexually irresponsible as Blake was suggesting.

The fury rose up in a huge, unstoppable surge. She was renowned for being amazingly easy-going and laid back in temperament until driven too far. And then sparks flew. They were about to ignite the touchpaper, big time, she thought grimly, heading straight for it.

'Are you trying to insult me or is it purely accidental?' she snapped.

The barb went home. He actually flinched. Or, rather, his mouth crimped in briefly before his very English self-control asserted itself again.

'I need to know if Luc is illegitimate,' he bit.

'Why?' she blazed. 'Don't you talk to the mothers of bastards?'

He flinched and went pale beneath his tan. 'It's not that!'

'Then what? Are you collecting gossip for the village magazine? Looking for fallen women to save?' she flung, getting well into her stride. 'Or doesn't the lord of the manor allow bastards in this village—?'

'That's enough!' Blake hissed, his entire body quivering with suppressed fury. 'Answer the question. Is he your legitimate son?'

'Yes!' she hurled back. 'Why is that so important to you? Tell me—or get the hell out!'

His hand shook slightly as it swept over his gypsy hair. He looked shell-shocked, his confident manner gone, his mouth compressed in a thin, hard line. And he seemed almost to shrink away from her as if she might be carrying the plague.

She gulped, even more apprehensive than before.

'I told you,' he grated harshly. 'I'm establishing facts.'

'Maybe. But for what purpose? You must tell me what's going on!' she cried in exasperation, so vehement in her movements that she dislodged Luc.

He protested long and loud. With her nerves skittering all over the place she quietened him and soon he was nursing again. That was when she looked up once more, her mouth set in a firm line of anger.

Again Blake appeared to be in the throes of a struggle with a powerful emotion. Twice he made to speak and stopped himself. Her fears increased. It was something to do with her father. And yet her Papa had been kind and generous, loving and loved!

Oh, Papa! she thought, dreading what was to come. A terrible revelation. Perhaps a criminal record, an injustice or maybe some misdemeanour in his youth with a village girl...

She closed her eyes in misery. Discovering a dark secret would destroy all her lovely memories of him and she wanted to hold on to them with a desperation that shook her to the core.

Blake had never known such indecision. There she was, the picture of aggrieved innocence, engrossed in the tender act of feeding her baby. Mother and child. A tiny defenceless baby, the rightful heir to Cranford.

He winced. Dear God! The shock had been more than he could bear for a moment. He'd seen his life—the life he loved—being brutally taken from him. The house, the land, his projects that he'd begun and those he'd successfully completed—all these would be no longer his to worry about, or his responsibility to guide to fruition.

He pictured Josef's face when he told him they were moving and his son's bewilderment as he struggled to understand what Granny had done and why they were leaving their beloved home, their friends, the life they had fondly imagined to be theirs by rights.

He felt the most terrible anguish tearing at his guts. It was a living nightmare. His whole life. All for nothing.

Fighting the knifing pains in his heart, he turned his back again on the touching scene as she gently rocked to and fro, an expression of deep anxiety creasing her clear forehead and drawing down those sensual lips into an expression of misery.

His brain seemed overloaded, every thought hurtling around and getting nowhere. First there had been the shock of meeting Giles's daughter, such a short time after his mother's revelation. Then the tender mother and child scenes. His sympathy for her. The terrible battle with his conscience. And, even more disturbing, the stirring—no, who was he kidding? The firing, the exploding, of his loins.

Incredible. She exuded sex from every pore, despite her motherly role. The sheer intensity of her sensuality had hit him like a physical blow, penetrating his cold indifference to women and setting him alight with almost unstoppable lust.

Every movement she made with that incomparable body, each wide-eyed glance and flicker of those impossibly long lashes, had attacked his celibate state and flung it so far into history that it was in danger of colliding with the ancient Romans.

His feelings alarmed him. By rights he should run a mile from someone who could affect him so strongly. He had wanted to take her in his arms. Kiss that soft, pliable mouth till they were both breathless. Crazy, unbelievable. Unwise even to dwell on such urges.

And yet, unable to stop himself from doing so, he glanced over his shoulder, hungry, aching for the very sight of her. His pulses leapt. The blood throbbed in his veins.

Her bent head shone like yellow glass in the sunshine. He took in the perfection of her skin, the small straight nose, those softly parted lips and desire rose within him as he'd never known it before. Hot, hard, urgent. Forget the Romans. He'd reverted to caveman levels. What the devil was happening to him?

Although he'd been determined not to let his gaze wander any further he found himself ignoring that decision. Hating himself, disgusted and torn with battles between his better nature and the coarser urges of his body, he let his tormented eyes linger on the flawless hill of her half-exposed breast.

And then, appalled and stunned by the sexual power she unknowingly wielded over him, he clenched his jaw and resolutely—with unbelievable difficulty—turned away again.

Struggled with his desire for a total stranger. His second cousin. Giles's daughter. A woman brought up by a man without morals. So what did that make her? It was inconceivable she could have remained totally untouched by her father's habits.

His entire system seemed to be in turmoil. But he knew one thing. This was when he should say to her, Your son owns this land and everything you can see. He owns a Tudor mansion, its mullioned windows and hammerbeam hall, the tapestries and treasures. He also owns stables, outbuildings, estate cottages and acres of land. Every month he will receive the rents that will assure his future and yours, as his legal guardian. You both have come into a fortune. And an ancient and historic dynasty.

The worst scenario of the evil Giles inheriting had been avoided by the man's death. Blake's duties were clear-cut. To announce Nicole's good fortune and bow out. Yet he couldn't bring himself to say the words.

Being a woman she couldn't inherit herself, but with eighteen years till Luc gained his majority she would be the one who ran the estate. And spent its money. But he knew next to nothing about her.

Except that she was beautiful and sexy. Earthy, even. Blake clenched his teeth, mentally killing his too-responsive leap of desire. This gut feeling for her was something raw and primal and utterly terrifying in its sweeping obliteration of his rigid self-control. It seemed that his safe, known world had been destroyed and with it his painfully acquired discipline over his wayward passions. His heart thundered. Had his mother's revelation released him from the strait-jacket of his emotions?

Was he the result of a union between two highly passionate people ruled by base needs? Fire was certainly coursing through his veins at this minute—and had been ever since he'd set eyes on Nicole.

He didn't like that loosening of control. Didn't know who he was any more. And that was terrifying, like being thrown into a deep hole and finding yourself forever falling.

Being freed from constraint was disturbing. Perhaps, he thought sourly, suppressing one's feelings had its compensations and could be a virtue after all.

He scowled at the ground. As for Nicole... What of her? She'd lived with her father. Couldn't have been ignorant of his ways—and yet she'd idolised him. Was that because she had similar tastes, or had she loved him *despite* his outlandish behaviour?

So many questions and no answers—though he needed them fast. Her character was the key to his next move.

Blake scowled, thinking of the way she'd responded to *him*, a total stranger, when his guard had slipped and he'd accidentally let his raw attraction surface. Her mouth had curved in a wanton smile, her eyes had issued an almost irresistible invitation. Which he'd almost grabbed with both hands.

It might be a mutual attraction. It might be her response to men. How would he know? He couldn't take risks with Cranford's future. If the land was mismanaged and drained of investment then the whole village would suffer. He had to know more about her before he took the irrevocable step of telling Nicole that her son was the heir.

Behind him he heard the sounds of her fingers fumbling with material. Buttons being done up. Life flared in his loins and he concentrated on timing some long controlling breaths even while his senses remained on high alert.

There came the zip of the baby bag. Her husky, deep-throated voice in that spine-tingling accent, speaking in French to the baby.

Here we are, my sweet. Let's get that bottom of yours sorted and then...

Her voice broke. He waited, the hairs rising on the back of his neck, tension in every sinew of his body as he strained to hear her low, secretive whisper in the language he knew as well as his own.

Then we'll get the truth from that man, even if I have to use all my wiles to do it!

Blake's eyes glittered. Fortunate that he had such good hearing. And that the Bellamie family—descended from a French ambassador who had 'gone native' in the reign of Elizabeth I and had been rewarded with Cranford for his loyalty—had not only adopted French names for the male heirs, but by tradition had sent them to France until they were fluent in the language.

So she wanted the truth. He'd tell her what he knew about her father, then, and see her reaction. Beneath those tears and the charm lay a strong will. He'd realised that when she'd defied him.

Unless he knew that she was of unimpeachable character he couldn't possibly hand over the house, or put the lives of people he cared about in her hands.

He thought of his mother, so close to death. His heart lurched with pity and he knew he couldn't tell her that the real heir had turned up. She would die a destroyed woman. It was his loving duty to protect her from harm at all costs. She had sacrificed everything for him. He could at least allow her to die content.

Filial love played tug-of-war with honour. And he found a way to satisfy both. He would deal with this later, he decided, putting off the evil hour. If he thought Nicole was worthy she would know the truth when she was ready to be told—and that would definitely be after his mother had died.

CHAPTER FOUR

WITH unusually clumsy hands Nicole finished changing Luc's nappy, her eyes warily flicking in Blake's direction. He'd keep. She had other priorities.

Tucking the now sleeping child into the sling, she fixed it in place and levered herself up from the bench, swaying a little as she did so. Her head felt full of cotton wool. Her stomach was running on empty.

Food, rest, and an explanation. In that order. Without the first two she'd never cope with the third.

'I'm going to the pub,' she announced to his uncompromising back. Her statement came out rather belligerently because she was trying to sound tough. No point in letting him think he could walk all over her. 'I'll ask them what *they* know about anyone called Bellamie.' He spun around with an intake of breath. She saw his eyes flicker in alarm and knew he hadn't liked that. Pleased with her tactic, she added, 'After that, I would like to meet up with you again. I have a right to know why you bear such hostility towards my father. And me.'

'You must come to my home, not the pub,' he grated.

'I'd rather eat worms,' she said tartly.

There was a flicker of something akin to alarm in his eyes. 'They're not on the menu. Nicole, you have to understand that this must be kept between ourselves,' he said ominously, striking fear into her again. His mouth twisted. 'No dirty washing in public. You know the expression?'

Mystified, she nodded. 'But what do you mean by it?'

There was a long tense pause. She could see that he was

steeling himself to say something he'd clearly prefer to keep to himself.

Eventually he said flatly, 'You are family.'

Her eyes widened in amazement. '*What* did you say?'

He stared then said with obvious reluctance, 'My name is Blake Bellamie. I am your second cousin.'

'*Cousin?*' she croaked.

There was no welcome. None of the easy charm she'd witnessed earlier. Just a coldly stated fact. She blinked, trying to gather her wits. He'd known they were cousins all the time he was interrogating her. And hadn't chosen to reveal their relationship.

'And when were you going to tell me this? Over coffee?'

He thought for a moment. 'Probably not.'

She gasped. That was unbelievable! 'How dare you? That's outrageous!' she stormed. It hurt even more because he'd been so kind before and they'd shared personal confidences. His change of attitude seemed almost like a betrayal. 'You knew I was upset,' she accused. 'You knew I wanted to find my family—' She paused. Drew breath. And hazarded, 'You only told me because I said I'd make enquiries in the pub, didn't you?'

'Yes. And you'll understand why in a moment. Where is your car?' he rapped out, grim-faced.

'By—by the post office—'

He nodded. Curtly. Strode off to the church without a backward glance and disappeared inside. Nicole wasn't sure what to do. Her legs wouldn't stop shaking. She could get in her car and vanish, keeping her father's memory safe. But, even as the idea came into her head, she knew with a heavy heart that for the rest of her life the mystery would fester in her mind.

She would wonder why a perfectly decent man—her kinsman, she thought in wonder—who loved his son and had shown consideration to a total stranger, should have reacted so adversely when he'd realised she was Giles Bellamie's daughter.

A cross-sounding child's voice penetrated her seething brain. 'But why, Daddy, why?'

Looking towards the church, she saw Blake pull a handkerchief from his pocket. He efficiently wiped Josef's chocolatey face and hands. All the while he spoke quietly to his son. He seemed appeased because he grabbed his father's hand and trotted along beside him, seemingly unaware of Blake's hard-jawed expression as he strode towards her.

'Hello,' chirruped Josef blithely. 'Hello, baby.' He patted the sling with small, dimpled hands, his beaming smile a contrast to his father's cold reserve. 'Daddy says I can have ice cream for pudding when we get home—'

'Only if you eat your lunch in the kitchen with Cook,' Blake warned.

'Sometimes,' Josef said with a hugely artificial sigh, 'I wish we didn't have cream sofas.'

Despite her worries, Nicole couldn't help but smile. 'It'll be cosy in the kitchen,' she observed.

'Shall we go?' Blake suggested coolly. 'I'll direct you. It's not far. Josef and I will walk.'

'But—!' Josef began. And was silenced by his father's glare.

Dear heaven! she thought. Blake can't even bear to be in the same vehicle as me!

With Josef chattering with surprising knowledge about the plants and flowers beside the churchyard path, and with his occasional diversion to admire a gaudy beetle and a bustling colony of ants, she and Blake proceeded in stony silence to her car.

Remote and disapproving, he gave directions then collected Josef, who had been dangling perilously over a drystone wall above a sparkling stream, and headed off up the road.

It took her a while to unfasten Luc and secure him in the car. It took even longer for her to force herself to switch on the ignition. She felt weak as if all the stuffing had been ripped from her. It was obvious that she was heading for something unpleasant. She wished she'd never set eyes on the man she'd imagined to be a helpful stranger.

By the time she caught up with Blake and Josef they were walking through a large and imposing pair of wrought iron gates. Nicole slowed the car to a crawl, her eyes wide with astonishment as she scanned the beautiful parkland beyond.

Everything pleased her artist's eye. Post and rail fences edged the wide drive and sheep grazed on emerald-green fields studded with specimen trees. Hills clothed with woods rose in the distance and the scent of wild honeysuckle permeated the air, pouring through the car's open windows and filling it with fragrance.

Josef broke away from his father and clambered over the fence, waving frantically at a figure on horseback who was cantering in front of a stand of ancient oaks. As the rider came closer she saw that it was a woman—young and shapely.

Blake's wife? she wondered nervously. Someone else to slice her with a contemptuous glance. Her mouth set in a grim line. Well, she wouldn't put up with it! She'd done nothing wrong. There was no reason why Blake should be so unfriendly.

She revved up the car and shot forward to where Blake and Josef were talking to the slim, fair-haired woman. When Nicole killed the engine and jumped out she noticed the flash of annoyance in Blake's eyes. But she wasn't to be browbeaten.

'Hello,' she said to the woman, holding out her hand in greeting. 'I'm Nicole Vaseux. Blake and I are c—'

'This is Susie,' he broke in icily. 'She's just off.'

Susie looked faintly bewildered but hastily took Nicole's hand and shook it. 'How do you do?' She raised a questioning eyebrow at Blake.

'I know you're busy. See you later,' he said with a perfunctory smile.

'Daddy's in a funny mood. He's been walking all stiff and cross,' Josef confided to Susie. She did her best to hide a grin. 'Must go. 'Bye. Be good, Joe.'

'Goodbye, Mrs Bellamie,' Nicole said, taking a crafty shot in the dark.

'Susie,' Blake said in tones cold enough to freeze lava in its tracks, 'is a groom.'

It wasn't a word she'd come across before. Josef saw that and came to her rescue. 'She looks after the horses,' the little boy supplied, as Susie hurriedly left. 'Rides them. Keeps the tack clean. Shovels out the—'

'Thank you, Josef,' Blake said drily before his son became too explicit.

Nicole went pink. 'I thought she was your wife.'

'I don't have a Mummy,' Josef said amiably. 'She went off with the shuvver when I was little—'

'Chauffeur,' rasped Blake, scowling. 'Who told you that?'

'Oh, people,' Josef said vaguely. 'Can't remember, I talk to so many. I always wondered what a shuvver was. It's all right,' he added, seeing Nicole's look of alarm. 'I don't remember her. And Daddy makes a good Mummy. Then there's Cook and Maisie who cleans and—'

'Josef—' Blake said drily '—see how long it takes you to reach the front door from here. Take the short cut. I'll time you.'

'I expec' he doesn't like to remember,' Josef explained to Nicole.

But, as Blake opened his mouth with none-too-pleased an expression on his face, the little boy scampered away, apparently knowing when his father had reached the end of his tether.

Nicole said nothing. Although her gaze was directed towards Josef, who was disappearing into a vibrant stand of rhododendrons ahead, she was too busy digesting two new facts. Blake's wife had left him. And he seemed to have a battery of staff. What was his house like? It wasn't even in sight!

'You...'

'Yes?' he murmured.

She licked her lips, flushing at the sweep of his glance, which took her in from head to toe. There was something sexual about the curl of his mouth and it threw her off-balance for a moment. He was the most disturbing male she'd ever met in her life. Especially on an empty stomach. She must eat. Not indulge in idle chit-chat. But her curiosity won out.

'You *own* this incredible place?'

The curving line of his lips thinned. 'This is Cranford Hall. The Bellamies have lived here for centuries.'

'Oh! What about my father? Where did he fit in?' she began croakily, wondering about his part in this wealthy family of landed gentry. She couldn't imagine him here. Her father had never liked routine or convention. Was this why he had left such luxury? Before his work became widely known, he'd struggled to make a living. Her fingers fiddled nervously with her bracelets. Her throat had dried and the questions remained unasked.

Blake's brooding gaze slid over her once more and she fancied it lingered on the narrowness of her waist and the gentle swell of her hips. Again she felt that dangerous

lurch in her chest, a tightness that signalled her suscepti-
bility to his intense masculinity.

'You'll learn soon enough. You'll need to be sitting
down when you do,' he muttered alarmingly. 'Let's get
this over with as quickly as possible.' His voice gave no
clue to his feelings. 'Park by the main steps and go into
the hall. I'll join you there.'

'I must eat first,' she reminded him faintly.

He took one look at her white face and trembling lips
and frowned. 'Get in the passenger seat. You look terrible.
I'll drive. I don't want you lurching over the verge and
ruining it.'

Charming! she thought crossly. But did as he said. She
knew her limbs were turning to wobbly lumps of jelly and
she didn't want to risk an accident.

The car started up as soon as she had slammed the door.
With annoying ease, he persuaded her ancient and tricky
gears to obey the confident, sensitive flicks of his large
hands and they shot off up the drive.

They passed between avenues of rhododendrons and
azaleas then breath-stopping arches of cherry blossom.
Meadows sprawled beyond them, thick with bluebells,
wood anemones and snake's head fritillaries.

Her heart missed a beat. Like their meadow at home.

Without knowing she did so, she looked for acer trees
and found them. Pears, too, laden with blossom. There
were drooping, strap leaves where daffodils had once flowered, seemingly acres of them. It must have looked spectacular a month ago, she thought. A sea of nodding yellow
trumpets.

A sadness fell on her. All these were plants that her
father had insisted should be planted around the cottage in
France. He had loved it here, she thought with sudden
insight. And must have longed to return.

But he didn't. She shivered involuntarily.

'All right?' muttered Blake.

'No.' She wasn't going to pretend. 'Awful.'

'Nearly there.'

The house came into view. Tudor. She recognised the style from her Fine Arts course. Imposing golden stone, heavy chimney stacks and mullioned windows. It basked in the warm April light, masses of wisteria vying with a huge magnolia to hide the walls.

Below, in the borders against the house, she could see scarlet tulips amongst the shrubs and perennials, all of which she recognised. Her heart ached because her father had obviously lived here and had missed this house desperately. And she, too, felt her emotions stirred deeply, falling irrevocably in love with Cranford Hall.

'It's the most beautiful house I've ever seen,' she said, her voice soft with awe.

Blake glowered and swerved to one side, driving through a stone arch and into a paved yard surrounded by outbuildings. Without a word to her, he leapt out of the car and began unfastening Luc's baby seat.

Slowly, daunted by the size of the house and the revelations to come, she slid from her seat and meekly followed him as he manoeuvred the seat through a narrow plank door.

Her footsteps sounded deafening on the stone flag floor of the corridor but she controlled the urge to tiptoe. Blake paused and put his head around a door. From his softer body language—the lowering of his tense shoulders and the relaxing of his muscles—she realised that his son must be in the room. Perhaps it was the kitchen, she guessed, where Josef had been banished.

'Well done, Joe, you sped along like a bullet from a gun!' Blake declared, a smile in his voice. 'Special treat for pudding, I think, Mrs Carter. And could you rustle a lunch snack for me and my guest in the morning room?'

'Pleasure, Mr Blake,' came jolly, rosy tones of affection. 'Just be a jiffy.'

Mr Blake? Why use his first name like that? She frowned.

Following Blake blindly as he disappeared into a room with Luc, Nicole then remembered how her father had suggested that their once-a-week gardener in the Dordogne, who did all the heavy digging, should call him *Monsieur* Giles. A very English compromise with long-standing staff, she mused, thinking of the novels she'd read about the aristocracy in the UK.

Her father had never abandoned his past life, she realised, hunger and apprehension making merry with her stomach. All the signs had been there if only she'd known. Only a traumatic event must have kept him away.

An unbearable misery came over her and, closing her eyes for a moment, she stumbled. There was the sound of hurrying feet and she felt two strong arms come around her. Heat flowed from his hands. His breath mingled with hers.

She flung up her lolling head and met his dark commanding eyes. The room seemed to swirl about her and she was swept off her feet and found herself hovering in mid-air. Then she was being pressed against the living warmth of his chest where she could feel the thunderous beat of his heart. Before she had time to wonder why she felt the urge to put her arms around his neck, she had been deposited, none too gently, on a comfortable sofa.

'It's irresponsible of you to miss meals. You have a child to think of,' he snarled as if she'd done something to anger her.

Her head cleared. 'Luc!' she croaked, looking around wildly.

'Safe,' came the growled reply.

Following Blake's curtly angled head, she saw her son,

sleeping in blissful ignorance. The car seat had been placed in front of a table, evidently antique and of such highly polished oak that it must have had an army of servants working on it for a good few hundred years.

'I've never half-fainted before,' she mumbled crossly, struggling to sit up. 'But then I've never been bullied so unmercifully on an empty stomach.'

'I apologise if I have upset you,' he said stiffly.

'Upset?' She took a deep breath, her eyes like blue beacons of rage. 'I've recently lost my father. I have a small baby to bring up alone. I've travelled across France knowing that my father had kept his birthplace and nationality a secret from me. And then I come across you! Kind and sympathetic—till you knew who I was—and then you gave me the third degree and all but strip-searched me!'

She saw a flicker of acknowledgement set his stony face alive and knew that he would have gone that far if necessary. And her mouth tightened in contempt... Even as her body betrayed her by responding to the thought of Blake removing her clothes one by one. Dear heaven! she thought in horror. What had this man done to her sense of decency?

'I did apologise,' he said in a low hoarse tone. 'You'll understand my reaction when...' Pausing, he slid his tongue over his lips and inhaled deeply. 'Look, would you mind adjusting your skirt?'

Looking down, she blushed scarlet. It had rucked up to her thighs and had become caught beneath her body. With some difficulty she yanked it free, horribly conscious of Blake's hard-browed scowl.

Before she could retaliate by asking if he'd never seen legs before, there was a discreet tap on the door and a merry-looking lady, plump and dusted strategically with flour, came bustling in bearing a tray.

'I heard that you've come to scatter your father's ashes

here, and I'm ever so sorry.' The woman—whose voice
she recognised as that of Mrs Carter, who'd spoken earlier—gave Nicole a genuinely sympathetic smile.

'Thank you.'

Shakily she smiled back, thinking that the bush tele-
graph worked fast here. But at least Mrs Carter wasn't
looking at her as if she'd murdered half the inhabitants of
Great Aston and pickled them in vinegar before feeding
them to their dogs.

'I thought some home-made soup and hot rolls might be
nice,' continued the comforting Mrs Carter. She flicked
something beneath the laden tray and legs sprang out of it
as if by magic. 'Then there's an assortment of cold meat
and some hot chicken and mushroom pie with new potatoes. Home-made lemonade in the jug—and our own
strawberries to follow.' She beamed at Nicole and then
caught sight of Luc. 'Oh, what a poppet! Is that your
baby?' she asked eagerly.

'Yes.' Nicole was grateful for a lull in the hostilities and
her voice softened. 'He's called Luc.'

'Aaah!'

The woman's sentimental expression prompted Nicole
to elaborate. 'He's seven weeks old.' And she glanced at
Blake, wondering if she'd be going too far if she added,
And he's legitimate. The warning look he gave her sug-
gested that might be unwise so she turned her attention to
Mrs Carter, who was cooing over little Luc.

'Pretty as a picture,' beamed the woman. 'And look,
how extraordinary! His hair is as fair as the Bellamies!'

She felt Blake stiffen as she followed the cook's finger
and saw that the woman was pointing to a series of oil
paintings on the walls. Unaware of her surroundings up to
now, Nicole realised that every painting depicted blond
men, mostly from the nineteenth century. Presumably
Bellamies. One even had eyes like her father's.

'But—' Nicole said, puzzled, and surveying Blake's Mediterranean colouring with curiosity '—not all of them are fair.'

'Always get throwbacks, dear,' Mrs Carter confided with a teasing wink at Blake.

He responded with a tight smile that didn't reach his eyes. 'Very true. Right, we'll make a start on this. Thank you, Mrs Carter. The lunch looks delicious,' he said in tones of polite dismissal.

Nicole realised that he had no intention of introducing her as a relative. She paled. A family secret. So she wasn't good enough? Or…her father wasn't. She bit her lip.

'Okeydokey.' The cook bustled to the door. 'I'll bring coffee when you ring. And some of your favourite chocolate thins.'

Blake muttered his thanks. 'Presumably Josef's been filling you in on the events of the morning, has he?' he asked lightly.

The cook gave a broad grin and nodded. 'While helping me finish making the cake for tea. As you can see.' Laughingly, she brushed at her hair with her sturdy fingers and a fine shower of flour formed a cloud around her face. 'Well, I must check if he's washed the pans properly—or maybe he's drowned himself and flooded the kitchen in the process!'

With another half-hearted smile Blake nodded and waited till she had rolled out of the room before ladling soup into a bowl and passing it to Nicole. The aroma was enticing and she dipped her spoon in it eagerly, giving herself up to the hedonistic pleasure of fresh, well-cooked food. It was rather, she thought ruefully, like a prisoner eating a last meal before being executed.

He ate little, she noticed—a few mouthfuls of the creamy watercress soup, a minute wedge of pie. Conscious of her need to fuel herself, she tucked in heartily.

It wasn't until she was well into her second bowl of strawberries that she realised he was watching her. Since her gaze was directed on her pudding at the time it rather shook her that it was a sudden pressure in her chest, not eye contact, which had alerted her to his attentions. Some power he had! she marvelled.

'You're ready to talk,' she said, her shaking fingers dabbing at her mouth with a linen napkin. 'I'm ready to listen.' Her eyes widened with apprehension as she met his gaze.

His chest rose and fell. There was an odd expression in his eyes. Sultry and intense. It made her head swim as if she'd drunk too much wine.

'Coffee,' he muttered and jerked to his feet, walking stiffly towards a tapestry bell pull. There was nothing sultry about him, after all, she realised. Just a brooding edginess, she decided, wondering how she could have misinterpreted his expression so badly.

A silence descended—hot, thick and suffocating. Nicole watched Blake striding up and down, her nerves in shreds. She could stand it no more. It would have looked silly if she'd paced up and down like him—however much she wanted to—so she went over to Luc and checked him then pretended to be sorting out the baby bag.

Surrounded by disposable nappies, wet wipes, little toys and changes of clothes, she heard Mrs Carter's knock with relief. Cups rattled on a tray accompanied by heavy footsteps and even heavier breathing.

'There we are! My, you've had a good meal. That's splendid! Never liked women who pick at their food. Shows a mean nature, I always—'

'Thank you,' Blake interrupted meaningfully.

Nicole had turned and was smiling at the cook, disarmed by the woman's jolly manner and total lack of ceremony. She guessed that Mrs Carter had been with the family a

long time and felt able to state her opinions every now
and then.

'It was a lovely meal. Thank you very much. I was
starving.'

The cook beamed. 'No trouble at all. Don't tell Mr
Blake—' she said, in a pretend whisper that he could hear
perfectly well '—but I'd do anything for him, and that goes
for his friends too.' Deftly, the trays were being swapped
over with Blake's help. 'Oh,' sighed Mrs Carter, 'isn't it
good to see a baby in the house? Those dear little
hands...the dinky little nose...and the pretty toys... Does
your heart good, doesn't it, Mr Blake?'

'Children are a source of great delight,' he agreed.

His tone had been soft as he eyed the sleeping Luc. Then
a shadow fell over his face and he averted his gaze as if
irritated by his thoughts. Nicole felt her stomach somer-
sault. Perhaps he knew that her father had carried a rare
disease that she and Luc could have inherited, she thought
wildly, panic making her leap to all kinds of irrational
explanations.

'Oh, well. Must get on and make some bread,' the cook
said briskly. 'Ted's taken Josef off to sow lettuce, if you're
wondering where he is.'

Nicole watched Blake open the door for his cook. Saw
the true warmth of his eyes when he smiled his thanks.
And then the shutters that closed his lively, expressive face
the moment the door was shut.

Her huge eyes followed his every movement. That feral
stride, so grim and determined, towards the sofa opposite
her. The way he avoided meeting her gaze. The folding of
his long, lean body when he sat down and the frown that
brought thunder to his face.

When his chiselled lips parted to begin she gripped the
arm of the chair in nervous anticipation and tried to calm
the tumult in her mind. This was it. The explanation.

CHAPTER FIVE

I COULD get used to this, Nicole thought, luxuriating in perfumed suds. She closed her eyes, quite exhausted, and let her mind drift.

There had been a mistake about her father, of that she was sure. The stories Blake had told her an hour earlier bore no relation to the man she knew at all. And she'd let him know that, in no uncertain terms. Well, she'd shouted at him, if she was honest. But how dared he make such ridiculous and disgusting accusations? Still, they were so silly that she could rest in peace.

Under the circumstances, it had surprised her when he'd offered hospitality. Perhaps he was worried she'd contaminate the villagers, she'd thought tartly.

However, since she hadn't booked accommodation for that night, she'd agreed to stay in the manor house. Providing Blake talked about non-controversial topics like religion, politics, capital punishment and the state of the economy rather than the vile things he'd accused her father of doing.

'You don't believe me,' he said flatly after relating his improbable stories about her father's sexual rampages as a teenager.

Her eyes flashed a warning. 'If I weren't so angry I'd be laughing. My father was amiable and easy-going. He lived for his work, his painting.'

'And sex.'

'Hardly. He had a couple of female friends after my mother left, yes. Nothing wrong in that. Consenting adults—'

63

'Why did your mother leave?'

Nicole made a face. 'She met someone richer and more famous! My father was still struggling to make his name and she was fed up with poverty. Some women can't handle being poor,' she said defiantly when he frowned.

'I know,' he said tightly and she wondered about that. He would have been wealthy all his life, surely? 'Why did she marry him if he was so poor?'

'A misunderstanding,' she replied sadly. 'When they first met, he had a Bentley and some valuable personal jewellery. Mother told me she'd been misled by this until he started selling things to pay the rent.'

Blake pursed his lips. 'Money slipped through his fingers—'

'No, it didn't!' she cried indignantly. 'He saved hard. Went without so I was clothed and fed—'

'But he indulged himself too,' Blake growled. 'You can't tell me that your father was never drunk.'

'No, I can't,' she conceded. 'But—'

'I thought so!' Blake said in triumph.

'Once and once only!' she defended. 'And with good reason!'

She couldn't speak for a moment. It hurt to remember. The shock of hearing about her father's terminal illness had stunned her into silence and for a moment the world had stopped turning.

She pictured him—tragic, wracked with pain, his voice breaking as he'd gently given her the news. Anger surged. What did this cushioned, protected lord of the manor know about despair and tragedy?

'My father was drunk that one time because he had the hardest thing in the world to tell me,' she gritted, her eyes flashing with fury. 'He wasn't thinking of himself. Only me. He knew how I'd feel.' She flung back her head, misery and rage tightening the muscles of her small, defiant face. 'He told me that he only had a short time to live. I think anyone's entitled to get a little drunk under those circumstances, don't you?'

Blake didn't look convinced by her explanation. 'Alcoholics are skilled at keeping their weakness from members of their family—'

'He was not an alcoholic!' she cried hotly.

He shrugged as if her opinion couldn't be trusted. 'Or deviant? You don't recall any wild parties?'

She'd felt like hitting him. 'Never deviant! How *dare* you!'

'No parties?' he drawled.

'Are they illegal now?' she snapped.

His eyebrow hooked up cynically. 'Depends what went on.'

'You could have invited the vicar,' she snapped. 'Sure, we had parties. Noisy ones. If you call music and singing and laughter and excited chatter "wild" then yes, we had parties like that! Never anything bad. People brought their children. Do you think they'd subject them to anything indecent?' she cried indignantly. 'In all the years I knew him he never hurt anyone or anything—'

'Your mother wasn't so thrilled with him,' Blake pointed out, his expression scathing.

'If I were mean-minded,' she answered sharply, 'I could say the same thing about your ex-wife. And my ex-husband. But does that make us monsters?'

He gave a little smile of grudging admiration, his glittering eyes boring deeply into her as if they intended to penetrate the whole of her brain and lay it out for analysis. 'If you're so feisty after harrowing experiences and an exhausting journey,' he mused surprisingly, 'I wonder what you're like when you're on top form?'

'Dynamite.' So beware, her silvered eyes told him.

'Yes... I can believe that.'

The low husk of his voice curled into her and the inky blackness of his eyes created havoc throughout her body. She could feel his sexual aura drawing her inexorably towards him. So she folded her arms as a barrier between them. Then realised that the action had pushed her breasts into greater prominence than was wise. And that was when she flailed around for some way to escape and asked if she might have a bath and a rest.

With a sigh, she slipped deeper into the foam, letting her body float in the enormous Victorian tub. The bathroom was the most opulent she'd ever seen, with rich and heavy gold curtains at the window, looped up with heavy tasselled ties.

When she'd walked in her bare feet had almost disappeared into the cream carpet and she was looking forward to snuggling into one of the giant bath towels, which were as soft as a baby blanket. Freed from her fears that her father had done something dreadful, she could now relax. Blissful music from a discreetly hidden stereo filtered into her semi-consciousness.

After this glorious soak she would draw the hangings of the four-poster bed and shut out the world till it was time to feed Luc, who was currently chortling away in one of Josef's old cribs. She glanced over at it with admiration. It was a family heirloom and sixteenth century, judging by the coat of arms on it.

She smiled. How the other half lived! But she had no reason to stay. She had what she'd come for. The link had been made with her father's family. The mystery was solved.

There had clearly been a falling out between her father and someone. Stories had been invented by Blake's family to explain why a Bellamie should want to leave the paradise that was Cranford Hall. Blake had even admitted that he'd never known her father, who'd apparently disappeared one night at the age of twenty or so. Though Blake wouldn't reveal who'd fed him those terrible stories.

Instead, he'd personally escorted her up to a suite of rooms in the west wing and had said that he'd come for her at seven to take her down to dinner.

'I can find my own way,' she'd said huffily.

'Please wait here,' he'd insisted. 'I would be failing in my duties as a host if I left you to wander the corridors and possibly get lost.'

Odd that, she mused, clambering out and cuddling into the towel. He'd been quite tense at that moment. It was almost as if he didn't trust her not to poke about in the other rooms and perhaps slip a few antiques into the baby bag!

'Well, Blake Bellamie—' she said cheerfully, vigorously rubbing herself dry '—by this time tomorrow I'll be on my way home. And you and your precious family can keep your prejudices and nasty minds because I want nothing to do with you. Despite the fact—' she added ruefully, slowly studying her ripe and totally wasted curves '—that you are the sexiest man I've ever seen.'

Her breasts swelled before her eyes. Hazily she watched her nipples harden and she groaned at the liquefying of her loins. She throbbed there. And wanted Blake at that moment more than she'd ever wanted a man before.

Stunned by the power he had over her, even when he wasn't anywhere near, she lifted her head and stared blindly at the full length window across the room. Then her eyes focused on something moving in the far distance.

Wrapping the towel securely around herself, she hurried over. Someone was riding like the wind across the park. A tall dark figure on a gleaming black horse. She quivered.

Blake.

The flames rose in her body, consuming her. And she berated herself for falling for such a hackneyed, romantic image. Man on horse. A symbol of power and mastery, physical energy and virility.

And Blake would be virile. All that unleashed vitality. The tightly controlled emotions. In bed, a man like that would be a tiger set free from a cage. Little shivers ran up and down her body, electrifying it. And she felt ashamed of her thoughts.

She'd been untouched for too long and was fantasising. Blake didn't even like her. Every time he'd come near he'd been tense with suppressed anger because she'd sullied his house by being the daughter of the family scapegoat.

Dinner would be a cold and icy affair. She sighed, turning from the window and determinedly banished the distant figure from her mind.

Beginning to prepare for Luc's needs, she told herself that she'd eat in silence, go to bed immediately after, and leave the next morning for the long journey back to France without saying goodbye. He didn't deserve courtesy. Besides, he'd be glad to see the back of her.

His entire body tingled from the elation of his ride. Unusually, it had taken a long time to rid himself of his pent-up feelings. Nicole had wormed her way into the very tissues of his body, it seemed, and all but pulped his brain. What a fool he was to lust after her when he'd remained indifferent to dozens of willing women far more suitable!

But she was a woman who knew all about pleasure. You could see that in the sway of her body, the knowing, flirty glances and the provocative pout of her lips. She'd be unbelievably abandoned, he'd thought.

And had been obliged to wipe her from his mind and straining manhood by galloping as far as the outskirts of Broadway.

Pleasantly exhausted, Blake spent an hour with his

mother telling her the events of the day—leaving out any mention of Nicole at all, of course.

Mrs Carter and the rest of the staff had been puzzled by his request that his mother should not know about their unexpected guests, but he knew they'd carry out his wishes.

It was a slight risk having Nicole around for the night but it was better than having her talking to the villagers. And despite her spirited defence of her father she'd looked tired and drawn. The main thing was that he should keep her from wandering about and stumbling on his mother's suite of rooms by accident.

He didn't have the heart to send Nicole on her journey without time to recover. It was the least he could do for a member of his family. A new mother with a baby to manage. A woman who aroused terrible longings in him...

Impatiently he blanked out his mind, scowling as he began to dress for dinner. She'd seemed to accept the situation. He'd shown her the family tree. For a moment he'd had to put a hand out to steady her because she'd gone white and had swayed at the sight of the neat square which had been cut in the parchment where her father's name should have been. He'd always been told the genealogist had made a mistake in drawing up the tree but now he knew that Giles had been deliberately removed.

His arm had slid around her shoulders and he'd almost given in to his compulsion by hugging her to him in sympathy. But she'd drawn in a massive breath and shrugged him off, noting coldly that they had great-grandparents in common.

'Yes. My grandfather and yours were brothers. Our fathers were first cousins,' he replied.

'Until my father was obliterated from your lives,' she muttered, her face set in mutiny. 'Someone in your family is lying, Blake! Someone who wanted him gone!'

That shook him for a moment. But he couldn't believe that of his mother, not when she knew she was dying.

'I can understand why you want to believe that. But it's not true. Accept it, Nicole.'

'I can't!' she cried, her eyes haunted.

It was hard, not touching her then. She needed comfort. Somehow he steeled himself to resist. 'Give me your address,' he suggested instead. 'We'll keep in touch.'

And she did. It was his intention that some time in the future he'd invite her over to see if she could be trusted with Cranford. But for now it was better for his mother's sake that she stayed away.

'Hello, Daddy!' A small whirlwind flew through the door and launched itself at his thoughtful figure. Deftly he caught Josef and flung him, laughing, on the bed where they wrestled for a bit.

'Don't you ever knock?' he grumbled amiably, escaping the giggling Josef. He sucked in his lean, muscled stomach and tucked in his shirt.

'Why? Nobody's in here, only you!'

It flashed into his mind that he could have been making love to Nicole. For a split second he saw her lush body writhing invitingly on his bed and then he fiercely rejected the idea. Though his arousal was less easy to dismiss.

'You're in your best suit,' mused his infuriatingly observant son. 'Does that mean Nicole's here for dinner? Can I stay up too?' he asked eagerly.

'You've eaten. I saw you demolish a huge plate of spaghetti bolognaise, two crusty rolls collapsing under mountainous lumps of butter and two portions of strawberries.'

'I am a bit full. I could watch you eat, though!' Josef attached himself like a leech to Blake's leg. 'Oh, please! Please, oh please!' he begged, for all the world like a silent movie heroine pleading with wicked Sir Jasper. 'I'll tidy my room. I'll even *wash* again—'

'Good grief! That's a bit drastic!'

Grinning, Blake hobbled over to the mirror, dragging Josef with him as he went. He tried to concentrate on getting his tie to sit right. His fingers seemed to be clumsier than usual. And why the heck *was* he making such an effort? He thought of being with Nicole. Candles on the dinner table. Intimacy...

'I'll ring ChildLine,' Josef threatened, still casting himself as the victim. 'Show them my wet pillow where I cried myself to sleep—'

'Idiot!' he said affectionately. Suddenly Josef's presence seemed a good idea. Blake yanked at the stubborn tie and started again as his son began to sob unconvincingly. 'Boo hoo isn't a very good impersonation of someone who's upset,' he drawled, fighting his laughter. And went in for some bargaining. 'Tidy your room and do your teeth for a week without complaining. Then you can come with me to collect Nicole for dinner—'

'I could practice making polite conversation for a bit,' Josef said craftily.

Blake nodded 'After that, you're going to bed without arguing and you'll tuck yourself in.'

Blake felt rather pleased with himself. Josef would remind him of his fatherly role and wipe out all thoughts of an evening's seduction by the earthy Nicole. He cleared his throat, which seemed to have become husky and finished dressing.

'You're making an awful fuss tonight. You've brushed your hair four times,' his son accused.

'It's a mess. That's why,' Blake growled, irritated to be found out. He flung the brush down, impatient with himself. 'Come on. Let's go.'

'Piggyback!' demanded Josef and, to his surprise, his father readily agreed.

Jogging along the corridor with his son's two bony

knees crushing his upper ribs, Blake reflected—not entirely with relief—that their arrival would kill even the lustiest woman's desire for casual sex.

Hopefully it would kill his, too. He'd never wanted a one-night stand before. Had never imagined that he could desire a woman so fiercely that he could contemplate satisfying his lust in a no-strings-attached, rollicking orgy of mind-blowing sex.

Hell. He was getting hot again. He had to get a grip.

'Come on, Daddy!'

To his surprise, he discovered he'd stopped. And his jockey was urging him on with impatient whipping movements. Blake felt the warmth of his son's body through his jacket, the sweet breath that fanned his face and the pressure of a soft cheek against his.

This was more precious, more lasting and more worthwhile than anything in the world. Overcome with love for Josef, he threw back his head in a magnificent whinny, pawed the ground and took off at top speed.

He and his jockey roared with laughter as they careered madly from side to side and occasionally jumped an imaginary fence. By the time he knocked on the guest room door they were both breathless and in hysterics. Josef was clinging to Blake's neck—nearly throttling him—and, like him, was quite helpless with laughter.

Nicole heard them coming long before she heard the rap on the door panel. It gave her time to compose herself. And to check her appearance in the mirror.

Alarmed, she saw that the flush on her face almost matched the scarlet of her dress. In panic, she wished she'd worn something more modest. It looked as if she was putting herself up for grabs. She hesitated, torn between answering the door and dashing back for a wrap to cover her almost bare shoulders. And the even more daring cleavage.

But Josef was shouting outside and so she grabbed Luc

and hurried to the door. Blake would be too taken up with managing his son to disapprove of the outfit she'd worn so many times without comment... Until that farewell dinner in France, she remembered in dismay, as she opened the door. And that was when she knew she'd made a mistake.

At first Blake's appearance made her go weak at the knees. Laughing at his son, his face wreathed in smiles and with that devastatingly infectious grin, his joy went straight to her heart and dug a little place for itself there.

Leaning over Blake's shoulder, Josef was a smaller version of his father—tumbled black curls rioting everywhere, black brows and eyes, mischief dancing in every line.

But Blake's countenance had become dark and scowling the moment he set eyes on her. Sliding his son to the ground, he even took a step backwards after flashing a cursory glance up and down her body. His mouth thinned. He narrowed his eyes. Clenched his fists.

Nicole's spirits fell. He thinks I'm parading myself. That I'm cheap, she thought in dismay. And cradled Luc protectively over her offending bosom.

'Are you ready?' he asked in a husky growl.

She gulped, her eyes huge. And opted for a cover-up. She couldn't nurse Luc like this all evening! She'd never be able to eat a thing!

'I—I have a wrap to collect.'

His head jerked in a nod of approval. 'We'll wait.'

Perhaps she ought to pull on a fleecy sweatshirt, she thought moodily. Or an anorak and a woolly scarf plus a duvet. Then he couldn't complain.

She groaned at her stupidity. Why had she worked through every item she'd brought and yet opted for this outfit, when she could have chosen something less in your face?

Vanity, she sighed, and carefully placed the wriggling

Luc on the clothes-strewn bed. She knew she looked good in the slim-fitting red dress. Aware that it would be a difficult evening, she'd wanted to feel her best. To impress the hell out of Blake and make him respect her. Instead, she'd ended up making herself look over-eager. Crossly she rummaged in her case for the silk wrap, conscious that Josef had bounced into the room.

'Wowee!' she heard the little boy's voice pipe up behind her bent back. 'You're as messy as me!'

'Joe!' barked Blake.

Flushing with embarrassment, she turned, wishing they hadn't seen the evidence of her dithering over what to wear.

'I've never eaten anywhere this posh,' she explained hurriedly, neatly dodging the truth.

'It's only Dad. Mind you, he *is* all done up like a dog's dinner tonight,' agreed Josef equably.

Her glance flew to Blake's. Inky-black met anxious blue. And she felt as if she'd been electrocuted. Delicious tingles were reaching hitherto unknown parts of her body. She could hardly breathe.

'He looks very nice,' she said in a garbled croak, making the understatement of the year.

Nice! Edible, more like it. Groomed, beautifully turned out in a soft charcoal suit that had been cut to flatter his broad shoulders, well-developed chest and slim waist and hips. A turquoise shirt and emerald tie deepened his tan. He was gorgeous and she felt heartily relieved that Josef would, it seemed, be dining with them.

'Shall we go?' Blake suggested loftily, scooping up Luc from the bed.

Her initial protest at the cavalier takeover of her child died on her lips. Luc had spent so much time with her— and her alone—that he didn't go to strangers readily. And yet her son was cooing merrily to Blake, another convert to the wretched man's charm!

Still, she thought, tossing the silk around her shoulders and drawing the wrap closely around her, Blake toting a baby was less of a sexual danger to her wayward hormones. Then, as she headed off down the corridor with Josef on one side and Blake on the other, she realised that she was wrong. Again. Blake's tenderness, his air of gentle protection and the sight of his huge hands carefully cradling her beloved son, combined to turn her heart over.

Help, she wailed silently. And help came.

'It's been nice weather today, hasn't it?' ventured Josef cheerily, hopping up and down beside her as they reached the landing.

She wondered if this was his version of polite conversation. 'Just lovely,' she agreed, glad of the child's presence. And, seeing his joyful face, she impulsively reached out and took his hand.

The little boy looked up at her with blinding delight. 'Have you come far?' he enquired as they began to descend the grand staircase.

Nicole hid a giggle. 'From France. A long way,' she replied.

Josef broke away from her, straddled the banister, slid down to the bottom and then raced up the stairs to them again.

'Much traffic?' he asked politely.

She met Blake's eye, caught its amused gleam, and they both convulsed with laughter. So much so that she had to sit on the stairs.

'What? What did I say?' demanded the perplexed Josef.

'Oh, sweetheart!' she said, hoping she hadn't hurt his feelings. He tucked himself next to her and she put her arm around him lovingly. 'It's... Well, you sounded so grown-up but not like *you* at all. Though it was a very good…er…'

'Impersonation of adults at a cocktail party,' Blake supplied.

'Yes, absolutely brilliant,' she agreed, seeing the little boy brighten. She got to her feet and took his hand again.

As they entered the sitting room, she thought contentedly that the evening was turning out better than expected. It was a long time since she'd felt so much at ease.

'Time for your story,' Blake said softly to his son. He brought Luc over and tucked him in a heap of cushions next to Nicole.

Josef looked appealingly into Blake's eyes, heaved a huge, wistful sigh and said hopefully, 'If you're ever thinking of getting a new Mummy for me—'

'I'm not. Did you know about the little boy who found a baby dragon in his pocket and it was crying because it was stuck to a half-sucked boiled sweet?' Blake said with a masterly diversion tactic.

The story unfolded with much drama and over-acting till she was consumed by giggles like Josef. The unlikely tale ended on a hilarious high note and gales of laughter. Then, unbidden, Josef ran over to kiss her goodnight, pecked Luc on the cheek and flung his arms around his father who hugged him hard.

'I love you, Daddy.'

'I love you too,' Blake said huskily.

The adoration in Blake's eyes as he followed his son's exuberant, cartwheeling departure made a lump come to her throat. This family evening had been a revelation. A startling insight into Blake's character.

She was overwhelmed by a need for him to like her. To accept the truth about her father, instead of believing those vicious rumours. Blake wasn't a hard and vindictive man. He'd just been misinformed. His family had made out that

her father was some kind of monster and Blake had believed the stories unquestioningly. That was understandable. Why should he do otherwise?

But she couldn't leave it like that. There and then, she
decided to stay in the area till she'd convinced Blake that
her father should be reinstated on that wretched family
tree. And, she vowed, she would insist that a memorial
plaque be made to join the others in the church, which
apparently recorded the existence of every Bellamie descendant since the fifteen-hundreds. She smiled, feeling a
warm glow as she imagined herself unveiling that
plaque…

'Shall we go in to dinner?' Blake murmured softly.

There was an unnerving glitter in his eyes. Just a reflection of the chandelier, she was sure, but for a moment
the illusion of intense interest in them had unsettled her.
She swallowed, telling herself to stop being so fanciful.

'Yes. Sure. Is…anyone else joining us?' she asked, her
heart thumping madly at the thought of eating with him
alone.

'Just us. Is that a problem?'

She looked at him but couldn't hide her doubts. 'N-
no—'

His mouth curved in a heart-stopping smile. 'We could
make polite conversation like Josef. The weather—'

'The traffic!'

She laughed in delight at his chuckle and blessed Josef
for lifting the atmosphere between herself and Blake. At
least, she thought, holding Luc closely as they headed for
the door, she could always fuss over her baby if there were
any sticky moments.

But she found herself reckoning without Mrs Carter,
who surged in with starters of crab, leek and Gruyère tart
and whisked the gurgling Luc off before Nicole could
voice more than a token protest.

'He'll need a feed in an hour or so,' she reminded Blake.

'No problem. But for a while you can have a break from being a mother.' Blake's eyes kindled and she felt her heart bumping erratically. 'I want to thank you,' he went on. 'I'm grateful for your tact with Joe over his efforts at polite conversation.'

She beamed. That was a safe subject. 'I couldn't hurt his feelings.' Her voice softened. 'He's terrific, Blake. Very loveable. I only hope Luc grows up to have half his spirit and lust for life.'

He poured himself a glass of wine, nodded when she refused one and filled a tumbler of mineral water for her. 'He likes you a lot.'

Those dark, intensely brilliant eyes were fixed on her and destroying her brain cells again. She sighed. 'I feel enormously honoured. I don't imagine he suffers fools gladly.'

Like his father, she almost added, but restrained herself, not wanting to spoil the amicable atmosphere.

There was a long pause during which Blake studied her thoughtfully. 'No. He doesn't.'

It was a small victory, getting him to admit that, but it meant a great deal to her. She had won over Josef without any effort on her part. Now she needed to bridge the chasm between herself and Blake. That might take some doing— but she had to gain his trust if she was to convince him of her father's good character.

He bent his head and kept his attention on transferring a forkful of crab and pastry to his mouth. In the flickering candlelight, with the silk shawl draped over her smooth shoulders and her face alive with tenderness for his son, she looked too good to be true. Unbelievably beautiful. Huge intensely blue eyes, a sweet face and a mouth made for kissing. All that he could have handled—blocked out, with an effort of will. But she'd bonded immediately with

Josef, which made her special. And for a short time during the story-telling Blake had felt a pang of longing for a deep relationship with a woman who could instantly fit into his family set-up. That period before dinner had been how he'd always dreamed a family should be. A relaxed atmosphere in which laughter and warmth and love could flourish.

'Not too windy today, was it?' he heard her say.

He looked up and laughed. 'I'm sorry,' he said, his eyes twinkling. 'I was miles away.'

'Miles away... Hmm. Much traffic?' she teased.

He grinned and saluted her wit with his raised glass. 'Only in my head. You know the next stage of the conversation, don't you?' Pushing his empty plate away he leaned forward, trying not to notice the rise and fall of her breasts. 'Tell me about yourself.'

Her eyes glowed brightly as if he'd given her the opportunity she'd craved. OK, he thought, sell yourself.

And all through the main course he listened and prompted, encouraging her to reveal more of her true nature. Increasingly impassioned, she spoke of the small cottage, her father's modest fame, her own work in restoring antique ceramics.

He looked at her hands—slender, delicate, sensitive. He went to the sideboard and brought over a Lalique vase with a small chip in the base, which she handled with loving care, stroking it sensually.

In his fevered imagination he could feel those hands caressing him. And, as she described how she would repair the vase, he almost believed her words became slower and more slurred to match his own drugged senses.

'You inherited your love of beautiful things from your father,' he said throatily. And a sour voice reminded him that this had included beautiful women by the dozen. Giles had loved women but he had also abused them. The highest and lowest pleasures of the flesh.

'I hope I've inherited his nature, too. His kindness. Tolerance. Boundless hospitality.'

Her worship of her father shone through everything she said. But those traits she'd described could be taken too far.

'He was very much a party animal from what you've said,' he probed.

'I'll say!' Her eyes sparkled with enthusiasm. 'He loved people and they loved him,' she said, naively innocent of the slant he might put on that remark. 'There was a constant flow of friends visiting with their families. They were always welcome.'

'Tell me more about the parties. What they were like.'

Her voice became wistful. 'We'd sit late into the night beneath the stars, children lolling on parents' laps, vigorous discussions raging around the table, punctuated by laughter.' She smiled. 'I adored it.'

'You like dancing? Music?'

Her eyes glistened. 'Oh, yes! I'd dance till I dropped sometimes. Music sets me on fire. It has the power to make me cry or laugh. We would all abandon ourselves to it during those parties.'

'Oh?' His eyebrow lifted and in that 'oh' was a wealth of meaning.

'Not the way you're thinking!' she declared indignantly. 'We just let ourselves respond to the rhythm, whether it was fast and furious or slow and dreamy. Children, adults, grandparents...' Scathingly she accused, 'You wouldn't know about that. You've probably never done anything reckless or spontaneous in your life!'

'I have responsibilities,' he snapped, stung by the truth of her words.

'But you need to live, too!' she declared passionately, her face alive with vital energy.

Yes. He did. Increasingly so. All his life he'd been mindful of his position. Careful not to say or do the wrong thing. And now Nicole was taunting him with her freedom from restriction, unwittingly goading him to crush her in his arms and make frenzied love to her.

No wonder he desired her. She was everything he longed to be. She epitomised the kind of person he'd always been, deep down, beneath the self-control. At that moment he would have willingly exchanged life-styles.

There was a striking contrast between her description of carefree living and his own sober upbringing. So many times he'd balked at the straitjacket of being the 'son' of an English gentleman. And more than ever he envied her the freedom he'd been denied.

Growing in confidence, she became more expansive, less inhibited in her movements. A glow lit her eyes. And he was mesmerised by her, drawn to her because of everything she represented. And wanted.

'I beg you—' she said softly, perhaps sensing the softening of his brain '—ask people here about my father. Keep an open mind till you have evidence of his supposed wickedness.'

Her sweet, hopeful smile would melt the stoniest heart, he thought, sternly resisting such a fate. She drew in a deep breath and he felt first a kick of need and then pure anger. She must know how her body moved, he thought cynically, loathing women who used sex to get their own way.

And yet, despite knowing that she was deliberately enticing him, his anger turned to a hunger, a longing to possess part of this free-living woman who had lived the kind of life he had always yearned for.

She was offering. Why not take?

Blake sat back in his chair, his expression giving no hint of the passions that raced through his body. But she was destroying his control inch by inch, leaning forward in her eagerness to paint her father white, gesticulating in a typically Gallic way, graceful, fiery and intense.

All he could think of was touching that silken skin. Cradling her delicate face in his hands. Drawing her close and feeling the soft curves melt against him and her lips parted for his inevitable kiss... Surrendering at last to the need that raced excitedly through his body.

'Blake?'

He blinked. Felt close to exploding. Had to move. Abruptly he got up and removed their plates, carrying them to the sideboard.

It had been an error, going close to her for that brief moment to pick up her plate. She had looked up at him and murmured her thanks, her eyes two deep silver wells in the candlelight, and he'd almost jumped in head first to drown a happy man.

The memory of her perfume stayed with him as he briskly cleared the vegetable dishes. She didn't offer to help but remained in her seat looking rather forlorn. An act again? he wondered savagely. Grimly controlling his urge to haul her up and rain a torrent of kisses on that pouting, lush mouth, he cut them both a slice of raspberry pavlova. He slid hers in front of her then regained his seat, moving like a stiff automaton because if he allowed himself any fluidity at all he'd be surrendering to the little voice inside his head which kept saying, *Respond. She's interested. Go for it.*

Discipline prevailed. The meringue tasted like sandpaper to him but it was probably excellent as usual.

'You weren't listening. I've been boring you,' she said unhappily, her pudding untouched.

Boring him! If only. He registered the sexy pout of her

mouth and felt angry that she was able to affect him so deeply.

'I heard every word.'

Keeping his head down, he scooped up some raspberries and tried to look as if he was enjoying them.

'Then you'll understand—' she said, her voice unfairly throaty and low and making a mess of his intentions to stay detached '—why I can't allow you to think—let alone say—those awful things about my father.'

He had to get up again. Strode towards the window and flung the curtains back, then the French doors, to let in the starlit night. He breathed the air for a moment till his head cleared. She was using her femininity to persuade him, he thought angrily. Flirting with him. Lowering her voice and occasionally her eyes to weaken his resistance and get her own way. Meaningless tricks. And he was falling for them, big time.

'My source is unimpeachable. My source would not lie,' he said firmly.

He heard the scrape of her chair. The sound of her feet in the gloriously feminine high heels tapping towards him. And his loins melted.

'Well, something's wrong because I know I'm not lying!' she cried fervently, just inches behind him. 'I knew him and you didn't. I'm more likely to be right about him!'

Her breath teased the hairs on the back of his neck. If he turned around he knew he'd take her in his arms and make an utter fool of himself. He tried to make his addled brain focus more clearly. It was clear that she genuinely believed her father to be a good man. That left him with a dilemma. To accept her at face value and question his mother's version of events, or to keep silent as he'd intended until he knew more about her.

Her hand touched his arm and he stiffened automatically.

'Please, Blake,' she breathed jerkily. 'I know you don't like me, but you're a good man and I'm sure if you think about this dispassionately you'll realise I—I…'

He flung his resolutions to the wind and turned around in a violent movement. Nicole's upturned face swam before his eyes. Unable to stop himself, he took a step closer. Caught hold of her arms in a fierce grip.

And saw the drowsy flutter of her lashes, the sultry pout of her mouth as she signalled with every languid bone in her body that she, too, was aroused. He frowned, registering the shortness of his breath.

'Nicole,' he grated harshly. And he knew he'd reached the point of no return.

CHAPTER SIX

SHE couldn't move. Of course she'd heard of the *coup de foudre*—that bolt from the blue that could strike unexpectedly and fatally. But she'd never believed that instant attraction could possibly exist until now.

Not this deep, this obliteratingly single-minded, need to touch someone, be with them, follow their every move.

Alarmingly, her quest was being wiped from her mind by the urgency of her need. It was a wonderful feeling and her entire body was driving her to give in to the inevitable consequences, to strain forward and kiss Blake's stubborn, grim mouth until it softened. Until he flung away his rigid manner and let blood flow into his veins.

She lifted her head till her mouth was inches from his. 'Yes?' she murmured invitingly.

And, just as his frown deepened, she heard a wail.

His hands dropped away abruptly. 'Perfect timing,' he drawled.

Her eyes narrowed. What did he mean by that? Shaking, she began to stride across the room to the kitchen. Did he think that the interruption meant that he could successfully evade her questions?

Or…that he'd been saved the bother of rejecting her unwanted advances? She went hot with embarrassment.

How could she have been so stupid? Yes, she could hardly breathe for the ache of physical emptiness. Yes, she wanted Blake to make love to her. Badly. But that didn't mean she had to bat her lashes at him like a besotted schoolgirl!

It was all that talk of behaving like a flower child, she

thought with a rueful sigh, and hurried into the kitchen to console herself with cuddling her baby. 'Hey, sweetheart! You're hungry again, aren't you?' she murmured fondly, weakly smiling her thanks as she took Luc from Mrs Carter's soothing, sudsy arms.

'Now, you shouldn't be dashing in to him the minute he cries,' the cook chided amiably. 'Poor lamb. You look quite pale. Shall I do you a cocoa?'

'I'll see to Nicole,' came a low growl from behind her.

Nicole tensed as Blake came in to dominate the room. Her skin burned. The atmosphere seemed to thicken and she even looked up from under her lashes to see if the cook had sensed it and was puzzled. But Mrs Carter was busily stacking plates as if the electrical charge in the air didn't exist.

'I can manage,' Nicole jerked out. 'Honestly, I don't need anyone—'

'Why don't you pack up for the night, Mrs Carter?' Blake suggested, ignoring Nicole's babbling. 'You've done more than enough for us. Maisie can clear away the rest of the things in the morning.' He put his hand on the cook's broad shoulder. 'You did us proud. Dinner was superb,' he said more gently. 'Thank you for all your trouble. Goodnight, then. Sleep well.'

'If you're sure…'

'Positive.'

Nicole's heart sank as Mrs Carter rinsed and dried her fingers then trundled heavily out to a chorus of goodnights. Now Blake would read the riot act, Nicole thought glumly. Accuse her of low morals. Declare that any woman who offered herself to a virtual stranger must have come from a sexually liberal household…

'Your child is crying.'

Her huge eyes swivelled to Blake's. 'Do you think I don't know that?' she flared. 'I'm waiting for you to go!'

He studied her coolly, never taking those piercing, coal-black eyes from hers. And all her body was melting—bone, flesh, sinew, while her blood surged and raged till every cell felt energised and frighteningly alive.

This wasn't good for Luc. She must calm down. But she couldn't, not while Blake remained in the same room, pushing out all that testosterone at her.

His eyes seemed drowsy. Sternly, she told herself he was tired.

'Do you want cocoa?'

The banal words were spoken in a husky undertone that caused turmoil within her. She sat down quickly with her back to him.

'No!' she grated. 'Just get out!'

His hand touched her shoulder and she jumped. His fingers idly pushed her shoulder strap to and fro. For a moment she thought he was going to slide it down to reveal her breast. She felt every inch of her body tingle in anticipation and she willed him to do it, even though she knew it would be the act of a man who thought she was a slut.

'Goodnight,' he muttered in hard, crisp tones and left.

The door banged shut. Trembling, she eased off the strap, intensely aware of the burning imprint of his fingers still branding her skin as if he'd claimed her for his undisputed possession.

'Oh, Luc! My little sweetheart,' she whispered in despair as she settled him for his feed. 'I've made such a mistake. He despises me. I've failed your grandfather.'

She leaned back in the chair until the tumult of her thoughts grew less frantic. Gazing down at her son, she reflected that he was the most important thing in her life. He would not grow up with the spectre of a wronged grandfather hanging over his head. She could never rest while people were thinking such awful things about her father. It pained her. She couldn't bear injustice.

In the morning she would ask her own questions. There would be plenty of people around who'd remember Giles Bellamie. To hell with washing her dirty linen in public! She wouldn't be beaten by Blake's refusal to consider he might be mistaken.

Maybe she'd never gain his respect where she was concerned. But she'd force him to grovel and admit he was wrong about her father. She must, for Luc's sake.

Six o'clock. Silently, she packed her case and got Luc ready for the day. He didn't seem hungry and was unusually grizzly, so it took her a while before he was dressed in his little blue romper suit.

But that morning she felt she could cope with anything. Despite her mind teeming with thoughts, she'd had a good night. It wasn't surprising since the day before had been exhausting. Seemingly a lifetime had been lived in just twenty-four hours.

Refreshed, she slipped on one of her favourite flowing summer skirts and a cropped top then tidied the room so Mrs Carter or Maisie wouldn't have to do too much once she'd gone.

Her pre-breakfast playtime with Luc was briefer than usual. Just a few cuddles, a tickle of his round tummy and some kisses and words of love. 'Things to do,' she murmured, nuzzling his little pink toes. 'People to see, reputations to uphold. Come on, sweetheart. You wait here in your crib while I get things organised.'

She started up the musical mobile which Mrs Carter had attached to the crib and for a moment Luc stopped grizzling, his huge blue eyes fixed in wonder on the whirling musical farmyard.

Hoping there were no burglar alarms, and steeling herself for the sound of screaming sirens just in case, she tiptoed down the stairs and left her case in a corner of the hall. Then she returned for Luc, who seemed to be fretting again. 'Hush, sweetheart, hush. Mummy's here now. She's going to have breakfast—' she whispered into his miniature ear as she hurried down towards the kitchen '—and then we'll explore the village. All right?' She deposited a kiss on the screwed-up nose and he stopped whimpering for a moment. 'After that, we'll have an early coffee and then get rooms somewhere—*oh*!'

In the doorway she stopped in confusion. A tousle-haired, unshaven and bleary-eyed Blake was sitting at the kitchen table and scowling at her over a bone china mug of steaming coffee. He looked so disheveled and disreputable and utterly gorgeous in tight black jeans and the torso-embracing T-shirt that she was lost for words. And her heart was thumping crazily. All her embarrassment of the previous night was forgotten. This Blake was dangerous—almost feral. With an animal quality that made her shiver with fear and excitement at the same time.

'You!' he growled ungraciously.

She gulped at his hostility. But wouldn't be cowed. Maybe in his eyes she was cheap, but he had no right to be rude to a guest in his house. She'd made a mistake. Read the signs wrongly. Did that make her so contemptible? Men made passes without being labelled as tarts!

'Me.' Her chin lifted in defiance. 'Why so surprised?'

'You're up early,' he complained and looked as if he might lock her up for such a crime.

Nicole boldly marched in. 'You didn't mention there was a curfew,' she said sarcastically. 'I must remind Luc not to wake up till eight if I'm ever in this house again.'

That should shut him up! Head high, she stalked over to the kettle and carried it to the tap, intending to juggle the grizzling Luc in one arm and prepare her breakfast with one hand and the occasional use of an elbow, as mothers had probably done for centuries.

The kettle was tugged from her grip. 'See to him.' He wrenched open the tap. 'I'll make you some tea.'

It sounded as if he'd prefer it to be arsenic and strychnine combined. She glared. 'I was going to cook something—'

'I'll do it.'

'I'd prefer to do it myself,' she retorted, 'than have you curdling the eggs with your bad temper.'

'Luc needs you. He's not settled. Give your attention to him and let me do your breakfast then you can both get out of this house and be on your way.'

Grumpily, Blake aimed the plug at the socket and pushed it in then snapped on the switch. She watched him stomp over to the fridge and grab bacon, eggs and sausages. If he wanted to be a martyr, then let him.

'A tomato would be nice, too,' she commented perkily.

He scowled and she giggled. 'Glad it's amusing,' he muttered.

She paused in trying to cheer Luc up and laughed. 'You just look so cross! Are you always such a grouch in the mornings?'

'Are you always so darn cheerful?' he countered.

She made a face. 'I don't have much choice. Luc is usually ready for fun and games by the time the sun rises. Hey,' she said to her son. 'This grumpiness is catching! Where's your happy face? Look. Here are the little piggies, one goes to market, one stays home...'

'When are you off?'

'Immediately after breakfast.' She saw him cover up a yawn. Noticed how slow his movements were. And put two and two together. 'Have you been out all night?' she enquired caustically, remembering his sarcastic references to her father's supposed excesses. 'Spent the night partying, have you?' And wondered with a sudden vicious spurt of jealousy who'd kept him up, who'd exhausted him, who'd put him in such a bad mood.

'Walking.' Expertly, he turned the sausages, scowling at them so hard she thought they might be horribly charred from his glare alone.

'In the dark?' she asked, intrigued and relieved that he hadn't been with a woman. Stupid. *Stupid!* she told herself.

'Full moon.'

'Hmm. You don't have any Transylvanian blood, do you?' she asked, her eyes big and innocent, her lashes batting up and down like mad.

He crushed her merriment with one scornful glance. 'If I were a vampire,' he said tightly, 'I'd have claimed you last night.' Avoiding her wide-eyed look as she coped with the wicked thrill that curled through her veins, he raked through his already mussed-up hair then massaged his temples as if they hurt. 'Why don't you amuse your child and leave me in peace?'

'Oh,' she said with exaggerated understanding. 'Hangover!'

He slammed a knife and fork on the table, then the salt and pepper were similarly tested to destruction.

'Not on two whiskies,' he growled.

'So there's no excuse for your bad temper,' she countered in a flash.

His breath sheared in. 'I have reasons.' It seemed that his eyes glittered with anger. 'You're definitely one of them.'

'Oh!' She felt crushed.

There was a silence, broken only by the sizzling food in the pan and her increasingly desperate attempts to make Luc smile. Suddenly a plate was banged in front of her.

'Give him to me while you eat.'

'No, thanks. He's not too happy today and...' Her voice

died away. Blake had thrust his face very close to hers and she could see he was explosively angry.

'I want you to leave as soon as possible,' he said through his teeth. 'If you hang on to Luc then I'll be forced to cut up your food for you and feed it to you, mouthful by mouthful. Is that what you want?'

The image of being fed by Blake was inescapably erotic. Her heart began to pound as if it might leap from her body. There was passion in his face and a wild, almost uncontrolled blaze in his eyes. She almost said yes. That was what she wanted.

Gulping, she pushed Luc at him and Blake was forced to move back. She felt as if she'd come up for air after being half-drowned.

With trembling fingers she picked up her knife and fork and went through the motions of eating. She pushed food into her mouth—but only because he'd realise how disturbed she'd been by his threat if she left it untouched.

After a moment she had recovered her composure a little. Enough to notice Blake lightly tossing Luc in the air. Her son betrayed her totally by squealing with laughter and thoroughly enjoying every stomach-swooping second.

While she scurried through her meal they went on to more delights. Like 'see how near the ceiling you can get' and 'whirl around like a pancake' games. Blake's enjoyment of her son—and Luc's joyous surrender to the rough and tumble of inescapably exciting male bonding activities—made her blurt out, 'I am going. But I'm staying in the village, you know.'

The pancake spun to a sudden halt and looked rather surprised. Blake looked as if he'd been told she ate babies for lunch. 'I don't think so!' he hissed, tucking Luc over his shoulder in an infuriatingly expert way.

'I have some enquiries to make,' she said smugly, tackling the last piece of bacon with great satisfaction.

He studied her thoughtfully. 'No one will accommodate you.'

She shot him a suspicious glance. 'Because you're Mr Big around here?'

'Something like that,' he replied laconically.

Her jaw dropped open. 'Are you telling me that you'd order people not to give me bed and breakfast?' she cried in astonishment.

'If necessary.'

'But that's…that's…'

'Unfair use of authority.'

He didn't seem at all bothered by that. On the contrary, he seemed positively proud of his intended behaviour.

'Why?' she demanded.

'Simple. I don't want you pestering people just because you can't accept that your father was—'

'Don't say it!' she yelled, leaping to her feet. 'You may make everyone here dance like puppets on a string, but somehow I'll discover the truth! There are other villages nearby. Other pubs to stay in. Give me my son. I want to get out of this house.' She took Luc from him and felt unbelievably upset when her baby began to grizzle again. 'I'll be back with evidence, Blake Bellamie, and then you'll apologise to me on your bended knees!' she snapped.

'On my knees to you?' he queried, his eyes hotly dark and lustrous. And she was instantly alight with a terrible sexual hunger. He smiled speculatively. 'Forgive me if I don't hold my breath,' he drawled.

'Just you wait!' she muttered, furious with herself for responding so eagerly every time he put on that sexy look. Hair bouncing angrily, she spun on her heel and stormed to the door.

'Just a minute!' he commanded.

'What now?' she asked, turning to face him defiantly.

'Something you forgot,' he growled and she felt a *frisson* of danger rip through her body.

'What?' she mouthed.

She knew what he was going to do but she couldn't move, couldn't stop him. Their gazes clashed. His was black and pouring out hungry fires that seared her flesh and made it burn. Her parched lips parted as she struggled for breath, hope and fear tangling in her mind and a wild need destroying her urge to turn tail and run.

In seconds he had closed the gap between them, his closeness almost suffocating her. Before she could move a muscle he had caught her shoulders and his mouth had come down hard on hers in a hard, thorough and intensely erotic kiss that made her moan with desperate longing.

Only seconds later he stepped back, his expression utterly non-committal. She couldn't breathe at all. Her mouth felt hot. As if it had been abandoned. Wide-eyed, she stared at him in bewilderment.

'Why…what…?' she choked out.

'I believe you were expecting that last night,' he said scathingly, his body and face rigid with tightly controlled emotions.

It was true, of course. That made it worse. Her skin turned to flame. 'I—I don't understand—' she stumbled.

'Just to let you know that things happen only when I want them to. I call the shots around here—'

'Oh, Mr Very Big indeed!' she flung.

'That's right.' His eyes darkened. 'A warning, Nicole,' he added with soft menace. 'Set one foot on my land or pester people in the village, and I will broadcast your father's misdemeanours, even if it means shaming my family name.'

'You mean…?' She gulped. 'No one knows about this rumour that he was wicked?'

'Of course not. It was a private family matter,' he answered curtly. 'But make no mistake about it, if you pursue this matter then I'll drag his reputation into the mud. Contrary to what you might think, I don't rule here as a tyrant. I am respected. My word is unquestioned. So, if you know what's good for you—and your father's memory—get out of Great Aston and don't come back until you're invited. Or you'll find yourself in a hell of your own making.'

CHAPTER SEVEN

'HELLO, Daddy! Hello, Nicole, hello, baby!'

They both jumped as the irrepressible figure of Josef came leaping in, dressed in a Monsterman outfit over his school clothes.

'Oh, dear,' he muttered, skidding to a halt and looking from one tense face to the other. 'You're having a row. Shall I go out and come back in again so you can pretend everything's all right?'

In that split second Nicole knew that he must have witnessed his mother arguing with Blake. And that the perceptive child had probably slipped quietly away until a false polite atmosphere was restored. Her heart went out to him and she was desperately thinking of a way to reassure him when Blake spoke.

'What,' he asked with frightening self-control, 'are you doing up at this time?'

'I woke up and went into your bedroom and your bed hadn't been slept in. So I got dressed and went to see Granny and told her all that, but she didn't know where you were either.' Josef beamed at his father. 'I said a pretty lady had stayed here last night and she raised her eyebrow like you do. Did you sleep in Nicole's bed, Daddy?'

'No!' he and Nicole shouted in unison.

Josef jumped back, startled, his lower lip trembling. 'What did I say?' he complained. 'Granny said, "Aah, so that's it!" as if you *had*. And she asked me to bring her some orange juice and tell her more about—'

'I'll do that,' Blake muttered, striding to the fridge. He poured juice into a glass.

96

'So you weren't arguing 'cos you took all the duvet and left Nicole cold, Dad?'

Blake's mouth tightened. 'No! You get yourself some breakfast.' He made for the door. 'I'll be back in a moment,' he muttered, and disappeared.

Nursing the fretful Luc, Nicole smiled consolingly at an unusually subdued Josef. 'Your Daddy and I have only just met,' she said gently. 'It's usually only married people who share a bed—'

'Debbie Barker's not married to Pete's Dad and they sleep together,' announced Josef, pouring cereal into a bowl.

Nicole sighed. You couldn't fudge things with children. 'I expect they know each other very well, though,' she suggested.

'Oh, ever so. Pete says they have baths together. Will you and Daddy do that when you're proper friends?'

'I prefer showers,' Nicole said faintly.

'There's room for two in Daddy's,' Josef informed her helpfully. 'But you couldn't play with Monsterman slides or motor boats or anything like that.'

'I think,' Nicole said hastily, behaving like an abject coward and avoiding any further comment, 'that Luc needs changing. Excuse us a moment.'

Hurrying over to the sofa, she laid out the changing mat and placed the wailing Luc on it.

'I told Granny you were nicer than any of Daddy's lady friends,' the irrepressible Josef announced through a mouthful of cereal.

'That's very flattering. Thank you,' she said, wondering how many 'lady friends' the little boy had endured. Probably dozens, she thought, judging by Blake's testosterone levels. Did they all coo over Josef or had they found his frank outspoken manner disconcerting? Granny clearly knew what the arrival of a female meant in this house. Blake must be something of a womaniser.

'I didn't know you had a granny here,' she said idly.

'She's in bed all the time. I only get to see her once a day with Dad. I think she's got leg trouble. Maisie said she was on her last legs, anyway.'

'Oh! I'm so sorry,' Nicole cried, her face falling in dismay. Poor Blake, she thought. It must be hard for him with his mother so ill.

Her mind was occupied with this as she was unbuttoning the little romper suit. It was a moment before she realised to her horror that Luc's skin was covered in a rash that hadn't been there earlier. With shaking hands she quickly changed her son and, in as level a tone as she could manage, she called out to Josef, 'Would you bring a glass tumbler to me, please?'

'Does he drink orange juice too?' the little boy asked with interest, meandering over with nail-biting slowness.

'No!'

In panic, Nicole snatched the glass from him and pressed it against Luc's skin to test for meningitis. The rash disappeared. She sank back on her haunches in relief. The glass dropped from her nerveless fingers and was caught by a large, tanned hand.

'Trouble?' Blake asked urgently.

She put her hand to her forehead, trying to compose herself but she was shaking dreadfully. After a moment, Blake's arm came around her.

'Take it slowly. Breathe deeply,' he rasped. 'That rash—'

'It's not meningitis!' she whispered, burying her head in Blake's accommodating shoulder. He was probably annoyed with her for being so bold, but she needed comfort and he was the only person available. 'It's something else—but it's not that!' She raised a tragic face. 'Oh, Blake! I thought... I thought...'

'OK, OK.'

When she continued to shake, he hesitated for a moment and then with a half-suppressed sigh he hugged her tightly, his arms wrapping around her securely. She inhaled the musky maleness of him, felt the firmness of his warm body, and was instantly reassured.

Then a little hand inserted itself into hers too, and she pulled away to see Josef's small, anxious face.

'It's all right,' she said jerkily, calming herself for the child's sake. She found a weak smile because his lower lip was trembling, and squeezed Josef's little hand. 'I thought Luc might be very ill but it's probably nothing dreadful at all.'

Blake released her, leapt to his feet and moved swiftly over to the phone, saying with measured authority that brooked no refusal, 'But we'll get the doctor round, just to be sure. Joe, finish your cereal, make some toast and get yourself ready for school. Susie will take you this morning. You'll find her in the stables. All right?'

'Yes, Dad. Will do. If—if anything's wrong, will you—?'

'I'll ring the school either way. Promise. Good lad.' Blake gave his son an approving nod and began to speak in low, urgent tones into the phone.

Nicole's heart was pumping hard. Sinking to the comfort of the sofa, she cradled her beloved son, praying that the rash wasn't serious. It could have so many causes—and she couldn't bear Luc to be in danger. He was her whole life now. She had to keep him safe. She'd do anything, *anything* to protect him. Her lip trembled and she felt alarmingly close to tears.

'He'll be here in a few minutes. Hey. Don't worry,' Blake said when she raised blurred eyes to his. 'Everything will be fine.' He came to sit beside her and surprised her by taking her shaking hand in his.

She looked up at him gratefully. 'Thank you,' she whispered. 'I—I can cope with almost anything, but the thought of—of...' She couldn't say it. Her father's death had been hard enough to bear, but the idea that her little baby might... 'I'm sorry!' she gulped, choking back the tears.

A handkerchief dabbed at her eyes. His face was very close and it seemed less angry than before. Warmer. Kinder.

'It's all right to be upset. I understand,' he said in a gravelly voice. 'I felt exactly the same helplessness when Josef had gastroenteritis once.'

'I remember,' chirped in Josef. 'I was mega-sick everywhere. Dad kept clearing it up. Yuk! And that's not all. I had the most awful—'

'Do your toast, Joe, and save us from the less pleasant details,' Blake said drily. He turned back to Nicole, who gave him a sympathetic roll of her eyes at Josef's lack of delicacy. His finger lightly touched her wryly smiling mouth and she held her breath. 'Embarrassing he might be,' Blake murmured, 'but he's made you smile.'

She mastered her racing pulses. 'He'd make a slab of stone smile,' she said ruefully.

'I deserve a reward, don't I? Can I ride my pony to school, Dad?' Josef asked, clearly taking advantage of this highly satisfactory praise.

'No. You walk like everyone else. And don't reel off a list of children who come by car. You know what I mean.'

Josef closed his open mouth and Nicole smiled again, seeing that Blake had guessed right. Then the little boy perked up and adopted another tack. 'Will Nicole and Luc be here when I get back?' he asked hopefully.

Blake let out a long hiss of breath that managed to sound resigned and irritated at the same time. 'Probably.'

'Good. I can show them my beetles.'

'Depending on how Luc is,' Blake warned. 'He might not be up to beetles.'

She couldn't read anything into his tone but she knew he didn't welcome her enforced stay. He'd made his feelings about her clear enough last night, however kind he was being about Luc now. But he wasn't a monster. His sympathy lay purely with her baby, not with her, so she needn't kid herself that he'd had a change of heart.

'I'm very sorry about this,' she said awkwardly. 'I really was intending to leave—'

He grunted. 'Now you can't,' he said and she still wasn't sure from the low growl if he was annoyed or reluctantly accepting that fact. 'I can hardly turn you out with a sick baby, can I?'

'Blake…'

She hesitated. More than anything she wanted to assure him that she respected and admired him. And as a consequence she wanted to make discreet enquiries to clear her father's name. Deep down, she longed to be accepted by him as a member of the family. For a relationship to build up between them all—Blake, Josef, Luc and herself. He was her kinsman. The only family she had, other than Luc.

How could she say what was in her heart? But then, what did she have to lose?

Blake was perplexed. It felt so right, holding her hand, protecting her, trying to ease her worries. He didn't understand why, only that his entire being was rebelling against his decision to keep her away from Cranford at all costs. Something told him that she had qualities he might appreciate and value. She'd consistently been thoughtful towards his son and she was a devoted mother. He frowned. Only a short time ago, when he'd taken up the glass of orange juice, his mother had expressed a hope that he'd met 'a nice girl' at last.

He'd smiled wryly and assured her that he hadn't indulged in a night of passion and that his appearance was due to a lack of sleep after badger-watching in Sawpit meadow rather than romping all night in a nubile girlfriend's bed.

'Shame,' she'd said, surprising him. 'Be happy, my darling,' she'd urged. 'Go with your heart and your gut instincts. Don't make my mistake.'

Tactfully, ruefully, checking his retort that it was she who'd taught him to suppress his feelings, he'd kissed her, promising to read to her before lunch and to tell her a little about Nicole. Though how much he'd reveal he wasn't sure yet.

And now his heart and his guts were telling him to give Nicole a chance. To let her stay and to see if she could be trusted with Cranford.

'You were about to say something,' he murmured.

'It's nothing,' she said.

'It's troubling you. I can see that by your frown.' Again he had to touch her. The faint V between her brows. She lowered her lashes and bit her lip. 'Why don't you say what you want to?' he suggested, his heart and guts churning at the tenderness of her expression as she rocked and kissed her tiny baby.

He felt her take a deep breath. 'When the doctor's been,' she said. 'I can't think straight before that.'

'Of course.'

There was the sound of crunching close by. Blake looked up to see a worried Josef munching on a partially burnt piece of toast.

'He'll be all right, won't he, Dad?'

Disregarding the shower of sooty crumbs, Blake pulled his worried son on to his knee and gave him a cuddle. 'We have the best doctor in the Cotswolds. Of course he'll be all right. Now. Got everything you need?'

'PE kit, lunch money, hanky, string, Monsterman swaps, banana, chocolate bar, owl's pellets, lucky stone, empty matchbox, strip of leather and magpie feathers,' Josef replied in a solemn chant.

Nicole looked at Blake questioningly. 'Don't ask,' he muttered and slid from the sofa, taking his son with him. After a chorus of goodbyes and hugs, he managed to push Josef through the door just as Steve ushered himself in.

'Morning, Blake! Is that the patient over there? Blond as a Bellamie, isn't he? Morning, young lady. I'm Dr Steve Mackenzie. Let's have a look at the little man while Blake makes me some tea, shall we?'

Blake took one look at Nicole's white, frightened face and at that moment he would have done anything to stop her worrying. He was astonished. He cared about her. Why the devil was that? Perhaps his capacity for human sympathy was greater than he'd imagined. Perhaps he'd feel like this about any woman whose baby was ill. He dismissed his doubts as to the truth of that and focused on making Steve a mug of tea.

But he couldn't stop his heart thudding like crazy as the doctor examined little Luc and very gently asked a battery of searching questions.

Silent and restraining his urge to yell at Steve to make a diagnosis and put Nicole out of her misery, Blake placed the incongruous Monsterman mug on a side table beside Steve.

'Well, Nicole,' he said eventually and Blake found himself leaning forward for the verdict.

Steve flashed a reassuring smile at her and she looked slightly less anxious. At that moment, Blake wanted to catch her in his arms and shield her from the troubles of the world. Hell. He was going mad.

'What is it?' he demanded, far more abruptly than was proper.

Steve blinked his surprise then turned back to Nicole.

'Probably nothing to worry about—'

'Oh! *Grâce à Dieu!*' she said huskily, snuggling her face into Luc's small body.

Blake's throat developed a huge lump of emotion inside it. 'He's not in any danger?' he grated. He felt Nicole's eyes on him. Knew she was thinking that now she'd be thrown out. And so he smiled at her in reassurance.

Steve coughed for attention and they both gave a little jump. Blake could see his friend was wondering what was going on between them. Their gazes had held for a fraction too long.

Briskly he said, 'OK, Steve. Let's hear it.'

Looking slightly amused, the doctor turned his attention to Nicole again. 'You're doing all the right things. You're breast-feeding so that rules out many contagious diseases because that protects Luc from them. I reckon he's had an allergic reaction, perhaps to the crab you had last night—so don't eat any more shellfish, just in case.'

'I caused this?' she cried in horror.

'Don't beat yourself up,' advised Steve with a genial smile. 'You've tested his immune system and given yourself a bit of a shock, nothing more. If you want punishment, I imagine you've had enough in the past ten minutes or so.'

'You're right!' she muttered. 'I died a thousand deaths in a split second.'

'Then relax. Things will only get better. Keep him cool. I'll call in later to see how he's doing but ring me if he seems feverish or any worse—though I don't think this'll be the case. No aspirin for him or you...'

Blake listened to the instructions and felt a wash of relief flood through him. And, to be honest, a small surge of elation. Totally against his better judgement, Nicole was being forced to stay in the house. And to his amazement he felt overjoyed.

Steve waved a cheerful goodbye, extracted a promise of a game of tennis later that week, gave him a conspiratorial wink that was entirely superfluous and they were alone again.

Blake went over to her immediately, drawn by the fragile vulnerability of her drawn face. 'It's good news,' he said, his stiff tone at odds with his joyous feelings.

'Yes.' There was a long pause. She stared miserably at Luc, who seemed more settled. 'I could... I should be able to leave when the doctor's been this afternoon.'

'I don't think so.'

He saw her swallowing. When her huge, wet-lashed eyes lifted to his he felt a kick of tenderness ripping through him, as fierce as any anger.

'But you don't want me here,' she said in a low voice.

How could he answer that? With the truth—that he did want her around but couldn't trust himself not to keep his hands off her? And that he feared the release of the volcanic passions he was storing up?

'Come into the garden,' he said. 'Luc's asleep. I'll fetch the baby buggy and you can sit in the shade beneath the cedar. You can tell me what you wanted to say.' He took a deep breath and decided to give her a chance. 'And I can explain why I've been so determined to get you out of the house as soon as possible.'

CHAPTER EIGHT

IMMEDIATELY she stepped outside a sensation of serenity stole over her. Despite the grandeur of her surroundings she felt at home. Maybe this was because she recognised so many of the trees and shrubs, but also because the garden had been designed to please the eye and was a clever combination of formality and apparent, but well-ordered, chaos.

Blake brought Luc's buggy and then carried over two hugely comfortable steamer chairs which looked as if they might be Edwardian. Nicole sank into the deep cream cushions and gazed around, enchanted.

The unrestricted view across the mirror-still waters of a large lake to the wooded hills beyond was quite breathtaking and she felt calmer just by sitting there and looking at the view.

Eventually she turned to Blake, grateful that he'd given her time to let the lovely garden bring peace to her troubled mind.

'What do you think of it?' he asked, watching her intently.

She smiled. 'That I've never seen anywhere more beautiful,' she answered with a quiet sigh and his consequent smile of delight was just dazzling.

'I've spent years changing it from the stark, formal avenues of yew and box favoured by my…father,' he confided, his voice ringing with justifiable pride after the odd but brief hesitation.

'You?' she cried in astonishment. 'But this is the work

of someone with an artist's eye. And a love and knowledge of plants—'

'When you take over a place like this you have a great responsibility to ensure that it survives in good heart.' He looked at her intently, as though it was important she knew that. 'Those who inherit historic land and estates are only trustees. It is a duty to preserve everything that is good and to make the land financially viable. I made it my business to learn about landscape design and the use of plants.' He smiled to himself. 'There's something about being outside, even in the worst weather—digging, planting, weeding and tending—that lifts my soul,' he said to her surprise.

And she detected an underlying passion, too, that conveyed his enthusiasm even more than his words. Sparkling with animation, his eyes devoured the riotous borders, the foaming blossom and much-loved plants.

'You love it very much, don't you?' she murmured.

'Every bit of it. It's my creation. Part of me. Like Cranford itself,' he said quietly.

'And does Josef feel the same?'

Blake frowned. 'Passionately. He helps. Whenever he's missing I know I'll find him in the garden doing something useful. He needs to be out in the open air, like me, engaged in a physical activity.'

'I wonder that you have the time to be hands-on, with the estate and that huge house to manage,' she mused.

'It's not easy but I have a good staff who've been with me for years. I pay them well and they love Cranford enough to take care of it. But I have little spare time, it's true. Of course,' he said, his tone changing oddly, 'I was brought up knowing I'd inherit. I followed my...father around the estate much as Josef follows me.' He looked away and she could only see his jaw but it was tense and she wondered why. 'My son would be lost if he had to

leave this house. **Absolutely** devastated,' he said, almost
with a tinge of harshness in his tone.

'I—I'm sure that's **true**,' she said, aware that he was on
edge but not knowing why. Then a reason occurred to her.
In dismay she cried, '**You're** not thinking you might have
to sell for financial reasons, are you?'

He gave a short, oddly mirthless laugh. 'My finances
are in good heart. We were in debt when I took over but
now the estate is profitable because I dared to make
changes. Apart from the farm, there are estate cottages
bringing in rent. I employ a blacksmith, a potter and a
printer, all of whom make items for the tourist trade.'

'My goodness!' she murmured, impressed.

'That's not all. We have Pick Your Own soft fruit and
a farm shop, lease fishing rights on the lake and river, and
hold weddings and functions in the old orangerie. The diary is full. In fact,' he said, 'there's a conference taking
place this afternoon.'

'Oh. Do you need to go off to organise it?' she asked,
feeling a lurch of disappointment at the prospect of losing
his company.

'My PA is doing that. But I'll put in an appearance to
check everything and I'll wander over in the evening when
the fireworks are let off.'

She gazed at him in frank admiration.

'You've probably saved the estate from being broken
up.'

'I can't argue with that,' he agreed. 'It was in a bad
state when I took over.'

'What an achievement,' she mused. 'It must make you
feel good inside to know that it'll continue in your family
for your descendants to enjoy. No wonder Josef is full of
self-confidence. His future is utterly secure.'

She smiled, thinking how comforting it must be to be
part of such an inheritance. Not for the financial security

but the sense of belonging, of being part of a community. And she wished her background wasn't so complicated by secrets and diverging opinions.

'Nothing,' Blake said quietly, 'is ever secure.'

'Well, with all those activities providing income you're hardly going to lose Cranford Hall to some outsider!' She laughed at such a ridiculous idea. 'No one would run it as well as you clearly do, anyway. You and Josef are absolutely right for this place, I can see that.'

There was a long silence while Blake stared out at the view to his far right. Perturbed at the idea of talking to the back of his head, she lightly touched his arm. He flinched and she bit her lip. That wasn't the reaction she'd hoped for.

'Blake. Please. We are cousins. I want us to be... friends.'

That was untrue. She wanted more. Heaving a deep sigh, she plucked up all her courage and continued. Her father had always told her to face up to mistakes and to see yourself as honestly as possible, warts and all. It was time she apologised for batting her eyes at him the previous evening.

'I know what you thought of me last night,' she ventured bravely.

'I doubt it,' he drawled.

She bit her lip. He wasn't making it easy for her. Fair enough. He didn't like being propositioned by women he didn't fancy.

'OK. I'll level with you. I was encouraging you because I find you very attractive. If I embarrassed you then I'm sorry. I've never behaved like that before in the whole of my life.' She gave a small, deprecating laugh. 'I'm totally inexperienced, to be honest. My ex-husband, Jean-Paul, was my only lover, the only man who's ever kissed me till...till...'

'Till I did.'

He turned his head and for a moment his eyes lingered on her mouth, making it tingle. She swallowed and resisted the urge to lick her lips. Too much of an invitation, even though she wanted to feel his mouth on hers again. She gave an inward groan as he jerked his head away again. How shameless she was!

'Yes. I—I don't know what happened to me last night. Perhaps the emotions of the day… I have no explanation, only that I wanted to be kissed by you. It was an impulse that I regret. Since you have no interest in me, it won't happen again.'

He turned to her then. 'Won't it?' he asked with a frown.

Reaching out, he stroked her cheek but was still frowning as he did so and she wondered if he was testing her. Even so, she quivered and marvelled at the power of his touch to arouse her. She gritted her teeth and forced herself to concentrate hard on what she wanted to say because it was so important that she cleared the air of any misunderstanding.

'I can take a hint. You made your feelings clear. Blake, I want you to forget what happened,' she went on doggedly. 'I am used to expressing my feelings and I can see that I must have seemed pushy and…' She remembered one of her father's favourite words, usually used to describe scantily dressed celebrities who flaunted their attributes in public. 'I was brazen, I know, and I apologise. Please forgive me!' she begged. 'We got on so well before you knew who I was. It was fun talking to you during dinner, too, after Josef broke the ice between us. If you block me out of your life, I have no family other than Luc.'

Eager to plead her cause, she leaned forward, her eyes beseeching him. 'You can't turn your back on us. There's been a misunderstanding about my father and I think we can sort it out, given time.' She held out her hand, her gaze steady and level on his dark, unfathomable eyes. 'Be my family. Be my cousin, for our children's sakes,' she begged.

It was a risk, he thought. But one he desperately wanted to take. Both honour and instinct were urging him to give her this chance to prove her father's innocence. And he knew he would forever regret it if he sent her away without searching for the truth.

There was something extraordinarily dignified about her manner. He thought of the way she'd responded to Josef and of the adoration in her eyes whenever she looked at her baby or touched him. There was a goodness in her, he felt sure.

Besides, she was a Bellamie and he couldn't turn his back on her. Wryly he acknowledged that his life had become confusing and unpredictable where it had once been stable and uneventful. Not long ago he'd known what the morrow would bring. But with Nicole around life had suddenly changed. One day he was threatening her, the next saw him welcoming her into his home.

It was the baby's illness, of course—that had forced his hand. And while Luc and Nicole waited under the protection of his roof—how could he do otherwise?—it did make sense to make some enquiries about Giles. And to find out more about Nicole.

Yes. He was acting sensibly. Couldn't reproach himself for changing his mind. And as if knowing he'd capitulated, his pulses leapt with an almost uncontainable excitement that swept through his body with a force he could not deny. He knew that all his logical reasons for letting her stay were as nothing compared with his need for her. To make love to her. Possess that body. Touch her, breathe in the scent of her, sate himself until the destructive hunger abated and he could think clearly again.

Nicole watched the changing expressions on his face

with apprehension. He stared at her for a long, breathless moment.

Then, to her delight, he took her hand in his. There was a new warm liquidity to his eyes and she felt dizzy with hope and longing.

'Cousin,' he said huskily. 'How could I resist such an impassioned plea?'

'Uhuh,' she managed, her lips parting as she fought breathlessness.

'I think we might be...*kissing* cousins,' he whispered.

She was astonished. Slowly, as his face came closer and closer, her eyes began to close. The anticipation was sweetly painful.

But the moment his mouth touched hers she felt something inside her snap. With a groan she caught his strong face between her hands and deepened the kiss till her senses reeled from the onslaught of his hard, demanding mouth.

She found herself being drawn on to his lap. Passionate kisses rained on her face and throat even as she struggled to grasp the fact that he had wanted her after all. She felt wonderfully wanton and desirable. With a featherlight movement his hands had slid to the warm nakedness of her back between the hem of her cropped top and her skirt and she arched against him with a small moan of pleasure.

Then, reluctantly, she gently pushed against his chest and was released.

'Because of Luc,' she explained, panting heavily.

'Of course.'

She slid from his lap and sat shakily on her chair. Her mouth felt as if it had been brought to life. And unbelievably smiley. Her shining eyes met his and she didn't know how she didn't ravish him then and there, her need was so strong and his magnetism so incredibly powerful.

'I—I can't...while he...'

'I know,' he whispered. And his eyes promised 'later'. She felt a thrill electrify her entire body. Later. *Later!*

In her wildest dreams she'd never thought… She gave a slow, sexy smile and rejoiced when he clenched his teeth and tensed up in an effort not to reach out for her again. He did want her!

It seemed the fireworks had already begun. Something was certainly rocketing through her. A kind of wild joy, a hope and a growing certainty that their relationship would be very special. Perhaps even someone she could love. Her head whirled. Even from the very beginning she'd known there was an extraordinary chemistry between them. A bond, fiercer and even more urgent than blood itself. That was why she'd been confused by his rejection of her. In her bones, despite his apparent indifference, she'd had a suspicion that she'd been responding to the signals his body was sending out. The chemistry had been two-way. In future she'd listen to her instincts, she promised herself!

It quite shocked her that she could hardly keep her hands off him. At the same time it excited her that he felt the same, however hard he tried to hide it. She wanted to know, to feel, and to be the reason and an essential part of the passion that simmered beneath his restraint. Felt a wicked urge to be the one who drove him crazy till he forgot everything except making love to her.

She looked up at him from under her lashes, unknowingly alluring, unknowingly aping the seductive techniques of women out for all they could get.

Blake froze, remembering other women who'd thought to entice him into their power with their sexuality.

'Blake…you will let Luc and me stay for a while, won't you?' she breathed. 'I want to. So very much.'

It was an alluringly husky plea that came so close to her eager kisses and her sudden withdrawal. A trick he was well used to. His entire body tensed up.

Had she responded to him to get her own way? He felt sickened at the thought. He'd had enough of that from his ex-wife, who'd only agreed to have a child if she could profit financially. The memory of those months of cold-blooded bargaining chilled his ardour. He wouldn't be taken for a sucker again. Wouldn't be manipulated. Would never be a woman's victim again.

Nicole realised that he had withdrawn from her even though he had not actually moved. The closed look came into his eyes where once there had been glowing desire.

They were back to square one again.

'You don't trust me, do you?' she blurted out in dismay. 'You think I'll pervert Josef or the people here—'

'I don't know,' he muttered, pushing his hand through his hair till the black waves bounced in angry disorder. 'I'll level with you. I can't be sure about your motives for flirting with me—'

'My *motives?*' she flared. 'I don't have motives! I just *am*! Don't you think my behaviour might be something to do with sexual attraction?' she added indignantly.

He shrugged. 'You could be using sex to make me change my mind about you,' he said bluntly.

'Is that the kind of woman you're used to? A woman who sees her favours as a bargaining tool?' she asked in horror.

He gave a short laugh. 'Yes. I suppose I am.'

'Well, I'm sorry for you! But there are also women without…' She frowned. '*L'astuce.*'

'Guile.'

'That's right.' She made a mental note to ask him why he spoke French like a native. 'And women like that—like me—enjoy sex for what it is, not for what it can do for us.'

'Really,' he said in a husky croak.

'If I had any sense,' she said with a sigh, 'I'd behave

modestly and wear unrevealing clothes. Then you might question your belief that I've been brought up in a house of ill repute by a dissolute father.'

'So why—' he muttered, glaring as he angrily fingered her bare midriff and made her draw in her breath sharply '—are you doing exactly the opposite?'

Her eyes darkened. 'Because this is how I dress normally and...' She took a gamble. 'Where you're concerned, *and only you*, I can't help myself.'

From the startled look he gave her she knew he wanted to kiss her. That her honesty had rocked him. And it had also given him a free hand. Take me in your arms! she pleaded silently. Trust me.

She watched him struggling with his desires and her mouth parted in longing. When he tore his gaze from it and sat stubbornly back in his chair she felt a shaft of disappointment spear its way through her yearning body. She did so badly want him to like her as well as to lust after her.

'I have to remain objective about this,' he muttered. 'I can't just do as I please.' And added under his breath, 'So much is at stake.'

'I don't see the problem,' she argued. 'We're attracted to one another. We are free.'

'I want to stay free,' he growled.

Her face flushed. 'I'm not intending to behave like a nagging wife just because we make love! It's simple, Blake. We want one another. What's the big deal?'

'Are you always that frank about your feelings?' he asked.

He'd tried to sound cool and curious but his voice had shaken. At least, she thought, he does have the same urges—even if he's better at controlling them.

'Not about wanting someone. I've never felt this way before. I know women aren't supposed to be so...up front, but what am I supposed to do? Play coy and hard to get? I'm not like that, Blake. Everyone says I'm too open, though. I say what I feel. I don't believe in hiding my emotions, unless what I say or do might hurt someone,' she said quietly. 'My friends tell me I'm naive—childlike in my innocence and my inability to pretend.' She smiled, seeing that he had relaxed and his suspicious expression had vanished. 'Perhaps that's why I feel so close to Josef. He's refreshingly honest, isn't he?'

'To a fault,' Blake growled.

'But you don't correct him and make him into a social robot, do you?' she argued.

His brows drew hard together. 'No,' he said shortly. 'I had enough of that in my own childhood. My aim is to teach him to be kind and thoughtful and to put himself in other people's shoes.'

'Then we think alike. My father told me always to speak the truth and never to play games, especially with men.'

He rubbed his piratical five o'clock shadow. 'So you don't tell lies.'

'I'm hopeless at it! It's too complicated when you do!' she cried passionately. 'You have to remember what lies you told. It's far easier to be truthful.'

'Your husband.' Blake narrowed his eyes speculatively. 'Did he appreciate your honesty?'

She sighed. 'That was the problem.'

'Would you tell me why you broke up?'

'If it will help.'

'Possibly.'

With a flick of her finger she pushed back her hair behind her ears, her expression sad and reflective. 'OK. He wanted me to stay the same and never to get pregnant because that would change me from a wife into a mother.'

'He wanted your body to remain unchanged. Sexy and

unmarked by the ravages of motherhood,' Blake said quietly.

'Yes!' she cried in amazement. 'But how did you know?'

'My ex-wife was worried about her figure,' he said, his expression bitter.

'But,' argued Nicole, 'she did choose to be a mother. She had Josef—'

'Only because I promised her a hefty chunk of my fortune,' he muttered.

Nicole's eyes rounded in shock. 'That's awful!'

Blake gave a small shrug. 'I should never have agreed to such blatant blackmail. But I was trying to keep my marriage together. I thought that when Josef was born she'd be different, she'd love her child and would welcome motherhood.'

'But she didn't,' Nicole said with gentle sympathy.

His eyes darkened. 'She wouldn't even look at him. And I could never forgive her for neglecting her own flesh and blood. She stayed because she enjoyed her position here as lady of the manor. But she tired even of that. And she knew everyone in Great Aston disliked her for rejecting Josef. So, seeing that she wasn't going to get anything more from me, she left when he was almost three years old.'

'Is she happy, do you know, with the chauffeur?' Nicole asked tentatively.

'I've no idea. She hasn't even sent birthday cards to Joe.'

Nicole stared at him in horror.

'I can't understand that,' she said slowly.

Blake gave another perfunctory shrug. 'Some people think only of their own good. Their own needs. Their lives are dedicated to pleasing themselves and they are incapable of generosity or sacrifice for others.'

'I'm sorry you had that experience,' she said fervently.

'My fault. I was warned that my money and position would attract the wrong kind of woman.'

'But you loved her,' she said with understanding.

'I don't think so,' he said, surprising her. 'She was beautiful and lively and charmed her way around the social circuit. I mistook that for a loving nature. She's not wicked, Nicole. Just too immature to cope with anyone's needs but her own.'

She sighed. 'I can understand why you're wary of my motives. It's difficult to trust people after an experience like that. I suppose day after day you had to handle the fact that your wife was trying to manipulate you. But you have to risk trusting people, Blake, or you spend your whole life missing all the good, honest friendships you can make.'

He shook his head. 'I prefer that to being hurt again.'

'I'd rather be hurt than live like a hermit without someone to love, someone to give your heart to!' she declared.

He looked pained. Haunted.

'Let's get back to your own marriage,' he said, deftly changing the subject. 'You obviously became pregnant. I gather your husband didn't like that situation.'

'Worse than that. He was furious,' she confessed. 'Luc wasn't planned, you see.'

'You didn't want him?' he cried, aghast.

'Oh, yes!' she cried, clasping her hands in a passionate gesture. 'I *longed* to have a child! I was overjoyed when I knew I was pregnant. It seemed to complete my life.' She smiled lovingly with a long, lingering glance at her sleeping child and then her face grew sad again. 'I'm afraid Jean-Paul never forgave me. He stayed out late a lot. I told him I didn't like that in no uncertain terms. My friends said I should lure him back to me with intimate meals and sexy dresses that showed my cleavage.' She shrugged her slender shoulders. 'I felt that if he loved me he'd want to care for me and be with me.'

'A mature man would have coped with the changes to his life and yours,' Blake observed with contempt.

'Precisely. He was being selfish and just didn't love me enough. And, knowing that in my heart of hearts, I wasn't in any mood to put on an act and seduce him.'

'Presumably he had an affair.' Blake's gaze was very direct, very searching.

She wrinkled her nose in disgust. 'In our house, our bed, under my nose and with my best friend!'

'Doesn't get much worse than that!' he commented drily.

'Oh, it does, when you've caught him once, forgiven him and then find him and your friend in your bed again!' she muttered.

Blake frowned and swore.

'Yes,' she said bitterly. 'He was that and more. After the divorce he disappeared. He doesn't even know if he has a son or a daughter.'

He cursed again. 'So you've had no moral or financial support for Luc?'

'Oh, yes. From my father at first—'

'Just a minute.' His brows drew hard together. 'Luc's seven weeks old. Your father was alive till recently?'

She took a moment to speak, her eyes sad and haunted. The memories made her heart ache.

'Very much so. Dear Papa,' she mumbled to herself. 'He was so thrilled to be a grandfather. He'd sit and stare at Luc and smile as if he was the most precious thing on earth. And sometimes he'd be so moved that a little tear would drop to his cheek. I'd go to him and hug him and say he was going senile in his old age and…and he'd laugh and hold me tight and say he was happy for the first time since he was a young man. That shook me. I'd no idea he'd never been content with my mother.'

'Exactly when,' Blake murmured softly, 'did he die?'

The pain touched her eyes and drew down the corners of her mouth. 'A little over three weeks ago,' she whispered in a shaky voice.

He looked genuinely shocked. Her hands were gently caught in his. Compassion showed in his softened face and the sincerity of his sympathy brought tears to her eyes.

'I can't tell you how sorry I am. I've been hard on you. And you've been through hell,' he said huskily. He lifted her hands, one by one, and pressed a tender and deeply impassioned kiss on them.

'I loved him very much,' she choked. 'Miss him so badly.'

Blake's grip tightened but he didn't comment. His thumb lightly stroked the back of her hand while she struggled to push back the tears. She knew that she could never rest until Blake honoured her father's memory.

'How are you managing now?' he asked quietly.

'Papa had sold a couple of paintings and the buyer very kindly paid the money direct to me. I inherit his cottage so I have a home, and eventually there'll be his savings too when the executors have done their work. I can earn my living even while Luc's small because I can convert the piggery and put in an extractor fan for the glue fumes. Then I'll be able to repair and restore ceramics at home when Luc sleeps—either outside or in the house. I'm lucky, really. Luckier than most.'

'You have your future mapped out,' he said with a frown.

'I have Luc to think of. I must provide for him.'

'You are happy where you live in France?'

She wondered why he asked. Why he should care. Perhaps he was just being polite.

'I was,' she said honestly. 'But my father's death has changed everything. And I'm afraid that now I'm divorced my male friends think I'm fair game and my female friends are wary of me.'

'I can't blame them,' he said drily.

'But I'd never threaten their relationships!' she objected.

'You couldn't help it.'

'No! I'm not like that!' she insisted. 'I'm not a marriage wrecker—!'

'Nicole. You are sexy and you are alone. Men will find you irresistible.'

She gave an exasperated sigh. He was exaggerating. But there was some truth in what he said. 'I'll have to shave my hair and wear old clothes,' she said dejectedly.

'That,' Blake commented, 'would be a waste.'

'Perhaps,' she mused, 'my situation brings out men's chivalrous instincts. They want to console me.'

'Perhaps,' he clipped. 'You've certainly suffered over the past months.'

'And worrying about my father's reputation is adding to my worries,' she pointed out softly.

In the silence that followed she knew that Blake was making up his mind about her. So she kept quiet while he did so, hoping he believed that she was absolutely straight in everything she did and that she wasn't defending a monster of a father.

'I think,' he said eventually, 'you might be genuine—'

'Not,' she said, so delighted that she was unable to resist the mischievous impulse, 'a prostitute or a drug user or—'

'Nicole.' He frowned. 'I know I must sound stuffy and cautious, but all my life I've been brought up to protect Cranford and the Bellamie family and to think of its best interests.' His frown deepened. 'Anyone who inherits this land must be prepared to put Cranford before their own needs. That's how it's survived for the past five centuries in the same hands. We have traditions to uphold. Like becoming fluent in French, for instance, merely because our ancestors came from across the Channel.'

'I understand,' she said, contrite. 'You've learnt to weigh your decisions carefully. But you've got things out of all proportion. I'm no threat to Cranford!'

He inhaled deeply as if she might be.

'OK. So you think I was over-reacting. That's because you don't know the problems involved—'

'Then tell me,' she prompted.

'I can't. One day, maybe. But for now, perhaps we both need to know the evidence stacked against your father. If you do stay for a while—'

'Yes?' she asked, her eyes filled with hope.

He eyed her speculatively. 'I'm taking a gamble here. But there's something I must ask of you in return. It entails being…economical with the truth.'

That was unexpected. 'You want me to lie?'

'Not exactly. Let me explain. It seems that fate has thrown us together. And fate has decreed that we might be living in the same house for a time, till we're sure that Luc can travel safely.'

'And you'll get to know me,' she cried eagerly. 'You'll find out that I am an open book—'

'Part of which,' he warned, 'must remain closed.'

She frowned. 'How do you mean?'

'Nicole, I can't let you stay anywhere near this house unless you agree to keep it a secret that we are second cousins. Otherwise I must insist that you and Luc are transferred to a private nursing home some distance away, till you are happy that he's fit for the journey home.'

She didn't want that! She wanted to be with Blake, to learn more about him, to curl up in his arms...

His eyebrow crooked, asking for her agreement, and she forgot her dreams and pulled herself together.

'I'm not sure,' she said slowly. 'I'd be accepting the fact that you're ashamed of me—'

'It's not quite that, Nicole.'

'Then what is it?' she demanded impatiently.

'It's complicated. You realise that I have a sick mother.'

Immediately her expression became sympathetic. 'I do. Josef told me. It must be a terrible worry for you to see her so ill. I remember the feeling exactly.'

'I've had to come to terms with it. There's nothing I can do. To be blunt,' he said, in a horribly tight voice, 'she's dying.'

'How awful!' And now it was her turn to be the consoler. Her turn to stroke his strong, powerful hands. 'Are you very close?' she asked.

His eyes brooded on this. 'She gave up a great deal for me,' he replied quietly.

'That's quite a burden of guilt for you to carry,' Nicole said, unable to hide her disapproval. 'Sacrifice should be willing—and never referred to.'

'You're right, and it *was* like that. In fact, I only learnt about it a short time ago—and she only told me because it was necessary. She loves me very much, Nicole. And I love her.'

'What an awful time for you. I do know how you feel. It's terrible, losing a parent!' she declared passionately.

'Yes. And you'll understand why I didn't want you around, why your arrival shook me. She's very frail and I want her last days to be as peaceful and happy as possible—'

'Of course, but how could I—?'

'Because you're Giles's daughter. And she'd go berserk if she knew you were in the house.'

'She was your source, wasn't she?' Nicole blurted out unhappily. 'She's the one who told you all those lies—'

'She was very certain of what she was saying,' he defended. 'She became almost hysterical when she told me about him. I knew nothing about him until that moment. No one had ever spoken his name or referred to him. There are no photographs or portraits of him. Don't you think that suggests something disastrous must have happened? We Bellamies stick together. And yet this one has been wiped from the family tree—literally.'

She felt helpless. Blake loved his mother. Under the circumstances he'd naturally believe her. Nicole thought that *she'd* even believe the stories if she hadn't known her father so well.

'I don't want to upset you,' she said firmly, 'but she's *wrong*, Blake! Terribly wrong!'

He pulled in a long breath. 'We're going round in circles. I'll suspend judgement till I know for sure, one way or the other. So let's forget for a moment whether she's misguided or not. The point is that she mustn't know anything other than the fact that you are a friend of mine. Anything more will not only hasten her death but she'll die an angry woman.' His voice changed. Became harder, more determined. 'I won't have that. Do you understand?'

She admired his defence of his mother—even though he was wrong. It showed great loyalty.

'I do! Of course you want to protect your mother at this time. And under the circumstances I wouldn't want her upset either!' she cried vehemently.

'So you agree?'

'Absolutely,' she said. 'I'm happy for it to be known

that I'm a friend, staying for a while. No one else knows of the family connection.'

She would do anything for the sake of the future she wanted to create with him. An excitement skittered within her. She knew she'd disprove those awful stories about her father. And then she and Blake would be free to give rein to their true feelings. Her face became wreathed in smiles.

'Trust me,' she continued, gazing into the dark depths of his eyes. 'For your mother's sake I can keep my mouth shut about our kinship until you want to reveal it.'

He kissed her fingertips, the thickness of his lashes on his cheeks making her heart flutter. 'Thank you!' he murmured with heartfelt relief. Looking up, he gave her a crooked smile. 'Hell. I just hope I'm doing the wise thing—'

'Oh, you are!' she cried happily. 'We'll solve the mystery and we'll become proper cousins. Josef and Luc can get to know one another. Perhaps you can visit us in France in the summer holidays. It'll be lovely, Blake, knowing I have roots, knowing I have family. I can't have wished for anything better.'

It was as if, she thought, delirious with delight, she'd removed an intolerable burden from his shoulders. Leaning forward, he gently kissed her on the mouth.

'You can have the benefit of the doubt—for the time being—kissing cousin.'

'You won't regret this,' she promised him, her eyes starry.

'I hope not. And now—' he declared, leaping energetically to his feet '—I have things to do. Like have a shower and a shave, for a start!' He grinned, suddenly looking carefree. 'Make yourself entirely at home. Mrs Carter starts work at eleven—though Maisie will be around, doing the housework, in case you need anything. You know where the kitchen is. Make a list of shopping you'll need and it'll be done for you. Lunch will be at one. I'll see you then—but tell someone if you're worried about Luc and they'll reach me on my mobile. OK?'

Nicole nodded, her smile soft and unknowingly inviting. He hesitated, then bent his head and kissed her long and hard.

'Farewell for now,' he muttered, his breath hot and harsh against the plushness of her lips.

And then he was off, striding rapidly towards the house.

CHAPTER NINE

THE morning was very relaxing. Free from her fears that Luc was seriously ill and that Blake might throw her out before she had finished her quest, she was able to enjoy herself.

He was going to investigate the rumours about her father. That was progress. So, she thought, brimming with anticipation, was his acknowledgement of the extraordinary chemistry between them. Her fingers tentatively touched her mouth and she sighed, luxuriating in the memory of his kiss. Life suddenly seemed rosy. Blissful, even. She sighed with utter contentment.

Happily she played with Luc, fed and changed him, made herself a hot drink and filched a couple of biscuits from a large cookie jar, then chatted amiably to Mrs Carter. Who had nothing but praise for Blake.

Nicole listened avidly, hugging herself in well-hidden delight as she listened to the tales of Blake's saintliness from infancy to the present day. And, reading between the lines, Nicole picked up a few clues about Blake's wife. Tania had indeed been very beautiful and dreadfully spoilt. And, as Blake had said, it was clear that she'd not been popular in the village.

'Now...' Mrs Carter bustled around, flipping beautifully rolled pastry over a dish of home-bottled peaches and crimping the sides with a surprising deftness. 'That little baby is a lot better. You can hardly see his rash now, so why don't you go for a nice walk while he sleeps here? It's sunny outside and he can stay in the shade of the wisteria outside the kitchen door where I can keep an eye on him. You look as if you need a break and the sun'll do you the world of good.'

'I'd like to,' she demurred, 'but—'

'Go on.' Two hefty hands pushed her towards the open French doors. 'You've got an hour. Then come back for lunch. No argument. You've been devoting all your time to him and no one could fault you as a mother,' she said approvingly. 'But you've got needs too. You'll feel all the better for a good wander in the garden. Mr Blake always does, I know. Likes a bit of freedom, that one.'

'Does he?' She was avid for stories about him. And knew what that hunger implied.

'Always has. He'd get that het up being cooped up indoors when it rained that he'd sneak out and come back hours later, soaked to the skin and muddy but bursting with happiness. He can't be contained for long. Like quicksilver, I always thought. Never happier than when riding or working outside and pretending he's as free as a bird, even though he's got the weight of this place on his shoulders.'

'Was he…?' She hesitated. It seemed as if she was prying. But the cook smiled at her in genial encouragement and so Nicole ventured, 'Was he like his father, or…his second cousin?'

Mrs Carter gave a snort. 'Never like his father! Not for me to speak ill of the dead, but Mr Darcy ran Cranford into the ground. Mr Giles, mind, he was a kindly lad. Polite to me—and I was just a lowly maid in those days.'

'But he left,' Nicole said cautiously, pleased to hear someone speak well of her father at last.

'Some trouble.' Mrs Carter's mouth suddenly buttoned up tight. 'I'll say no more. Family business, not mine. Go on. Have that walk then you'll be up to doing justice to my lunch.'

Nicole laughed, knowing she'd get no further. Another time, she thought. 'You're an angel!' she declared, turning and kissing the plump red cheek. 'Thank you. I'll be back to help with lunch—'

'Don't you trespass on my patch!' cried the cook in horror. 'I'll be out of a job. Get outside. Be off with you. You're under my feet,' she grumbled unconvincingly.

Giggling, Nicole dashed out in mock alarm, turning to wave at the beaming Mrs Carter. How she loved it here! Happily, she wandered through the gardens, admiring the plantings and itching to sketch and paint the views as soon as she had a free minute.

Passing through a wrought iron gate in a high and ancient brick wall, she found herself in a stable yard. In a field beyond she could see several horses grazing, but the sound of irritable snorting and whinnying close by suggested that one stable was still inhabited.

'Hi!' she called to the slim, energetic figure she recognised as Susie.

'Hello!' Susie rushed over, looking anxious. 'How's that baby of yours?'

'Much better, thanks. I think he'll be OK,' Nicole said, touched by Susie's genuine interest. *'Mon Dieu!'* she exclaimed, jumping with fright at the sound of hooves battering the nearest stable door.

'That's Midnight,' Susie explained with a laugh. 'Blake's stallion, complaining because he hasn't been taken out since he was ridden at dawn. He's a devil. No one can manage him except Blake and I leave it to him to put him in the field because Midnight's such a handful. Blake's a whiz with horses. Can do anything with them. They all but lie down and let him tickle their tummies, like dogs! Ah. He's coming.'

Nicole cocked her head to one side but failed to hear anything. 'I'm impressed. You must have ears like a bat!'

'No! The horses have! Look!'

In the field every horse had raised its head and even at

a distance she could see that their ears were pricked forward. Nicole was conscious of the hot breath of Blake's stallion and the restless tossing of its head behind her as it waited impatiently for its master.

Then she saw him riding into view. She held her breath as he approached the gate into the field but his mount cleared it effortlessly. The grazing horses flung up their heads and whinnied in greeting, galloping over to him.

'I wish I had that power,' Susie said enviously. 'He has an affinity with all animals. Wounded birds, injured foxes and badgers, that sort of thing. He's nursed no end of road casualties back to health. Josef has the gift, too. He has no fear and I think animals sense his love for them.'

'In France—' Nicole mused, fascinated by Blake's communication with the horses, which were jostling for his attention '—we'd say someone like that had gypsy blood.'

Susie grinned. 'Well, maybe there's a bit of gypsy blood somewhere. It'd explain his colouring, wouldn't it?'

Nicole giggled. 'The Bellamies would be appalled to hear you say that!'

After a while Blake trotted away, leaning down to open the gate into the yard and jumping down lithely when he arrived, with a look of delight on his face when he saw Nicole was there.

'Hi!' he said cheerfully, busy with unsaddling his mount. Midnight kicked the stable door meaningfully and Blake laughed, his white teeth gleaming in his dark face.

Yes, Nicole thought, seeing something different in those black sparkling eyes and the furiously tousled curls. He does look as if he has a Romany ancestor. Though that couldn't be right because he'd inherited Cranford. There must have been a Mediterranean wife in the Bellamie family long ago, she decided. And reflected that it was interesting how a strong gene could emerge—even, perhaps, after centuries of dormancy.

That might be why she found Blake so intriguing. He was a combination of contrasts... She jumped again as the stable door received a flurry of angry kicks.

'I'll deal with Flouncy,' Susie said to Blake, taking the reins. 'You sort that one out.'

He laughed again. 'Midnight or Nicole?'

Susie giggled. 'Take your pick!'

'*Flouncy?*' queried Nicole with mock horror, in retaliation.

'Josef's choice.'

She grinned. 'Might have guessed!' But it described the horse very well. It did flounce.

'It's good to see you here,' Blake murmured, ignoring the snorting beast trying to batter down the reinforced stable door.

Nicole felt her heart beat faster. He looked so alive. Sweat beaded his forehead. His eyes gleamed, his face glowed with vibrant health. And there was something so achingly sexy about his crisp white shirt, tight jodhpurs and high boots that her throat closed up in sheer longing.

'I imagine Luc's better or you wouldn't be here,' he said when she didn't speak.

'Much improved,' she said huskily. 'The rash has nearly vanished.'

For a moment her radiant face stopped him in his tracks. 'I'm very, very pleased,' he said, smiling idiotically at her.

Susie threw him a towel and he busied himself with wiping his sweaty face and hands. It gave him something to do. He would have preferred to grab Nicole and kiss her and think of doing unspeakable things to her. Instead of quietening his passions, the ride had made them fiercer. He wanted her with an all-consuming urgency. Dangerous ground, his common sense told him prissily. Why not? every other sense replied.

Earlier on he'd issued that ultimatum to her—that she

wasn't to set foot on his land—because he'd been appalled by his lust for a woman who might be something of a harlot.

But his feelings about her had changed. He did believe her to be essentially kind and innocent of the effect she had on men. That old friend of his, common sense, had told him to steer clear, to let well alone. But his gut feelings had rebelled. And morally he knew he couldn't just send her home. He must learn more about her. And her father.

It had disturbed him how happy that decision had made him. It was as if he had opened a door and let the light shine in. This time he *was* doing the right thing. His troubled conscience would rest in peace.

However, he had no intention of telling her that he was a bastard—yet. If she proved to be the daughter of a rogue, if she had inherited some of Giles's unpleasant traits, then he could send her packing without endangering the estate and its dependants.

However, if she was above suspicion... He put the towel down on the mounting block with a slow deliberation. Then he didn't know what he'd do. How could he leave? Josef would be desolate...

'Blake!' yelled Susie. 'Stop staring at that yukky towel and see to that brute of yours!'

'Sorry. Miles away.' He glanced up at Nicole, who seemed to be looking at him with some curiosity. 'Won't be a minute,' he said with unreal jollity. Quite fearless of the flying hooves of his ill-tempered stallion, he unbolted the stable door.

'I don't know much about horses,' Nicole called nervously, backing away.

'Wise to stand clear of this one,' he cried in warning over his shoulder.

As usual, Midnight skittered out in a blur of gleaming

black muscle and flailing hooves while Blake tried to keep his grip on the bridle and his feet on the ground. As usual, Blake felt awed by the animal's beauty and thrilled and privileged that the spirited horse regarded him as a friend to be trusted.

'Gently, gently,' he soothed, stroking with a mesmeric rhythm. There was a token toss of a powerful head, a low hrrumph, and then Midnight was all his. 'I know,' he whispered, snuffling into his stallion's nostrils. 'You hate being cooped up. Me, too. But you needed a long rest after our ride last night. Come on.'

At a run, he led the now reasonably docile Midnight to the field and set him free. With the gate safely closed, Nicole came to join him.

'He's fabulous,' she marvelled as Midnight kicked and bucked his way around the field in sheer joy of living.

'Pure Arab. My indulgence,' he replied, following the glorious shift of muscle beneath the racehorse flanks. There was something uplifting about Midnight's exhilaration. It touched a chord in him. He, too, could set himself free. He could run wild if he wanted. He could rip off the imposed restrictions that he had railed against for years and follow his impulses, like Nicole.

He shot her a sideways glance. The wind was blowing silken strands of hair over her face. Eyes fixed on the now cantering Midnight, she lifted a graceful hand and her long tapering fingers absently tucked the hair behind her small ear.

Her face was uplifted, the sun lighting her high cheekbones and the inviting curves of her breasts. An ache hit him so hard that he had to grit his teeth and turn away. He was hot and sweaty. This wasn't the time.

Angrily he glared at Midnight, envying him the freedom he denied himself. He took a deep breath. To hell with denial! He knew what he wanted. And he wanted it *now*!

'Come.'

Without waiting for her agreement, he caught her hand and led her through the yard and up the steps of the hay-loft.

'What...?' She took one look at the piles of sweet-smelling hay and the penny dropped. 'Why, Mr Blake!' she murmured with a good mimicry of a country wench. 'What can be in your mind, sir?'

'You,' he growled with a curt impatience.

Her eyes grew huge and melting. The smile that parted her lips was mischievous and utterly ravishing.

'I'm so glad,' she said huskily, and held out her arms.

Roughly, he pulled her to him. Bent her supple spine with the ferocity of his kiss. Pushed her back to the straw where they fell. Felt blood surge through his body when he lay on her, kissing her with a sweet passion that made him want to groan.

And she urged him on with wicked words in his ear, telling him what she liked, what she wanted, refusing to allow him to hold back because she needed his passion to match hers.

His head was whirling. He couldn't think, couldn't order his body to obey him any more. This was truly making love. No studied moves. Just pure and perfect harmony of one body with another, with hands, lips, teeth, exacting the greatest pleasure.

The softness of her skin awed him. When his lips brushed her midriff it was like feeling the smoothness of satin. Somehow she was naked—though he couldn't say how—and his shirt had been dispensed with, so that they were skin to skin and he could feel the hectic thunder of his own heart and the rapid pounding of hers.

She tasted so sweet. He couldn't get enough of her

mouth, even as her legs twisted around his and the heat of her made him cry out in need. Her fingers deftly hooked open his jodhpurs and he felt her hands caressing the tight, hard muscles of his buttocks.

She was beautiful. Unbelievably, heart-stoppingly desirable.

'Nicole,' he said thickly, dazed, bewildered by the frightening power of his rioting emotions.

There was a little flicker of her tongue and she licked the corner of his mouth. A huge shudder went through him and then another as she slid her hand down and touched him. He couldn't wait. He had to tell her so...

'I—can't—I—'

His eyes closed. He was there. Warm, liquid, welcome. And then he took his freedom, suddenly elated, intoxicated with it, sharing himself with Nicole, knowing only the gloriously liberating movement of their bodies as they united and the unstoppable joy that flooded every cell, every inch of his being.

Nicole jerked as a series of unbearably exquisite spasms rewarded her body. Blake looked down at her, unshed tears making his eyes glisten. And at that moment she fell head over heels in love with him. She read his heart in those longing, loving eyes. And knew that she would be bound to him for the rest of her life. Whatever happened.

'Oh, my darling!' he whispered, touching her face tenderly, wonderingly. 'I'm sorry. I was too—'

Her finger pressed against his lips. Panting with exertion, weak with love and satiation, she smiled her radiant smile. 'It was perfect. Hot, hard, furious. So much passion. Wonderful,' she breathed.

Gently he bent his head, his hair tumbling over his forehead in glistening black curls and she was reminded of the stallion—impatient, angry and frustrated then full of joy to be free. They were both dark, both touched with the same magic and powerful masculinity. Creatures who needed space and no restrictions if they were to flourish.

Blake's mouth claimed hers in a long and tender kiss. Her arms wrapped around his neck and she sighed into it. His liquid black eyes danced with happiness and she felt thrilled to be the cause of it. With the lightest of touches he caressed her face and throat, his finger drawing a path between her breasts. As his tongue lapped the beads of milk quivering on the peak of each nipple, she caught hold of his thick, tousled hair and moaned with pleasure, saying in a reluctant whisper, 'I should go. Feed Luc. It must be late—'

Blake groaned. 'Time! It's the enemy of lovers. I want to stay here all afternoon with you. But…yes. I must shower and spend some time with my mother before lunch. I promised.'

'Yes,' she said, but he kissed her and wouldn't let her go. 'Blake.' Gently she pushed him away. 'I must go!' she said with reluctance.

'You know what you've done,' he said huskily.

Her heart seemed to bounce. 'Yes!' she whispered.

He smiled and hauled up his jodhpurs. 'I wonder if you do. The way I feel at the moment, I'm going to want to be with you twenty-four hours a day and I'll resent any time spent elsewhere.'

She giggled with delight and hurriedly dressed, stopping every few seconds to fend off his kisses. 'You're insatiable!' she pretended to protest as his mouth enclosed hers once more.

'Driven crazy by a witch of a woman,' he growled and stood still in evident bliss as her hands slowly shaped the beautiful contours of his chest.

'Blake,' she whispered, hugging him tight, 'I'm so glad we found one another.'

With lowered lashes, he smoothed back her hair, for all

the world as if he were a fussy hairdresser with a client. 'There. You'll do.' A kiss was dropped on her lips and then he was drawing her to the barn door.

As she hurried back to the house alone it seemed that her heart was full to bursting. So she sang and let her happiness ring out across the garden. Not long ago she'd been in despair. Now... She had never felt so content in the whole of her life.

CHAPTER TEN

BLAKE felt guilty at his sense of relief when he finally left his mother. But she'd questioned him about Nicole with surprising vigour for someone so ill. And he'd hated not being honest with her. It seemed a betrayal, somehow.

God, he was torn! Josef had always come first in everything. Before his duty, before his mother, before Cranford itself. And now, in even contemplating the idea that Nicole might one day guide little Luc to his rightful inheritance, he could be throwing away his son's future. Let alone his own.

In turmoil, raging against his mother's lover despite the fact that the man had given him life, he strode with a grim, rapid gobbling of the ground towards the idyllic scene beneath the cedar tree.

A light lunch had been set there. Nicole sprawled on a rug beside the old teak table with its snowy white cloth and assorted cold dishes. As he approached, his stride and his temper mellowed. Magic.

The fact that she turned to smile at him just melted away his hammering problems. She could do to him, he mused, what he could do to Midnight. Soothe the savage breast. Make everything seem all right.

He'd changed into a short-sleeved summer shirt the colour of pollen and had scrambled into a pair of faded old jeans. Dropping down beside her, he peered at the naked little baby on the changing mat. Luc was crowing happily and waving his arms and legs in glee.

Blake smiled at the perfection of the child and then at Nicole. 'He looks fine. I can't see any rash.'

138

She tickled Luc's tummy and was rewarded with a chortle. Her beatific smile reached the depths of Blake's heart. 'Isn't it wonderful? I think he'll get the all-clear when the doctor calls,' she said happily.

He let Luc grip his finger, enchanted by the gurgling child. 'Such a tiny body,' he marvelled. 'It's amazing to think he'll grow into an adult. A miracle.'

The heir to Cranford, he thought with a pang. And frowned because he couldn't wish this child anything but a full and happy life. Did that mean granting him his birthright?

'Can I hold him?' he asked, by way of apology to the little boy. 'I remember when Joe was this small. I felt choked up every time I saw him. I couldn't believe he was my son and kept creeping up to touch him to make sure he was real.'

'Be my guest,' she said softly. And she leaned over and kissed his cheek.

He caught her face in his hands, turning it so that he could taste her mouth. She smelt of baby. That fresh, talcum smell. Her hair...he nuzzled her neck...reminded him of apple blossom scent. Her skin...was all woman.

Before things went too far he pulled away. Picked up the squirming little Luc and cuddled the plump bottom in the palm of his hand. Blue eyes stared at him trustingly. He felt a swoop of love which mingled with a very large twist of guilt.

'He's gorgeous,' he said huskily.

'Mm.'

It was a strange sound that had come from Nicole. She'd turned away and seemed to be unnecessarily fiddling with things in the baby bag. Tucking Luc over one shoulder with reckless regard for the consequences, Blake reached out his hand and gently drew her to face him. Her eyes were glistening and she looked as if she might be struggling for composure.

'There's no need to be sad,' he said, caressing her face.

She pushed her fists, child-like, against her eyes and found a smile for him. 'I'm not. I just go to pieces when I see a strong, masculine male with a tiny baby in his arms. It's so poignant, so sweet.' She laughed. 'I know! I'm an idiot! But it's lovely to see you adoring Luc. Shall we have lunch?' she added lightly, jumping up.

It wasn't possible for her to tell him that she'd felt a visceral tug of motherhood. That she wanted to have Blake's babies. Wanted him to cherish and love her and their children. What on earth, she wondered, appalled with herself for such fantasies, would he say to all that? Probably run a mile and ban her from England itself, let alone Cranford!

'Now. How was your mother?' she asked briskly when Luc had been deposited on the mat again and Blake had come to sit at the table beside her.

'Suspicious,' he replied drily.

Nicole's eyes widened. 'Why?' she asked, cutting herself a slice of quiche.

He grinned ruefully. 'Even after I'd showered and changed I think I must still have been glowing rather more than usual. To be honest, I felt as if I could conquer the world and still dance the night away, I felt so good. I suppose it showed. She all but put me under a searchlight to interrogate me!'

Nicole's eyes sparkled with amusement and delight. 'What did you say?'

Blake concentrated on transferring a fillet of cold salmon on to his plate. 'I told her a bit about you. I think she put two and two together. My offhand, casual tone didn't fool her a bit. She knows me well. She knew I was

141

still flying. And guessed we'd become lovers.' He shot a questioning glance at her. 'Do you mind?'

'I don't, no. We're free agents, we can do what we like. But does *she* mind?' She was pleased when he leaned forward and kissed her. His hand stroked her arm. She heaved a happy sigh.

'I don't think so. She's probably glad to see me happy.' His hand dropped away. 'That's all we want for our children, isn't it?' he added, suddenly frowning at a baby tomato on his plate as if it had no right to be there.

She had to touch him, to reassure this mercurial, complex man. Her fingers slid over his shoulder, felt the tautness of the muscle running to his neck then teased the small tendrils of defiant hair which curled so appealingly at the nape despite all his attempts to control them.

With encouragement from her he had released his emotions. Had flung himself into a kind of abyss that was unknown. Although he'd surrendered joyfully and wholeheartedly to his instincts he would naturally find it unnerving to abandon all those years of self-restraint.

'We owe it to our children to be happy, too,' she murmured in his ear.

'Sometimes—' he said in a low tone, disappointing her by not responding more enthusiastically '—that may not be possible.'

'Are you talking of your mother's sacrifice for you? Has she led an unhappy life?' she asked gently. 'I can't believe that to be true. She loves you and has seen you grow into a man she must be proud of. And there's Josef, too, surely the apple of her eye—'

'Yes. Of course,' he said roughly, but there was pain in his voice.

From his grim profile she knew he was keeping something from her. Something important—perhaps connected with his mother's illness. That meant he didn't trust her.

Unaccountably distressed by this, she reached over and kissed him lightly on the corner of his tense mouth.

'Your mother's not the only one who doesn't like to see you unhappy,' she said quietly.

He shot her a quick look and suddenly his mouth was full on hers, searching, demanding and desperate. 'Nicole,' he whispered throatily. 'Nicole!'

Loving him, she responded passionately, hoping that he'd forget his worries for a short while and find solace in her.

'Better?' she murmured when they broke apart for a moment.

'Sure.' He flashed her a smile that wasn't entirely believable. 'Let's eat. We've a lot to do this afternoon.'

'Have we?' she asked brightly.

There wasn't any point in pushing Blake to confide in her. She could wait. But the disappointment sat sourly in her stomach.

'If you'd like to.'

He was getting further and further from her every second. She bit her lip. 'Doing what?'

His fork idly toyed with the salmon. 'I thought you might like to come with me on my rounds. Things I need to do on the estate,' he said casually.

She beamed. That was inclusive enough. 'I'd enjoy that. I'll need to sort Luc out first and settle him for his sleep—'

'We'll leave him with Mrs Carter,' Blake said firmly. 'There'll be a lot of getting in and out of the car and chatting to people. OK?'

'Providing she doesn't mind—' she began, looking doubtful.

He looked directly at her. 'I want you to come. It's important to me.'

'Oh!' She felt flustered by this admission. 'Then...yes. Of course. I'm sure Luc will be in good hands.'

When they'd finished eating she dressed Luc and curled up on the rug with him on her lap. Quite unselfconsciously she began to feed him while Blake waited.

'All done, sweetheart?' she murmured to her sleepy baby and gently tucked him in his buggy. 'Right,' she said, straightening and slowly buttoning herself up. 'Oh!'

Blake followed her surprised gaze and stared at the house, his eyes narrowed. 'What is it?' he asked warily.

'A face. At an upstairs window.' She blushed, hating to be spied on.

'What kind of a face—and where?' he retorted.

'I just saw white hair. See where the coat of arms is? Well above that and two windows to the left.'

Blake frowned. 'My mother.'

She heaved a sigh of relief. 'That's all right, then! She must be feeling better.'

'Or insatiably curious,' he drawled.

'I should think she reckons I'm rather shocking, feeding Luc in front of you,' Nicole mused. And she looked at him in sudden alarm. 'I did want to make a good impression,' she complained. 'And now if she ever finds out who I am, she'll think—'

'She won't find out who you are!' Blake hurled with a sudden sharpness. 'She mustn't.' There was a cold silence and then he said a little more calmly, 'Now, if you're ready, we'll make a start.'

She hung her head. He was so distant and stern suddenly. Her day was blighted. But she had to hold on, to give him space. She loved him enough to do that.

He felt as if he was walking a tightrope. One that stretched far into the distance with no end in sight. And he swayed from one side to another—surrendering to his wild passions one moment and jerking himself back into his old, suppressed self the next.

But the next few hours would extend his knowledge of Nicole. His tenants were direct and called a spade a spade. Maybe he was blinded by sexual longing, but they'd suss her out.

Back at the house, he packed a box of peaches into the four-wheel drive together with a pile of magazines and several romances he'd bought from a village stall the previous week, then flung in his overalls. Nicole chattered cheerfully as they drove to their first call—Mrs Lee in the small ex-gamekeeper's cottage. He answered tersely, increasingly nervous about the outcome.

He realised that he wanted her to be accepted by everyone. That was madness, of course. If she was as pure as the driven snow then he'd have no choice but to vacate the seat of lord of the manor. It would suit his purpose, he scowled, if she made a complete hash of this afternoon and then he could pack her off home none the wiser.

Except that if she went he'd feel as if his right arm had been torn off and minced for cat food.

Hell. He ground the gears and irritably fought with them. For the first time in his life, after being renowned for crisp, wise decisions, he couldn't even make up his darn mind.

'Mrs Lee,' he said crisply to the strangely silent Nicole as they bounced down the narrow track and the cottage came in sight. He ignored her huge, soulful eyes and concentrated on the job in hand. 'Courtesy visit. She's elderly and doesn't get out much.'

'Oh. Are the novels and magazines for her? Shall I bring them—?'

'No. She'd think I was playing Lord Bountiful.' He drew to a halt. 'Leave them where they are.'

After handing Nicole out he wiped the frown from his face and walked with her to the door, pulling the old-fashioned bell pull as he'd done so many times throughout his life. There was the sound of shuffling and a quavering voice called out, 'Who is it?'

'The wicked wolf, Goldilocks!' Blake shouted cheerily.

'Rascal!' Chuckling, Mrs Lee opened the door and lifted her gaunt cheek for his kiss.

'Hope you don't mind. I was on my way to the village with my friend—Nicole—and I thought I'd just drop by to see if you needed anything while I'm shopping there.'

'I might,' she replied with dignity. 'There again, I might not. How do you do, Nicole? Come in. I'll make us some tea.'

He saw Nicole's warm, ready smile emerge and charm the old lady. 'Thank you. I'd love some,' she enthused.

Full marks, Blake approved. She didn't offer to make the tea for Mrs Lee. The old lady was fiercely independent and Nicole hadn't made that mistake.

'Don't know of anyone who'd take some books and things off my hands, do you?' he enquired, when they were all nursing steaming mugs of tea strong enough for a mouse to trot on. 'My mother's read them and I'm supposed to take them to a boot fair but I haven't the time.'

'Might. Let's have a look,' Mrs Lee said cautiously.

He hid a smile and dutifully hurried out, taking his time to stack the books in a neat pile on top of the magazines. When he returned Mrs Lee was squealing with laughter at something Nicole had said. He waited in the hall, fascinated.

'I'm a bit paranoid about it now.' She was giggling as the old lady rasped her delight. 'I don't think I'll ever wear a baby sling again, for fear of being taken for Quasimodo's sister!'

Of course. The episode with Josef. He grinned, remembering it. And his first glimpse of Nicole, the first time he'd ever been socked between the eyes by a woman, never to recover.

'Smashing kiddie,' declared Mrs Lee. 'Like his Dad. Never liked the father, though. The cousin, though, that was a different kettle of fish.'

Blake froze. She was talking about Giles.

'You remember them both, do you, Mrs Lee?' Nicole asked and he could hear the tension in her voice even though she'd tried to sound casual.

'Mr Darcy was an arrogant little pup,' grumbled Mrs Lee. 'Glad to see the back of him. Mr Giles was kinder, a real gentleman. Liked to paint, I remember. Did that portrait for me, up there. It's unfinished; that's why it's unsigned. But it's his all right.'

He heard the swish of Nicole's skirt and reckoned she'd gone to look. He knew the painting well but he had had no idea who had painted it. It was of Mrs Lee as a younger woman. He'd always admired it. There'd been a running joke where he'd make some ridiculous offer for it—five hundred thousand pounds, usually—and she'd regally refuse, saying she liked it and what would she do with all that money, anyway?

'It's…'

Blake swallowed. Nicole's voice had cracked. She would have recognised her father's work. And she'd feel upset. It was a beautiful portrait of Mrs Lee, depicting her as a handsome and generous-natured woman, done with love and feeling. The work, he'd always felt, of a man with perception and insight, who had seen beneath the skin and bone and somehow teased out the real nature of the person during the sitting.

'It's excellent,' Nicole said tenderly. 'He's captured the real you.'

'You can see it, can't you? I know a kindred spirit when I see one. That's why Mr Giles and I got on. We were all very fond of him. Pity he had to go abroad so suddenly.

Never came back. Never finished my painting.' She cack-
led. 'He wouldn't recognise me now, would he?'

'Actually, I think he would,' Nicole said quietly.
'You're the same inside, aren't you? And that's what he
saw.'

'Clever girl.' There was the sound of a hand being patted. 'Now. Where's that young man of yours? He hasn't
finished his tea.'

'He's not my—' Nicole began as Blake tiptoed back to
the front door, intending to make a noise coming in.

'You can't fool me. I saw how he looked at you. I hope
he snaps you up before someone else does— Ah. Here he
is.'

'Sorry to be so long,' Blake announced, his mind teeming with strands of thought. 'Had to sort out the sexy
ones—'

'Oh, I like those!' protested the old lady.

He gave her a withering look. 'I know. Those are the
ones I sorted out for you! I left behind the books with a
sweet aproned figure on the front. You've got any which
show passionate clinches and rippling muscles.'

The two women laughed and exchanged girly glances.
Blake had to award Nicole maximum points on the visit.
Mrs Lee was notoriously blunt and could tell false smarm
from forty paces.

As he joked and defended himself against the combined
forces of the women he reflected that his eavesdropping
had been an eye-opener. Perhaps his mother *was* mistaken.
He felt a ridiculous surge of happiness at the thought and
wondered why on earth he was merrily advancing towards
his own ejection from Cranford. Then he looked at the
laughing Nicole and knew.

And the revelation came as a terrible shock.

CHAPTER ELEVEN

'IT's compelling evidence,' he agreed when Nicole excitedly told him of the conversation with Mrs Lee while he was supposedly out in the car sorting the books. 'I'll talk to my mother. Try to get to the bottom of this.'

'Oh,' she cried, clasping her hands together in delight. 'Thank you, Blake! Thank you!'

'Blacksmith next,' he announced, controlling the urge to first stop the car and kiss her parted lips and then rush back to confront his mother. 'He's teaching me his craft.'

'Why?' she asked in surprise.

Because he loved it. Felt a stirring in his soul when he hammered out the softened, malleable iron. When sheer physical labour and an unerring eye resulted in a work of lasting beauty and usefulness.

'Why not? I'll be about an hour. That's all he'll allow me of his time,' he said with a grin. 'The potter's nearby, or you can wander around the village if you're bored—'

'I'll watch you for a while, see what a mess you make of things,' she teased. 'Then I'll do those bits of shopping for Mrs Lee.'

Nicole shook hands with the short, stocky Joseph Croxford, the blacksmith, who looked just a little older than Blake. Her hand was dwarfed by the man's huge fist but his handshake was gentle and his smile welcoming.

While Blake stripped off his clothes somewhere in the backyard and shrugged on his overalls and a heavy leather apron like Joseph's she looked around with interest. It was dark inside the small, high-roofed barn and, peering in the gloom, she could see tools of all kinds hanging from the timber and plaster walls.

'How long has the forge been here?' she asked Joseph.

'Long time.' He picked up a heavy hammer. 'Been Croxford blacksmiths and master blacksmiths in the village for hundreds of years,' he said proudly as Blake came in the back door. 'Long before those upstart Bellamies wandered in, anyhow.'

She laughed as Blake threw Joseph a mock glare. 'Newcomers, are they?' she sympathised.

'Furriners. Came over from Calais. We're mentioned in the Doomsday Book,' the blacksmith replied.

'As sheep stealers, if I remember,' grinned Blake.

'Prob'ly right.' Joseph chuckled. 'Least my family has decent English names, not fancy furrin ones. Your mother had sense, not calling you Darcy.'

'Or Giles,' Nicole offered.

'Don't know that one. Here. Grab that rod, Mr Blake, and see if you can make more'n a pig's ear out of it.'

For all their joshing the men were comfortable with one another, Nicole realised. She leaned against the grimy wall and watched them. Blake had pulled his overalls up to his waist and tied the sleeves in a knot there, leaving his chest bare. Soon it was glistening with sweat as he worked at the white-hot forge.

Scarlet sparks flew into the air and the sound of a bell-like ringing resounded around the small forge as he beat the rod into shape on the massive anvil. There was something wonderfully primitive about the scene.

Blake could have been any ordinary man from any time down the centuries, skilfully fashioning everyday items from a lump of metal. She watched him, crazy with love for him, tenderly smiling at his deeply engrossed expression as he struggled to meet Joseph's exacting standards.

'Relax your grip, man!' bellowed the smith. 'Let the

hammer bounce! And stop checking with your audience for approval,' he grumbled.

Blake seemed to redden, though it could have been the light from the fire.

'How's he doing?' she whispered when the smith collected a huge pair of pliers from the bench nearby.

'Not bad for an amateur.' Joseph paused. 'Heard about your father. Must have been hard for you. He can't have been very old,' he said with surprising gentleness.

Nicole looked into the thoughtful grey eyes. 'He wasn't. It was cancer,' she explained quietly.

'Like mine too, lass. Comes hard to see them go like that.' He hesitated. 'Like me to make a cross and put it under the old yew?'

She felt overwhelmed by his kindness. 'I'd like that very much,' she said quietly. 'Tell me what it would cost and—'

'I don't charge Mr Blake's friends. This place would be about my ears if it wasn't for him. You'll do me a favour in return, one day.'

'But... I live in France,' she began uncertainly.

'At the moment,' Joseph said, moving away. And, before she could ask him what he meant, he yelled at Blake, 'Come on you, put your back into it! Can't hang about all day—'

'Tyrant! I'll put your rent up,' Blake yelled back over the din as his hammer flew up and down in a silvery arc.

'Don't pay none!' cried Joseph triumphantly.

Blake paused and flashed a dazzling grin at them both. 'Forgot!' Laughing, he drew his forearm across his brow and left streaks of dirt there. He was panting, his chest heaving, and never had he looked more desirable.

She caught Joseph's sharp, speculative eyes on her and hoped he hadn't identified the naked adoration in her eyes. To show how casual she felt, she reluctantly decided to leave. 'I'm going to the shop!' she shouted at Blake, who'd resumed his hammering.

He thrust the bar into the fiery embers. 'Wander round the village, too. I'll meet you in the pub. Three o'clock.'

'How did you get on?' he asked when she walked into the old pub ten minutes late. Though he knew very well.

She'd been accepted. Taken to the hearts of those villagers she'd met. Joseph, Joan who ran the shop and several locals who'd been shopping there, Tim the potter... His heart thudded at the implications.

She came to sit with him on the high-backed settle and gave her version of events while the darts team roared one another on in the background.

Fresh from his naked dunking under Joseph's cold tap in the back yard and a vigorously applied scrubbing brush, he leaned back with his pint glass of well-earned local apple juice and watched her enthusiastically reporting on the friendliness of everyone in Great Aston.

'Can I get you a drink?' he asked politely when she paused for breath.

'Something soft, please. Same as you?'

She smiled and nodded in a friendly way at a group of farmers at the bar. To a man, they raised their glasses to her and she beamed as if they'd presented her with rubies.

Perhaps they had, he thought, weathering the farmers' comments as he waited to be served. This one afternoon's success could result in her controlling Cranford's fortunes.

'Get your own French lessons,' he retorted drily to a risqué comment about her presence from one of the farmers. He hurried back across the stone-flagged floor to where she sat. 'I've got some fences to check and then I thought we'd go into the hills after,' he said casually.

'Erm...what's happening there?' she asked, checking her watch.

'Sex,' he retorted. 'I'm going to make love to you. I'm managing to keep my hands off you for the moment but soon I'll be forced to touch you. Kiss you all over—'

'Blake,' she said, sounding wonderfully husky, 'I'd like nothing more. But I have to get back soon to feed Luc.'

He screwed his eyes tightly shut. Took a few deep breaths. Swigged his juice. Tried not to let that unpleasant little voice intrude and tell him that she was evading him and keeping him dangling.

'Of course. I'll just take another cold shower. Sit in a freezer for a week or two. Don't mind me.'

She giggled. 'They say anticipation is sweet.'

'They're wrong. It's agony,' he growled, dumping his glass on the table.

Her eyes flirted outrageously. He was conscious that everyone was looking at them and he didn't care. Leaning forwards, he took her face between his hands and gave her a long, slow kiss.

Somewhere in the background the farmers were making encouraging noises. He didn't need their encouragement. He was doing fine all by himself.

'To hell with anticipation,' he muttered.

'Now you've done it!' she breathed. 'The entire village will know what you've been up to.'

He touched her sultry mouth. Lusted after her straining breasts. Knew that he was captivated by her, caught hook, line and sinker. In that moment he decided to throw away the rule book and to 'wing' it. He'd follow his instincts and his impulses and see what happened.

And the moment he could, he'd turn the searchlight on his mother and interrogate *her*. As far as the problem of himself and Josef being turned out on the streets was concerned, he'd solve that somehow. There *must* be an answer. If only his chaotic brain could come up with it...

*   *   *

Thwarted by his mother's worrying relapse after her venture to the window, he had stayed by her bed for a long time after dinner, talking to her about the events of the day.

But he couldn't ask her about Giles. She seemed too frail to be questioned. His mind whirled and whirled until he felt as if he'd been in a tumble-drier for a week and all his brain cells had been spun dry.

'How is she?' Looking anxious, Nicole jumped up from the sofa where she'd been waiting for him.

'Asleep, and much better after I made her laugh by giving her a blow-by-blow account of Josef's beetles,' he said with an absent smile.

Nicole chuckled and sank elegantly back against the pale damask cushions, her long dress a vivid, life-affirming streak of red.

'Dung beetles!' she murmured fondly.

He thought of his beloved son, sleeping innocently upstairs, unaware that his future hung in the balance. He had to turn away because his heart had wrenched so fiercely that he couldn't hide his anguish.

Josef had been home from school when they returned from dropping off the shopping for Mrs Lee. He'd met them with a joyous welcome, squealing that Luc wasn't spotty at all and did that mean he could show him and Nicole his beetles.

'I'm only keeping them for a bit,' he'd explained when Nicole had solemnly agreed. 'Animals need to be free. They like to be outside finding their own dung, you see.'

Of course Blake had already seen Josef enthusiastically demonstrating the technique used by the beetles as they rolled and heaved the dung across fields that must be the size of Britain to them, but he still found the performance very funny. And he'd noticed Nicole wasn't daring to look at him because she must surely have been convulsed with laughter inside.

Ironically, the perfect day had only made things worse. She'd gone down a storm. Josef doted on her. Elderly ladies softened at the sight of her. Old men dreamed of their youth when they looked into her eyes and found themselves eagerly engaged in a conversation about their personal interests.

He doubted that anyone would mind if she replaced him. He went cold. And forced himself to face reality. Pictured Josef's bewildered, tear-stained face as they drove away from Cranford, never to return.

His guts twisted. No. He couldn't do that to his child!

There *was* an answer, of course. He could have his cake and eat it. His conscience would be salved if he said nothing and she stayed as his mistress. Then Josef would inherit and perhaps half the estate could be settled on Luc.

But it was such a momentous decision that he dared not risk making a fool of himself without giving it cold, deliberate thought. She might refuse, of course. The thought gnawed at him, churning away inside and ruining his digestion. Too much rested on this. For Josef's sake, he must not make another mistake in his love life.

'Come and kiss me,' she murmured softly.

His resolve almost melted away. He gritted his teeth. Knowingly or not, she was seducing him, inch by inch, softening his brain and, for his son's sake, he needed a clear head. Brains that worked, not loins.

'No time,' he said shortly. Fiddling busily with his gold cuff-links, he tried not to feel the sudden chill in the atmosphere. 'I'm going over to see the fireworks in a minute. Want to come?' he asked casually.

'What's the matter?' she countered in an anxious voice.

'Nothing.'

'Liar. You're worried about your mother, aren't you?' she said gently.

He groaned. He'd heard the swish of her silky dress as she rose. The soft pad of her feet. The warmth and the scent of her that told him she was near.

She came to lay her head against his chest. He stroked the gleaming cornfield hair, wishing there wasn't this terrible secret between them.

'All you can do—' she said in her soft, soothing voice '—is to make her as comfortable and as happy as possible. Show her you'll be all right when...when she's gone. That's what my father worried about. I told him how I'd manage and put his mind at rest. So make sure she knows you have everything you want.'

'But I don't,' he muttered.

Innocently she gazed up at him. 'What else could you possibly want?'

'You!' he growled and took her mouth by storm. 'Come and dance with me,' he urged thickly. 'I want to hold you in my arms in public. To feel your body against mine, like this... To look into your eyes and know that you need me as much as I need you.'

'The children—' she gasped, as stunned as he was by his outburst.

'Maisie is sleeping next to the nursery tonight and babysitting Josef.' He grinned lopsidedly. 'Or it could be the other way round! I knew I'd be putting in an appearance at the dancing and the firework display. She'll be thrilled to be in charge of Luc, too. He sleeps well. He'll come to no harm.' He brushed his lips against her cheek. Nuzzled the softness of her neck. 'Is it a date?' he asked, barely able to breathe for hoping.

Her mouth found his. And then she was dreamily smiling into his eyes.

'Only if you take your mobile so Maisie can reach you

in any emergency,' she murmured, her fingers wonderingly stroking his face.

Hand in hand they wandered across the gardens to the orangerie. Everyone seemed to be looking at them when they walked into the crowded room. He knew that the men were openly admiring Nicole and he felt a kick of pride that she was with him—and that her sparkling eyes and delighted smile were for him, and him only.

Whatever the future brought, he knew that he wanted Nicole now. He would do what his mother had suggested. Follow his heart.

Concealing his impatience, he introduced Nicole to the organisers and the dignitaries. Then managed to slip away with her, leading her to the dance floor. Taking her in his arms, he felt utterly content with life. As if he'd started to be himself. The soft silk of her dress flowed warmly against him, the heat of her body penetrating the thin material as she responded to the sensual blues rhythm. He had eyes only for her. She for him.

The room didn't exist. Just the two of them. Her heart beating against his chest. The pounding of his heart echoing in his head. Her slender, supple body in the enclosing circle of his arm, bending with his every movement as if they were glued together in an inseparable bond.

Her breathing sounded as short and shallow and as laboured as his. The scent of her was driving him crazy. The slipping of her body, as she swayed languorously to the music, rubbed provocatively against his aching, burning loins. Every time she encountered the hardness of him she gave a little shudder of suppressed delight.

He must ask her. Now.

'Nicole.' Huskily he whispered into her ear. Half-afraid, unsure. They'd only known one another for a short time. He had nothing to lose by asking her to be his mistress. But did she?

'Mmm?'

Her smile dazzled him. She was wonderful, he thought hazily.

'I feel I've known you all my life,' he marvelled, still blinded by her shining eyes and happy smile.

'That's how I feel about you,' she said with a sigh.

'You know I want you!' he said urgently.

A mischievous glance. 'I had noticed!'

'I mean… Nicole, there's something I want to say. Will you come somewhere private with me?' he said huskily.

She nodded, wondering affectionately why he didn't just tell her that he wanted to make love to her. In a blissful daze, she let herself be tucked against his hip and led out of the orangerie. His arm lay heavily around her shoulders and he seemed tense. She'd relax him soon, she thought happily.

They stopped by the lake. It was still and an inky black, except where the moonlight was turning it to silver. The scent of honeysuckle was almost overpowering her senses.

He turned her to him and kissed her, long and hard, and she stood on tiptoe, her hands clasped around his beautiful head to intensify the pressure of their mouths. It seemed they kissed for hours, unable to get enough of one another's mouths.

I love him, she thought, beginning to feel as if she was floating.

'Nicole.' It was barely a whisper in her ear.

'Will you…' He drew in a shuddering breath as she looked deeply into his eyes, telling him yes, she would make love to him here. Here, anywhere. Any time. 'Will you marry me?' he asked.

CHAPTER TWELVE

HE COULDN'T believe what he'd just said. How had that happened? Appalled, he sought for a way to turn his mistake into a joke.

But Nicole forestalled him. By saying, 'Yes.' And kissing him with such tenderness that he found himself drawing her gently to the ground, his head a whirl of delight and panic, though with his body entirely sure of itself.

Nothing seemed real. Not the fever that possessed him, the softness of her yielding, eager body, the hasty stripping of their clothes. They melted into one another, the hot curls of sweet agony sending his entire being into spasm as her wicked fingers teased and tormented their way to the sealing of his fate.

She cried out his name—a raw, feral cry that reached right into his heart. And then, when he could hold back no longer, she whispered in a low moan, 'I love you, Blake! I love you so much!'

His mind seemed to shatter into pieces. An emotion rushed in, making him want to shout and cry and punch the air at the same time. Shuddering, he devoured her soft, trembling mouth with a tenderness that brought pain to his heart.

He had no idea what was happening to him, only that this must be an explosion of all his long-suppressed feelings.

Gently he teased apart her thighs. Stroked the silkiness of her. Watched her eyes close in ecstasy as he began those slow, minutely delicate movements that aroused her so sensationally.

She bucked beneath his fingers. Pleaded. Moaned. Glared and took her own sweet revenge by closing her fist around where he throbbed with such unbearable heat and hunger and sliding her hand with exquisite timing until he thought he'd lose his sanity.

'Love me,' she whispered.

His body obeyed. Every inch was for her, dedicated to her pleasure. Every word, caress, impassioned glance.

Their bodies were insatiable. He took her with passion, with gentleness, with laughter. He took her fiercely with fast, urgent strokes that left them breathless. And then, after kissing every inch of her skin he made love to her with a slow deliberation that had them both moaning with need.

When the sky began to lighten he helped her to dress. Stumbling together, silent and stunned by what had happened, they made their way back to the house. Drugged. Intoxicated. Sated and trembling with emotion.

'Sleep,' he said, when he had seen her to her room. 'Sleep as long as you need, as long as Luc will allow you. Goodnight.'

He leaned forwards and brushed her lips with his. Stared deeply into her eyes. Touched her cheek as if he couldn't believe what they'd done. And slipped quietly away.

Bright-eyed and bursting with happiness, she danced downstairs in the morning with Luc in her arms. It was mad and reckless committing yourself to someone you hardly knew, but she had no doubts about Blake, none at all.

Her love for him, and his for her, reached deep inside her, giving her life new meaning. And it would be like that till she died.

There was a note on the table from Blake, saying he'd be back for lunch. And so, happily she played with Luc and then when Mrs Carter arrived she helped by making an open French tart until the cook shooed her out for some fresh air.

'Surely you're not going to hog that baby all to yourself?' Mrs Carter complained, cuddling the squirming Luc. 'If you take the path to the wood,' she said craftily, 'you might meet Mr Blake on his way back from the farm.'

Nicole laughed. 'There's no fooling you, is there?' she murmured.

The cook chuckled. 'I'm not blind. Hurry up, child! Go!'

Nicole kissed her son, nibbled his little bare toes and waved a cheerful farewell to the approving cook. Living here would be wonderful, she thought, her face radiant with happiness.

Being with Blake anywhere would be heaven. But here... She hugged herself with delight, not unaware of the huge step he'd taken in proposing to her. He must feel very sure of his love for her, she thought dreamily. It must have been as instant and as catastrophically life-changing as her love was for him.

Marriage. She heaved a huge, happy sigh. Never had she been so sure of someone. They were soul-mates. And she was the happiest woman in the entire world. Dreaming of their future, she wandered aimlessly through the wood until she came to a small hut by the path. Intrigued, she opened the plank door and stepped inside.

It was then that she heard the thundering of hooves outside and a man's voice calling in a strange language. The hoof beats slowed and stopped.

Cautiously Nicole peered through the glassless window. And felt a shock freeze her where she stood.

Standing beside the fretting Midnight was a man with dark hair like Blake's, though it was long and caught at the nape of the neck with a thin black ribbon. He was older and leaner but he had the same presence—and the same piercing eyes the colour of the night sky.

Her heart raced. To her amazement the man was managing to calm the wild, untameable Midnight, whispering into the stallion's ear. And Midnight nuzzled the man's neck and face almost as if he was caressing him.

Intrigued by the man's uncanny resemblance to Blake, she was about to go outside and challenge his right to be there when Midnight suddenly stilled and the man cocked his head in an attitude of listening.

Soon after, Nicole heard the sound of someone running. And she relaxed when she realised it was Blake. But her cry of greeting died on her lips at the sight of Blake's face.

He knew at once. Skidded to a halt, the feeling of shock so fierce that it almost threw him backwards.

His father.

Emotion welled up, depriving him of the ability to speak. For several seconds the two of them just stared at one another, transfixed.

The older man recovered first, lowering his head deferentially. 'Morning, sir,' he said, his voice low and deep. 'This your horse? Fine animal. Got a bit spooked, I reckon. He's all right now.'

'Josef,' Blake said hoarsely, his voice shaking.

There were tears in his eyes. Agonised longing in his heart.

The deference vanished. His father seemed to grow taller, his head held proudly now. And Blake fancied that there was an answering glow of affection and yearning in his father's eyes.

'You know then?' his father said gently.

Blake nodded dumbly. Strode into his father's welcoming arms. A little choke emerged from his throat. His eyes closed and the tears squeezed out.

Both of them were shaking with emotion, muttering and exclaiming their delight. They remained locked together for several long seconds, as if unwilling to part in case this was a dream.

Finally they separated, though keeping their hands on one another's shoulders. Gazing into his father's extraordinary black eyes, he saw the tears that had spiked the dark lashes and trickled down the dark-skinned face.

'Father!' he croaked, choking on a ball of emotion that had lodged in his throat. This was the love he should feel for his father. The love he'd never felt for Darcy. He was overwhelmed with delight. 'You came back!'

'I didn't mean you to see me,' his father said soberly.

'I'm glad I did,' Blake said huskily.

'Me, too. Though it raises problems. Truth is, I've come to see your mother before she dies. Then I will leave her to God and turn away.'

'Why go?' cried Blake, desperate not to lose his father now.

'You know why, son.'

Blake bit his lip. 'I want to get to know you—'

'You will. There'll be time for that. Will she see me, do you think?'

He smiled. 'She'll welcome you with open arms. She still loves you,' he said softly.

That evoked a wry, sad smile. 'I thought so. She said I was just a wild fling, but I knew better. You can tell when love hits you. It obliterates everything else.'

'Then…if you knew that, why did you leave her?'

'Because,' Josef said quietly, 'it was what she wanted. And I was prepared to give her everything in my power that she desired. It was the hardest thing I ever did,' he added, 'walking out on the woman I loved and my unborn child.'

Tentatively he touched Blake's chest and his face as if

reassuring himself that this was his son and they had found one another at last. Blake grasped his hand and squeezed it in his. The two men grinned at one another, faintly embarrassed by their intense feelings.

'You're a gypsy,' Blake said, suddenly realising. And understanding of his restless nature flooded through him in a welcome realisation.

'You're not ashamed? Plenty would be,' his father commented drily.

'It's the man I see. Not his label.'

Josef smiled. 'I gave up wandering long ago. Became a craftsman in the village where I live with my mother and my brother and his brood. Always worked for my living. Never dishonest. Never disloyal. True to my family, in the Romany way. You're like me in that. With a touch of wildness and passion. I can see you have the light behind the eyes.'

Blake felt his body ease into itself. 'I feel that I understand myself better,' he said slowly. 'Now I know why I feel so deeply, why I need to feel that I'm free, why I hate routine.'

'Aye. Once we all had wings. Only the gypsies remember how it is to fly,' his father said with a grin.

He thought how apt that was. But he knew someone else who knew how to fly, how to show due wonder at the wonderful world, enjoying every second of life. Little Josef.

'I have a son—you have a grandson named after you. He's very much a free spirit,' Blake said eagerly, longing for his father to meet his namesake.

'I know. I've seen him. Fine lad. And you, Blake, I hear nothing but good, about you.' He grinned at Blake's querying eyebrow. 'I know how to blend into the background. I often sit in the pub with a hat over my head and my collar turned up and listen to the people in the village.

You've done good, here. I'm proud of you. Live. Be happy. You only come this way once.'

'I know!' Blake replied fervently. 'My mother says the same. I mean to be what I am—and to go for what I want.'

Frozen to the spot and with all the colour drained from her horrified face, Nicole watched Blake and his true father embrace again.

What he wanted. What did he mean? Her heart thudded painfully.

'My existence was supposed to be a secret,' Blake's father reproached.

'It was, until a short time ago. But, because she is dying, she wanted to unburden herself,' she heard Blake say. 'At first I could hardly believe I wasn't Darcy's son. And then she showed me the picture of you she carries and I knew it to be true. I suppose I'd *felt* it to be true all my life.'

Josef looked delighted. 'My picture,' he said softly. 'Well, well. Take me to her. And don't worry. No one will see me, I'll make sure of that. The resemblance between us is so strong that it would be obvious you're not Darcy's spawn. And you don't want anyone to find out you're not the heir, do you?'

She didn't hear Blake's quiet reply. There was a roaring in her ears like thunder. Now it had been said. Not the heir. *Not the heir!*

That man was Blake's father! Not Darcy Bellamie, but another man who had loved Blake's mother and got her with child, whom she had pretended was the heir to Cranford!

Dizziness attacked her and she almost lost her balance. But the terror of being discovered helped her to steady herself. Trying to control her violent shaking and fighting to stay quiet when she wanted to scream questions at Blake, she became aware that the two men were moving away, talking too quietly for her to hear, with the devoted Midnight trotting submissively behind them.

When it was safe to do so she collapsed weakly against the window, gripping the glazing bar for dear life.

It was then that the nightmare began. Horror flooded through her. If Blake wasn't the heir at all...then she was. That meant... The implication hit her like a blow to the stomach. Blake knew very well that he had no right to Cranford. But, by marrying her, he would be the husband of the true heir.

Her fist went to her mouth to stop the primal wail that fought to emerge and she bit into the flesh, tasting it.

Surely, she thought, he hadn't been covering his back by proposing to her? But it all made a horrible kind of sense. She forced herself to think.

There had been Blake's initial hostility when he knew who she was. His lies about her father and his determination to send her home, then his change of tack when she'd insisted on staying. And finally he'd shown a personal interest in her...

She felt sick. Perhaps everything had been a sham! Blake had been so scared of losing his position that he'd...he'd...

'No. *No!*' she moaned.

He couldn't have faked that raw hunger. Nor the love in his eyes, surely? Was it a coincidence that they'd fallen in love? Or...had it been a calculated act to secure the Bellamie inheritance for ever? She shivered, feeling chilled to the bone.

Questions piled up in her head so thick and fast that she put her hands to her ears to block her senses. Her stomach lurched and she ran out and was sick.

With distaste she cleaned herself up. Now she had to face him. But what would she do, what would she say? Denounce him as a liar and an impostor?

If she did, then she'd pull the wrath of the village about her ears and she and Luc wouldn't be able to manage Cranford. And if his mother knew that her deception had been discovered then maybe that might hasten her death.

But this land was hers! Eventually it would be Luc's! She couldn't let Blake get away with this scam. He didn't deserve to. Yet…what would she do as mistress of Cranford, alone in that great house with her baby?

Confused and miserable, she stood there in the beautiful woodland, recognising it was rightfully hers and yet knowing she was incapable of claiming it. She couldn't run the estate, even with the goodwill of everyone behind her. The thought of managing such a huge enterprise without any experience at all was terrifying.

Besides, she wanted Blake. Wanted to pretend that everything was fine and that he loved her for herself alone, not because she had Bellamie blood. She acknowledged that the marriage might be one-sided. She'd be unloved, eventually rejected. Would it be worth that humiliation to be with the man she loved so stupidly, so obsessively that her brain had gone into hibernation? She didn't know. Couldn't decide.

Pale and trembling, she slowly began the walk back, turning everything over in her mind. Perhaps he did truly love her.

A nasty little voice queried cynically, After such a short time? But she pushed it away. She had to believe in Blake. To do otherwise would destroy her.

'Well! Your walk didn't do you much good!' exclaimed Mrs Carter when Nicole shuffled disconsolately in through the back door. Wan-faced, she immediately went to Luc and hugged his warm, loving little body to her for reassurance.

'I have a terrible headache,' she mumbled, preparing to feed her son and hoping she'd be forgiven the lie this once.

This was her future. Loving Luc. Protecting him and ensuring that he learnt how to run Cranford. But, her conscience nagged her, what of little Josef? She put her hand to her throat as she gagged.

'Nicole!'

At Blake's voice—kind, concerned and deceptively loving—she closed her eyes, fighting the nausea and concentrating on Luc. The tug at her breast. Her child. Her flesh and blood. He'd never betray her. He was all she could rely on for undying, uncomplicated love.

'Sweetheart!'

There was a rustle as he crouched down in front of her. The familiar electric charge making the air between them tremble. His hands steadied her arms and a false sense of calm and security soothed her.

'Just a sick headache,' she forced out. And suddenly it became real, hitting her with such splitting ferocity that she moaned aloud.

His gentle fingers stroked her forehead. 'What can I do?' he asked tenderly.

Love me! she wanted to cry. Tell me that you don't care that I am your means of keeping Cranford, that you feel as passionately for me as I do for you!

'A nice cup of tea. What do you think?' came the kindly tones of Mrs Carter.

She'd throw up. Her head shook imperceptibly.

'No, thanks,' she whispered. 'I want to be alone. In the dark.'

Her head was being stroked again, the finger-light movements so delicate and caring that she could almost pretend he loved her.

'I can't bear to see you like this,' he said softly.

No, she thought bitterly. Until we're married your future isn't certain! You'll look after me like a gardener caring for his prize marrow! And then... She gritted her teeth.

Once they were married her purpose would have been served. Her head tipped back in despair.

'I'll take Luc when you've finished—' he began.

'No!' Her eyes opened, wild and frantic. He wasn't going to have her child! She blinked, seeing Mrs Carter's open-mouthed astonishment. Sensed Blake's surprise in the cessation of his soothing fingers. 'I want him with me,' she whispered. 'He'll be ready for his sleep, anyway.'

When Luc had finished feeding and she had winded and changed him, Blake helped her up the stairs. The touch of his hands and the close hug of his body was driving her to distraction. He was living a lie! she told herself miserably.

But hope and love made her wonder if that was true, and if perhaps he did really adore her. Because, she thought with a scowl, he was giving a darn good impression of loving concern!

He drew the curtains, bringing coolness and darkness to the room.

'Do you want me to stay?' he murmured when he had coaxed her into stripping down to her underwear and sliding into bed.

'Hold my hand!' she muttered before she could stop herself.

He clasped it firmly, for all the world as if he was willing her to get better because she was one of the most important people in his life. Which she was, of course, the nasty little voice said. She was bringing him the inheritance he coveted.

'What…?' She licked her dry mouth. The question had to be asked. She must know her position. 'What would have happened,' she said weakly, 'if you had been a girl?'

'I would have worn dresses,' he murmured, amused.

Her brow furrowed in irritation. There was no time for humour. 'I mean to Cranford.'

His hand brushed the hair from her forehead and she noticed that his fingers were shaking slightly. Then his mouth touched the deep frown line between her brows.

'Your father would have inherited,' he said in an odd, husky tone.

'So...it goes through the male line.'

'Yes, darling. But why bother your head with that now?' he asked, a slight tension underlying his words.

'Why indeed.'

For the first time in her life she was keeping something back. Now she knew that Luc was the heir she felt frightened for her son. Terrible, uncharitable thoughts were streaming unchecked through her mind. Fiercely, she tried to reassure herself. Blake wouldn't hurt Luc. He was a good man.

And yet he was keeping Luc's inheritance a secret. Was marrying her as a safeguard.

'My darling,' he murmured. 'Are you daunted by the thought of becoming my wife and mistress of Cranford?'

Her eyes filled with tears as she gazed into his glowing eyes. 'Yes,' she said honestly, in a small, pinched voice.

'You'll be fine. I'll guide you,' he murmured, kissing her cheek tenderly.

'Blake...' She searched his face for the truth. 'You...do love me, don't you?'

He smiled as if she were being silly. 'You are the most wonderful thing that's happened to me—apart from Josef's birth,' he assured her.

She closed her eyes, trying hard to regulate her breathing, because that wasn't what she'd wanted to hear at all. Her suspicious mind was telling her that she might be the most wonderful thing that had happened. But not because Blake had fallen in love with her.

She put her hand to her aching head. He'd been in danger before she'd arrived. Someone might have learnt the secret of his birth. But as her husband he could rest easy. Till he grew tired of being polite and pretending, and abandoned her.

'I'll leave you.'

Her eyes snapped open in instant fear. 'What?'

'Just for a short time. Let you sleep it off.' He gave her a quick peck on the cheek. 'I'll get on with the arrangements for the wedding. I hope you're in as big a hurry as I am!'

He flashed his dazzling grin, blew her a kiss and walked softly out.

Nicole stared up at the ceiling. A hasty courtship, an even hastier marriage! How suspicious was that?

'Oh, please let him love me!' she moaned.

But she had no idea how she'd ever know—until it was too late. Or how she could salve her conscience where Josef was concerned. The child expected to inherit. If she said nothing, then he would. If she stuck up for Luc and for what was right, then little Josef would be utterly devastated.

It was a terrible situation. And she had no idea what to do.

CHAPTER THIRTEEN

SHE refused lunch. In the semi-darkened room she stared up at the ceiling, her mind a merciful blank because her headache was so bad she couldn't think about her situation any more.

Blake crept in and she closed her eyes, hoping he'd go away, but he sat by the bed. She couldn't stand being watched any longer. What was he doing? she thought irritably. Guarding his meal-ticket?

Her eyes opened. He looked so anxious and loving that her heart turned over. His lips lightly touched hers.

'Anything I can get you?' he whispered.

The truth! she wanted to scream. Instead, she weakly muttered that she'd be better on her own. And then decided to test him. It sickened her that she was playing a game and not confronting him, but she wanted to give him a chance to confess.

'I was in the wood earlier,' she mumbled.

He flinched visibly and it was a while before he answered. 'Nice walk?'

'I thought,' she whispered faintly, 'I saw you. With someone.'

The silence was so thick it seemed to close around her like a blanket.

'A man who used to know my mother,' Blake replied.

She waited. But he said no more.

'A visitor to see her?' she asked, the misery filling every cell in her body. 'She only lets you and little Josef into her sick room. She hasn't even met me.'

'This man was a special friend.'

Nicole tried to sound amused. 'An old lover?' she asked with a raised eyebrow. Please tell me, she begged with her eyes. Tell me.

Blake shrugged. 'I must go. You'll be all right?'

And he had kissed her, his lips cold and his eyes distant, and had reached the door before she could say anything more.

She closed her eyes tightly. He needed time. He'd had a shock when his father had turned up and would need to think things through.

'Fine. I'll sleep.' She even managed a weak smile. 'See you later.'

With a look of relief, he hurried out as if he had been released from jail.

Nicole lay there trembling. When he'd had time to consider his options he'd realise what he must do, she told herself. It was wonderful that he had met his father. It had been an emotional moment for both of them.

And a devastating one for her.

The afternoon dragged. Eventually she slept. Refused supper. Allowed herself to be coaxed with a small bowl of soup and nodded when Blake told her that Josef was anxious to see her.

On the tip of her tongue was the question, Which Josef? But she didn't ask it and raised herself against the pillows when the little boy tiptoed in, heartbreakingly the image of his father and grandfather.

'Are you any better?' Josef asked in a loud stage whisper.

'I am a little. And will be fine in the morning,' she said, thinking how much she loved this child. Her eyes filled with tears and Blake, seeing this, took her hand in his.

'I brought you something I made in school today,' Josef hissed, taking huge, exaggeratedly soft steps on his way to her bedside.

Her heart melted. 'Did you?' she said fondly.

He thrust a strange concoction at her—a painted cereal box with precarious additions. Conscious of the honour he was bestowing on her, she received it gravely.

'I dropped it on the way back,' he explained, tugging at a drunken piece of an egg box. 'We were playing football and it sort of ended up in the bushes with the ball. Do you like it?'

She recognised the wisteria that had been painted over the neatly scissored front door. 'Cranford.' she smiled. 'Thank you.' And said from the bottom of her heart, 'I will treasure it always.'

Josef beamed at her and his father. 'She would make a lovely Mummy, Dad,' he said wistfully.

Blake drew in a breath. Smiled at her. And she froze. But it was too late. 'I think so too,' he said.

Josef's eyes widened. 'You mean…?'

His father laughed. 'I mean.'

'Wow—oh!' Josef clapped a hand to his mouth to stem his exuberant yell. 'Wow!' he whispered. 'Oh, wow, wow, wow!' he squealed as quietly as his joy would allow. 'Are you going to be married?'

'As soon as possible,' Blake replied.

The look he gave her was one of pure love. And she responded, smiling with blind happiness, because her brain just wasn't connected to her heart at all.

'And you'll be my Mummy?' Josef snuggled up to Nicole.

She tucked her arm around him, praying that everything would be all right.

'You have a mother. I will be like a mother,' she said gently.

'Make cakes with chocolate drops on and gooey icing?'

'Yes,' she replied, breaking her heart with love for Blake and his motherless son.

'And we'll have picnics and you'll tell me off when I fall in the river and things?' he said earnestly.

'Definitely.'

'I'm so happy,' Josef sighed. 'I can teach Luc how to ride. And how to catch fish. And he can be my brother and share *everything* with me!'

She felt Blake stiffen. 'I think we should leave Nicole to rest now,' he said, clearing his throat.

Gently Josef wound his arms around her neck and kissed her on both cheeks. 'Goodnight,' he said with such infinite tenderness and love that it stopped her heart for a moment and she couldn't breathe for the pain that ripped through her. 'Oh, Daddy, isn't it wonderful?' he cried. 'I want to go out and shout for a bit before I go to bed, if that's all right. I've got all these yells and "wow"s bottled up inside me and they've got to be let out or I'll bust.'

'Sure!' chuckled Blake. 'I know how you feel.' He sobered. 'I have the same feelings.' His voice shook. 'It's how we are, Josef.'

With a loving kiss, he left her too and she heard Josef's excited chatter echoing down the corridor and then his erupting delight as he let rip once he thought he was out of earshot.

Blake loved her, she told herself. Didn't he?

Then she remembered how he'd said what Josef meant to him. She knew that sense of protection too and understood that he might do anything for his son. Even marry a woman he didn't love.

The bones of her spine seemed to turn to ice. Blake had deceived her. Deceived everyone. He and his mother had lived a lie for their own ends—and they'd said terrible things about her father.

That hurt so much that she was beyond crying. In the white heat of pain she recognised that Blake would keep his secret for his son's sake. And the lie would fester between them like a sore until it became an open wound.

He slipped into bed with her later. Held her very gently as if she were precious china. And she lay awake when he slept, adoring him and torn between staying silent for ever and confessing that she knew the truth.

She grew cold in his arms and that must have woken him.

'Headache worse?' he murmured drowsily. 'I could get you something for it—'

'No,' she whispered. 'It's gone. Hold me, Blake. Hold me!'

Surprised by her passion, he wrapped her in his arms, kissing her face tenderly. 'Headache!' he said in mock reproof. 'And we're not even married!'

She managed a little laugh but couldn't speak because her distress filled every cavity of her body.

'Have you…loved before?' she asked shakily.

'No. I haven't even dated since my marriage broke up.' She waited for him to say the words she longed to hear. But waited in vain.

'We must tell Mother. Introduce you.' His mouth drifted over her cheekbone and down her jaw. 'Josef is thrilled. I could hardly get him into bed. I'm afraid he has a long list of what mummies and daddies do. One of which is to share a bath.'

She did smile then. 'I'm glad he's pleased. He's very important to you, isn't he?'

'Yes.' Blake's voice was husky. 'I want to protect him from hurt. The trouble is, I know that's impossible,' he muttered. 'He will be hurt. It's inevitable.' The bleakness of his face caused a pain to slice through her. He was finding this situation impossible too, she realised. The suffering radiated from him in waves and she wanted to take that suffering away.

Nicole couldn't bear to see him like this. And suddenly she knew what she must do. Loving him as she did, finding his pain worse than her own, she had to make the sacrifice.

'Make love to me,' she whispered, suddenly frantic to be as close, as intimate with him as possible.

They both seemed to need one another with the same desperation. They tore at one another's clothes. He was hot and hard and urgent and she didn't care if he felt just lust or if it was love because she felt impelled to give him everything—her heart, her soul, her mind and body. This was how she felt. How much she loved him. And she would give him all she could and he would know that her love had been unfaltering.

The night was a magical one. It seemed that he worshipped her and she allowed herself to believe this.

She could keep silent because she loved Blake so much. Because she felt the same about Josef. And because she knew Joe would look after Luc's future. That was her decision.

She moaned beneath Blake's fierce loving. Urged him on, writhing and arching her body, taunting him and luring him until he groaned with frustration.

And then they slid together, united, each shuddering with pleasure. Slowly, with agonising tension, they moved in perfect rhythm, watching one another, drowning in each other's eyes until she saw Blake's head go back and heard his breath shorten, felt his heart accelerate and then lost herself in the exquisite pleasure of their mutual climax.

'I love you,' she whispered as he kissed her passionately afterwards.

'Oh, Nicole!' he rasped, and buried his face in her neck.

She clenched her jaw. No word of love. And that was what she must accept, even if it broke her heart in the process.

*   *   *

She woke early the next morning and Blake had already gone. She fancied she'd heard the clatter of hooves on the cobbles in the stable yard. She smiled at that, realising he would be riding off his tension and guilt. There would be many fast gallops in the future, she imagined. And wondered what she would do to keep her own sanity.

After feeding Luc and making herself breakfast, she decided to go for a walk to blow away the cobwebs and to come to terms with her decision to say nothing.

Pushing the buggy and with her head down as she frowned and thought, she didn't realise until too late that she was heading straight for Blake, who was standing by the lakeside with Midnight and watching her approach. She stopped, disconcerted. Her heart thumped as usual because he looked so handsome. Her body came instantly to life and she wanted to run to him and fling herself into his arms.

But he seemed detached and distant, his brooding eyes dark and his brows meeting in a fierce scowl. Nicole gulped, suddenly apprehensive and a chill settled on her body.

'What is it?' The wind tossed her hair as she remained a few feet away. His manner wasn't welcoming.

Pain wrenched across his face. 'I must talk to you,' he growled.

Instantly she felt afraid. If he was going to confess then she didn't want to know. It would end their relationship because he'd leave—

'Nicole,' he said curtly. 'Come and sit down. You must listen to me.'

'No!' Petrified of the consequences she backed away. 'I—I have to go back—'

He let go of Midnight's reins and strode towards her, grim and stony-faced. His hands caught her arms and he reached out a foot to toe the brake on the buggy, then pulled her to the ground without ceremony or gentleness.

'No,' she protested, struggling to free herself from her tangle of long skirts. 'I don't want to listen—'

'You must!' he said hoarsely, holding her down. 'It has to be said. It's about your father.'

Surprised, she stopped fighting him. 'My father?'

'I spoke to Mother about him,' he said quickly. 'She has admitted that she lied about his behaviour. She doesn't know why he left. He just disappeared overnight. But all my enquiries confirm that he was a good man, Nicole. A brilliant artist. Everyone was fond of him and you were right. I apologise. I was mistaken to believe her. Please forgive me.'

'Of course,' she said mechanically. 'I understand why you believed her and not me.'

'Forgive her too, if you can. She was only trying to protect me. All her life she has put my interests first. She deeply regrets maligning him. Don't you want to know why she lied?'

'No!' she whispered. Desperate to finish the conversation, she made to get up and was prevented.

'You must be curious why she blackened your father's name!' he grated harshly, his face contorted with misery.

She could see how painful this was for him. She flung him a reassuring smile and wished she could escape his imprisoning grasp. Make a quip. Pretend everything was fine.

'Not at all,' she began lightly.

'Listen, Nicole!' he growled, forcing up her chin so that she had to look at him. 'This is something that will change your life—'

'I don't want it changed!' she blurted out wildly, scared now he was close to confessing. 'I just want you! To love

you, to be your wife! Nothing else, Blake! Do you understand? I want nothing else!'

She saw the anguish ripping through him, felt the contraction of his muscles as he steeled himself to deny the
inheritance and to ruin his son's future. So she kissed him.
Hotly. Passionately, tasting his mouth, driving him to the
ground.

Until he rolled away impatiently, his face like thunder.
They stared at one another for a moment, his chest heaving, her breasts straining at her shirt. And she knew with
a terrible sinking feeling in her stomach that he would not
be stopped.

'The truth is inescapable. She wanted me to think badly
of your father because she thought he was still alive. In
her pain and misery she blurted out the first things that
came into her head. She didn't want the risk that I might
contact him. You see... I am not the rightful heir to
Cranford,' he said in a hoarse whisper.

She closed her eyes. He had chosen to do what was
morally right. And his action had broken him.

'Nicole?'

He could see by her anguished face that the truth was
hitting her. Soon she would wonder if he'd proposed to
her as a means of keeping Cranford in his grasp.

'No,' she moaned, shaking her head.

She sat there, a tight ball of tension, her lip quivering
and misery in every line of her face. She would see this
as a betrayal and nothing he could say would ever make
her trust him again.

Never in his entire life had he felt so desolate. Not only
would he lose Cranford, but Nicole as well. But he
couldn't cheat her of what was her son's right to own the
estate.

A frustrated fury burst from him. 'I have to tell you! I
can't keep it a secret any longer! My mother had a lover.

I am the child of that lover. Therefore I am a *bastard*! That man you saw was my real father.'

She bit her lip. He knew what she was thinking so when she said it he wasn't surprised. 'Is that why you're telling me?' she asked in a small voice. 'Because he's turned up and therefore you were about to be exposed as an impostor?'

'No. He said he'd keep a low profile. But I don't want him to hide! I'm not ashamed of him! I wanted it all: Cranford, you, him. And now I know that's impossible. I had decided to tell you before we were married—even before he arrived. I was waiting for the right moment. So there it is. I have no Bellamie blood. The inheritance cannot pass down my line. That leaves you as the nearest next of kin. It means that Luc is the heir.'

He paused, waiting for her to speak. She seemed to be in shock and no wonder. He swallowed, taking the final step, the words lurching out hoarsely as emotion claimed him and he spelt out her fears for her.

'I know you will think that I wanted to marry you because it would allow me to stay here—'

'Did that ever cross your mind?' she whispered, looking terrified.

He couldn't spare her. He'd told himself that she would get the truth, nothing less.

'When I first knew who you were, and when I realised there was a sexual attraction between us,' he replied with a sense of scouring shame, 'I thought you might be willing to live with me, to share the benefits of the estate—'

'Not…marriage.'

God. This sounded so bad. 'Not then.'

'What changed your mind? Why did you propose?' she asked mournfully.

Her eyes haunted him. For the rest of his life he would

remember their reproach. 'I don't know,' he admitted in a harsh whisper. 'It—it just came out.'

'Not very flattering,' she said jerkily.

He pushed his hand through his hair. 'I'm trying to be honest here. The proposal surprised me. I've no idea where it came from. Somewhere inside me. My soul... Hell!' he groaned. 'You must hate me and I wouldn't blame you for that. I'll go as soon as I can. Leave the estate to your care.' He swallowed, unable to bear the prospect. 'I just need time to tell my mother and Josef and to organise somewhere for them to stay. And to say goodbye to everyone.'

Nicole felt as if her heart was tearing in two. He turned his head away but the broken, haunted look on his face stayed with her. It had come from his soul, she thought. What did he mean by that?

'Say something!' he whispered. 'For God's sake, say something!'

'You can't do this to Josef,' she said shakily.

The strong jaw clenched. 'I have to. He will understand.'

From his soul...

Her head lifted. She couldn't put Blake and Josef through this. She'd never live with herself. She would gladly sacrifice everything for his happiness.

'He won't need to.'

Blake frowned. Turned to look at her. 'What?'

Now that the truth was out in the open she couldn't stay if he really didn't care for her. She would leave the coast clear for him.

However...if he *did* care—as she believed he did in her heart of hearts—then he could have everything he desired.

Her body grew erect. Her future happiness hung on a knife edge.

From his soul. Let that be true!

'I'm going back to France,' she announced, taking the gamble. His brow furrowed and she made it clearer. 'Blood isn't important. It's the man,' she said, partly echoing something Blake had said to his father. 'And you and Josef will run Cranford better than I could. Luc doesn't know anything of this and will be none the wiser. Keep Cranford. You've given it your love and tender care all these years and you deserve it.'

He just stared at her. For several seconds it seemed he was trying to make sense of what she'd said. 'You…you would give up a life of luxury and wealth…for my benefit?' he eventually asked in a cracked voice.

She smiled. 'Of course. I love you more than I can say,' she told him simply. 'I want what makes you happy.'

'But I wouldn't be! How can I ever be happy?' he raged.

It was her turn to stare. Her pulses began to race. 'Why's that?' she asked with as much innocence as she could. 'You would have Cranford. Josef. What more do you need?'

Blake scowled at the ground. Fixed her with his penetrating glare. '*You*! You wouldn't be with me!' he growled.

'No,' she said, hardly able to conceal her delight. 'Not if I'm in France.'

'Then I'll follow you there!' he cried grimly, capturing her in his arms. 'I'll prove I love you if I have to set up home next to you and court you for the next ten years!' he cried passionately. 'I *have* to be with you, Nicole. Life is unthinkable without you. I knew that some time ago and the intensity of my feelings scared the hell out of me! I probably loved you from the moment I first saw you, but I was too dim to realise it. If you want my happiness, then that includes you. If you love me be my wife. I want nothing less. I know you can't trust me and I'll wait for as long as it takes for you to realise what I truly feel. I want *you.* Selfishly, for myself. For Josef too. I want us to be a family. To have picnics together—'

'Take baths together,' she suggested in delight, a wicked look in her eyes.

He pushed her back and scanned her amused face. 'Let me follow you!' he groaned. 'I love you, Nicole! So much that it hurts as if I'm being knifed! I can think of nothing else but you. Want to be with you all the time, touching you, looking at you…'

His mouth closed on hers, possessive and demanding. She wound her arms around his neck and surrendered to his kiss.

'It seems a shame to go all the way to France,' she murmured in his ear some time later.

'Nicole? My darling?' he whispered, hope making his voice shake.

Her mouth found his. 'I believe that you do love me. We were both shot by the same arrow, I think. It pierced both our hearts very early on.'

'The moment I set eyes on you,' he agreed.

She smiled. 'So we might as well stay here, don't you think? The boys can share Cranford. And any other children we might have can share it too.'

'Other…children?' he croaked.

'Mm. Am I being forward? Brazen?'

He grinned and their lips met in a long, lingering kiss. 'Oh, I do hope so,' he murmured. 'Do you mind if I let off steam somehow? I have all this energy inside me waiting for me to shout and yell and go ''wow''!'

'We could combine the two,' she suggested, looking deceptively demure. 'Link up our plan to have more children and you letting off some of that energy.'

'Good idea,' he breathed, drawing her to her feet.

But they stood there for a very long time, just kissing tenderly, holding one another.

And, gazing into his rapturous face, Nicole felt such a profound love for him that, for a while, just being with him was enough.

'I love you so much!' he murmured dazedly.

And she lost herself in the gentle wonder of his kiss.

'It's getting dark. Draw the curtains back a little more and let the last of the daylight in, my darling Josef,' wheezed Kay Bellamie.

It wasn't dark at all. The light streamed in but Josef knew that, for her, the light was fading.

He made a pretence of dragging the drapes back and stood at the open window, watching his son and Giles's daughter stand up and embrace lovingly where before they seemed to have been locked in some kind of stand-off.

'I hope Blake understands why I lied about Giles. I feel so bad about it. I've been selfish and wrong,' Kay fretted. 'And his pride and honour will ensure that he loses Cranford—'

'No. By some miracle it is securely his,' Josef said gently.

She had to know. He sat beside her and told her how the young Giles had secretly fallen in love with a village girl who'd died tragically when she'd been working on Cranford farm. Josef explained how he'd made some silver bracelets for the girl who'd died before Giles could give them to her. How the distraught young man had been unable to bear the sight of Cranford after that and had fled the unhappy memories.

'After that he would only have given those bracelets to someone he loved deeply,' he murmured. 'To his daughter. The girl who came to scatter her father's ashes around the churchyard, the girl who is so like her father that it touched my heart when I saw her. The woman Blake has fallen in love with. The pattern of life has come full circle and completed itself. They will be happy together, you can be sure of that.'

He saw the silent tears and hoped he hadn't given her too great a shock. 'Kay,' he said tenderly, stroking her hand in his. 'Are you happy at last?'

She smiled at him, the old, dazzling smile, her eyes the colour of the summer sky. 'I am. Thank you for telling me. For being here,' she said faintly. 'I am very, very happy. I love you, Josef. And always will.'

'And I have always loved you, Kay. No other woman. Just you.'

He choked back his own tears and kissed her tenderly on the lips. As he did so he felt her relax and her life ebbed away in a soft whisper.

Looking down on her, he didn't see a woman old before her time because of severe pain but the beautiful girl with whom he had fallen head over heels in love.

'We'll meet again,' he said softly.

Raising his head, he saw through the blur of tears that Blake and Nicole were walking hand in hand back to the house. He would tell them later about Kay. How content she'd been. That her love had burned, like his, down the years and eventually she'd been at peace with herself.

And then into his vision came a Common Blue butterfly, the colour of the sky. It fluttered into the room, beating its wings frantically against the window. The old Romany legend had come true for him.

Gently, reverently, he cupped his hand around the fragile butterfly. And, with love filling his heart, he set it free.

Turn the page for a sneak preview of

The Greek Millionaire's Marriage
by Sara Wood,

*coming in the thrilling collection of
Mediterranean romances called*

IN THE GREEK'S BED

*available from Mills & Boon By Request®
in November 2008*

The Greek Millionaire's Marriage
by Sara Wood

DIMITRI ANGELAKI braced his powerful legs as his launch surged forwards, its streamlined hull scything cleanly through the glittering sea towards the little fishing port of Olympos. He sang softly to himself, an old Greek love song, in a throaty voice that conveyed his passion for life and love.

It had been an odd day. One with stark contrasts of delight and anxiety, during which his senses had been utterly sated—and his nerves had been tested to the utmost.

Glancing around, he allowed himself an indulgent moment of pleasure, letting his gaze linger on his wife's incredible body, and enjoying the gleam of her golden-goddess skin against the luxurious cream leather seat. To his approval, her bikini was minimal: three small turquoise triangles barely concealing the essence of her womanhood.

The dazzling light was turning her hair to white fire where it fanned over her slender shoulders and he felt a helpless little jerk in his chest when he recalled just where that hair had been that day, slithering and sliding over the most sensitive parts of his body in an erotic dance that had driven him to paradise and beyond.

His chiselled mouth curved sensually and a throb began yet again in his loins. That was the joy of sex with Olivia. First would come the anticipation: the fiery glances that ripped his brain to shreds, the messages of hunger and need clearly projected in her sea-blue eyes.

5

Then, as surely as night followed day, came their un-inhibited lovemaking: inventive, crazy, wild and tender—but always intensely satisfying and releasing the steam valve of their mutual passion.

Finally, he thought, now fully aware of her and with all his senses on high alert, he could enjoy a rerun of every erotic second, from the first glance they'd exchanged to their final sighs of release.

A growl of pleasure rose to his throat and his hands were less than steady when he belatedly turned his attention to steering a straight line again. She got to him, right in the gut, and he loved that because it made him feel alive and utterly male.

Sometimes he wanted to shoot his fist up into the air after their lovemaking, and shout Yes! like a kid who'd just scored a goal. He grinned to himself at the very idea. He, a tycoon whose coolness under pressure was admired the world over! But property deals didn't excite him nearly as much as these exquisite encounters with his wife. It was unfortunate that his work took him away from home so often and that the hectic nature of his breakfast-to-midnight schedules meant that it was pointless for Olivia to travel with him.

Still, the time they were together seemed all the more sweet. That day they had anchored offshore to swim naked in the silken sea. Then they had made love in a lemon grove, the intoxicating scent of a thousand blossoming trees adding to his delirium. Later, she'd fed him lobster and grapes on a hillside overlooking the ruins of an ancient temple dedicated to Aphrodite, the goddess of love.

'Venus,' he'd explained to her. 'A poor second to you, my darling.'

Amazingly, he could still feel the thrilling touch of

Olivia's fingers on his mouth, his throat, his chest...and everywhere else. Each deeply pulsing inch of him bore her imprint. It had been one of the most sensual experiences in all the thirty-two years of his life.

Everything would have been perfect—if it hadn't been for his increasing concern for Athena. A frown creased his sun-bronzed forehead as he willed Athena to ring from the hospital to say she was all right. He felt the tension screwing him up again, ruining the memories of the day. But then it was understandable. He loved Athena with all his heart...

Olivia stiffened when she heard the trill of Dimitri's mobile. It had been ringing far too often that day, but with infuriating stubbornness he'd refused to turn it off.

'Greek moguls,' he'd said with a pretence at pomposity and referring to a standing joke between them, 'need to stay in contact with their minions.'

'Then find a minion you can delegate to,' she'd protested, but had been fatally diverted when his mouth had closed firmly on hers and he'd kissed her complaint away with a breathtaking thoroughness.

Looking back, though, she could be more objective. His obsessive devotion to work had been a problem for some time. When he was away, and she only had her disapproving mother-in-law, Marina, for company, she felt increasingly lonely and unhappy. Her insecurity and doubts over Dimitri's true feelings were painfully reinforced by Marina's sly hints about Dimitri's long absences.

Olivia clenched her fists. From the day of her marriage six months earlier, Marina had taunted her.

'All Greek men have mistresses,' Marina had purred. 'Don't think my son is any different.'

A mistress. Would that explain his lack of consideration? Even this long-anticipated trip today, to the ancient Greek theatre at Epidauros, had been marred by his inattention. She sighed. It could have been deeply romantic. Dimitri had demonstrated the acoustics of the two-thousand-year-old theatre by whispering 'I love you' from the performing area far below. Amazingly, she had heard every impassioned syllable from where she had been sitting, fifty-four rows up.

Quite enchanted, she'd risen to her feet to blow him a kiss. Unfortunately just then he'd received another of his infuriating calls and he had hurried out of the arena so that she couldn't eavesdrop on his conversation.

Recalling how offended she'd been, and with her eyes flashing in anger, she curled up crossly in the luxurious seat of his launch, glaring at Dimitri. He handled the boat expertly with one hand, the other holding the loathed mobile to his ear.

Although his back was to her, she'd seen the tension of his body when the phone had rung. And now that he was engaged in an earnest discussion she wondered at the reason for his relief, which was apparent in the easing of those taut muscles that she knew so well. Something was going on.

Her heart cramped. He was almost cradling the phone, his magnificent body fluid with tenderness. A sense of dread played havoc with her stomach. She sucked it in, not breathing. Perhaps her mother-in-law was right.

Yet...Dimitri couldn't keep his hands off her. Almost from the moment she'd become his secretary two years ago, at the age of twenty-four, they'd been

mad for one another. Every moment in public together
had been a deliciously tensioned ordeal; every second
alone had become a shattering explosion of hunger and
raw need. They had been blind to sense, reckless in
surrendering to the volcanic passions that had seized
them.

Thinking of those blissful stolen moments of abandon caused an instant arousal in her and she shifted her
slim thighs, pressing her legs tightly together to control
the pulsing heat that had begun to massage her with its
irresistible rhythm.

Clouds of helpless longing confused her brain and
ruefully she realised that the pressure of her bikini top
had become unbearable because of the sudden fullness
of her breasts and their tingling tips.

Focusing on him, she noticed that he was laughing
now. The honey-gold naked shoulders shook with
amusement as he murmured something intimate into
the wretched phone.

A fierce stab of jealousy ripped through her. Dimitri
was *hers!* Body and soul, heart and mind! Immediately
she felt appalled by her irrational suspicion and, contrite, she went over to stand behind him, wrapping her
arms around the warm, satin skin of his narrow waist
in a gesture of remorse, the jutting peaks of her breasts
pressing provocatively into his back.

Dimitri jumped as if she'd ambushed him, muttered
into the phone something incomprehensible in Greek—
which *might* have been 'see you tomorrow', though her
Greek was still minimal—and with a hasty *'Adio!'* he
broke the connection.

Beneath her hand, his heart thudded fast and loud.
In fear? she wondered, alarmed. Maybe he did have a
mistress. Business took him away so often he could

even be serving a whole harem of women for all she knew!

Yet when he swung around, his eyes were smouldering with intent. Hauling her slender body against his, flesh to flesh, he kissed her with slow deliberation, one deft hand killing the engine, the other untying her bikini straps.

He was fully aroused. Magnificently, thrillingly, urgently. Whilst she revelled in the hardness of him, she couldn't help but wish she knew if it was for her, or the woman on the phone.

'Who was that?' she demanded, an ominous frown flattening her arched brows.

He was intent on an erotic stroking of her hair, the pale ash-blonde strands slithering over her sun-kissed shoulders. He disturbed the sprigs of lemon blossom, which he'd arranged around her head like a crown, and they drifted to the ground in a generous waft of intense perfume.

Dimitri's marauding mouth savaged the golden skin of her throat before he answered lazily and with a satisfying huskiness.

'A friend.'

To her suspicious mind, that sounded a shade too casual. And he hadn't looked at her, his inky lashes dropping to hide his eyes.

'Do I know him?' she asked with even more studied carelessness.

There was a very slight hesitation but it was long enough for her to know he was about to be economical with the truth.

'No. Forget it, my darling. Concentrate on what I'm intending to do to you, mm?'

She firmed her mouth but he teased it open easily

with his tongue. The magic of his fingers, tantalisingly laborious as they undid the ties of her briefs, ensured that she did forget. The glorious surrender of her body began. Throatily whispering outrageous things to her, describing in detail what he had in mind, Dimitri eased her gently to the warm teak deck.

Her hands clutched at the waistband of his swimming trunks and slid them from his body. Beneath her avid fingers, the muscles of his small buttocks contracted and she ran her hands lovingly over the firm curves.

As a lover he was insatiable. Sometimes his hunger startled her, but she, too, could be as wild and demanding. Then there were times, like now, when his tenderness made her heart contract and his thought for her pleasure knew no bounds.

Olivia began to lose control as Dimitri's wicked fingers slipped with unnerving accuracy to the swollen bud of sensation that lay close to her liquefying core. He did love her, she thought in an ecstatic haze. He'd married her, hadn't he?

Celebrate 100 years of pure reading pleasure with Mills & Boon®

To mark our centenary, each month we're publishing a special 100th Birthday Edition. These celebratory editions are packed with extra features and include a FREE bonus story.

Plus, you have the chance to enter a fabulous monthly prize draw. See 100th Birthday Edition books for details.

Now that's worth celebrating!

September 2008

Crazy about her Spanish Boss by Rebecca Winters
Includes FREE bonus story
Rafael's Convenient Proposal

November 2008

**The Rancher's Christmas Baby
by Cathy Gillen Thacker**
Includes FREE bonus story *Baby's First Christmas*

December 2008

One Magical Christmas by Carol Marinelli
Includes FREE bonus story *Emergency at Bayside*

Look for Mills & Boon® 100th Birthday Editions at your favourite bookseller or visit
www.millsandboon.co.uk